ENDGAME

THE COMPLETE FUGITIVE ARCHIVES

Endgame series

Novels:
The Calling
Sky Key
Rules of the Game

Digital Novellas:
Endgame: The Training Diaries Volume 1: Origins
Endgame: The Training Diaries Volume 2: Descendant
Endgame: The Training Diaries Volume 3: Existence
Endgame: The Zero Line Chronicles Volume 1: Incite
Endgame: The Zero Line Chronicles Volume 2: Feed
Endgame: The Zero Line Chronicles Volume 3: Reap
Endgame: The Fugitive Archives Volume 1: Project Berlin
Endgame: The Fugitive Archives Volume 2: The Moscow Meeting
Endgame: The Fugitive Archives Volume 3: The Buried Cities

Novella Collections:
Endgame: The Complete Training Diaries
Endgame: The Complete Zero Line Chronicles
Endgame: The Complete Fugitive Archives

ENDGAME

THE FUGITIVE ARCHIVES

VOLUME 1

PROJECT BERLIN

CHAPTER I

Boone
December 24, 1948

"How you doing, Peterson?" Driscoll asks as we descend through the thick fog. "You look a little green. Do me a favor and try not to lose your lunch all over my plane, okay?"

The C-54, buffeted by a crosswind, shakes fiercely, rattling us like peas in a can. It's been like this the whole flight. Driscoll grins at me.

My name isn't Peterson, but he doesn't know that. He also doesn't know that I've been in far more nerve-racking situations than a rough approach. I may look like any other 19-year-old GI, but I'm far more than that.

"Last time I flew over Berlin, I was *dropping* eggs on their heads," Driscoll continues, shouting to be heard above the roar of the engines. "Now I'm bringing them eggs for their breakfast." His joke about the bombing raids that destroyed huge parts of the city during the last days of the war isn't funny. I smile anyway. I need him to think I'm just one of the guys, at least for a little longer.

The truth is, I *am* a little bit nervous. I've been training for war since I was a kid. I've been through more than Driscoll and all the other soldiers on the plane ever saw in boot camp. But this is my biggest mission yet. A lot is riding on it. And yet I don't even know exactly what it's about.

I know the basics. I've got to find a man and get him out of Berlin. I know his name and his suspected location. And I know that if he won't come with me, or if someone else gets to him first, I have to kill him.

A simple plan. That's why I know there's more to it than the council has told me. For some reason they don't want me to know the details of why this man is so important, which means they don't want anyone *else* to have that information either. If I get captured, my enemies can try as hard as they want to get me to talk, but I can't tell them what I don't know. Not that I would talk anyway. I'd never do anything to jeopardize the safety of my line. The council knows that, so it bothers me a little bit that they're taking this precaution. More than a little bit, if I'm honest. This is the first time since I became the Cahokian Player that they've kept me in the dark about something. I don't like the feeling.

I push that irritation from my mind as the Tempelhof airstrip appears—seemingly out of nowhere—and meets the wheels of the plane. The rumbling intensifies, shaking my bones, and I hang on as Driscoll applies the brakes. Through the cockpit windows I see groups of children standing on top of piles of debris that line the runway. They wave at us, grinning and clapping their hands.

"Look at that," Driscoll says. "It's like we're Santa Claus."

In a way, we are. After all, it's Christmas Eve. And along with the ten tons of eggs, milk, meat, flour, and other basic supplies in our hold, we're bringing bags of wrapped gifts to hand out to the people of the city. Chocolate bars for the kids. Cigarettes for the men. Perfume for the women. The war ended in 1945, but more than three years later, Berlin is still trying to recover. And since the Soviets cut off all sea and land access to the city's western zone earlier in the year, life has gotten even harder.

Thankfully, the airlift organized by the American, French, and British militaries has been successful in bringing supplies to the city. It's also provided me with a handy way inside. Posing as an American soldier has been easy enough. There are so many young men being assigned to the dozens of daily airlift flights coming out of Rhein-Main Air Base that no one notices one more. All I had to do was put on a uniform and start helping load the plane.

When the Skymaster comes to a stop, we reverse the process begun three hours earlier, transferring everything in our cargo area onto the trucks that pull up one after the other.

"Nobody disappear!" Driscoll shouts as we launch into action. "General Tunner's orders! We get this stuff off, turn around, and land back in Frankfurt in time for eggnog and cookies!"

The airlift is a well-oiled machine. Planes land at two-minute intervals, and the total time from unloading to takeoff is 25 minutes. Everything moves like clockwork, and everyone has a job to do. I can't make a break for the main terminal or someone is bound to notice the missing pair of hands. But when we're almost finished, one of the mobile coffee trucks arrives filled with pretty German girls who hand out drinks and smiles, and I take the opportunity to slip away while the others are distracted. I don't look back, and nobody calls Peterson's name. Even when they finally notice he's gone, it won't matter, as the United States Army has no record of him anyway.

Once I'm away from the airport, I make my way into Berlin. In an attempt to maintain a balance of power, the city has been divided into four sectors, each one controlled by one of the Allied superpowers: Great Britain, France, the United States, and the Soviet Union. In reality, though, it's become the Soviets on one side and everyone else on the other. Fortunately, Tempelhof is in the American sector, and a GI walking through the streets is a common sight. I'd prefer to be dressed like a civilian, but at least wearing a uniform means that nobody questions me. And in case they do, all my identity papers carry the name of Alan Peterson.

It's early evening, a little past seven, and already dark. A light snow is falling. And even though the streets are dotted with rubble—some of the buildings I pass have shattered windows and walls that have crumbled, so you can see into living rooms and kitchens still filled with furniture—it somehow manages to feel like Christmas. There are wreaths on some of the doors, and trees decorated with ornaments are visible in the parlors of some of the houses. The shops I pass don't have much displayed in their windows, but signs reading FRÖHLICHE WEIHNACHTEN are taped to the glass.

Bells chime, and when I turn a corner, I see people walking into a church. The inside is lit by candles, and the sound of a carol being played on an organ floats from the open doorway. This makes me think of my own family back in Illinois. It's just after noon there, and I know my mother is getting ready for the Christmas Eve gathering. She's been cooking all day. The Tom and Jerry bowl and glasses that only come out once a year are set out on the sideboard. She's probably already hung the stockings from the mantel over the fireplace, one for each kid, arranged in order from youngest to oldest: Marnie, Evan, Lily, Ella, Peter, me, and Jackson. In the morning, the stockings will all be filled to overflowing. Even mine, although I won't be there to open it. And even Jackson's, although it's been three years since he died. The people of Berlin aren't the only ones who've lost something to the war.

I hurry by the church, clearing my mind by focusing on the address the council gave me. I memorized it, as well as the best route to reach it. Writing things down is risky. As my father told me repeatedly when I started my Player training, the brain is the only notebook nobody can steal.

It takes me another 20 minutes to find the house. It's in a section of the city that was hit hard by the Allied bombing, one of a row of connected brick town homes. Most of the buildings are empty, uninhabitable because of the damage. This one looks empty too. Most of the windows are boarded up, and the front door has an official notice on it warning people not to enter due to unsafe conditions. But looks can be deceiving. Just because you can't see somebody, it doesn't mean nobody is there. Sometimes, you just have to look harder.

I don't announce myself by knocking on the front door. This isn't a social call. Instead, I go into the bombed-out house next door, climb the stairs to the third floor, and step through a shattered window onto a narrow ledge that runs along the front of the whole row of houses. I press myself against what's left of the wall and slowly move one foot at a time toward the house next door. If anyone notices me, maybe they'll just think I'm Saint Nicholas coming to deliver presents. When I reach the closest window of the target house, I pause beside it and look inside. The bedroom behind the cracked, dirty glass is empty. When I push on the window frame, the window slides up.

I slip inside, turn on the small flashlight I carry in my pocket, and look around. It's just as cold in here as it is outside, and I can see my breath. There's no heat. But coal is in short supply, and no one is supposed to be living here anyway, so this might not mean anything. More telling is that everything in the room is covered with a thick layer of dust. No one has been here in a long time.

Then I notice the footprints. They start just outside the door, run along a hallway, and disappear down a flight of stairs. A faint glow emanates from the second floor. Someone is here after all. I creep to the end of the hall and pause. I can hear voices. There are two speakers, a man and what sounds like a younger woman.

This is a problem. There's supposed to be only one person here. A man. I haven't seen him yet, but even if the man I hear talking is the one I'm after, who is the girl? Is she a wife? A daughter? Something else? I need to get a look at them.

I draw my M1911 standard-issue military pistol and walk down the stairs. It's not my weapon of choice, but it's what Private Peterson would carry, and nobody would think twice about me having it, so it's what I've got. The voices grow louder as I descend. When I reach the landing, I pause. The speakers are in a room just to my left.

"I wish Oskar and Rutger were here with us," the man says.

"You know how Oskar is," the young woman says. "He didn't want to risk anyone following us to you."

"I think everyone must have forgotten about me by now," says the man. "Still, he's right to be cautious. I worry about you making visits here."

"Perhaps it's time for you to leave," the girl says. "You've shut yourself up in here long enough. Pass the duty on to someone else. Oskar and I—"

"Lottie, please," the man interrupts. "How many times have we talked about this? I cannot leave."

"You mean you will not," says Lottie. "Do you want to spend the rest of your life here?"

"I'm already a dead man. Remember?"

The man's words chill me. What does he mean? And who is this girl? Maybe it doesn't matter. Maybe I'm better off if I don't know who Lottie is. I know from experience that it's easier to kill someone when you know nothing about her.

"Let's not discuss it further," the man says. "It's Christmas Eve. Play something for me. You know I always love to hear you play."

A moment later, I hear the sound of a piano. It's badly out of tune, but the melody is familiar. "Silent Night." The girl begins to sing, and the man joins in.

I risk moving closer and looking through the doorway. Inside the room, a scraggly pine tree stands in front of a boarded-up window, its branches hung with silver tinsel and a handful of colorful glass balls. The piano is against a wall, with the young woman seated at it. The man stands beside her. Both of them are wearing long, thick coats.

I recognize the man from the photo the council showed me. It's Evrard Sauer. I'm in the right place. But the council said nothing about the girl. Now I have to decide what to do about her. My orders were to leave no witnesses, which gives me only one option. I know what I should do—what I've agreed to do for my council and my line—but the thought of actually doing it doesn't sit right with me. The girl is simply in the wrong place at the wrong time. I hate to make her pay for that with her life.

They finish singing, and the man takes something from the pocket of his coat. It's a present wrapped in newspaper and tied with plain white string. He hands it to the girl, who carefully opens it. A happy smile spreads across her face.

"Toffees!" she says. "Wherever did you get them?"

She doesn't wait for an answer before taking one of the candies from the box and unwrapping it, the cellophane crackling in her fumbling fingers. She puts the toffee in her mouth and sucks on it, her eyes closed. I don't think I've ever seen someone enjoy a piece of candy so much.

She opens her eyes and reaches into her own pocket. She takes out a package, this one wrapped in brown butcher paper. She gives it to the man. He opens it and holds up a red knitted scarf.

"I unraveled one of my sweaters for the yarn," the girl says, sounding embarrassed. "Wool is still rationed."

"It's beautiful," the man assures her as he wraps it around his neck. "Thank you."

The girl turns back to the piano and begins to play again. This time the song is "O Tannenbaum."

I've obviously interrupted their Christmas Eve celebration. And if I do what I've been instructed to do, I'm about to make it a whole lot worse. I still feel like something is off, but there's no time to contact my council for further advice, so I have to make a choice based on the available information and what I've been told. That means completing the mission according to plan.

I accept the reality of my situation, even though I don't like it, and prepare to act. Then the sound of a door being kicked open comes from the first floor. Wood splinters. Heavy footsteps pound up the stairs. The man and the young woman stop singing and look at each other. I have just enough time to dart back to the stairwell before three figures burst onto the landing. Two of them have guns drawn.

"Evrard Sauer," one of them, a man, says. "You are under arrest for collaborating with the National Socialist German Workers' Party."

He's speaking in German, but with a heavy Russian accent. And although he's used the more formal name for them, I know he's just accused Sauer of working with the Nazis.

"Who are you?" the girl asks.

"Be still, Lottie," says Sauer. "Do as you're told."

His voice is quiet, sad. As if he has feared this moment for a long time.

I huddle on the stairs, my pistol at the ready. Besides the two men, there is a woman in the room. She stands slightly behind the men, her hands in her pockets. As I lean forward for a better look, my foot presses against the floorboards, making a faint creaking sound. I see her tense. She turns her head toward the stairwell, and for a moment I think she's seen me. But I can't look away. She's younger than I thought. My age. And beautiful. She has long dark hair and dark eyes, and for a second I'm sure that I've seen her before. Then it hits me—she looks like Wonder Woman from the comic books my sister Lily loves so much. I find myself frozen in place.

Then she turns away, and it's as if a switch has been turned off and I can breathe again. I blend into the shadows, my finger on the trigger of my gun in case I need to use it. I know I *will* need to use it. I can't let these people take Sauer. I think I know who they are. MGB. Russian intelligence. And apparently they want him because of his association with the Nazis. What he did for them, I don't know. Just as I don't know why he's so important to my council. What I do know is that I can't let them leave with him.

"If you come quietly, there will be no problems," the first man says.

Sauer nods. He motions to Lottie, who stands up.

It's time. I start to raise my pistol, aiming it at one of the Soviet agents.

Before I can fire, the woman draws her hand from her pocket. She's holding a Tokarev TT-33. There are two shots, and her companions collapse to the floor. She lowers the gun.

"You have a choice," she says to Sauer and Lottie. "Come with me and live, or join them."

CHAPTER 2

Ariadne

Sauer and the girl look from the bodies lying at their feet to the gun I still have trained on them. Their fear is obvious. They know who the dead men are, or at least who they work for, but they don't know who I am or why I'm here. They're trying to decide if I am a greater or lesser danger.

"I'm not going to ask again," I say, giving them their answer.

I point my gun at the girl. It has the desired effect.

Sauer holds up his hands. "We'll come."

He's made the right choice. Had they resisted, I would have shot them both. If I had, they would have been my third and fourth kills. The men on the floor are my first and second.

I'm surprised how little I feel about the killings. I'd expected something more, a sense of excitement perhaps, or pangs of remorse. Instead, there is simply an awareness of having done what was necessary. It probably helps that the two MGB agents were not good people. After six months of working undercover within their organization, I'd come to despise them. For one thing, they'd been dismissive of me because of my gender and my age. That was a mistake.

Three weeks ago, I turned 18. But I grew up long before that. I don't actually remember a time when I didn't feel the weight of responsibility. As a child, when I played, I played games of war. And always, I had to win. Even if it meant defeating someone close to me. When I was chosen as the current Minoan Player out of my group of trainees, it was simply the next logical step. This is a role I've been studying for my entire life.

I don't have time to waste thinking about the dead men. I motion for Sauer and the girl to walk ahead of me. They start to leave the room, which is when a figure detaches itself from the shadows of the stairs and rushes at me. I have only a moment to curse myself for not heeding an earlier feeling and checking to make sure no one else was in the house before a man is tackling me. He hits me low and hard, and before I can get off a shot, I'm falling backward. I land on the floor, and my breath is knocked out of me. Also knocked away is my gun, which my attacker sweeps out of my reach.

He, however, is still holding a weapon. He straddles me and points it at my face. "Who are you?" he asks in German.

I take inventory, trying to figure out who he might be. He's wearing the uniform of an American soldier. Then, as I look up at his face, an odd thought passes through my mind: his eyes are the same blue color as the cornflowers that grow in the fields around my grandparents' house outside Kamilari. The same color as the Aegean Sea in summer. I feel a pang of homesickness, and I'm so shocked that this is what I'm thinking about in this situation that I don't say anything for a moment. He mistakes my silence for not understanding and tries again in Russian.

"The only reason for you to know my name," I say in English, "is so you know who it is who has killed you."

I thrust up hard with my hips, trying to throw him off. I am surprised when it doesn't work.

"I've been riding horses bareback since I was four," he says, grinning down at me. "You'll have to do better than that."

"Or what?" I ask. "You'll shoot me? You should have done that when you had the chance. You won't get a second one."

Before he can answer, I lift my torso and grasp him around the chest, pulling him down toward me. My right leg traps his left foot while I hook my right arm over his shoulder. Then I push up on my left foot while swinging my left arm over. The next moment, our positions are

reversed and I'm the one on top.
"I guess you were too busy riding horses to get in many street fights," I say.
He surprises—and annoys—me by laughing. Then he says, "You'd better hurry up and decide what you're going to do next, because those people you want so badly are getting away."
That's when I realize that Sauer and the girl have disappeared. I can hear their footsteps in the hallway, so I know I still have time to catch them. But only if I go now. I look down at the man—a boy, really, or at least not much older than me. I don't know what he's doing here. Is he working with Sauer? Do the Americans (I assume he's American because of his uniform and accent) want the man too? Or is he somehow connected to the girl?
"What's the matter?" the soldier says. "You trying to decide whether to kiss me or kill me?"
I pick up his gun, which is on the floor beside us. "I've decided," I say, pointing the pistol at him.
He doesn't flinch. "Come on," he says. "You wouldn't shoot a guy on Christmas Eve, would you?" Then his eyes flick to the bodies already on the floor. "Actually, I guess you would."
I probably should kill him, just to be safe. Unlike the MGB agents, however, I don't think he's a real threat, just an inconvenience. A GI who happens to be in the wrong place. Besides, there are those blue eyes that make me think of a place I love. For this small gift, I will spare him. "Merry Christmas," I say, and bring the gun down on his temple. His body slumps beneath me as he passes out.
I scramble to my feet and run after Sauer and the girl, who are trying their best to get away from me. They've already reached the first floor. But they don't run out the now-open front door. Instead, they run for the kitchen at the rear of the house. I assume that they're going to try to escape through a back entrance. They won't.
What they don't know is that I don't want to have to kill them. They're worth much more to me alive. To me and my entire line. If

Sauer really has the information that we believe he does, it could change everything about how Endgame is played—that is, when it finally begins. And whoever controls that information might just be unstoppable.

The MGB agents were not lying when they said that Sauer used to work for the Nazis. Whether he agreed with their politics or not is another story, but that doesn't concern me. I'm only interested in what he knows. The Minoans don't believe other lines are aware of Sauer and what he might have discovered while working for the Nazis. But they could be. After all, we aren't the only ones with agents planted in strategic places. And the American solider I just ran into suggests that some world powers might be interested as well. I obviously know the Soviets want him. Multiple parties looking for him makes sense.

Of course, none of this matters if I can't get Sauer to cooperate. I was hoping that my killing the MGB agents who came for him would be proof enough that I'm one of the good guys. Then again, maybe I'm not. At least not in Sauer's eyes. It's funny how your perspective changes depending on which end of a gun you're on.

I reach the kitchen in time to see Sauer step through a door to a pantry. The girl is ahead of him. "Run, Lottie," he shouts as he pulls the door closed. "Go now!"

He's holding the door shut from the other side. Or trying to. I step back and aim a kick at the handle. The wood splinters as Sauer cries out. I kick it again, and it flies open. Inside the pantry, Sauer stands staring at me as, behind him, the girl disappears through another door that was hidden by shelves filled with jarred foods. A secret passage.

Sauer turns, grabs a jar of pickled beets, and hurls it at me. I dodge, and it hits the wall behind me, shattering and staining the wallpaper with red juice. He grabs another jar, and another. He's panicking. This gives me an advantage over him.

"I don't want to hurt you," I tell him, keeping my voice low and calm, as if I'm speaking to a frightened animal. I set the American's gun on a nearby tabletop and hold my hands up to show him that I'm now unarmed, at least as far as he knows. In reality, I remain as deadly as ever. "I want to help you," I continue. "I can get you out of Berlin. You and the girl. To safety."

He pauses, a jar in his hand. "Who are you?" he asks.

"A friend," I tell him.

"Some friend," says a voice from the hallway.

I turn and see GI Joe standing there. He's holding my own gun, and it's pointed at me.

"I figured since you coldcocked me with mine, you wouldn't mind if I borrowed yours," he says. Then, addressing Sauer, he says, "She's going to turn you over to the Soviets. They have a bounty on your head, and she plans to collect it."

I see Sauer's face contort in fear. Then, with a glance at the American, he throws the jar of sauerkraut in his hand at my head. I duck. Sauer turns and darts into the opening behind him. He pulls the shelves shut with a bang. I start to run after him, but a bullet whizzing past my head stops me. It just misses, and inside the pantry, several jars of pickles meet their deaths.

"I missed on purpose," the soldier says. "Next time I won't. Now turn around."

I do as he says. But even as I do, my mind is working out my options, formulating a plan. "He's getting away," I say.

"That's kind of the idea," he tells me. "Well, the idea is for him to get away from *you*. I can find him again."

He sounds sure of this, and I wonder why. Was he assigned to protect Sauer and the girl? But then why did they run away when we were fighting? If they were so sure of him, wouldn't they stay? Maybe, I think, he wasn't protecting them; maybe he was waiting to claim them for himself. Still, I can't help but be impressed by his confidence. Also by the fact that he came to much sooner than most people would have after I've hit them.

"Why don't we start by you telling me exactly who you are?" he says. "I made up that stuff about the Soviets, although it's obviously true that they want him, right?"

There's no point in lying about this because he's going to be dead in a minute, so I nod.

"But you're not Russian, are you?"

"No," I tell him. "I'm not."

"And I don't think you're German," he says. "So what are you? French?"

I snort. I wonder what he would say if I told him I was Minoan. Would he even know what that means? Instead, I say, "I'm Greek."

"Greek?" he repeats. "How about that. Well, I guess Greece has no love for the Nazis either."

This is true. Hitler's army did untold damage to my country and killed many of our people. But I'm not here to discuss history with an American soldier, and with every second we spend talking, Sauer is getting farther and farther away. I say nothing.

The soldier waves the gun at me, as if this will encourage me to answer him. "What's your business with Sauer?"

Does he really not know? I don't see how this is possible. Anyone who would take the time to find Evrard Sauer would have to know who he is. For one thing, he's been living under a different name.

Maybe, I think, the American is testing me to see what *I* know. Since he's wasting my time, I decide to play with him. "The Nazis took many things from my country. Including works of art from our museums. They've been hidden somewhere and haven't been found. Sauer knows where they are."

He looks puzzled. "You just killed two people so you could kidnap a . . . museum director?"

"An art historian," I lie. "And what was taken from us is priceless. It's our history. Your country is young, so perhaps you don't understand."

He shakes his head. "This doesn't make any sense." He sounds as if he's speaking to himself, not to me. I take the opportunity while his attention is elsewhere to look around the kitchen. I see a knife on the counter beside the sink. I could use that, if I could get to it. But even closer is a bag of flour.

I snatch the bag and hurl it at the soldier's head. He reacts immediately, bringing the pistol up and firing, exactly as I'd hoped he would. The bullet hits the bag, and the paper wrapper explodes. A cloud of flour erupts, filling the air like a snowstorm. The soldier is completely hidden from view, which means he can't see me either.

I run into the pantry and pull on the shelf hiding the secret entrance. Luckily, there's no trick to it, and it flies open. A set of stairs leads down into a brick-lined tunnel. I step inside, pull the shelves closed, and look for a way to secure it so the soldier can't follow me, at least not easily. I'm surprised to discover that the back of the door is covered in metal sheeting, and that there's actually a very solid bolting mechanism attached to it, making it easy to secure from this side and virtually impossible to open from the other. Sauer must have been in too much of a panic to bother with it. Or he hoped that I wouldn't be in any condition to chase him.

I lock the door. A moment later, the pounding begins.

I ignore it, knowing that the American can't get through, at least not for a while. Now it's time to turn my attention back to Sauer. I wonder how far he's gotten and if I can catch up with him. Everything is now in question. At least the American is no longer in my way. I run down the tunnel I now find myself in, leaving him to whatever the Fates have in store for him. My own destiny lies ahead of me in the darkness, and I rush to meet it.

CHAPTER 3

Boone

It becomes clear pretty quickly that I'm not going to be able to open the door. From this side it looks like an ordinary door, one I should be able to kick down, or at least shoot my way through. But as my aching foot and the bullets lodged in the wood prove, this isn't the case. This door has been designed to keep anyone from getting through it. Whoever installed it meant business.

Berlin is riddled with former safe houses, places where people who might have reason to hide could hole up and wait until the coast was clear. My line has a safe house here as well. I'm supposed to take Sauer to it and await extraction instructions. Now, unless I can get through this door and catch up to him, I'll be waiting in that house alone, trying to figure out how to explain to my council how I let a girl get away with my prize. An amazingly smart girl, and one who was able to knock me out, but nobody's going to care about that part. All they'll care about is that she took what should be mine.

I stare at the door, trying to figure out a way through it, my frustration growing. Then I hear my trainer's voice in my head. *If you can't go through, then go around, go under, or go over.* He used to put me in seemingly impossible situations and make me figure a way out. A nine-foot wall I had to scale. A rushing river to get across. A trap to get out of. Anything to force me to think differently. There's always a way. Always.

I start by asking myself what's behind the door. While it's possible that the door leads to just another room, it's more likely that it leads to some kind of an exit. And if there's an exit, I should be able to find it. But I've already lost a lot of time trying to get through. I have to hurry.

The kitchen has another door leading to the backyard, but it's boarded up, and there's no time to pry the boards off. So I run back down the hallway and out of the house, a cloud of flour flying around me. I have to admit, the girl's trick was pretty clever, even if she has made me look like a fool twice now. And I still don't know who she is or what she's doing here. She's become a mystery that I'm determined to solve. First, I have to catch her.

Getting into the backyard of Sauer's house is as simple as running through the downstairs of the deserted house next door and climbing over a fence into the small yard. I stop and survey, sketching a map in my head. There is a set of steps leading down to a cellar, but I know this isn't where the secret passage comes out. The whole point is to get as far away from the house as possible before you have to come up into the open. Most likely, it runs the length of the yard, then opens up into a sewer system or some other network of already-established tunnels.

I cross the yard and climb over yet another fence. This street looks much like the one I've just left, a row of town houses, many of them bombed out and empty. The tunnel could lead to, or pass under, any of them. With each second taking Sauer farther away from me, I run in one direction, hoping to find something that will provide a clue.

I find it in the form of a garden. It appears as a small break in the line of houses, really just an empty space where normally another building would have been. Instead, there's a gated fence behind that sits on a lot that contains a small fountain, a bench, and a toolshed.

It's the shed that interests me. It's the perfect spot for an underground tunnel to come out. Then, as I peer through the bars, I see something else: footprints coming out of the shed. Everything in the garden is covered in snow, so the footsteps are easy to see. And there's more than one set of them. They lead to the opposite side of the lot, where another gate opens onto another street. The gate is open, and the footsteps continue through it. My guess is that the girl has recently passed through there with Sauer and Lottie.

The gate on my side is locked, but it's easy enough to scale the fence and get inside the garden. I run to the other side and follow the footprints. The street is deserted, so it's easy to see them. But then they turn onto another street filled with people and disappear into the crowd. I scan the block for the mystery girl, Sauer, or Lottie, but there are too many bodies, and everyone seems to be wearing heavy coats that look the same. Between that, the dark, and the snow, my chances of finding them are almost nonexistent.

Then something crunches under my foot. Curious, I bend down to see what it is. It's a candy. A toffee, wrapped in cellophane. I think back to the gift that Sauer gave the girl. It can't be a coincidence. Candy is heavily rationed, and it's unlikely someone would just drop one by accident.

I start walking and find another about 20 feet farther on, then another. Now I'm certain that they weren't dropped by accident. Someone has left me a trail to follow.

It's not easy searching for them in the snow, and I'd look crazy shining my flashlight around, but the light from the streetlamps helps. I see a sparkle and find another candy. I pick it up and add it to the growing lump in my coat pocket. Approximately every 20 feet, I find another one, although sometimes there are gaps where either the candy has been kicked away or perhaps picked up by somebody else.

The trail of toffees leads down the street and around a corner, where it comes to an end. Then I notice a child, a little boy of about four or five. He and his mother are standing together. He's holding something in his hand. As I watch, he unwraps it and puts it into his mouth.

"What is that?" his mother asks.

The boy shrugs. "Candy?" he says doubtfully.

His mother, clearly alarmed, snatches the wrapper from his hand and looks at it. "Where did you get this?"

The boy points. "A man gave it to me," he said. "As he was getting on that streetcar."

I turn my head just in time to see a streetcar rounding a corner at the end of the street, tethered to the electric line above it. I run to the boy and his mother. "Where does that streetcar go?"

The woman puts her arm around the boy and draws him closer to her. "To the Soviet sector."

I thank her and take off after the streetcar. It's not going very fast, but it's difficult to keep pace running on the slippery pavement. Also, if the mystery girl is keeping an eye out for me, I don't want her to see me running behind the streetcar like a madman. I still don't know if she's caught up with Sauer and Lottie, or if she's trying to follow them too. Until I can figure out which of them—or any of them—is on the streetcar, I need to be careful.

Fortunately, the streetcar makes frequent stops to let people on and off, which gives me a chance both to rest and to try to get a glimpse inside. Unfortunately, the cold has made the windows frosty, and I can't see through them. And if the girl is with Sauer and Lottie, I don't want to get on and risk a confrontation in front of so many people. So I watch to see if Sauer or either woman gets off, but they don't. I can only hope that I'm right about them being on it.

Once again I wonder who the girl is. Twice now I've had the chance to kill her, and twice I haven't. I can't explain why, except that, for reasons I don't entirely understand, I want to know who she is. And it's not just that she's undeniably beautiful. It's more than that. There's something about her that at the same time feels both very familiar and completely foreign. For one thing, she also could have killed me but didn't. And I know she has no problem killing. She took down the two MGB agents without blinking. No ordinary soldier would do that—or even be able to. You have to be a certain kind of person to kill so easily, or at least to make it look so easy.

Someone like a Player, I think.

Maybe my line isn't the only one that's after Sauer. Maybe the girl is Playing too.

She's the right age. Also, she's a, well, she. Most militaries don't train women to fight. They're mainly nurses or some other kind of noncombat personnel. Yet she fights like a soldier—a highly trained soldier. She had to learn it somewhere, and despite her remark about street fighting, there's no way she got this good from a couple of brawls on a playground.

If she is Playing, then the question is: for which line? She said she was Greek, so if she wasn't lying, she's a Minoan. If another line wants Sauer badly enough to kill for him, then what he knows has to have some bearing on Endgame. I don't believe for one second the girl's story about him being an art historian. Something bigger is happening here. Once again, I question why my own council hasn't told me what it is.

I think again of how she reminds me of Wonder Woman. The Amazon princess. What was her real name? Diana Prince. Maybe that's what I should call her. Diana. Diana was also the goddess of the hunt, so it fits there too. We're both hunters, after the same quarry. Has she already caught them? I still don't know.

The streetcar stops, and again the doors open. I peer through the open door as people get out, and just for a second I see a face looking back at me. It's Sauer. Our eyes meet, and a look of panic appears on Sauer's face. His eyes dart away, then back to me, and for a moment I think he's about to run off the streetcar. Then the doors close.

What did the look mean? Was he afraid because he saw me? Or was it because Diana was with him, making sure he didn't get away? I don't know. But now at least I know that he's on the streetcar, and it renews my desire to follow it wherever it goes.

When the streetcar crosses from the American sector to the Soviet sector, I worry for a moment that I might be stopped. Although people are still free to move around the city, an American soldier walking into Soviet territory could be suspicious. But it's Christmas Eve, and lots of people are going back and forth to visit friends and family, so I risk it. As I walk past the big sign announcing YOU ARE LEAVING THE AMERICAN SECTOR, I barely get a glance from the grim-faced Red Army soldiers standing around cradling their rifles in their arms.

Even though it's the same city, the Soviet sector of Berlin feels different. There's a tenseness here, as if the residents and even the buildings are holding their breaths. The people walking around seem to be in a hurry to get wherever it is they're going. Instead of looking at one another, they look at the ground. Even the snowfall seems heavier here, the cold more biting. I pull up the collar of my coat and glance over my shoulder, more on guard than usual.

The streetcar makes less frequent stops as it moves deeper into Soviet-controlled territory. Thanks to the snow and the outdated and unreliable overhead wires that power the streetcar, it moves slowly enough that I can keep up with it without having to do an all-out run. Then it stops at the corner of a street lined with nondescript apartment buildings, and half a dozen people get off. Three of them detach from the group and walk away, and as they pass through the glow of a streetlight I see that one of them is wearing a red scarf. Sauer. And the other two are Lottie and Diana.

The trio walks quickly. Diana stays one pace behind the other two. I wonder if they've come willingly or if she's got a gun to their backs. If she's a Player too, Sauer is the one she wants, so perhaps she's told him she'll kill Lottie if he doesn't play along. As my father always says, love is the greatest danger of all. It's why he's warned me not to fall in love until I'm no longer a Player. When you have something you're afraid of losing, it gives your enemies a weapon to use against you.

Three blocks later, the group walks into a building that looks like all the other ones on the street. Five stories tall. Surprisingly undamaged. They disappear through a door, and I wait outside across the street. I keep my eyes on the windows, scanning the floors in an orderly manner from top to bottom, then back up. As I'm scanning for the fourth time, a light goes on. I note which apartment it is. Fourth floor, third from the left.

"Bingo," I say aloud. "Got you."

CHAPTER 4

Ariadne

I am not happy about how things have played out.

As I draw the shade on the window facing the street, I wish that the Minoans had a safe house in Berlin. But we do not, and so advance agents set up this apartment, which is occupied by an elderly woman of our line who calls herself Lydia. Sixty years ago she was known by another name, one that is familiar to all Minoan Players. She was one of our greatest, a legend. Often when one of my class of candidates was struggling during an exercise, our trainers would yell, "Europa would be at the top of that cliff by now!" or some such thing. Often, I pictured her in my mind, fighting or swimming beside me, urging me on. Now she looks like one of the *yia yia*s who crowd the markets of Greece, haggling over the price of olives and fish, yet still I feel I am in the presence of a great fighter.

"Do you think you were followed?" Lydia asks as she stirs the pot of avgolemono soup on the stove. She tastes it, then adds more salt. As I smell it, my mouth waters.

I've told her about the American soldier. I had to, as his interference prevented us from following our original plan, which was to have my compatriots meet me at the house where Sauer was hiding and take him by car out of the city. Instead, I had to take the extremely risky move of getting on the streetcar and coming here. By now, Theron and Cilla will have realized that something has gone wrong and should also be making their way here.

"I don't think so," I say.

"You're not sure?"

Once a Player, always a Player, I think to myself.
"I didn't see him anywhere," I tell her. "But it's dark, and I was focused on making sure Sauer and the girl didn't try to run."
Lydia ladles soup into a bowl and carries it to the table. "You worry too much," she says, patting me on the cheek.
"Perhaps you don't worry enough," I reply gently. I am not arguing with her, as I respect her too much. Also, she reminds me of my own grandmother.
She laughs. "Sit," she says. "Eat. Theron and Cilla will be here soon, and then you'll be on your way."
"In a minute," I tell her. "First, I need to speak with our guest."
I pass through the living room, ignoring the girl, who is tied to a kitchen chair, a cloth around her mouth to prevent her from calling out. I go into one of the bedrooms, where Sauer is likewise tied up, and I shut the door behind me. I go to him, remove the gag, and sit on the edge of the bed.
"Who are you?" he asks.
There is no point in lying, so I tell him. "My name is Ariadne Calligaris."
"You are not Russian," he says.
"No."
"What do you want with me?"
"You were working on a project involving a weapon," I say. "We want that weapon."
"Who is *we*?"
This I do not tell him. Instead I say, "The weapon is of alien design. You were asked to build it, or rebuild it, from plans that the Nazis discovered."
He looks genuinely surprised but says nothing.
"There is going to be a war," I continue. "A war that will make this most recent one look like a child's game. The weapon you discovered may decide who wins and who loses."
He shrugs. "Why do I care who wins?"

"Maybe you don't. Maybe you don't care if you live or die. I think you do care whether the girl out there lives or dies."
Sauer looks at me, and I know that I'm right. Actually, I knew already, as my threat to shoot her if either of them tried to run is what allowed me to get them here after escaping from the American. At first I was irritated by the unexpected presence of the girl. Now I am grateful for her, as I can use her as a bargaining chip in dealing with Sauer.
"I don't have the weapon," he says.
"Where is it?"
"Destroyed," he says. "In the bombing. Along with the blueprints."
I stand up and take my weapon from its holster. "Then I have no need for you or the girl," I say, chambering a round. I walk to the door and put my hand on the knob.
"Wait," he says, as I knew he would.
I turn and look at him, saying nothing.
"I don't have them," he says. "But I know where they are."
"Are they in Berlin?"
He nods.
"Can you get to them?"
"I don't know."
"You have half an hour to decide," I tell him as I open the door. I shut it behind me, leaving him to think about his situation. I don't know if he's telling the truth or not. He might be trying to buy time. If he's lying and the weapon and the plans really have been destroyed, it will be unfortunate for him. Some of what he's discovered will still be in his head, and we can't allow him to live with that information. It's too valuable.
I return to the kitchen and sit down at the table. Lydia sits down across from me. She doesn't speak, but her lifted eyebrows ask a question.
I know the girl is listening from the living room, and even though I have no reason to think that she speaks Greek, I don't want to say too much. "The soup is wonderful," I say to Lydia. "You'll have to give me

the recipe. I had it, but it might have been lost."

She nods to show she understands my meaning: Sauer might or might not have what we want. And as I told him, he has until Theron and Cilla arrive to make up his mind. Until then, there is nothing else I can do, so I eat Lydia's soup and think about how, if all goes well, in a few days I'll be back in Greece with this mission behind me, and perhaps something that will greatly strengthen the Minoan line's resources. If I am successful, my name will perhaps join Europa's in the list of the great Players. Second only to winning Endgame itself, this would be a great achievement, and it would show my council that they chose the right Player.

When there's a knock at the door, Lydia stands. "Theron and Cilla," she says.

As Lydia goes to answer the door, I get up and go into the living room. Although there is a short hallway between the door and the living room, and the girl is out of sight, I train my gun on her anyway as a reminder not to make any noise.

"Who is it?" I hear Lydia ask.

"Dagmar, from next door," says an elderly woman's voice. "Can you help me? My stove has gone out, and I need a match."

"Just a moment," Lydia says. As she comes back to the living room she tells me, "The gas is always going out in the building. I'll pass her a match through the door. It will look bad if I refuse."

Again I wish that we were not in an apartment building. There is nothing to be done about it, however, and soon the old woman will be gone. I keep my eye and my gun on the girl as Lydia fetches a box of matches and returns to the door. I hear the click of the lock as she opens it.

"Here you are," she says.

A moment later Lydia returns to the living room—but she's not alone. There's a man behind her. He has one arm around her neck and is pointing a gun at me. A second man appears, holding an old woman I assume is Dagmar. She's whimpering softly, saying, "I'm sorry, I'm sorry, I'm sorry."

"Shut her up," the man holding Lydia says.

The man holding Dagmar places a knife at her throat and slices it, as if she's nothing more than a chicken being readied for the stewpot. The old woman's eyes widen, and her hands flutter to her neck. The man lets go, and she crumples to the floor. He looks down at her, grinning, her blood on the blade of the knife in his hand. I consider shooting him, but I can feel the other man watching me.

"Put your gun down," that one says now. "Or she's next." He tightens his grip on Lydia's neck.

"Don't. Kill him," Lydia says to me in Greek.

"Quiet," the man orders.

I look into Lydia's eyes and try to telegraph a message to her as I hold my hands up and gently place my gun on a nearby end table.

"Good girl," the man says. He looks at Lottie, who throughout all of this has remained in her chair, watching everything. Then he says to the other man, "Go find the engineer."

The other man disappears down the hallway to the bedrooms. I know I have very little time. Once he finds Sauer, these men will have no use for me or Lydia. I don't know why we aren't dead already.

The man holding Lydia watches me. "Why do the Greeks want Sauer?"

So he understood Lydia. And now I know why we're still alive—he needs information from us. If I can keep him waiting long enough, perhaps Theron and Cilla will arrive and all of us will get out of here alive.

"Why do the Russians?" I counter.

He smiles. "You should know," he says. "Isn't that why you killed Sergei and Pavel?"

The MGB agents. But is he also MGB? Or is he with another group? And how did he find me? I have questions of my own.

Before I can ask them, or answer his, Lydia acts. The Player she used to be comes to life, and she throws her head back and hits the man in the chin. At the same time, she brings her foot down as hard as she can on top of his. He cries out in surprise and pain, loosening his hold on her neck. She breaks free, whirls on him, and with surprising strength for someone her age, knocks the gun from his grasp, sending it flying across the room. Then she draws a paring knife from her apron pocket. She brings it down toward his chest, but he deflects her hand and she ends up stabbing him in the shoulder. As he shoves her roughly away, I grab for my gun on the table.

Lydia stumbles backward and hits the table hard just as I'm picking up the pistol. It slides onto the floor, and before I can get it, the man pulls the knife from his shoulder and rushes at me. I abandon the gun and prepare to meet him. As he nears me, I center myself and deliver a kick to his groin that sends him to his knees, clutching himself. It's not a pretty trick, but it's the first one I learned when fighting boys on the playground, and it remains effective.

As he moans and curses me in Russian, I go for my gun to finish him off before his cohort comes in and round two starts. That's when I notice Lydia still lying on the floor, unable to get up.

"My leg," she says, and I see it twisted cruelly beneath her. She must have fallen on it. I start to help her, but she waves me away. "Finish them first," she says.

I nod, proud of her resolve, and reach for my gun. But before my fingers grasp it, someone kicks it away. I look up to see an enormous man standing over me. How he got in without me noticing, I don't know. It seems impossible that such a large figure could move that quietly. Yet here he is, a gun pointed at my head. He looks at Lydia, then at her leg.

"When horse break leg, of no more use," he says in broken English, and fires a bullet into her head.

I let loose a bellow and spring for him. His foot hits my chest, knocking me back, but I barely feel it due to the rage rushing through me. I leap back up and go at him with my bare hands, but stagger when a huge fist hits me in the side of the face.

"You want to play?" he growls. "Okay. We play."

He holsters his gun and faces me with just his fists. A smile plays on his lips. He thinks he has me defeated already because of his size. I don't flinch, don't show any sign of fear. I'm a Player. I've faced worse. Even so, my heart quickens when the man on the floor gets up and the third man emerges from the hallway. The two of them stand back, watching, as if this were a spectator sport.

If a show is what they want, that's what they're going to get. I'm not just fighting for my life now, I'm fighting to avenge Lydia. I hurl myself at the giant and land a blow to his solar plexus. It feels like punching a steel door.

The next few minutes are a whirlwind of fists and feet. I've had the best training in the world, but this guy is MGB trained, and he is my match in hand-to-hand combat. He also seems immune to pain. Only when I bust his lip with a well-placed punch does he show any sign of faltering.

The other two join the fray like jackals coming to the aid of a weakening pack member.

No matter how well trained I am, it's me against three huge men. They manage to shove me to the floor, all three of them pressing their knees into my back to keep me there. I buck and kick wildly, trying to throw them off. But a rag is forced against my face. It smells sweet, and I know I'm being drugged.

"I think we will have a little fun with her before we kill her," the giant says.

My head begins to cloud as the drug takes effect. This is not how I want to go out. I want to fight these men to the death. Every fiber of my body cries out to me to fight. But I can't. Despite all of my training, I can't stop the drug from washing over me. My last thought before I pass into oblivion is that I have failed my line.

CHAPTER 5

Boone

I've been standing across from the building where Diana is holed up with Sauer and Lottie for twenty minutes, keeping myself hidden in the shadows, when four figures approach the front of the building. They stop and look up at the windows, pointing in the direction of the same one I've been watching. I wait for them to do something, but as a car turns onto the street and comes toward us, the figures disappear into an alley along one side of the building.

The car stops, and two people get out. As they too walk toward the building, they pass by the entrance to the alley. I watch as they're pulled into the darkness. A moment later, three figures come out and go to the front door. As they disappear inside, I rush across the street. There's one man still alive in the alley. His back is to me. Before he can turn, I walk up behind him and snap his neck. As I lay his body on the snowy ground, I look at the two bodies already in the alley. They were shot, and the white snow is turning pink from their blood. If the snow continues to fall as it is now, all three bodies will be covered within a few hours. Not that it will matter when someone finds them. If all goes well, I won't be here.

The other two dead are a man and a woman. Who they are, I have no idea. There's nothing in their pockets to identify them. As for the man I killed, a search of him turns up an identification card in Russian. I assume it's a forgery.

I leave the dead and go after the living. There's no time for stealth. I take the direct route through the front of the building and up the stairs. I see no one in the halls, and I hope that I'm correct about

which apartment I think Diana has taken Sauer and Lottie to.
I arrive on the fourth floor and see that one of the doors is ajar. I was right—it belongs to the apartment I identified. But before I can reach it, the door shuts. I pause, listening, and hear voices coming from behind the wood.
"I think we will have a little fun with her before we kill her," a man says.
I don't know if he means Lottie or Diana. And I don't care. The excitement in his voice enrages me. I've done some things in my short life that I would rather not have done, but it's always been out of necessity. I would never hurt someone just for fun. Not even during Endgame. And this, what he's suggesting, is unthinkable.
I test the door. It's unlocked, which is a surprising but welcome piece of luck. I open it a crack to peer inside and draw my gun, ready in case anyone is waiting there. The first thing I see is the body of an old woman. Then another one. And then I see Lottie, tied to a chair and looking at me with frantic eyes.
My first instinct is to untie her, find Sauer, and get them out of there. That's what a Player should do. But I'm not just a Player. I'm a brother, and a son, and when I think about what I heard the men say, it makes me think of my sisters and my mother. Lottie isn't going anywhere, and although the girl in the other room might be my enemy, she doesn't deserve what those men have planned for her. So even though I hear my trainers yelling at me to get the prize and get out, I choose to make a detour.
Lottie struggles, scraping her chair against the floor. I wish I could untie her, but that's a bad idea. She could escape, or run into more thugs. At least tied up, she's out of harm's way. I put my finger to my lips to keep her quiet and move down the hall.
I follow the sound of voices in the back of the apartment. There are three doorways. When I reach the first one, I look inside and see Sauer tied to a chair. He's wearing a gag, but he gives me the same frantic look that Lottie gave me. But he's safer here tied up, so I put a finger

to my lips and back out of the room. The second door is to an empty bathroom. I take a deep breath outside the third room, steady my gun, and push open the door. Diana is lying unconscious on a bed. The three men are standing around her, arguing in Russian about who is going to go first.

I shoot the biggest guy through the forehead. He's a giant of a man, and I want him out of the way. He falls across the girl with a heavy smack. One of the others pulls a gun, but I shoot him quickly as well. The last guy fumbles for his gun—I'm quicker. But when I fire at him, the Soviet pistol jams, and nothing happens. I try again, and this time a gun explodes—but it's not mine. Pain rips through my arm. I don't know how he's missed so badly, at such close range, but I don't stop to think about it. I throw myself at him and knock the gun from his hand.

We fight with our hands. We're evenly matched, but my opponent keeps punching me where I've been shot. It hurts like hell, but it's not the first time I've battled through this kind of pain. I grit my teeth, ignore it, and fight. This thug isn't going to stand in the way of my mission.

The room is small, and we keep crashing into furniture as we grapple with each other. A lamp tumbles from a bedside table and shatters. A bureau is overturned. We slip in the blood of the dead men as we perform a dance in which we keep changing positions.

Then my opponent pulls a knife from his boot. The next thing I know it's being thrust at my stomach. I turn to the side, and it slides across my thigh instead. The fabric of my pants splits neatly, and blood begins to flow. It's not a mortal wound, but it hurts like the devil, even more than the bullet graze on my arm, because it goes deeper.

I can feel my strength waning, and I know I have to finish this. So when my opponent attempts once again to push his knife into my gut, I grab him by the back of the neck and use his forward momentum to slam his head down on one of the metal knobs that decorate the footboard of the bed. The first blow stuns him, but he still attempts to break away from me, so I repeat the motion, over and over, until his face is a bloody mess and he's no longer moving. It's not a pretty victory, but I'll take it.

I toss his body to the floor. Then I pull the dead brute from atop Diana and make sure she's still breathing. She is. I leave her snoring peacefully on the bed and I go to check on Sauer and Lottie.

But when I check the second bedroom, I find it empty. An empty chair sits in the middle of the living room, rope coiled around it on the floor. They're gone.

I rush to the windows and look out. The street is empty. I check the hallway, but I know it will be deserted as well. It is.

Damn it. If I hadn't chosen to help Diana, I'd have them in my custody now. I think about running down to the street and trying to find them, but they could be anywhere—and what am I going to do, run after them with a bullet wound and a bleeding leg? Besides, Diana is still unconscious in the bedroom. As much as it angers me to lose Sauer and Lottie yet again, I have a feeling that the girl in the bedroom might have information that will help me find them again. I make the decision to stay in the apartment.

I shut the apartment door and lock it, then tend to my own wounds. The bullet seems to have only grazed me, so I clean the abrasion with soap and water and tie a strip of towel around it. The cut on my leg is another matter. I'm going to need to stitch it up. For now, I tear off another strip of towel and tie it tight to stop the bleeding. Then I return to the bedroom.

I drag the three bodies into the living room, where I lay them next to the bodies of the old women. I feel bad about making them keep company with their murderers, but there's not really anything else I can do with them.

Despite the ruined furniture and the blood splatter, Diana looks like some kind of enchanted princess asleep in a tower, waiting for a prince to wake her with true love's kiss. Her hands are resting at her sides, and her lips are parted slightly as she breathes.

I sit down on the end of the bed, watching her and thinking about my next step. Finding Sauer is my main objective, one I've already ignored in order to save this girl. I hope I made the right choice and that she really will have some information that will make helping her worth jeopardizing my mission. Then her eyes flutter open. She looks at me, frowns, and starts to rise up with a roar. I grab her wrists and hold them.

"It's all right," I say as she thrashes. "You're safe."

It sounds so stupid to say that. Of course she's not safe. Neither of us is safe. We need to get out of this place, and soon. But I don't know how else to calm her down.

"Let me go!" she says, her voice still heavy from whatever sedative she's been given.

I do. I wait for her to attack me, but she pulls back. I see her trying to focus her eyes.

"I'm not going to hurt you," I tell her.

This makes her laugh. I want to be angry, but I can't be. I laugh with her. She shakes her head, as if shaking off the last of the drug, and looks around the room. "Is that mine or yours?" she says.

"The blood?" I say. "Most of it belonged to the men who were going to kill you."

Her face hardens, and I know she's remembering everything now. "Where are Sauer and Lottie?" she asks me.

I shake my head. "Gone. While I was dealing with our Soviet friends."

"What!" she exclaims. "You should have watched them!"

"And let you die?"

"Yes," she says, and I know she means it. The look she's giving me makes it clear what she thinks of my decision. "If they escaped on foot, we could still catch them." She tries to get up, but she's still a little groggy, and lies back, an expression of frustration on her face.

"You really are an Amazon, aren't you?" I remark.

"What?"
"Nothing," I say, embarrassed to tell her how I've been thinking about her.
"Maybe Theron and Cilla took them," she says hopefully.
"Colleagues of yours?"
She nods.
"I wouldn't count on that," I say, and tell her about the bodies I saw in the alley downstairs.
She looks furious. "I don't know how they found us." She looks at me. "How did *you* find us?"
"Sauer left a trail of candies."
"I can't believe I didn't notice," she says.
I ask the question I've been wondering about since we met. "Why did you want them anyway? And who is this *us* you keep talking about?"
She stiffens. I know she still doesn't trust me. I need to give her a reason to.
"My name is Sam Boone," I tell her. "But everyone calls me Boone."
She looks into my eyes. "Do you like to Play, Boone?" she asks.
She says it just like that. I can hear the capital *P* in her voice. I also feel a shiver of excitement running through me. I decide to take a risk, a big one. "I do," I tell her. "And I think you do too."
"Cahokian?" she asks.
"How did you know?"
She points to my uniform. "Your American accent," she says. "It's obvious under your German and Russian."
I ignore the insult. "And you?" I say. "Minoan?"
She nods. "My name is Ariadne Calligaris."
Now I know her real name. I'm in shock. I've never met any other Player. Has she? But there are more important things to discuss.
"Why do the Minoans want Sauer? And don't give me the art historian bullshit."
"The Minoans want him for the same reason the Cahokians do," she says.

I know she's testing me to see what I know. And I don't know much. Obviously, this is about Endgame. Apart from that, I'm in the dark.

She lifts an eyebrow. "You really don't know about the weapon, do you?"

It's too late to pretend that I do, so I tell her the truth. "All I know is that I'm supposed to get Sauer and take him out of Berlin."

She hesitates. "Never mind," she says. "I shouldn't say anything."

"I saved your life," I said. "I think you owe me for that. I could easily have let them kill you," I remind her. "Or killed you myself."

She waits another minute before she talks. I know exactly what she's doing, because I do it too—weighing the benefits and risks of telling me what she knows. It's strange to see someone else doing what I would do myself. I wait to see if she would make the same choice I would. It's strangely exciting.

"Sauer is an engineer," she says. "He was working with the Nazis during the war. They discovered something." She hesitates. Makes more calculations. Comes to another decision. "Alien technology. A weapon of some kind. Sauer was brought in to help them build it. Or rebuild it. We don't know if they found any actual parts, or just plans."

I feel like I've been punched in the gut. Alien technology. A weapon. Is she talking about the Cahokian weapon, the one that could be used to defeat the Makers? If so, this is bigger than I ever imagined. Much bigger. But how much does she know? I can't show her how surprised I am. "How did the Minoans find out about it?"

"We have spies," she says. "I assume you do too."

Of course we do. My brother Jackson was working as a Cahokian spy in Germany when he was killed three years ago. Now I wonder if Jackson is how my council knew about Sauer. If so, then why did they wait so long to do anything about it?

The Cahokian weapon. I can't quite believe that's what this is all about, or that my council didn't tell me. Unless they don't know either. And maybe I'm wrong. Maybe it's just a weapon, and not *the* weapon. More important right now is my worry that if the Minoans know about the weapon, other lines may know about it too. It's time to get going. And for right now, anyway, it looks as if the Minoan will be part of my plans.

"So, Ariadne Calligaris," I say. "What do we do next?"

She bites her lip. Then she points to the bandage on my leg, which has turned red with blood. "First, we sew you up," she says.

CHAPTER 6

Ariadne

As I pass the needle through Boone's skin, he says, "It looks like you've done this before."

"I have," I tell him. "Many times. When I was little, I learned to do it on dead pigs because their skin is so similar to human skin. Then, in training, we practiced on one another. Sometimes after we'd inflicted the wounds ourselves."

"They had you stab one another?" he asks.

I nod. "Not on purpose. We didn't try for lethal blows, but sometimes there were accidents."

I smile a little, thinking of one or two occasions when I "accidentally" gave one of the boys in my training group a lesson in underestimating me. Boone sees this.

"Goddamn," he says, laughing. "Sorry."

I pull the thread taut, closing the wound on his thigh. "We're sitting in a room painted with the blood of a man whose head you beat to a pulp," I remind him. "And you're apologizing for using a curse word?"

Boone laughs. "I guess you're right," he says. "But my mother always says you should never swear in front of a girl."

"Then it's a good thing I'm not a girl," I tell him. "I'm a woman."

Boone grins. I poke him again with the needle, and the grin turns into a frown. "Ouch!" he yelps, and I laugh.

"That's what hurts?" I say. "After you've been shot *and* stabbed?"

He grimaces. "I wasn't expecting it."

I smile. I want him to think I'm helping him because I'm grateful to him for saving my life. Which I am, even if I think it was a mistake on his part. Truthfully, I'm only sewing up his wound because it gives me an opportunity to find out more about him.

"So what kind of training do Cahokians do?" I ask him.

"Lots of wilderness survival skills," he says. "Living off the land. When I was eleven, my trainers took me to a forest I'd never been to before, in the middle of a blizzard, and left me there. Naked. With nothing. I had to find my way out."

For a moment, I picture him naked in a forest. Not when he was younger, but as he is now. The fact that he's sitting next to me in just his boxer shorts and a T-shirt makes it not that hard. Unexpectedly, I feel heat flash across my cheeks. If he sees it, he does not give any sign.

"Well," I say as I tie off the last stitch. "You apparently made it out."

"Barely," he says, inspecting my handiwork. "I just about froze to death."

"Two in my training group died," I say as I gather up the things I've used to treat his wound. "One was killed diving from a cliff into the sea. The other was poisoned."

"Poisoned?" Boone says. "How?"

"He chose the wrong date during a test," I say. "I suppose he wasn't paying attention when they taught us how to recognize food that has been tainted. He was always talking too much."

"Your trainers just let him eat it and die?" says Boone. He sounds shocked, and maybe a little disgusted.

"Would your trainers have let you die in the woods if you hadn't made it out on your own?" I ask him.

He looks away. I can tell that he has never considered this question.

I've never met a Player from another line, and part of me finds it fun to compare notes. I've never been able to talk about this with anyone before, except for my trainers.

"You trained alone?" I ask him.

"Mostly," he says. "But my brother was our Player before me, and I saw a lot of what he did and participated in some of his training."

"Minoans train as a group," I explain. "Starting when we are very young. After several years, one is chosen to be the Player and receives the golden horns."

"Golden horns?" says Boone. "What are those?"

"A symbol," I say. "Of King Minos, the first king of Crete. There's a ceremony where the new Player is presented to the people and the horns are placed on her head."

"Minos," says Boone. "Like the legend of the Minotaur." He snaps his fingers. "That's where I've heard your name before. Ariadne was the daughter of King Minos. She helped Theseus kill the Minotaur and escape from the maze under the palace."

I nod. Of course I have heard the story of the bull-headed Minotaur and the Athenian youths sent to him every nine years as sacrifices many, many times. I'm impressed that he knows it. "You know mythology," I remark.

Boone nods. "I like stories about gods and heroes," he admits. "Sometimes, when training got really tough, I pretended I was Hercules or Jason, trying to prove myself to the gods. It helped."

"It's very close to the truth, isn't it?" I say. "Isn't that what Endgame will be, a battle to prove to our gods which of us is the greatest?"

"They're not my gods," Boone says as he puts his shirt back on and buttons it up. "I don't know what they are, but they're not gods."

I say nothing. I don't want to argue about this with him. Besides, my feelings are my own.

"Anyway, in a year, it's the next Player's problem," Boone says.

I'm surprised. "You sound like you don't want to Play," I say.

"Oh, I like Playing," he says as he puts his pants on. "I just don't want Endgame to happen for a long, long time. Why would I want the world to end?"

"The world won't end," I remind him. "Not for the winning line."

"But it will for all the other ones," he says.

I've never heard anyone talk like this about Endgame. For me, it's always been a certainty. I've always been prepared for it to happen, and I was taught to believe it would happen during my turn as Player.

If it doesn't, then all of my training will have been for nothing.

"Think about all the people killed during the war," Boone continues. "For them, that was Endgame. Imagine being someone in Japan, watching those bombs fall and wipe out everything like that."

He snaps his fingers loudly. "Everything. Gone. Whole cities, and everyone in them. Imagine being in London, or here in Berlin, and listening to the planes flying overhead, filled with bombs. And you don't know if the next one that falls is going to land on your house, or on your grandparents' house, or on your best friend's house. It all depends on where some pilot decides to drop them. And there's nothing you can do about it."

"But we can win Endgame," I argue.

Boone holds up a single finger. "One," he says. "One Player can win Endgame. The rest die."

"I thought it was your brother who thought too much about these things," I remark.

Boone smiles. "Maybe I'm more like him than I thought," he says. Then a strange look comes over his face. "And maybe that's why the council—" he says, but he sounds like he's talking to himself now, not to me.

"Why the council what?" I ask.

He shakes his head. "Nothing," he says. "So, how are we going to figure out where Sauer and Lottie went?"

"We?" I say.

He shrugs. "We might as well work together, right? Now that we're not trying to kill each other?"

I roll the needle in my fingers back and forth. Boone cocks his head. "Or are you going to kill me?" he says.

"Since I've stitched you back together, it would be stupid to kill you now," I tell him.

He smiles. "Does that make me Theseus?"

I snort. "Hardly. Do you have any idea where Sauer and the girl might have gone?"

He shakes his head. "None. Do you?"

I don't. I know someone who might, though. Now I weigh whether or not to share this information with Boone. I always repay my debts, both good and bad, and he did save me from the MGB agents. However, I'm not certain he can be of any more use to me.

"I think they're running as far away from us as they can get," I say. "Finding them will be next to impossible."

"So we're just supposed to give up? Somehow I don't think that's ever an option for you."

"Do you have a better idea?"

"Not at the moment, no," he admits. "But if we put our heads together, combine information, we—"

"I work better alone," I say.

Boone laughs. "Yeah? Look where that got you. Drugged and pretty damn near dead."

"I already thanked you for your help," I snap. "And I returned the favor as well. I stitched you up and told you about Sauer and the weapon. As far as I'm concerned, we no longer owe each other anything."

He looks genuinely disappointed. He stares at me for a long time. I stare back. He blinks first.

"Okay," he says. "I guess I'll go, then. If you don't mind me giving you a piece of advice, though, I wouldn't sit around here much longer. I have a feeling our MGB friends will be back again, and they won't take kindly to finding three more dead."

"I don't plan on being here when they arrive," I say. I want to ask him where he's going, but I don't. I don't want him to think we're friends, because we aren't.

"I guess we're back to being enemies," he says, as if reading my thoughts.

"Not enemies," I say. "Competitors after the same prize." I stick out my hand. He takes it. "Good luck, Cahokian."

"Good luck, Ariadne Calligaris," he says.

That he's called me by name, instead of Minoan, does not escape me. Nor does the fact that he's still holding my hand. "Until we meet again," I say.

"I hope we don't," he tells me. "Not for two more years, anyway."

He lets go of my hand and walks out of the room. I follow him as he goes to the door. There he pauses and turns to look at me. He opens his mouth to say something, then seems to think better of it.

"Be careful," I say.

He smiles. Then he's gone.

I shut the door, then watch from the window until I see him emerge from the building. I wonder if this is the last time I will see him. I'm surprised that the idea makes me a little disappointed. I should be relieved to see the last of him, as it means he's no longer in my way. Eliminating problems is something I'm very good at, and I've handled this one well, getting useful information in the process. And that's all Boone should be to me—a tool.

I push any other thoughts away. If we do run into each other again, I can't afford to treat him as anything other than a competing Player. This is unfortunate, but it's how things have to be. I almost wish that I'd never met him. Now, if it comes to making a choice between his life and the success of my line, I will have to treat him as another obstacle to be removed.

It might not come to that if I can find Sauer first, so I refocus my thinking to deal with that problem. As I told Boone, I don't have any idea where he and the girl might have gone. And unfortunately for me, the people who might are the very ones I least want to deal with right now—the MGB. Boone is right that they will likely be here soon, but I don't want to face them here. Ironically, that means going to the last place they'll expect me to be: MGB headquarters.

CHAPTER 7

Boone

The strange, heavy fog that has covered so much of Europe for the past few months has once again settled over the city as I leave the apartment building. I half expect to be ambushed by waiting Reds as I exit the front door. As my uncle Anson would say, there are more hounds in this hunt than I anticipated. If the Minoans are interested in Sauer, and he has information that might change the course of Endgame, I don't know who might turn up to try and take him.

But nobody confronts me as I hurry out into the dark, gray morning. As I pass by the alleyway beside the building, I see that the bodies are still there, although now the snow makes them appear to be heaps of rubble or garbage. I try not to dwell on the fact that they're people, people who probably still have families somewhere. Families who will wonder where they are when they don't show up to Christmas dinner.

As I walk down the street, I also find myself thinking about Ariadne. I can tell that Endgame is everything to her. That's how it should be for a Player. If it's not everything to you, you're putting yourself, and your line, at risk. She knows this. I know this. I imagine all the other Players out there in the world know this.

This is more than just a job to her, though. She *wants* Endgame to happen during her time. I've seen this before. One of my trainers, a woman with the most unPlayerlike name of Fawn Flowers, was the Cahokian Player more than 40 years ago. She's still bitter that Endgame didn't happen during her five-year term. As a result, she was harder on me than anyone else, and she treated any failure, even hesitation during a training exercise, as a personal insult. Fawn would be furious that I didn't kill Ariadne when I had the chance. During the *three* chances I've had.

I think about the way Ariadne touched me while she was sewing up my cut. There was a tenderness in her then that I don't think she's ever let out, or at least not often. I saw it in her eyes when she thought I wasn't looking. She's armored, like a knight, and for good reason. I can't help wondering what she would be like with that armor removed. I wish I could find out. I wish we both could find out. Thanks to Endgame, though, we won't.

I don't have the first clue about where Sauer and Lottie are now. They'd be foolish to return to the place where I found them. My guess is that Ariadne is right, and that they're running as fast and as far as they can. And now that Sauer knows so many people are after him, he's going to make sure he disappears for good this time.

I also know that despite what she said, Ariadne is still going to look for them. She's not someone who gives up. It would be smart to try to tail her, see where she goes. She'll be expecting that, though, and will be sure to cover her tracks. What I need to do is regroup and think about my next step.

As I start to cross a street, a figure steps out of the fog. A voice says, "Merry Christmas, Sam."

A voice I know. I stop in my tracks.

"Jackson?"

I haven't seen my brother in more than three years. But when I turn around, he's standing there in front of me.

It can't be him. It can't. Yet here he is, like the Ghost of Christmas Past. I stand there, staring at him, waiting to wake up.

"We need to get off the street," Jackson says. He beckons me to follow, then walks to a Volkswagen parked at the curb. He opens the passenger-side door. "Get in."

I hesitate, still shell-shocked from seeing my dead brother. He tells me again to get in, and I do it. He shuts the door and goes around to the other side, gets in, and starts the engine. As he pulls away, he keeps looking at me.

"You look like Mom," he says.

I have no idea what to say to this person who was my brother. Who *is* my brother. I've spent so long thinking he was dead that this feels like a dream. But it's not. He's sitting a foot away from me. And yet I can't bring myself to ask him any of the thousand-and-one questions that are racing through my head.

"You're dead . . . I . . . What the hell is going on?" I finally manage to blurt out.

Jackson looks straight ahead. "I know it's not enough to say that I'm sorry," he says. "But I am. I can't imagine what it's been like for everyone to think I was dead."

"You have a headstone," I inform him. "In the cemetery. Mom didn't want one put up, but Dad told her it would give her a sense of closure."

"I didn't want any of this, Sam," he says.

"What happened?"

Jackson takes a deep breath. "So many things," he says. "I don't know where to start. Did the council tell you anything?"

I shake my head. "Just that you were in Germany, and that they thought you were killed during the bombing of Berlin. Do they know you're alive? Have they known all this time?"

"No," Jackson says. "I let them think I was dead. They sent me to Cappadocia to spy on the Nazis. I was feeding information back to them. That's how I found out about Sauer and the weapon. I assume you know about that, since you're here."

I nod. I don't tell him that the council kept me in the dark about the weapon, and that I had to find out about it from a Minoan Player. I also don't tell him that I suspect the reason they didn't tell me everything is because of him and what he did.

"The weapon is Annunaki, Sam," Jackson says. "I'm absolutely sure of it. And if it can be built, it could change everything."

"You told the council all of this?" I ask him.

"Of course I did," he says. "I was so excited, I was ready to steal the plans myself. But then things changed."

"How?"

"I fell in love with Lottie," he says.

"Lottie? The girl with Sauer?"

"She's my wife, Sam."

"What? That's insane." I don't believe what I'm hearing.

"Her father, Oswald Brecht, was Sauer's best friend. She used to come to the dig site sometimes, and we started talking."

"Her father was a Nazi?"

"Her father was a scientist. Like Sauer. He didn't have a political bone in his body. He was only interested in studying the artifacts."

"But he worked for the Nazis. Like Sauer."

"It's hard to explain, Sam. I don't expect you to understand. You just have to trust me. Sauer and Brecht had no love for Hitler and his madness. But they couldn't just up and leave. They had families in Germany, and they were afraid."

I don't know what to think anymore, so I don't say anything. Jackson keeps talking.

"After the war, a lot of the scientists were rounded up and put on trial," he says. "Oswald Brecht was one of them. He was found guilty of collaborating with the Nazis. Now he's sitting in jail."

"Why isn't Sauer sitting there with him?"

"He would be," Jackson says. "But Brecht told the Allies that Sauer had been killed by the Nazis because his wife was Jewish. It was true that his wife died in the camps, so they bought the story. Sauer went underground. Used a different name. Eventually they forgot about him because there were more important people to go after. Well, more important to *them*. They never did find out what Brecht and Sauer had discovered, and they wouldn't have believed it if they had. They thought Hitler's obsession with the occult and aliens was ridiculous."

"Looks like you went underground too," I say.

"After what happened to Lottie's father, it wasn't safe here for us either. I'd been working under a different identity anyway. I killed him off and created a new one. Lottie and I went to France. We have a whole new life there."

"Why didn't Sauer go?"

"He was born and raised here," Jackson says. "His whole life happened here. We tried to get him to come, but he has too many memories here."

There's something else that Jackson isn't telling me. I hear it in his voice.

"We come back from time to time to check on him and see if he's ready to leave. That's why we're here now."

"What's your name now?" I ask him.

"Bastien Abelard," he says with a terrible fake French accent. He pretends to twirl a nonexistent mustache, which is supposed to make me laugh. It doesn't. I'm too upset.

"I still don't understand why you disappeared," I say. "You could have just come home."

"No," he says. "I couldn't. I'd disobeyed the council. They wanted me to steal the plans and the few parts of the weapon that we had."

"Why didn't you?" I ask him.

"I didn't want it to get into the wrong hands."

"And you think Cahokian hands are the wrong ones?"

Jackson sighs. "It's not as simple as they want us to think it is, Sam," he says. "I used to think it was too. Then I lived through the war here. I saw what the Nazis did, and what the Soviets did when they got here." He gets quiet for a moment, as if he's remembering things he'd rather forget. "And then I fell in love. It might be difficult to understand what I'm saying. But it's true. When I fell in love with Lottie, it changed everything I thought I believed about how the world works. She's not Cahokian, Sam. Do you know what that means?"

I do know what it means. When Endgame comes, even if the Cahokian Player wins, she wouldn't be among those saved. Only those descended from Cahokians would. Then again, a truly dedicated

Player would never marry outside the line.

"The council is filled with brave, intelligent people," Jackson continues. "But they operate on one basic principle, which is that the continued existence of the line is the only thing we should focus on. But what if there's another way?"

"Like what?" I ask. "If we don't win, we lose."

"What if everybody wins?" Jackson says. "What if instead of focusing on how to defeat all the other lines, we try to figure out how we can work together to defeat the Annunaki? To defeat Endgame."

"You mean share the weapon," I say.

"Exactly," he says. "Look at what just happened in the war. Germany was winning. But then countries that used to be enemies banded together and stopped them. Stopped the evil. Every country could have looked out for itself, but then the Nazis would have picked them off one by one. But when the Allies combined their resources, they were able to stop this force that seemed unstoppable."

"So you suggested to the council that the information about the weapon be shared with other lines?" I ask.

"Yes," Jackson says. "And they told me to come home. They said I had lost sight of what was important, and that I was a danger to the line."

"That's why you stopped communicating with them, and let them think you had died," I say.

"This all happened right at the end of the war," Jackson tells me. "It was easy to just disappear. Still, I've lived in fear that the council would find out and send someone after me." He hesitates. "Is that why you're here, Sam? For me?"

I shake my head. "I don't think they know," I tell him. I don't say that maybe because of him, they don't fully trust me. Or, it occurs to me, perhaps this is all a test. "How did you know I was here? Where to find me?" I ask.

"I didn't," Jackson says. "We're staying with friends in Berlin. When Lottie didn't come back to the house after visiting Sauer, I was worried. I had no idea what happened. I even went by Sauer's house to check. When I found them gone, I didn't know what to think. Then she phoned the friends we're staying with. She said she'd been kidnapped, tied up, but had managed to escape by breaking the chair she was tied to and went into the apartment next door. She phoned for help, then she and Sauer left and my friends took them somewhere safe. I stayed behind. I had a feeling the Cahokians might be behind the kidnapping, and I wanted to see who they'd sent."

"Just me," I say.

"I'm glad," Jackson says. "I've missed you more than I can say."

It's not lost on me that he's said "the Cahokians" and not "we." Combined with the fact that he's let us think that he's dead, it makes me wonder if his allegiance has shifted, and to where. As much as I'm happy to see my brother alive, I have to accept that I really don't know anything about him anymore. And because he was also a Player, I know he's capable of hiding things from me, no matter how close we are. Or used to be. As painful as it is to admit, he might not be my ally anymore.

He pulls the car over in front of a house.

"Where are we?" I ask.

"Our friends' house," Jackson says as he opens the door. "Come on. It's time for you to meet my family."

CHAPTER 8

Ariadne

I know I'm putting myself in danger by lingering longer than I have to, but I can't help but stop in the alley and attend to the bodies of Theron and Cilla. I didn't know them well, as they'd spent most of their lives working for the council outside of our own country, but I'd met them a few times, and considered them friends. I wipe the snow from their faces and look at their frozen features. The cold and death have drained all color from them.

From my pocket I take two ancient coins. On one side is the image of the Minotaur. On the other is a rough approximation of the maze in which the monster was imprisoned, and in which he met his death at the hands of Theseus. The coins are Silver Staters, minted at Knossos centuries ago. They are priceless.

I work one between the lips of each slain Minoan, placing it on the tongue. This is Charon's obol, the symbolic payment for the ferryman of the River Styx for rowing the souls of the dead across to the underworld. I cannot offer my linesmen a proper burial, but I can give them this.

"May you find your way through the maze," I tell them.

The dead Russian I ignore. I don't know what his people believe about the afterlife, but I hope he's trapped in whatever form of hell they have. I am thankful to the Cahokian for killing him.

The Cahokian. *Boone.* For he is no longer just a nameless Player to me. I wonder where he is, what he's doing. I also think about the things he said about Endgame, and being a Player. I have never heard anyone speak this way, and I don't know what to think. Part of me thinks it's weakness to hope that Endgame doesn't happen during our time as Players. Another part admires him for being truthful about his thoughts.

I leave my linesmen and focus on the task ahead of me. Without any clues to Sauer's whereabouts, I have little to go on. I can't just run around Berlin, hoping to find them. I can, however, try to narrow down the possibilities. I don't know how Sauer and the girl escaped, although the shattered pieces of the chair Lottie was tied to suggest that she managed to free herself. Then what? Did she and Sauer simply run? Or did they have help?

I have a feeling that Lottie is the key. The intelligence I got on Sauer while undercover with MGB was substantial. But it said nothing about Lottie. I've never once heard her name or seen her photograph in a file. Until I discovered her with Sauer, I had no idea she existed. And since I had no time to interrogate her before her escape, I still know nothing.

I know someone who might. Utkin. The man who until very recently thought he was my boss. By now he surely knows that I betrayed him, that the six months I spent at his side were a lie. That the kisses I planted on his lips and the vodka I poured into his glass were tricks to get him to talk about things he shouldn't. This will make him hate me even more, as will the fact that the men he sent to find me are now dead.

That's another troubling question. How did they know where to look for me? Only a handful of people know who Lydia was. Two of them—Theron and Cilla—are dead. And according to Boone, the Soviets were already there when they arrived. Who told the MGB that the apartment might be a place of interest to them? And how long have they known about it? Do the Minoans have a traitor in our ranks? Or did I somehow make a mistake without knowing it? The thought annoys me. I don't like making mistakes. Especially not ones that result in the deaths of my linesmen.

My destination is a nondescript office building deep in the Soviet sector. Once, it housed a cadre of secretaries who processed supply orders for the German army. Now it's the main base of operations for an organization that officially doesn't exist, chosen precisely because nobody would think the building housed anything of interest.

For six months prior to attempting to extricate Sauer from Berlin, I worked there undercover. It was the culmination of much planning. I'd prepared by becoming fluent in Russian. Misha, a Minoan operative living in Russia for many years, became my handler. The Minoan Council has installed agents in many different countries, particularly ones we expect to have great influence in world affairs. Misha was able to establish me as his cousin and get me forged papers. I did the rest. The Soviets, unlike many if not most nations, actively encourage the participation of young women in their military and espionage activities. They promote this as equality of the sexes, but in reality it just means that everyone has the same chance to die for the cause, whatever that may be.

It helped that Utkin found me attractive, and that I pretended to return his feelings. It's astonishing to me how quickly some men will forget all of their training simply because you appeal to their need to be desired. This was the part of my training I disliked the most growing up. I was training in weaponry and warfare—why did I need to learn how to flirt and act seductively?

Now I understand how it can sometimes be every bit as effective.

When I reach the MGB building, I pause in the shadows to consider my approach. I can't walk through the front door. I'd be shot on sight. But there are other options.

I decide on the coal chute at the rear of the building. It's used, of course, for loading fuel into the building's basement, where it's then shoveled into a large furnace. It's not the cleanest way of getting inside, but it will do.

I pull the door open with only a minimum of squeaking. I have to enter headfirst, but this is a minor inconvenience, as is the soot that sticks to my coat during my slide into the cellar. Everything that comes after will be far more difficult.

Christmas means very little to the Soviets, who effectively banned it as a symbol of Western excess, so there is no day off for the people who work in this place. The good news is that Utkin's office is in the basement, where the thick walls and absence of windows makes what happens there less obvious. So the first part of my task is the easiest. I know that there is a network of ducts that pass through the ceilings of the rooms down here. I can use them to my advantage.

I locate one of the openings in the ceiling and, standing on a chair, remove the cover. Pulling myself up and inside, I find that the fit is snug but not impossible, and that I can inch along by placing my palms on the smooth metal and pulling myself forward while pushing with my feet. It's slow work, and it makes a bit of noise, but the building is notorious for being plagued by rats, and I hope that anyone who hears something will attribute it to the activity of vermin.

The main duct crosses the basement and enters a corridor. I am moving in complete darkness, but ahead of me I see a faint glow, which means I'm approaching one of the openings into a room. As I grow closer, I hear voices.

"Who is Strekalova?" a man asks angrily.

Strekalova. The name I have answered to since infiltrating the MGB. A name that, until just this morning, everyone in this building knew me by.

"We still don't know," answers a weary voice. "Misha told us nothing. We were lucky to find out about the apartment. And we had to kill him to get even that."

His words are like a punch to my heart. Misha is dead. He was a good agent, loyal to our line. I can't even imagine what they must have done to him to get him to give up the address of the apartment.

I try not to think about it as I crawl forward some more and reach the opening in the ceiling. Peering down, I see Utkin seated on one side of a desk. On the other side is a man who I don't recognize. Given his size and what he's just said, I assume he's one of the men who carry out Utkin's less pleasant tasks.

"That bitch has killed five of my best men in less than a day," Utkin says. "And now she's gotten away with the engineer."

So he doesn't know that Sauer has slipped away from me too. Also, he thinks that I've accomplished this all on my own. He doesn't know about the American—who, to be fair, killed three of those men while I was knocked out. I admit I feel a bit of pleasure at knowing I've angered him so deeply.

"And what of the other girl, the one seen going to the engineer's house?" Utkin says. "Have you identified her?"

The other man opens a folder and places a photograph on the desk between them. It's a photo of Lottie.

"Her name is Violette Abelard," the man tells Utkin. "A French citizen. We don't yet know why she was visiting Sauer."

Utkin picks up the photograph. He peers at it closely. "I've seen this girl before," he says. He sucks in his lower lip, which I recognize as a sign that he's trying to connect some pieces of information in his brain. Then he gets up, goes to a cabinet, and pulls out a file. He sits down again and starts flipping through photographs. After a minute, he takes one and sets it beside the one already on the desk.

"There," he says, pointing to the picture, which shows Sauer, another man, and Lottie.

"That's Sauer and Oswald Brecht," the other man says.

"And Brecht's daughter, Charlotte," says Utkin. "It's the same girl."

The man leans back in his chair. "Charlotte Brecht disappeared years ago."

"And apparently became Violette Abelard," Utkin says. "Like many of the Nazi children, she obviously reinvented herself." He sucks his lip again. Then he says, "There is a man here in Berlin. He calls himself Karl Ott now. It's said he has organized a group of sympathizers anxious to get revenge on those who brought down Hitler's Reich."

The man across from him laughs. "Ridiculous," he says. "They would be crushed immediately."

"Yes," Utkin agrees. "Unless they have a weapon of enormous power. A weapon like the one Sauer was working on."

The man stops smiling and frowns. "You think Strekalova is working with them?"

"I don't know," says Utkin. "If she is, she has just delivered them a prize—the only engineer who can reconstruct the weapon." He rattles off an address, which I immediately commit to memory. "Go to that address. Get Ott. Bring him here for questioning. And if Strekalova is with him, bring her as well. I will deal with her personally."

The man stands to go. I consider trying to stop him. But I can do that later. I know where he's going, and now I have the address of Ott's apartment locked in my brain. All I have to do is get there before the MGB agent does. Now that I've gotten what I came for—or at least gotten information I can use—it's time to go back through the duct and get out of the building.

As I'm backing up, though, Utkin starts talking again. At first I think his henchman has returned. Then I realize he's talking to himself.

"Stupid bitch," he says. "She'll find out what happens to little girls who cross me."

The vent opening into the room is not huge, but it's large enough for me to slip through—if I can get it open. I position myself over it, lift my arms, and bring my elbows down on the grate. The first time results in a lot of racket. Utkin, startled, looks up.

"Goddamn rats," he says as I bring my elbows down again.

This time, the metal clips holding the grate in place give way. The grate tumbles down, and I follow, pushing myself through the hole. I watch Utkin's eyes widen as I fall toward him, shrieking like an avenging Fury.

He breaks my fall. I waste no time, clawing at his eyes with my fingers. My thumbs find his eyes, and I press down. I feel them pop, and Utkin bellows like a bull. I take the knife that hides in my boot and advance on him, pressing the blade against his neck. He lashes out at me, but I pin him to the wall.

"Shut up," I say.

He obeys, which makes me smile. I like seeing him helpless, blinded, and afraid. I stand there like that for a long moment, letting him feel the steel against his skin. I watch his chest rise and fall in quick breaths. I know he would love nothing more than to kill me.

He cannot see me, but he can hear me. I lean forward so that my lips are almost touching his. "My name is Ariadne Calligaris," I whisper, and draw my knife across his neck.

I came here looking for information. Instead, I found revenge. I should have waited to kill Utkin after getting him to answer some questions. My temper has perhaps gotten the best of me. But it feels wonderful.

And perhaps I've gotten what I need after all. I recite the address I've memorized silently in my head as I leave Utkin's office. It's time to go meet Karl Ott and find out what he knows.

CHAPTER 9

Boone

When Jackson and I walk into the living room of the house, I remember that it's Christmas morning. There's a tree with decorations on it, and presents underneath that have already been opened. Seated around the tree—some on the couch and chairs, some on the floor—are six people. Two of them are Lottie and Sauer. Then there are a man and woman I don't know, as well as two small boys. One of the boys runs up to us on little, unsteady legs and holds up his hands.

"Papa!" he says.

Jackson lifts him up and gives him a hug. He speaks to him in rapid French, and the little boy looks at me. He grins. "*Bonjour*, Oncle Sam," he says shyly.

"*Bonjour,*" I say. I look at Jackson.

"Bernard," he says.

"*Bonjour*, Bernard," I say to the little boy. "*Joyeux Noël.*"

"*Joyeux Noël,*" he says, laughing.

Jackson sets him down, and he runs to Lottie. I watch the nephew I didn't know I had climb into his mother's lap. It feels like I'm dreaming. Not that long ago, I was fighting men to the death. Now I'm in the middle of a Christmas celebration with my brother's family.

The other man stands up and comes over to us. He reaches out to shake my hand. "My name is Karl Ott," he says. "Welcome to my home."

I take his hand. "Sam Boone."

He nods. "Your brother has told me a lot about you, Sam. He is very proud of you."

"Karl is one of our most trusted friends. He and Lottie have known each other since they were kids," Jackson tells me. "This is his house. That's his wife, Greta, and their son, Jürgen."

"Perhaps we can speak in the kitchen," Karl says. He looks at his wife. "Greta, can you and Lottie watch the boys for a moment?"

I look at Lottie and notice for the first time the bruise on her cheek. I remember how Jackson said she tipped herself over and broke the chair she was tied to, and although I'm not the one who tied her up, I feel bad about how she was treated, and about leaving her tied up while I went to help Ariadne. Maybe if I'd stopped to help her, she wouldn't look as frightened of me as she does right now. I also look at Sauer again. He hasn't moved, and to my surprise, Karl doesn't invite him to come with us.

We go into the kitchen, where we sit down around a table. I am across from Karl, while Jackson is to my left.

"Why isn't Sauer here?" I ask.

"It's better if we talk without him," says Karl. "For now."

"Why?" I press. "He's the reason I'm here in the first place."

"We know," Jackson says. "And now others want him too. Who's the girl in the apartment?"

I'm surprised it's taken him this long to ask about Ariadne. Now I wonder how much I should tell him. I'm about to lie, but this is my brother. He was a Player once. And he's still a Cahokian. He deserves to know.

"The Minoan Player," I say.

Jackson's eyes widen. "And you let her live?"

Part of me is happy to see that there's still a Player inside him. A bigger part is annoyed that he's treating me like his kid brother and questioning my choices.

"I have my reasons," I snap.

"Are you working with her?" Karl asks. "This Minoan?"

I'm irritated by his question. He's not a Player. Not a member of our line. He shouldn't even know about Endgame. I ignore him and speak directly to Jackson. "The Minoans found out about the weapon," I tell him. "That means other lines could be looking for it as well."

He looks worried. "That's what I'm afraid of. That's why we need to convince Sauer to give it to us."

"Us? What do you mean us? The last I heard, you weren't working for our line anymore."

It comes out harsher than I mean it to. But it's the truth. Jackson has been hiding from the council—from our family—for three years. If the council knew this, he'd be considered a deserter, a traitor. I don't know what I think myself yet.

"Sauer and Lottie say that you saved the girl," Karl says. "Why?"

I look him in the eyes. "Look," I say. "I don't know anything about you. I don't know who you are or what you have to do with my brother. And right now I'm not sure I know all that much about him either. So excuse me if I don't explain every move I've made to you."

I see Jackson look hurt. Karl, though, smiles. "Good," he says. "You don't trust me. I don't trust you either. Your brother is a friend. But from what he has told me about this Endgame of yours, I don't think anyone involved in it can be trusted."

"No," I say. "We can't. But to answer your question, I'm not working with the girl."

I don't tell him that I tried to get Ariadne to team up. I'm sure that would make him even more mistrustful of me. I also think about what Ariadne would say if she knew I was sitting in an apartment with Lottie and Sauer. I've managed to win this round, even if it happened accidentally.

"And to answer *your* question," Karl says. "We are a group of people whose lives were turned upside down by the war. We do not wish to see something like this ever happen again. Which is why we wish to have the weapon that Sauer was working on."

"So you can use it, or so you can stop anyone else from using it?"

"Your trainers taught you well," Karl says. "It's good that you think this way. Again to answer your question, we want to make sure that the weapon does not fall into the hands of people who would use it to destroy the world."

"Then why not just kill him?" I ask. "If he's really the only person who knows where the weapon, or the plans, or whatever there is are, then kill him so nobody else ever finds it."

Karl nods. "That might be a solution," he says. "But if the weapon or plans really do still exist, someone will always find them. In that case, it's best if we have them and are in control of them."

I can't help but laugh. "Or you could just use the weapon yourself to gain control," I say.

Jackson shakes his head. "You don't understand, Sam."

"What don't I understand?" I'm getting tired of him telling me I don't understand things, and my impatience shows in my voice.

"Karl's father was like Lottie's father and Sauer—a scientist. A chemist. The Nazis made him work for them. Then, after the war, they threw him to the wolves. Claimed he was responsible for a lot of terrible things he had nothing to do with. He was found guilty and imprisoned for life. And he wasn't the only one."

"Many innocent people were imprisoned or killed," Karl says. "The victims of the camps were not the only casualties of the Nazis."

I don't say anything. I know about the trials after the war. I know about the hangings. I also know that punishing a handful of people for collaborating with the Nazis isn't even remotely like killing millions of people for no reason. And I find it hard to believe that the Allied forces in charge of those trials wouldn't do a thorough job of investigating the crimes the men on trial were accused of. Ott seems to feel differently, but I'm not here to discuss politics.

"You know how I feel about Endgame," Jackson says. "Do you really think it's fair for one line to survive, while everyone else in the world dies?"

I think about the conversation I had only hours ago with Ariadne, where I asked her almost the exact same question. Now, though, I find myself strangely defensive when Jackson asks it. "I didn't make the rules," I say.

Jackson shakes his head. "You're right," he said. "You didn't. And you're just following orders because you've been trained to do that. You know who else said they were just following orders? The German soldiers."

"Don't you dare compare me to the Nazis," I snap at Jackson. I can't believe he's even said this.

"I'm not saying it's exactly the same," he says. "But the principle is, isn't it? Every line wants to prove that they're the best, the strongest, the most worthy of surviving Endgame. And every Player will do whatever it takes to ensure the survival of his or her line. Even if it means everyone else on the planet dies."

I guess Karl can tell I'm getting tense because he cuts in. "I don't know that I believe this Endgame is real. However, what I believe is not important. You believe it is real. Others believe it is real. My father's and Sauer's work on the weapon is real. And if it is real, and if what I understand is correct, if Endgame happens, I might die. My family might die. Lots of other families might die only because they do not belong to the winning group. So, if there is anything I can do to prevent that, I will do it."

"By getting the weapon and using it yourself," I say.

"By getting the weapon and either destroying it or convincing the lines to cooperate and use it to keep Endgame from ever happening," Jackson says.

I ignore him. I'm still angry about his Nazi comment. "And if Endgame isn't real?" I ask Karl.

"Then we prevent any other powers from using it," says Karl. "The Soviets. The Americans. The French. Anybody."

"And what does Sauer think?" I ask. "Why isn't he in here having this conversation with us?"

"Sauer doesn't think anyone should have the weapon or know how to build it," Jackson says.

"Then why hasn't he destroyed it? If he really believes that, he would have gotten rid of the weapon, or the parts they found, or the blueprints. Either he doesn't have these things or know where they are or he's already destroyed them or something is keeping him from doing it. Which is it?"

Jackson and Karl look at each other. "We don't know," Karl admits.

"I want to talk to him," I say. "Alone."

"I don't think—" Karl begins.

"Alone," I repeat. When no one says anything, I continue. "I was sent here to get Sauer and get him out of Berlin at any cost. I'm fully capable of doing that, as my brother will tell you. If you want my help, then get Sauer in here so I can talk to him."

I can feel the tension thicken. And I know Jackson is unhappy with how I'm behaving. I also don't care. I've been holding back my anger at him for letting us all think he was dead. And I've been tolerating the big brother / little brother routine. But I'm the one with a mission to fulfill, with a council waiting for me to report back that I've succeeded. If anything, Jackson has made that more difficult for me, because more and more, I'm pretty sure that this isn't only a mission, it's a test of my loyalty to the line.

"Get him," Jackson says to Karl.

Karl gets up and leaves the kitchen. When he's gone, Jackson says to me, "They've really convinced you, haven't they? The council. Probably Dad worked on you too."

"Nobody has convinced me of anything," I say. "I have my own brain, you know."

"I know you do," my brother says. "And I hope you'll use it." Then he says, "Would you kill me, Sam? If I got in your way of taking Sauer? Because that's what the rules of Endgame call for, right? Winning at any cost."

This is not how this is supposed to be going. After all this time thinking Jackson was dead, then finding out he isn't, I should be happy. Instead, I'm frustrated and angry. Jackson was always the person I was closest to in this world. I was gutted when I thought he died. Part of me even carried on Playing in his honor—because it's what I thought he would have done. And now I find out he's been alive this whole time, lying to me, his family—and to top it off, he thinks I'm the enemy.

Before I can answer him, Karl returns with Sauer. Jackson gets up, and he and Karl go into the other room. Sauer sits down across from me.

"I have one question," I tell him. "Do you really know where the weapon or the blueprints are?"

Sauer answers quickly, as though he's been expecting this. "If I say no, you have no reason to keep me alive," he says.

I've also been expecting his answer. "I think you do know," I say. "And I think whatever there is, it's here in Berlin, and not just in your head. I think it's why you've stayed here. When I first saw you, Lottie said something about it being time to pass the duty on to someone else. What did she mean?"

He rubs his face with his hands. "I'm tired," he says. "So tired."

I lean closer. "Then tell me what you're protecting."

He shakes his head. "No one should have such power," he mutters. "It's too dangerous." He sounds as if he's talking to himself, not to me.

"I've been sent here to help you," I tell him. "Let me help."

He gives a short laugh, almost a bark. "Help me?" he says. "How? By building a weapon that can destroy the world?"

I look him dead in the eyes. "We already have weapons that can destroy the world," I say. "Maybe this one can help prevent that."

This is a lie, of course. The only use for the weapon is to win Endgame. I need him to believe me, though, and so I don't look away, not even for a second. I will him to trust me.

He puts his hands over his face and leans into them. When he puts his hands down, he looks far older than he is. "There is a place," he says.

"A library of sorts. It contains some of the objects collected by the Nazis."

"What kind of objects?"

"Peculiar objects," he says. "Occult. Ones they believed held power or could be used to obtain power."

I know all about Hitler's obsession with the occult and his search for artifacts related to things outside the realm of everyday science. I also know that, so far, no one has found the things he is alleged to have collected.

"And the weapon is part of this library?"

Sauer nods.

"And you know where it is?"

"Yes."

"Where?"

Sauer shakes his head. "I won't tell you," he says. "But I will take you there."

I look at his face, weighing whether or not I think he's telling me the truth. "I could kill you if you don't tell me."

He shakes his head. "You are not a good liar," he says.

"I don't know what you're talking about," I say, proving his point.

Sauer smiles. "I have seen the face of evil," he says. "I know what it looks like. And you are not evil. You will not kill me. I also know that your people would use the weapon to help themselves, regardless of the consequences."

"Then why help me?"

It takes him longer to answer this time. "As I said, I have seen evil," he says. "I saw it consume my country, my people, my friends, my wife. And there was nothing I could do to stop it. These creatures—beings—who are behind what you call Endgame. If they are real, they too are evil. Perhaps this weapon can help you stop them."

"That's what Karl and my brother seem to think too," I say.

A dark look passes over Sauer's face, just for a moment. I'm about to ask him what he's thinking when there's a commotion from the other room. A child shrieks. I get up and dash into the room, my weapon drawn.

Ariadne is standing there. Her gun is trained on the group of people staring at her in fear. Jackson has his arms around Lottie and Bernard. Greta is standing beside the Christmas tree, holding Jürgen, who is crying. Karl is glaring at Ariadne.

When I appear, Ariadne swings the gun toward me. When she sees me, she looks surprised. "What are you doing?" I ask her, not lowering my gun.

She looks at me for a long time. I can practically see the wheels turning in her mind. It's like an entire war is playing out behind her eyes. "You have to get out of here," she says. "The Soviets are coming."

"How do you—"

"Boone, you have to trust me."

"Is this the Minoan?" Jackson asks. "You can't trust her, Sam."

I ignore him, keeping my eyes on Ariadne. The truth is, if she wanted everyone in the room dead so she could take Sauer, they would already be dead. Something is keeping her from doing that, and for some reason, although I don't know why, I think it's me. Jackson is right that I don't know if I can trust her fully. I can tell she's not lying, though. For some reason, she's choosing to help me, or at least not to kill me or leave me to face the Soviets on my own. Although I might be crazy for thinking this way, that's good enough for me.

I lower my gun. "Let's go."

CHAPTER 10

Ariadne

We are sitting at yet another table in yet another house. This time, the Cahokian safe house. I am relieved that Boone convinced the others to leave with us and come here. I did not want to have to threaten to kill anyone, particularly with the children there. Although nothing in my training prevents me from harming children, and in fact I have been taught that they can be a particularly effective tool to convince people to do what I want them to, it's something I vowed to myself that I won't do. Maybe this is a weakness, and maybe someday I will be forced to break my promise, but I can't imagine it. Having had my own childhood taken from me so soon by my Player training, I understand how precious it is.

I'm surprised that Boone chose to reveal the location of their safe house, but as we seldom use any one place for very long, it doesn't really matter. Next week, someone else will be sitting in this kitchen. Right now, seated around the table are me, Boone, Sauer, Boone's brother, and Karl Ott. Lottie, Greta Ott, and their children are in the living room. I find myself looking from Boone to his brother. I only found out about their relationship as we were driving to the safe house—Boone, Lottie, Ott's wife, and their children in Ott's car, and me, Sauer, Ott, and Jackson Boone in another.

I insisted on separating the families to lessen the chance of them trying to escape, although I was fairly confident that Boone wouldn't try anything. After all, he was the one who insisted on bringing Ott and his family. I would have been content with only Sauer, but Boone thinks that Ott may be useful in some way. Also, bringing him made it easier to convince the others to come. As a Player, I find Boone's tendency to want to save everyone problematic, but as a woman, I also find it appealing.

Boone looks up, and I realize that I've been staring at him. He grins, and I look away. Sauer is telling us about something he calls a library, a collection of artifacts that supposedly have occult significance. The Cahokian weapon, or what there is of it, is among them. I look at the map Sauer has drawn on a piece of paper and placed in the center of the table. It shows what is called Museum Island, a man-made island in the middle of the Spree River. There are five museums there. The one Sauer is pointing at is the New Museum, which despite its name is one of the oldest of the five.

"The collection is in the museum?" I ask.

"Not in it," he says. "Beneath it. The museum was closed at the beginning of the war, and many of its treasures moved elsewhere. It was heavily damaged during the bombings, and much of it is now destroyed. We should not have trouble getting inside."

"Except that it's in the Soviet sector," I point out.

"The island is not heavily patrolled," Sauer says. "If we wait until nightfall, we should be able to get inside easily." He pauses. "I have done it before."

"We'll need to limit the size of our group," I say. "You, me, and Boone. That's it."

"No," says Ott. "That is unacceptable."

He has not forgiven me for breaking into his house and interrupting his Christmas celebration, but he's fortunate that he's alive at all. If I had not found Boone there, and if Boone had not insisted on bringing him, he probably wouldn't be.

"Ariadne is right," Boone says. "We can't have that many people running around."

"So the two people who have sworn to get the weapon at any cost are to go, while the rest of us sit here to see which of you comes back?" says Ott.

"You seem to forget that if I wanted you all dead, you'd be dead," I remind him.

"Ariadne and I have an—understanding," Boone says. "Neither of us is taking the weapon for our own use. Right?"

He looks at me. After a moment, I nod. But he is not entirely right. Yes, we have agreed that we will work together. What happens once we have the weapon, I don't know. For now, I am letting him think that we are allies. Curiously, this deception makes me a little uneasy.

"How about this," Boone's brother says. "I'll go, but Karl, you'll stay here. You trust me, right?"

Karl nods. "Yes," he says. "I trust you. But you are no match for the MGB if they decide to take the weapon for their own."

"I've handled them well enough before," I say. I'm getting impatient with his games. It was strange enough discovering that Boone's brother is here in Berlin, and that he's Lottie's husband. Now things are further complicated by the presence of Ott and his insistence on having a say in what happens. I have not forgotten what I overheard Utkin say about Ott being a sympathizer. I don't know that this is true, and I haven't had a chance to discuss it with Boone. It's possible that Utkin was wrong. That Boone's brother seems to trust him makes me think this is likely the case. And really, it doesn't matter. All I want is the weapon, and for that I only need Sauer.

"Then that's the plan," says Boone before Ott can reply to me. "We'll leave as soon as it's dark."

We have several hours before that happens, time that the families spend trying to make this Christmas as normal as possible for the little boys. I stay out of the way. I watch them playing with the stuffed animals they clutched in their arms as we left Ott's house, and I think how fortunate they are not to understand what's going on around them.

"Cute, aren't they?"

Boone's question brings me back to the moment. "Yes," I agree. "Cute."

Boone studies my face for a long moment.

"What?" I ask.

"I'm just trying to imagine you playing as a kid," he says. "I can't picture it. I bet you were born with a knife in your hand."

"I cut the cord myself," I joke.

He laughs. Then he asks, "Do you have any brothers or sisters?"

"A sister," I tell him. "Cassandra."

"Younger or older?"

"Younger. By four minutes."

"You're twins?" Boone exclaims.

"Identical," I say.

He laughs again. "One of you is a lot to deal with. I can't even imagine two. Is she just like you?"

"Yes."

"You don't sound too happy about that. Don't you get along?"

The answer to this is complicated. "Maybe we did before we began training," I say. "Once it became clear that only one of us would wear the golden horns, we became rivals. And once those horns were placed on my head and not hers, the rivalry deepened to something else."

"I can't imagine competing against my brother," Boone says. "I mean, we had our fights like all brothers do. But nothing like that."

"Didn't you train with him?"

Boone shakes his head. "I did most of the things he did," he says. "But we never fought each other. And I wasn't supposed to be our Player anyway."

"Really?" I say.

"There was another boy. Tim Palhook. He was going to follow Jackson when he aged out. But he was killed."

"In training?"

"No. Plain old car accident. That's when I got called up from the minors."

Boone notices the confused look on my face. "Sorry," he says. "American baseball reference. It means I took his place."

So Boone was never meant to be the Cahokian Player. I wonder if this explains why he doesn't always behave like a typical Player. Also, why there seems to be some tension between him and his brother.

I still have the scar under my chin from where the point of Cassandra's knife caught me during a skirmish. I touch it now as I wonder what she's doing. Actually, I know what she's doing. Training. As always. Perfecting her strengths and correcting her weaknesses. In case I should fail.

Sauer approaches us, ending the conversation for now. "It's almost dark," he says. "We should go."

We get ready. Ott says very little, sitting with the children, but his eyes are on us. I ignore him. My goal is to keep an eye on Sauer and, once we have what we've come for, figure out my next move.

The four of us leave the house and get into Ott's car. Jackson drives with Sauer in the passenger seat. Boone and I sit together in the back. Nobody speaks as we drive into the center of the city and park a short distance from Museum Island. It's fully dark now, and the snow has started again, which is good. It will provide some cover.

Sauer is correct that Museum Island is not patrolled by Soviet troops. I'm not surprised. The museums suffered extensive damage during the war, and everything of value was removed from them before then anyway. Now the buildings sit unused and unattended. The riskiest part is the short walk over the bridge leading to the island, and even this is unremarkable. After only a few minutes, we are standing before the ruined facade of the New Museum.

Sauer does not hesitate. He walks up the short flight of steps that leads to the front doors. Snow-covered rubble is everywhere, and the doors are hanging from their hinges. It feels like walking into a cave more than walking into a building.

Once we are inside, we switch on the flashlights we have brought and take in the damaged interior. There is evidence everywhere of the bombing. Shattered pillars. Holes in the walls. Snow falling through gaps in the ceiling. Sauer walks us through the eerie landscape, leading us down a corridor that feels like walking through time. It reminds me a bit of Greece's ruined temples, like the Temple of Athena Nike, or my personal favorite, the Temple of Aphaia on the island of Aegina. Even partially destroyed as they are, the magnificence remains.

At the end of the corridor he turns into one of the galleries. The walls here are black from smoke and fire, the tiles on the floor shattered and covered in bits of stone. We pass through it, finally reaching another door. On the other side is a stairwell. Sauer descends, and we follow him.

"This leads to the rooms open only to staff," Sauer explains as we go down one, two, three flights. Each flight takes us deeper into darkness. At the bottom, Sauer leads us through another door and down another hallway. Now we are in a part of the museum most likely never seen by visitors. We are underground, and there is less damage here. Still, it looks as if the rooms have been ransacked.

"The Soviets took everything of value," Sauer says. "At least, everything they could find."

He leads us into what looks like an almost-empty office. There is a desk but nothing else except for some papers strewn around on the floor. I begin to wonder if we aren't being made fools of, or being led into a trap of some kind. I am on guard, ready should anything unexpected happen. I can tell that Boone is as well, although he is trying to look relaxed.

Sauer walks to a closet at the back of the room and opens the door. He steps inside, and for a second I flash back to the escape tunnel in his house and worry that he's attempting to get away. A moment later there is a grating sound, and he steps out again. He motions for us to look inside.

Boone and I step forward and peer inside the closet. A bar stretches across it, with empty hangers where coats would normally hang. But where there should be a back, there is now an opening.

"An elevator," I say.

"It holds only two," Sauer explains. "I'll have to go on the first trip. To open the door below. Who is coming with me?"

I look at Boone. I don't like the idea of Sauer being out of our sight. I also don't like the idea of another Player being with him alone.

"Jackson can go first," Boone says. "Then you and I will go together. All right?"

"Agreed."

"I'll send the elevator back up for you," Sauer says as Jackson gets in with him. "There's only one button. Press it."

There's a clanking as the elevator descends. A few minutes later, it returns. I step inside, followed by Boone. The two of us barely fit in there, and we're pressed closely together. Boone reaches up and presses the single button. The elevator door shuts, and now it feels as if we're trapped inside a coffin. As the elevator descends, I listen to Boone breathing beside me.

"What do you think we're going to find?" he asks me.

"I don't know," I tell him. "Maybe nothing."

"Or maybe the biggest thing to ever happen in Endgame," he says as the elevator comes to a stop.

The door slides open, and we step out into a square room that I estimate is 8 meters on each side. The walls are lined with cabinets. Behind us, the doors to the elevator shut.

"How deep underground are we?" Boone asks Sauer as he looks around the room.

"Approximately 60 meters," I say.

Everyone looks at me.

"That's right, isn't it?" I say.

"Yes," says Sauer. "The museum was built between 1843 and 1855. This room was initially built to store items sensitive to temperature and light. Later, it became a place to hide some of the many items collected by the team of researchers tasked with indulging Hitler's obsession."

He sounds dismissive, and so I ask, "You don't believe any of the findings are real?"
"I was only asked to lend my skills to the weapon found in Cappadocia," he says. "Of the rest, I have no scientific opinion."
"But the weapon is real," Boone says.
"Yes, the weapon is real," says Sauer.
"Then let's get it and get out of here," I suggest. "The longer we stay here, the greater the risk of someone else showing up."
"Only a handful of people know about this chamber," Sauer says. "And most of them are dead or imprisoned. I've been guarding the secret for a long time."
Something about the tone of his voice unsettles me. And he's making no move to open any of the cabinets or produce the weapon or whatever plans for it are kept here.
"I don't know what I was waiting for," he continues. "Now I see I should have done this a long time ago."
"Done what?" I ask.
Instinctively, I draw my gun. Boone notices and does the same, although for now we keep them aimed down. Suddenly, I am very aware of the closed door of the elevator. I turn and press the button on the wall. Nothing happens.
"It won't open," Sauer says.
"What have you done?" I ask.
Sauer speaks calmly, which worries me more than if he were agitated. "As I said, this room was designed to house objects. It was later modified to prevent those objects from getting into the wrong hands. There is a network of pipes connected to the Spree, which as you know flows above us. Some of them lead directly to this room. After you enter, you have five minutes in which to disable the mechanism that opens those pipes. If you don't, water will come through those openings." He points to a series of vents in the ceiling. "The room will fill with water. The cabinets themselves are watertight, so the

contents will be protected. Anyone inside, however . . ."

The implication is obvious. I calculate how long we have been in the room, but my answer comes when water begins to pour from the openings overhead. It's ice cold, and I step away from the nearest torrent as it falls to the floor.

"Evrard!" Jackson yells.

Sauer looks at him. Water is drenching him, but he seems not to notice. "I'm sorry," he says. "But I can't let anyone have the weapon. Not even you."

I advance on him, my gun pointed at him. "How do we stop this?"

He looks at me, and his eyes tell me everything before he even speaks.

"You don't," he says.

CHAPTER 11

Boone

The water is rising quickly. More quickly than I would have thought possible. It's already over my shoes. I estimate we have about 10 minutes before the entire room is filled with water.

Ariadne is shaking Sauer.

"Turn it off!"

Sauer says nothing. Ariadne pushes him away and points her gun at him. "Do it, or you die."

Sauer just looks at her. His meaning is obvious. He's going to die anyway. We all are. He'd rather kill all of us than have the weapon be discovered. I know nothing she says or does will get him to stop what's happening. Whether he's wrong or right, he sees her as the enemy. Her and me. And he's decided that nobody is getting their hands on the weapon or the plans.

Still, I think, there might be a chance. Jackson could get through to him. "Try to get him to shut this down," I say to my brother. Then I touch Ariadne's shoulder. She whips around, smacking my hand away. "We need to look for a way out," I tell her.

She starts to argue, then nods. With a last withering glance at Sauer, she comes with me as Jackson takes over for her. I tune out the sound of Jackson's pleading voice and focus on Ariadne.

First, I try to pry the elevator doors open. They won't budge. "They must be locked," I say. "We're not getting them open without tools or explosives. And those water pipes are too small to go through. We need another way."

I see her focus shift in an instant from thinking about Sauer to scanning the room for options. Despite the situation, I can't help but be impressed by her.

"There," she says, pointing.

I look. In one corner of the ceiling, barely visible, is a vent cover.

"Air has to get in here somehow," Ariadne says. "That must be the shaft."

"But where does it go?"

"Probably a simple supply and return," she says, walking over to stand beneath the vent. "It doesn't really matter where it ends, does it?"

"It does if we can't get out," I say. "Once this place fills up, the water is going to go right up that shaft. If we're stuck in it, we drown."

"We're going to drown anyway," Ariadne says. "I'd rather do it trying to get out. Lift me up."

I link my fingers together and make a kind of step. Ariadne puts her foot on it, places a hand on top of my head, and steps up. I lift her so she can reach the edge of the vent. She works her fingers under the grate covering it, and it pulls out. She drops it into the water and shines her flashlight up.

"What can you see?"

"It seems to go straight up," she says.

She jumps down, and I shake my hands out. I turn to see if Jackson is making any progress with Sauer. He isn't. Sauer is now sitting down in the icy water, leaning against the cabinets at a weird angle. Jackson is squatting beside him.

"He took something," Jackson says. "A cyanide capsule, I think."

Sauer's face is pink and heading for red. His eyes are closed, and he's shaking. A moment later, he's unconscious.

"Evrard!" Jackson says, slapping Sauer's cheeks. I can hear in his voice how upset he is, and I realize that he must have come to think of Sauer as a friend.

"He's as good as dead," says Ariadne. "Leave him."

Jackson glares at her. His anger at Ariadne's suggestion can be felt through the cold air of the room.

"He left us for dead, so why do we care about him?" Ariadne's not even looking at him, she's eyeing the air shaft, calculating our next move. "You've gotten soft since your time as Player. We need to go."

"We can't just leave him here," Jackson pleads. "Sam?"

I put my hand on my brother's shoulder. "Ariadne's right. There's nothing we can do for him."

Jackson looks at Sauer, now lying on the floor with water covering his face. He's obviously gone. "Jackson, we have to go," I say gently.

He nods. He looks at the opening to the vent, and the Player he used to be comes out. "Who's first?"

"You're the smallest," I say to Ariadne. "And probably the fastest. You go first. Then Jackson."

"Wait," Jackson says. "How will you get inside? You can't reach it, and we can't turn around to lift you in."

I point to the water, which is now up to our waists. "I'll swim," I say.

Jackson shakes his head. "It's too cold. You'll get hypothermia."

"I'll be fine," I tell him. "I didn't spend all those hours swimming in the frozen pond behind Grandma's house for nothing."

He starts to argue, but I stop him. "When the water reaches the ceiling, I'll be able to swim right in," I say.

"And then the water will fill the shaft," he says.

"I'll climb fast. Now let's go."

Jackson and I lift Ariadne up. She reaches into the vent, gets a handhold, and pulls herself inside. A moment later she yells out, "Clear."

I help Jackson up and watch him disappear into the vent. He's bigger than both Ariadne and me, and for a moment I think he'll get stuck. But he wriggles in. Then I'm alone in the room with Sauer's body and the freezing water. To distract myself from how cold it is, I look around at the cabinets. I try to imagine what's hidden behind the locked doors. I know Sauer was telling the truth about it being here. If he was lying, there'd be no point in killing himself.

I wonder if there's time to try to open the cabinets. I could try shooting at the locks. But how do I even know which cabinet to try? Besides, the water is rising fast. Being so close to the weapon but unable to get to it is the most frustrating thing I've ever encountered as a Player. As stupid as I know it is, I want to punch the cabinets, try to break them open with my bare hands. If only I had more time.

My only consolation is that the rising water means I'll soon be able to follow Jackson and Ariadne. When the water reaches my chin, I lie on my back and float. Slowly, I rise up toward the ceiling. An icy chill is soaking into my bones, and I close my eyes and picture myself sitting in front of a roaring bonfire. The mind trick works. I push the cold away, at least for now, and wait.

After another few minutes, the room is almost completely flooded. I open my eyes and tread water below the opening to the air shaft. When I'm finally close enough, I reach up and pull myself inside. It's difficult to get a grip with my frozen fingers, but the water helps a little, lifting me up.

"I'm in!" I shout.

Then I climb.

The cold metal beneath my hands burns like fire as every muscle in my body screams out that it can't do any more. My back scrapes as I press my knees against the opposite side of the shaft and push up. A rivet scratches a line of pain across my shoulder.

By placing my feet and pushing up, I make my way slowly up the shaft. Each new repositioning is torture, and within a dozen feet my thighs ache and my fingers are bleeding.

All I can do now is keep climbing, an inch at a time. Time slows down as every movement, every bit of forward progress, seems to take an eternity. Since I can't see anything anyway, I close my eyes and imagine that I'm exploring an underground cave. I've done it dozens of times back home, slipping my body through narrow crevices until I can't go any deeper, then making my way back to the surface. My trainer had me do it to get used to being in confined spaces. At first I would panic, sure I was going to be trapped underground. Over time,

I learned to control my breathing and my emotions, remaining calm and clearheaded. I do that now, picturing myself emerging at the top into somewhere bright and open. Even though I know that's not likely to be the case, it gives me the motivation to keep going.

I hear Jackson and Ariadne moving above me. Then I hear Ariadne's voice coming from far away as she shouts, "I'm at the top."

Her voice sounds close—not far to go now. Soon I hear Jackson call, "I'm out. Sam, are you there?"

"Right behind you," I call back.

I look up and see a faint change in the light above me. Instead of more claustrophobic darkness, I'm looking at a small square of slightly less dark space. Jackson's face comes into view, looking down at me. I put my hands through, and he pulls me out and into a small room.

"Where are we?" I ask him.

Ariadne is shining her flashlight around. "No windows," she says. "Probably a basement. This is about the same level as the offices were."

I remember how she accurately calculated how deep the elevator went, and I think she's probably right now. I'm soaking wet and freezing, but I'm alive and happy to be out of the air shaft. I look back in and see that the water isn't coming all the way up. It must have leveled off.

"We have to get dry," Jackson says. I hear the Player in his voice. It as if he's been sleeping, and what's just happened has awakened him.

"First we need to get the weapon," Ariadne counters.

"Are you crazy?" Jackson says. "How?"

"There's a way," Ariadne says. "I just need to figure it out."

"In case you've forgotten, that room down there is filled with water," Jackson says. "Besides, we don't know that there's even anything there."

"It's there," Ariadne says. "Sauer wouldn't have killed himself and tried to kill us if it wasn't there. He wanted to make sure nobody got their hands on it."

I agree with her about this. I think Jackson does too, because he doesn't say anything.

"Nobody's getting anything if we freeze to death," I say. "I agree with Jackson. Let's get out of here—"

"I'm not leaving the—" Ariadne says.

"*And* I agree with you," I interrupt, stopping her. "We can't just leave the weapon down there. So let's go get warm, regroup, and decide what's next."

Ariadne frowns. She's trying her best to hide it, but I see that she's shivering. "All right," she says. "We'll go."

We pick our way through the basement, which is filled with trash and pools of water. Rats scurry out of the way of our flashlight beams. Ariadne is in the lead, and Jackson is walking with me.

"You should kill her," he whispers to me. "That's what our trainers would tell you."

I don't say anything. For one thing, I know Ariadne is listening, and even if she can't hear us, she's thinking the same thing about us. Any Player would be. She now knows where the weapon is. She doesn't need me, and I don't need her. The smart thing to do would be to eliminate her and remove the Minoans from this particular equation. Still, I'm surprised to hear Jackson say it after everything he said to me about working together. Maybe seeing Sauer die has changed his mind. Or, more likely, he just doesn't trust Ariadne. Do *I* trust her? I don't owe her anything. So why am I not taking her out?

We come to a stairway. I walk beside Ariadne as we go up, leaving Jackson to follow behind us.

"Your brother raises an interesting point," Ariadne says, not bothering to keep her voice low. She doesn't care if Jackson hears us or not.

"What's interesting about it?"

"I think you don't want to kill me," she says.

"And that's a problem for you?"

"For me, no. But he's right. It would be the smart thing to do."

"So now you're my trainer too?"

She snorts. "If I were, many things would have been done differently."

"I bet," I say. "And do you want to kill me?"

"If I did, you would be dead already," she says. "You shouldn't have let me go first up the shaft either. I could have killed your brother and left his body to block your way."

Behind me, Jackson makes a sound to let us know he hears every word.

"But you didn't," I say. "Which means you don't want to kill me either."

"Mmm," she says. "Not yet, anyway."

Before she can say anything else, bullets whiz past our heads. Jackson yelps in surprise as Ariadne and I flatten ourselves against the wall on either side of the stairwell, draw our guns, and return fire into the blackness above us. There's a grunt, and then a body rolls down the stairs toward us.

"Up or down?" I say to Ariadne.

"Up," she says.

We run up the remaining stairs, not knowing what we're heading into. We burst through a doorway and into a hallway. Very faint light fills the corridor, along with a cold wind and swirls of snow. We're on the first floor of the museum, in a part where the walls have been shattered by bombing. The snow outside has increased to a blizzard and is blowing through the hallway.

Several figures run toward us through the snow. "Stay in the stairwell!" I yell to Jackson and start shooting. On the other side of the hall, Ariadne does the same. Our attackers return fire, and bits of the wall explode as the bullets hit them.

I briefly glance behind me. The hallway keeps going, but I don't know where, and running won't accomplish anything. We have to make our stand here. I concentrate on stopping the advancing enemies.

Ariadne brings one down. I get another. There are still two more. I aim at one, but when I pull the trigger of my pistol, it clicks. I'm empty. And I don't have another clip.

I pull out the knife hidden inside my boot and run. Ariadne follows.

She continues to shoot as I dodge, trying to make myself as difficult to hit as possible in a hallway maybe twenty feet across. The snow and dark at least provide a little cover.

One of the remaining figures falls. The other is close enough that I see him point his gun right at me. With a burst of speed, I let my feet slide out from under me on the marble floor. My body shoots forward in the snow, and I hit the man dead on. He falls on top of me. My knife is ready, and I drive it up and into his guts. He gasps, and a moment later coughs blood into my face. I push the knife deeper.

I push the body off me. Ariadne is scouting for more shooters. The hallway appears to be clear, though, and she comes back to where I'm kneeling beside the man, going through his coat.

"Who are they?" Ariadne asks.

"No idea," I say. "But I don't think they're soldiers. He's wearing civilian clothes."

"That doesn't mean anything," she says.

She's right. Still, they don't look like MGB or any military group I know. It doesn't really matter, though. Somehow they knew we were here.

Jackson emerges from the stairwell and stands beside me. His flashlight illuminates the face of the dead man.

"I know him," he says.

Ariadne and I look at him, surprised.

"His name is Emerick Fischer. He's a friend of Karl's."

The three of us come to the realization at the same time.

"We need to get back to the safe house," I say. "Now."

CHAPTER 12

Ariadne

The Cahokian safe house is no longer safe.

When we arrive there, it's empty. Ott, his wife and child, and Lottie and her child are gone. Every drawer has been rifled through, every closet opened, every possible hiding location overturned and ransacked.

"Was there anything here for them to take?" I ask Boone.

"No," he says. "I wouldn't have left them here alone if there'd been anything important. This place was temporary, only for this mission."

"What about weapons?" I ask him. "Passports. Cash."

Boone laughs. "You think I'd leave any of that here once other people knew about its location? Especially you? Are you carrying everything you had stashed at the Minoan place?"

Of course I'm not. I found a hiding place for it, an abandoned building so decrepit that no one would think to scavenge there.

"Actually," Boone says. "I did leave a little something here." He goes into another room and comes back carrying a small bag. He reaches in and hands me two clips. I reload. Then he hands me something else.

"What's this?" I say, looking at the thing in my hand. "Bazooka?"

"Bubble gum," Boone says as he loads his own weapon. He looks at me as he blows a bubble, which expands until it finally pops. "Give it a try."

"Maybe later," I say, shaking my head.

Jackson is not taking the new development well. He'd seemed like a former Player when we were escaping the basement, but now he's gone soft again, letting his emotions get the best of him. He keeps walking around the rooms, as if his wife and son might have only wandered into one of them and aren't gone.

"I don't understand," he says.

"I think it's pretty clear," Boone says. "Ott has ulterior motives for getting the weapon. And he's willing to kill us for it."

Jackson shakes his head. "No," he says. "It's not possible. He and Lottie have been friends since they were children. I've known him for almost five years myself. Something else must have happened."

I have my doubts. I know Boone does as well. We exchange a glance, but neither of us says anything. Instead I say, "We need to get into something dry."

The one thing Boone did not take out of the safe house is clothing. He gets some for me, and I go into a bedroom and change into it. It's all his size, and made for a man, so I have to roll up the sleeves of the shirt and the cuffs of the pants, but I don't care. It feels good just to be dry and more or less warm again.

When I come out, I find Boone in the kitchen, making coffee. His brother is elsewhere.

"We need to talk," Boone says, handing me a cup of coffee.

Before I say anything, I take a sip. The warmth feels good. I hold the cup in my hands, letting it soothe the chill that has settled into my bones.

"Are we working together now?" Boone asks before I can speak. "Because it feels that way."

"Is that what you want?" I ask.

He sighs. "Can't you ever just answer a question? I know you're always thinking three steps ahead, but—"

"Six steps," I say. "As any Player would."

"All right, six steps," he says. He sounds angry. "However many it takes, I guess. But what's at the end of all the steps?"

"The weapon."

"Right, the goddamn weapon," says Boone. "It's all about the weapon."

"Isn't it?"
"For you, apparently. In case you haven't noticed, my brother's wife and little boy are missing."
"That has nothing to do with me," I say.
Boone reaches over and pokes my chest with his finger. Hard. "Is there anything in there?" he says. "Anything at all? Or just a frozen block of ice?"
Part of me wants to throw the coffee in his face. But I calm myself. I don't want him to see that he's gotten to me. I set the cup on the counter, then cross my arms over my chest.
"Get your priorities straight," I say. "We're Players. This is Endgame."
"Not yet, it isn't," says Boone.
I shake my head. "Not the final battle," I say. "But it's still a battle. And in Endgame, people get hurt. They die. You know this. You've killed some of them yourself."
"Lottie hasn't done anything to anyone," Boone says. "And Bernard is a *kid*. I get it that Minoans do things differently than Cahokians do, but one thing we do is look out for our own, and not just ourselves."
"For all you know, Lottie is part of this," I tell him. "And she's not Cahokian," I add.
"And my brother? And Bernard?" says Boone. "Are you going to tell me he's working for the Reds, or the Nazis, or some other people who want to get their hands on a super weapon they think will make them invincible? Maybe he's really a Minoan operative, working with you."
He's being ridiculous, impulsive, because he's angry. I let him rant. Of course I don't like the idea that children might get hurt in a fight over the weapon. I myself made the decision not to use violence in Ott's apartment because there were children there. But there's more at stake to the mission than the life of a little boy. This is the fate of the world we're talking about, or at least the fate of my line, which ultimately is the same thing to a Player.
"We don't know that they're in any danger," I say when he calms down

a little, trying to reason with him.

He snorts. "Yeah, I'm sure they just went off to the park to go ice skating."

Neither of us says anything for a minute. Then Boone says, "We should probably just split up. Go our separate ways. I know you're going to try to go after the weapon somehow. I guess I will too, if only to stop the Minoans from having it. It's probably best if we don't even think about helping each other out, since one or both of us might end up dead when this is all over."

What he's saying actually makes sense, and is precisely how a Player should be thinking. It's what I would say in his place. So I'm surprised to find that hearing him say it makes me feel sad. My face must register something of what I'm feeling, because Boone looks at me and says, "What?"

I don't know how to answer him, because I don't actually know what I'm feeling. This is not something I've encountered before as a Player, this sudden and unexpected sense of doubt. But what am I doubting? My feelings about Endgame? My feelings about Boone? Everything feels tied together in a knot of conflicting thoughts, and I don't know which string to try to unravel first.

A banging sound shakes me from my temporary stupor. It's coming from the front door. I look at Boone, and we silently agree on a temporary truce. We draw our weapons and head to the hall. The banging comes again, followed by a weak voice calling for help. It's a woman's voice.

"That's Greta!" Jackson says, emerging from the hallway.

"Wait!" Boone says, grabbing his brother's arm and stopping him from opening the door. "I'll get it." He looks at me, and I nod, agreeing to cover him.

He opens the door. Greta collapses into his arms, sobbing. Her hair is awry, and there are tears frozen to her cheeks. A cut under one eye is crusted with dried blood.

Jackson rushes past me and goes to Greta. "What happened? Where are the others? Lottie and Bernard? Are they all right?"

Greta nods, but it takes her a moment to speak. "They have them."

"Who has them?" Jackson says, impatient for answers. "Who, Greta?"

"I don't know," she says. "Men. A group of men. Six of them, maybe more. They came to the house and ordered us to go with them. Karl argued with them, tried to fight, but there were too many."

"Were they Soviet?" Boone asks.

Greta shakes her head. "I don't know who they are," she says. "They spoke German."

"That doesn't mean anything," I say. "Boone speaks German. I speak German."

Jackson turns and looks at me. "Maybe they were Minoans," he says. "Maybe she told her people to come while we were gone." He runs toward me. "If they hurt my wife and—"

Boone lets go of Greta and grabs him. "Stop!" he says. "They weren't Minoans." He looks at me. "Were they?"

"No," I say.

"How can you believe her?" Jackson says. "She just showed up at Ott's house with the story about the Soviets. How do we know it wasn't all a lie to convince Sauer to show us where the weapon is?"

"Sauer tried to kill us," I remind him.

"But you didn't know he would do that," Jackson argues, refusing to let it go. He looks at Boone. "It's the only thing that makes sense, Sam. It has to be her."

Sam looks at Greta, who is now sitting on the couch, crying softly. "Did the men say the word *Endgame*, or talk about Minoans or Cahokians?"

"No," says Greta. "Nothing. They demanded to know where Sauer was. That's all."

I ask the question that has been on my mind since Boone opened the door and Greta came inside. "How did you get away?"

If someone took her, there's no way they would allow her to just escape. They would surely have stopped her or killed her. She's here for

some reason that she has yet to reveal.
"They brought me back," she says. "In a car. Pushed me out a few blocks away."
"Why?" I ask.
She reaches into the pocket of her coat and pulls out a piece of paper.
"To bring you this," she says. She holds the paper out to Boone. He takes it and unfolds it.
"It's a note," he says. His eyes scan the page. "They want us to bring them Sauer and the weapon."
"Or what?" I ask, knowing that there's more.
Boone's eyes flick to his brother, then to me. "Or they'll kill the others. One every hour starting at midnight."
As Greta cries out and begins to sob, Jackson looks at his watch. "That gives us only two hours," he says. "And we don't have Sauer or the weapon."
"They don't know that," I say. To Boone I add, "Do they say who they are?"
"No. It just gives an address." He reads it to me, but it isn't familiar.
"That's in the industrial part of town," Jackson says. "Probably an abandoned factory or something like that." He's now sitting beside Greta, rubbing her shoulders as she continues to cry.
I motion for Boone to follow me into the kitchen, where we can talk in private. "There's something not right about this," I say. "If the MGB wanted us, they wouldn't play this game."
"I don't know," Boone says. "Between us, we've already killed seven of their men, two of them inside their own headquarters. Maybe they think it's safer to take hostages and make us come to them."
"That's not how they work," I argue. "And how did they find this house? Something isn't right."
Boone sighs. "I agree it's weird. But what other option do we have?"
"That's exactly what these people are counting on," I say. What I don't say is that he's the one who cares about what happens to the hostages, not me. We've already had that argument, though, and there's no

point in bringing it up again. Besides, although he's accused me of not having a heart, I do appreciate how he feels, even if I won't tell him so.

"Well, we can't just storm in there and try to get the hostages out," he says. "And there's still the problem of us not having anything to give them. What reason do they have to keep anyone alive if we have nothing they want?"

"We know where the weapon is," I say.

"Neither of us would ever tell them where it is, though," he says. "And it's underwater now anyway."

"There's still Jackson," I remind him. "They have his wife and child."

I wait for him to say that Jackson would never give up the information. We both know that isn't true, though. He would do anything to save his family. He may have once been a Player, but now he's a husband and a father. Several times now we've seen him go against his Player training. With the fate of his family at stake, I have no doubt he would abandon it completely.

I think hard, following possible paths, then doubling back when they don't work out. I consider all the options, discarding one after the other as impractical. Finally, one remains.

"I have an idea," I say.

Boone lifts an eyebrow. "Am I going to like it?"

"No. It involves you trusting me. Can you do that?"

He looks into my eyes, looking for answers. Instinctively, I put up walls to keep him out. Then, slowly, I lower my defenses. I need him to believe me. I look back at him, not blinking.

"For now," he says.

"Good," I say as I draw my arm back. "Because I'm about to break your nose."

CHAPTER 13

Boone

Ariadne's punch sends me sailing out the door of the kitchen and back into the living room. I reach up to touch my nose and feel it crunch when I try to move it. She really has broken it. There's no time to think about it, though, as she's coming at me.

"The weapon will never be yours, Cahokian," she says as she pulls a knife out.

I counter the swipe of her arm with an elbow, and hesitate only a moment before hitting her in the chest with the flat of my hand. This stops her long enough for Greta to scramble out of the way and hide behind Jackson.

"Get her out of here!" I yell at Jackson. He disappears with Greta into the other room. Then Ariadne and I are squaring off again.

This time, I'm the one to charge. She kicks out, sweeping her leg to try to trip me, but I jump and her foot slides underneath me as I fall onto her. We roll around on the floor, trading blows that always land just a little bit off. They're real enough that anyone hearing us will believe that we're really fighting. Which of course is the point.

We continue our battle until Jackson returns. Then Ariadne slips her knife into my hand and whispers, "Stab me."

I don't want to do it. She knows this, and she wraps her fingers around my wrist and guides my hand to a spot at her side. I look into her eyes as I push the blade in. She doesn't even flinch. Then she lets out a roar and shoves me off her. I'm still holding on to the knife, and it comes out. She leaps up and runs for the door, her hand covering the bleeding wound on her side.

I pretend to chase her into the hallway, where I stop and wait a moment. When I return to the living room, Jackson says, "I told you she couldn't be trusted. Now she got away. And she knows where the weapon is hidden."

I sink onto the couch and nurse my broken nose. "She can't get to it any more than we can," I say. "And she's wounded. She's going to go hide somewhere and fix herself up. With a little luck, I hit something important and she'll die."

"What if she goes to meet the kidnappers?" Jackson says. "Tries to make a deal?"

"For what? They don't have anything she wants, remember?"

"Maybe they're Minoans in the first place," my brother says.

"If they're Minoans, they wouldn't need to kidnap anyone. Ariadne already knew where the weapon is. She was just trying to get it for her line anyway. That's always been what she wanted." I sound convincing, but inside I wonder what Ariadne's plan really is. She didn't tell me, which means I have to trust that she's not doing anything that will hurt me. I do, mostly, but I can't forget that she's a Player. Still, I think something has changed between us, and that we're now working together. I hope that I'm right.

"And now we've handed it to her," Jackson says.

"And it's still 200 feet belowground, in a chamber flooded with water, behind locked doors," I say. "No one's getting it. Not yet, anyway."

My brother is being more stubborn about this than I expected him to be. I need to refocus his thinking. "You should be more worried about Lottie and Bernard," I say. I feel bad about reminding him that his family is in danger, but I need him to forget about Ariadne for a minute.

"What are we going to do?" Greta says. She hasn't spoken in so long that I've almost forgotten about her. "You have nothing to give them."

"We have information. We can use it to buy more time." Before Jackson can throw out any more concerns, I say, "We need to leave."

"Greta should stay here," Jackson says.

I shake my head. "It's not safe. Too many people know about this place now. She comes with us."

"What about going somewhere else?" Jackson says. "Greta, is there anywhere safe you can go? A friend's house, maybe?"

"Jackson, she'll be with two Players. That's as safe as she's going to get right now."

When he looks at me with a confused expression, I realize he thinks I mean Ariadne and me. "Me and *you*," I say.

I can see that my referring to him as a Player upsets him, but he doesn't say anything. He only nods. "Then let's go," he says.

Karl Ott's car is still parked on the street from when we drove here, and Greta has the key, so we take it. My instinct is to steal a car so we aren't so easy to identify, but it really doesn't matter. The kidnappers are expecting us anyway, and if we're being watched—as I suspect we are—they'll know the minute we left the house.

Still, when we near the location of the meeting point, I park some distance from it. Jackson is right that we're in an old industrial part of town. As in most cities that saw heavy shelling, this area was particularly targeted by Allied bombers, who wanted to cripple the manufacturing centers. There are almost no intact buildings here, and most are nothing but burned-out shells.

The building we've been instructed to come to was not spared. Half of it is a pile of bricks. The other is scarred with war wounds: shattered windows, crumbling walls, toppled chimneys. According to the smoke-blackened sign over the front doors, it used to be a steel foundry.

I'm tempted to leave Jackson and Greta in the car. But even with Jackson's training, I don't think it's the best place for them to be. So when we approach the entrance to the factory, it's as a trio. Despite the seriousness of the situation, as we get closer, I have this flash to the scene in *The Wizard of Oz* where Dorothy and her friends are approaching the castle of the Wicked Witch of the West. Which one of them am I? I wonder. Is it my heart that needs fixing? Or maybe my brain? Courage I think I have plenty of. But maybe I'm wrong about that.

As we reach the doors, three men emerge. They have guns drawn and aimed at us, which is no surprise. I'd have been surprised if they'd done anything less. What is slightly surprising is that the guns are Berettas. Model 38 submachine guns. They mean business.

"Stop," one of them says. He points to Greta, then Jackson. "You and you, come forward."

Greta doesn't hesitate, but Jackson looks to me. I nod, and he walks toward the three men. He and Greta are handcuffed. Then the man who seems to be the leader points at me. "Now him."

He keeps his Beretta trained on me as the other two approach cautiously. One of them stands a little ways off, also holding me in place with his weapon, while the third orders me to put my hands behind my back. Again, I'm not surprised. It also tells me that these men are aware of what I can do and are taking no chances.

The man snaps a pair of cuffs around my wrists and closes them tightly. Only then does he take me by the upper arm and says gruffly, "Move."

"You're a real brave one, aren't you?" I say in a voice only he can hear.

He tightens his grip and pulls me along. As we walk, I wiggle my fingers. I can't move them much. Just enough to touch the cuff of my coat. When we reach the others, I'm given a pat-down by one of the men. My gun and knife are removed, along with two extra clips and a small coil of wire. The man in charge takes the wire and unrolls it.

"You never know when you'll need to slice some cheese," I say.

He puts the garrote in his pocket, then examines my face. "You seem to have been in an accident." He reaches out and pinches my nose, moving it from side to side. Pain shoots through my head.

"I ran into a fist," I say through gritted teeth. "But you should see the other guy."

"I suspect you mean girl," the man says. "I see your partner is not with you."

"She decided to break up the act," I say. "Thought she could do better on her own."

He makes a *tsk tsk* sound. "That's unfortunate. And probably a lie."

"No, she did," Greta says, trying desperately to be helpful. Just as I'd hoped she would at some point.

The man glances at her, then jerks his head at the others. We're marched through the doorway and into the factory. It's basically a cavernous space crowded with rusted and broken machinery. There are no electric lights, but lanterns have been set up here and there, and they throw pale, jumpy shadows over everything. It's difficult to tell exactly what's going on around us, or how many people there are inside. I see figures moving around, and more Berettas, but I have no idea if we're talking six men or sixty.

We come to the back of the room and stop. Lined up against a brick wall are Lottie, Bernard, Karl Ott, and Jürgen. Their hands are bound behind them. Greta, seeing her husband and son, runs forward. A guard pulls her back.

"Let her go," a voice says.

Greta goes to Jürgen and Karl. Because their hands are bound, they can't do much more than kiss and lean against one another.

"Papa!" Bernard shouts, and a soldier slaps his face.

Jackson strains against his captor. "Don't touch him!" Lottie crouches, trying to comfort her now-crying son, but is pulled away from him by another man. I feel my wrists strain against the cuffs as I'm filled with rage. I have to hold it together, though, if everybody is to get out alive.

"Now that everyone has been reunited, perhaps we can get back to business."

A figure steps out of the shadows. It's a man. I've never seen him before. He comes and stands in front of me. "I see you've brought nothing with you," he says.

"Do you think I'd bring a weapon of that power with me and just hand it over?" I say. "I don't even know who you are."

He smiles coldly. "Who I am is not important. And you are not in a position to be asking questions."

He pauses, as if expecting me to say something. I don't respond. I'm studying his face, memorizing it in case I need to recall it later.

"Your deadline to bring us the weapon was midnight," he says. He looks at his watch. "It's now half past twelve."

He removes a gun from a holster. "I'm a man of my word," he says as he chambers a round. "I do not, however, enjoy killing innocent people." He looks me in the eye. "So I will let you choose who dies first."

Someone cries out. Whether it's Lottie, Greta, or one of the boys, I don't know, as I'm staring into the man's eyes. "Kill me," I say.

He laughs. "If only I could! That would save a great deal of bother for everyone, wouldn't it? And it may yet come to that if we can't reach an understanding. Until then, I'm afraid your name is out of consideration. Choose again."

"No," I say.

"If you don't choose one, I'll have to kill them all," he says.

He turns and points the gun at Lottie. I see her pull back, but she doesn't say anything. The man then lowers the pistol so that it's pointing at Jürgen's head. The little boy turns and buries his face against his mother's side. Seeing him so afraid makes me furious. My fingertips work at the ends of my shirt cuffs, trying desperately to find the end of the wire I inserted there before leaving the house. If I can get it free, I might be able to undo the cuffs. But I need a little more time.

"I didn't say I couldn't get you the weapon," I say. "I only said I don't have it here."

The man turns around. "Very well," he says. "I'm an understanding man. I'll give you another chance." He breathes deeply. "But I'm afraid you still need a reminder that further failures to follow instructions will not be tolerated."

He points his gun at Jackson and fires. My brother lets out a surprised cry, then falls to the ground. Lottie and Bernard scream and lurch forward, but they fall back when several men point weapons at them. Jackson isn't dead. But he will be soon. He's looking up at me, blood trickling from his mouth as he tries to speak. It takes all of my will not to go to him. As it is, my fingers are searching for the hidden wire in my coat. I find it and draw the wire down into my palm as I silently plead with my brother not to die.

"Now," the man who shot my brother says. "Let's discuss what happens next." His voice is as calm as if he's suggested we have tea.

But we don't get to discuss what happens next because right then there's an explosion off to the left. A chunk of the factory wall blows away, and pieces of machinery fly through the air. Screams, both from the captors and the captured, fill the air. I throw myself to the ground as the sound of gunfire adds to the confusion.

I crawl over to Jackson and lie beside him as I finally manage to work the wire into the handcuffs. "Hold on," I tell my brother. "Hold on. You're going to be okay."

The lock springs, and I get one hand free of the cuffs. I quickly remove the other side, then look around to see what's happening. Lottie and the others have disappeared into the smoke, and I have no idea where they are. I see several dead men lying on the ground but can hear many more shouting throughout the building.

Then someone is next to me.

"Here," Ariadne says, handing me a gun even as she keeps shooting. "I saved a couple for you."

CHAPTER 14

Ariadne

It's obvious very quickly that the men we are fighting are not trained soldiers. There is no rhyme or reason to the way they attack, no leader or organization. They simply run around, firing at where they think we are, while Boone and I pick them off one at a time. Within minutes, the factory is silent. I make a search, ensuring that every body on the floor is a dead one, while Boone returns to his brother.

When I come back to them, Boone is sitting on the floor with Jackson's head cradled in his lap. Lottie is standing nearby, holding Bernard in her arms. The boy is crying, and his mother is whispering in his ear. There is no sign of Karl Ott and his family.

"Where are the others?" I ask Lottie.

She shakes her head. "They ran," she says.

I watch Boone with his brother, keeping a respectful distance. Jackson was shot in the stomach. He's lost a great deal of blood, and he's going to die. I know this. Boone knows this. I don't think Lottie knows, or if she does, she's too shocked to accept it. She stands there rocking back and forth with Bernard in her arms.

Boone is singing to his brother and stroking his face.

"Count the stars across the sky,
Count the raindrops on the roof,
Count my kisses on your head,
Close your eyes and dream, dream, dream."

He sings the song over and over. Jackson's eyes are closed, and his hand is wrapped in Boone's. His chest rises and falls, and the breaths become more shallow and further apart.

As I watch Boone with his brother, holding him, singing him into death, something inside of me breaks open, something I'd thought I'd forever sealed up long ago. It's so dramatic, so powerful, that I physically feel it, as if I've fallen from a great height and hit the ground hard. It's difficult even to breathe. I hate that it's happened, but it has, and I'm afraid it's going to change everything.

Jackson's breaths continue for a little longer as Boone sings. Then they don't come at all. Lottie cries softly, trying to be brave for her son.

I go over to Boone and crouch down. "It's not safe here," I say, touching his shoulder and hoping he doesn't notice how my fingers are trembling. "We need to get Lottie and Bernard away."

Boone nods. I know he understands the danger as well as I do. He scoops his brother up in his arms and stands. "Let's go."

I don't argue with him about bringing his brother's body. I don't know what he plans to do with him, but I know he won't leave him behind. I walk with Lottie and the little boy, who keeps asking his mother, "Will Papa wake up?"

I have no idea what we are going to do next. We have nowhere to go. Both the Minoan and Cahokian safe houses are compromised. The MGB will be looking for me. We don't even know who our most recent enemy is. And the weapon, or whatever remains of it, is still lost in the underground chamber. We have to go somewhere, though, especially because of the boy. If Boone and I were on our own, we would be fine. But we're not.

You could be, I tell myself.

It's true. I don't have to stay with Boone. I could leave, maybe try to get to the weapon on my own. It would be the smart thing to do. The right thing to do, according to the logic of Endgame. I am still the Minoan Player.

Boone walks us back to where he left Ott's car. It's not there.

"Where do you think they went?" I ask him.

"Probably as far away as they can get," he says. He doesn't sound angry or bitter. Only tired. I do the calculation in my head and realize that we've been going for more than 24 hours without sleep. We need to get somewhere safe where we can rest and think. If such a place exists for us. Berlin suddenly feels like the most hostile place on Earth.

Boone walks to a car parked along the side of the street. "Do you know how to hotwire it?" he asks me.

I open the door, which is unlocked, and get in. As Boone places his brother's body in the trunk and bundles Lottie and Bernard into the back seat, I work on getting the engine going. It doesn't take long. Boone joins me in the front.

"Where are we going?" I ask him.

He leans back against the seat, thinking.

"What about Karl and Greta?" Lottie asks from the back seat.

"We can't go anywhere we've already been," he says. "I'm afraid they're on their own." He looks at me. "You've lived in Berlin for a while. Do you know anyplace?"

I think about it for a minute. Then an idea comes to me. It's risky, but we don't have a lot of options. "There's a girl I was friendly with who worked in a café," I say. "The last time I saw her, she told me she was going away for the holidays and wouldn't be back until after the New Year. I know where her apartment is because I once saw her coming out of it."

"It's not my first choice," Boone says. "But it might have to do. Let's go check it out."

I drive. It's well past midnight now. The snow has stopped, but the streets are empty. After a few minutes, Bernard falls asleep. My heart breaks for him. This morning he was opening Christmas presents, and now he's seen his father killed and is on the run from people who would happily kill him to get what they want.

When we enter the neighborhood of the café, I drive by the building where the girl, Anaïs, lives. The windows are all dark. "Hers is the third-floor one," I tell Boone as I park the car across the street.

"You go see if anyone is there," Boone says. "If she is home, you can make up some story about needing her help."

I get out and cross the street. The building's front door is unlocked, and I go inside and walk quickly up the stairs to the second floor, then to the third. There is only one apartment, so I don't have to wonder which one belongs to Anaïs. I walk to it and knock. No one comes, and there are no mumbled words from anyone I might have woken up. Still, I am very quiet as I pick the lock of the door, which luckily is a simple dead bolt. It opens easily, and I slip inside.

A quick check shows me that the apartment is empty. I return to the car and get Boone and the others. We go back inside, and while Lottie attends to putting Bernard to bed in one of the two bedrooms, Boone and I see what there is for food in the kitchen. We find some cheese, bread, and sausage, which we eat as we sit at the kitchen table.

"I'm sorry I didn't get there sooner," I say. This has been on my mind ever since the fight at the factory.

"You got there," Boone says. "That's what's important."

There's more that I want to say, but I don't know how to say it. "I'm sorry. About your brother."

Boone nods. I don't ask what he intends to do with the body.

"How's your side?" he asks me.

Instinctively, I touch the place where he stabbed me. I haven't had time to sew up the wound yet. "It's just a scratch," I joke. "How's your nose?"

"I should be able to smell in a month or so," he says. "Take your shirt off."

I look at him, surprised.

"So I can stitch you up."

I feel my cheeks burn, and quickly pull up my shirt to cover the burn I'm sure is flushing my cheeks. Luckily, Boone has gone in search of something to treat my wound with.

He returns with a needle and thread. "Good thing your friend likes to do cross-stitch," he says. "Sit."

I sit on one of the kitchen chairs. Boone kneels on the floor beside me.

He tries to thread the needle, but his fingers are clumsy, and he keeps missing the eye.

"Here," I say, taking it from him. I push the thread through on the first try and hand the needle back to him. I could do it myself. Easily. But I can tell he wants to do it. Besides, I think it might help him take his mind off what happened to his brother.

He is gentle but awkward. I find myself wondering if he's ever touched a woman like this. Fortunately, the knife went in cleanly and didn't cut muscle, so closing the wound takes only a few stitches.

"There," he says when he's done. "Not bad, if I do say so myself."

I look down at his handiwork. "Maybe you should finish Anaïs's sampler for her."

We look at each other and laugh. It feels good. A relief after all the death we've faced tonight. Then Boone looks serious again. "I have to get Lottie and Bernard out of Berlin as soon as I can. They're not safe here. I think Ott is the one who sent the men to the museum, and he was behind the kidnapping."

"I've been thinking the same thing," I say. "But who is he working for?"

"Maybe himself," Boone says. "Or he's part of a group. The problem is, he knows where the weapon is."

"Not precisely where," I say. "Only that it's supposedly in the museum. He needed us to find it for him. For all he knows, we have the weapon now. And even if he does somehow find the room, it's flooded."

"Maybe," says Boone. "I don't want to take a chance, though. We have to get whatever is in that chamber."

"How?"

"I have an idea," he says. "It will depend on whether or not a buddy can help me."

"Another Cahokian?"

"No one involved with Endgame." He doesn't tell me who it is. "It means leaving here for a few hours, though."

I know what he's really asking me: Can I be trusted to come with him?

"Boone—" I begin.

"There's something else," he says, stopping me. "If I can't get to the weapon, I'm going to make sure it's destroyed."

The Player inside me recoils instinctively at this announcement. All of my training tells me that any weapon that can give us an advantage in Endgame needs to be protected.

"I honestly wasn't sure how I felt until tonight," Boone continues. "Until Jackson was killed. Sitting there on the floor, holding him while he died . . ." His voice trails off, and I can see that he's remembering. "It changed me."

"What are you saying, exactly? You don't want to be a Player anymore?"

He doesn't answer for a long time. So long that I'm about to ask the question again. Then he says, "I don't know what I want. I know how I feel right now, tonight. I also know that might change too. I'm not making any decision about that right now."

I don't press him. Only a few days ago, what he's saying would have made me lose all respect for him. Now it doesn't. Nor do I feel as strong an urge to make sure the weapon ends up in my hands. In Minoan hands.

"We should go," he says. "I'll tell Lottie."

He gets up and goes into the other room. I hear him talking. When he comes back, he says, "They'll be okay. And they have instructions on what to do if we're not back in three hours. Are you ready?"

"Yes," I say. "Let's go."

We leave the apartment and get back into the car. It feels odd driving around with the body of Boone's dead brother in the trunk. My curiosity about where we're going outweighs that, though, especially when I realize that Boone is driving toward the air base.

"It'll be best if you stay in the car," he tells me as we get closer. "If anything goes wrong, and I'm not back after half an hour, get out of here."

"What are you going to do in there?" I ask. "Steal a plane?"
He laughs. "Nah," he says. "I just need to see a guy about a submarine."
I have no idea what he's talking about. When he parks the car and gets out, I slide into the driver's seat, in case I need to make a getaway. I watch as Boone walks toward the base, wondering what he could possibly be doing.
I can't help thinking that all I have to do is start the car and drive away. I know where the weapon is supposedly hidden. I can't get to it at the moment, but I could probably assemble a team and get to it. Not before Boone makes his attempt, but he could be dealt with as well. So why don't I? Why am I sitting here waiting for the Cahokian Player to come back when I should be trying to outmaneuver him?
The truth is, I no longer feel like his enemy. We've been through a lot together in a short time, and it's made me see things differently. I still want the weapon. I still have that drive to succeed and reach my goal. What happens once I get there is the question.
I keep checking my watch. The thirty minutes tick by with agonizing slowness. I really have no idea what Boone could be searching for here, and not knowing is driving me crazy. When I finally see him coming toward me through the gloom, he's carrying something that seems very bulky.
He reaches the car, opens the back door, and lays something on the seat. I turn my head to see what it is. There's an air cylinder with something attached to it. There's also a large bag.
"It's called an Aqua-Lung," Boone says when he gets in. "Invented by a guy named Jacques Cousteau."
I've heard of the invention but never seen one up close.
"That hose thing is called a regulator. You breathe through it."
"You've used one before?"
"No, but Smitty gave me a crash course."
"Smitty?"
"Supply sergeant here. I met him on the flight into Berlin the other

day. Told me to look him up if I ever needed anything. So I did."

"In the middle of the night," I say. "On Christmas. Didn't he think that was strange?"

"Fifty bucks makes any request seem totally normal," Boone says. "Now let's go. I want to get this over with before Ott or anyone else tries first."

I turn the car around and head back toward Museum Island. "I assume you think you're going to go back down that air shaft with that," I say. "But what happens once you're in the chamber? How are you going to get the doors open?"

Boone grins. "That's the easy part," he says. "With a key."

CHAPTER 15

Boone

Before we go back to the museum, Ariadne and I make a couple of stops at our respective cache points to retrieve weapons and ammunition. By the time we get to the New Museum, in the cold, still hours before dawn on the day after Christmas, we're armed for battle. I hope it won't come to that, but I have a feeling it will. A lot of people have died since I arrived in Berlin on Christmas Eve, and a lot of other people aren't going to be happy about that.

There's another pressure that I haven't told Ariadne about. If I don't check in with the council within 48 hours, they'll assume I'm dead and will send someone in to find out what happened to me. That gives me only about ten hours to get the weapon and figure out where to go. I'm thinking that we'll head for France. Having Lottie and Bernard along complicates things, but I'm afraid to leave them alone, especially if Karl Ott really is involved with the people trying to get the weapon. And I'm positive he is.

The question is: What about Ariadne? Would she come with us? She's sitting beside me as all these thoughts run through my mind. Although I feel like we're actually working together now, instead of just tolerating each other until one of us can make a move, there's no way to be a hundred percent sure. Still, when I feel with my gut and not just my head, I think she's someone I can trust.

As we drive, I go over the plan I've come up with once more.

"I'm going to use the Aqua-Lung to go down the air shaft," I say, "assuming it's still flooded, which I hope it is because that will slow down anybody else who is trying to get in there. Once I'm in the

chamber, I'll get the key and open the cabinets."
"How are you so sure that there even *is* a key?" Ariadne asks for the fifth or sixth time.
I'm *not* sure. But I say, "Sauer kept talking about how the items were locked inside the cabinets. If there's a lock, there's a key. And I'm betting that he had it on him."
"Why?" Ariadne says. "If he didn't want anyone to have it, wouldn't he have just thrown it away? Why bring it into the very place where it could be used if someone found it?"
"I hate that you're a Player right now," I tell her.
She makes an exasperated sound. "It's not only Players who would think this way," she says. "Anybody with any common sense would."
She's right. And of course I've thought this very thing myself. But I also have a hunch. "I think Sauer wanted it buried with him in there," I tell her. "He was a scientist. Methodical. Organized. I don't believe he would have ever given up the key, not after keeping it a secret for so long."
"That's a big if," Ariadne says. "And if you're wrong, you're going to be down there with no other way to open those cabinets. We should have gotten some explosives."
"Can't use them in such a small space," I say. "The pressure wave would probably kill anybody in the room."
"What about dropping a grenade down the shaft? You wouldn't have to be in there at all."
"True. But it might collapse the room, or the shaft, and then we'd be screwed."
Dropping a grenade down the air shaft is my plan if I can't get the cabinets unlocked, but I don't mention this. I know Ariadne isn't in agreement with me about destroying the weapon if we can't get it.
"I don't like any of this," she says. "We don't even know what we're looking for. A weapon? Pieces of a weapon? Plans? Sauer never said exactly what's in there."
"Well, we're going to find out," I say as I bring the car to a stop on a deserted street.

Our first worry is encountering anyone else who is out to get the weapon. Because I'm carrying the diving gear, Ariadne is the one responsible for keeping her eyes open for possible trouble. I can feel her tensed for action, and despite all the pressure and worry, I can't help but find it attractive. I've never met anyone like her before. She's a walking contradiction, and I still don't know where I really stand with her. I like being a team, though, and having someone besides my family who understands what it means to be a Player.

We don't enter the museum through the front door, but through one of the many holes in the walls. Ariadne leads us through the hallways as if she has map of the place in her head now after being there once, which she probably does. We encounter nobody, which is both a relief and a worry. At every turn I expect to be met with gunfire or confronted by an enemy. It would almost be better than the anticipation. A flesh-and-blood body is easier to deal with than a ghost.

But we pass through the museum without seeing anyone and find ourselves once more in the basement, where the opening to the air shaft is located. I set down the air tank and gear bag and shine a flashlight into the shaft. The light reflects off the surface of water about 20 feet below.

"It's still flooded," I tell Ariadne, and start to strip down to my undershirt and boxers.

"It's going to be freezing," she says.

"I'll work fast," I promise her. "Smitty didn't have any dive suits. We're lucky he had this stuff."

"You can't get through the shaft with that on," she says, nodding at the tank.

"I'm going to lower it in and go down after," I tell her. "I'll have to hold my breath to make it through the shaft, but once I get into the chamber, I should be fine. I'll carry the mask and fins with me."

"But—"

"Are you my trainer now?" I tease. "Trust me. I can swim a long way holding my breath. I used to practice swimming under the ice on the pond behind my grandmother's house. My trainer would drill a hole on one side and have me swim to the other and make another hole from underneath. I'll be fine."

She sighs but doesn't put up any more objections. A few minutes later, I lift the Aqua-Lung through the air shaft opening and lower it using a rope I've tied to the tank. When I run out of rope, I let go.

"Now it's my turn," I say, taking the mask and fins I've brought out of the bag. "Wish me luck."

She comes over and, to my surprise, kisses my cheek. Then she kisses the other one. "Good luck. Bring back the weapon."

I grin. "Hell," I say. "Forget about the weapon. I'm coming back for more of those kisses."

"Go," she says. "If there's trouble up here, I'll take care of it."

Now things get serious. "If there's trouble up here, you drop a grenade down this shaft," I tell her. "Promise me."

She nods.

I'm not convinced, but I don't say anything. I push the upper half of my body into the opening of the shaft. I'm going in headfirst. I pause for a minute, suspended on the edge. I take three deep breaths, inhaling and exhaling to expand my lungs. Then I take one final breath, hold it, and dive.

I've steeled myself for the shock of the water, but when I hit it, it's almost enough to make me gasp. I fight my instincts and swim as well as I can in the tight space, which isn't well at all. I wish I could use the fins, but there's just no room. But gravity is on my side, and I sink through the freezing blackness like a stone, the fins and mask held against my chest with one arm. It seems to take forever, but finally I'm through the opening in the chamber roof.

I hit the floor and turn on the flashlight Smitty gave me. It has O-rings and wax to seal it, but Smitty warned me that it might not be totally waterproof, as it's meant to withstand rain, not being submerged 200 feet underground. The light comes on, and I pray it holds.

Next I open the valve on the Aqua-Lung, put my arms through the straps, and place the regulator in my mouth. I take a breath, and my lungs fill with air. I take a moment to let my body adjust to breathing again, then get to work. The frigid water is already making me sluggish. First I slip the mask over my head. When it's on, I lift the lower edge away from my face and blow through my nose. The water inside is forced out, and I settle the mask back on my face. Then I pull the fins onto my feet.

I swim over to Sauer's body and start searching him. Between his coat and his clothes, he has a lot of pockets. Each one turns up nothing, and I start to think maybe Ariadne was right, there is no key. Then, in the last one I check, I find something. I pull out an ordinary-looking skeleton key, the kind that could fit a lock on a door, a trunk, or a hundred other things. Will it work on the cabinets?

I take it and go to the nearest cabinet. My fingers trembling, and not just from the cold, I try to insert it into the lock. It doesn't go. I try again, and again I'm met with resistance. The key does not fit this lock. I go to the next cabinet and have the same result. And the next. It's clear that the key from Sauer's pocket is not for anything in this room.

I return to his body and search again, hoping that I've overlooked something. I turn every pocket inside out. But there's nothing.

Despair presses down on me like the icy water. The excitement and hope that was helping keep me moving evaporates, and now I feel every bit of the chill. I know the weapon is here. I know it is. And I have no way of getting to it. After everything—all the killing, the running, the death of my own brother—I'm left with nothing.

Then I hear what sound like tiny explosions. They come again, and I realize that it's the sound of gunfire echoing through the air shaft. Something has happened up in the basement. Something bad.

I shine the flashlight at the opening in the ceiling. There's no way I can get up there to help Ariadne. It would take too long, and I would be an easy target. My frustration and rage double. I'm useless down here.

Nothing I can do will help anyone.

A tiny shadow detaches itself from the hole in the ceiling, a small circle of blackness that falls quickly through the beam of the flashlight. I know immediately what it is. A grenade. Ariadne has chosen to employ the final option.

That option means killing me too.

Still, my survival instincts kick into gear. As the grenade rolls to a stop, I swim as quickly as I can in the opposite direction, which means toward the elevator. As I near it, I see that the doors are open a crack. I don't know how or why, as I know they were sealed the last time I was in here. Maybe the water has short-circuited something. I don't really care, I'm just grateful for the possibility of escape. But is it enough to get through? Not with the air cylinder on my back.

I take a final breath and abandon the Aqua-Lung. As I force the doors open enough to pull myself inside the elevator, the grenade explodes. Only moments later, the wave of pressure comes. Even inside the elevator, it's enormous. The doors buckle. My whole body feels as if it's being squeezed. The glass on my dive mask cracks. My lungs are gripped so tightly that I can't breathe. I know I'm dying.

And then I don't.

I'm still alive. But I can't breathe. All the air has been sucked out of my lungs. So now I'm going to drown.

The flashlight is still in my hand and still working. I look out and see the Aqua-Lung cylinder. The regulator has been ripped from it, and air is bubbling from the broken valve. I grab the tank and put my mouth in the stream of bubbles. I sip at them, getting enough air to take a breath. Then I survey the damage done to the chamber.

One wall has been ripped open. The contents of the cabinets are strewn around the floor. It's difficult to see clearly through the cracked mask, and I have no idea what anything is, or if any of it is related to the weapon. I shine the flashlight around, hoping something will point me in the right direction. Then I see a metal box. It's dented and battered from the explosion, but still intact. I swim to it, take the key I took from Sauer's pocket, and insert it. When I turn it, I feel a click. I quickly turn it back, locking the box again. I don't know exactly what's inside, but I don't want to get water in there if I can help it. I have to assume that since Sauer was guarding the key to the box, whatever's in it is what I'm after.

Now I have to get out of the chamber. The only way out is the air shaft. But what's waiting up there? I don't know who Ariadne was facing, or if she survived. The fact that she dropped the grenade makes me think she might not have. If I go that way, I might be walking right into the hands of death.

Then I remember the elevator. I swim back to it and look at the ceiling. There's a hatch to access the machinery on top of the car. I turn the handle, and the cover flops down. The shaft above seems to be filled with water too. I push the box in my hands through the hole, take a last breath from the almost-empty cylinder, and pull myself up and through.

Standing on top of the elevator car, I take the box and put it under my shirt, knotting the material to hold it in place. Even then, it's incredibly awkward. Then I grip the steel cable that the car is attached to and start climbing, using the fins to help propel me upward. After a dozen pulls on the cable, my head breaks through the water. The rest of the shaft is dry. I rip the mask from my head and drop it, then lose the fins, as they'll do me no good out of the water. Being able to breathe doesn't make the climb much easier, though. I still have to pull my tired, freezing body up the entire length of the shaft. My muscles scream in agony as I go hand over hand, and I'm afraid to stop to rest in case I can't get them going again. I feel as if I'm crawling toward a finish line that keeps moving away from me just when I think I'm about to cross it.

Finally I'm at the top. The doors there are shut, but it's easy enough to pry them open. I stumble into a closet, then into an office. It's empty. So are the galleries and hallways outside. My feet leave footprints in the snow as I walk, then run, toward the steps that will take me to the basement. What I'm doing is stupid. I have no weapon. I'm freezing. I'm practically naked. But I have to know what happened to Ariadne. The steps to the basement are covered in blood. I slip in it as I go down them, my heart pounding harder and harder. There are bodies here, but most of them are from our previous fight. I see no new ones. I also don't see Ariadne.

I call her name. My voice echoes back at me. I call again, louder, not caring if anyone else hears me. I know I'm not thinking straight, not doing what a Player should do, but I don't care.

Then I hear someone behind me. I whirl around and see Ariadne coming down the steps. She's holding her pistol in her hand. As she runs, she takes off her coat, which she puts around me.

"I got it," I say through shivering teeth as I show her the box. The key is still in the lock. I turn it, and this time when it clicks open, I lift the lid. Inside is a metal cylinder, along with a handful of pieces of machinery. Ariadne lifts the tube out and unscrews the end. She tips some rolled-up papers into her hand. Unrolling them, she shows me what is obviously a blueprint of some kind. I can't read the writing on it, but the images are unmistakable. It's a design for a weapon.

"That's it," I say. "We did it."

I look at her face. She's smiling. She rolls the plans back up and returns them to the cylinder, which she places back in the case. She runs her fingers over the pieces of machinery, then shuts the lid.

"We did," she says.

There's something about her voice that troubles me, a coldness that I haven't heard since our first encounter.

"Ariadne?" I say.

She steps away from me and holds up her pistol. "No," she says, shaking her head. "Cassandra."

ENDGAME

THE FUGITIVE ARCHIVES

VOLUME 2

THE MOSCOW MEETING

CHAPTER I

Ariadne

As I stand beside Cassandra, watching Boone's eyes move between my face and that of my twin sister, a single thought keeps running through my mind: *He's going to die.*

I'm still shocked at Cassandra's unexpected arrival in the museum, where Boone and I have been working to extricate the alien weapon that's been hidden there by Evrard Sauer, the scientist who was studying it after its discovery by the Nazis. Sauer is now dead, entombed in the water-filled chamber 60 meters below our feet. The same chamber from which Boone has recently escaped for the second time.

I look at the metal box Boone is holding in his hands. It's the whole reason he descended into the room. Part of me is excited to see that he's gotten it, and to know what's inside it. Another part wishes he'd never found it, because I know what's going to happen next.

I'd hoped that by throwing the grenade down the shaft and into the underground room, I'd have warned Boone that something was wrong. Maybe he was too excited about finally getting the box. Maybe he thought he could help me. I'm thankful the blast didn't kill him, which was a very real possibility, but I'm not sure it matters now.

"Put the box on the floor," Cassandra says.

Even if we weren't twins, I would have known this was coming. Cassandra might not be our Minoan line's official Player, but she is a Player nonetheless. Maybe even more than I am. We trained side by side, and although I was the one who was presented with the golden horns at the choosing ceremony and have served our line to the best of my abilities, Cassandra has always longed to wear them. If she had been sent to Berlin instead of me, Boone would already be dead. Now she is toying with him, enjoying the confrontation.

Boone glances at me. I can tell he's confused. He doesn't know if I knew about Cassandra being here or not, if I'm working with her or still teamed up with him. I wish I could let him know that my sister's presence here is a surprise to me too, but I don't dare risk showing any hint of caring about what happens to him. If I do, Cassandra will make things worse. For both of us. I keep my face blank and stare back at him coldly, trying to still my wildly beating heart.

Boone crouches down, setting the box on the floor. Then he stands up again. Underneath Cassandra's coat, which barely stretches across his shoulders, he's wearing only boxer shorts and a thin undershirt, both of which are soaking wet. He's been swimming around in ice-cold water, and the temperature in the room now is well below freezing. I can see him shaking as his muscles seize up and his body attempts to warm itself. He's trying to control the trembling, but he can't. He's rapidly becoming hypothermic and needs to get warm. Although I want to go to him and wrap my arms around him, I can't. I have to watch him suffer, and it makes my heart ache.

Cassandra has had her pistol trained on him this whole time. She keeps it leveled at his chest as she says to me, "Go get it."

I don't like her ordering me to do anything, but the situation is delicate, and I don't want to risk upsetting her. I walk toward Boone. I consider placing myself between him and my sister, screaming at him to run and giving him a slim chance of escaping. But it would only put off his death for a short time. Cassandra would never let him get out alive. And she'd probably kill me as well for getting in her way.

When I reach Boone and the box, I kneel down and pick it up. It's not as heavy as I expected. As I stand and back up, holding it in my hands, I risk a look at Boone. He won't look at me. He's staring straight ahead at Cassandra, a furious expression on his face even though his lips are bluish and I can see that he's clenching his teeth together with enormous effort to keep them from chattering. But he still has enough strength to defiantly shrug off her coat, which puddles around his feet.

I walk back to Cassandra, who glances briefly at the box and says, "How clever of you to trick him into retrieving it for you." She smirks at Boone. "Just like a pet dog." She makes a woofing sound, and laughs. "Fetch, boy."

She's taunting him, but I know she's also taunting me, letting me know what she thinks about my not going after the box myself. But I don't react. Instead I smile and say, "You know I don't like to get my hair wet if I can help it." It's the kind of thing she would say, childish and inappropriate given the situation, so of course she laughs.

Cassandra turns her attention back to Boone. "Unfortunately for you, we no longer need you."

"Wait," I say, placing my hand on her arm.

She looks at me, one eyebrow raised in question.

"I'll do it," I tell her. I lift my shirt and show her the bandaged wound on my stomach. "There's a debt that requires repayment."

Cassandra nods. I know she's annoyed that I'm depriving her of making the kill herself, but she also recognizes that I have first right. "Do it quickly. We need to be on our way. Would you like to use my gun?"

She says this loudly enough for Boone to hear. She's enjoying playing with him, and I'm reminded of how during our training sessions she would often let her opponents think they had a chance just before she landed a victory blow. She enjoys offering a bit of hope, then snatching it away. I shake my head as I set the box down, reach into my boot, and pull out the knife tucked inside. "You know I prefer a blade."

She laughs again as I turn and walk back to Boone. "He's not a *kolios*, Ariadne. Make sure you gut him properly."

Another taunt, a reminder of the time we were four and our grandfather took us fishing and I wouldn't stick my knife in the flapping, gasping mackerel I hauled out of the ocean on my line. I felt bad for it. Before I could throw it back, Cassandra grabbed it and plunged a knife into its belly, slitting it open and scraping its insides out before it was even dead. At dinner, she'd eaten it fried, with lemon, grinning at me from across the table as our grandfather boasted about how brave she'd been.

I stop in front of Boone. He hasn't said a word, and I know this is mostly because he can't. The cold is forcing his body to conserve its resources in an attempt to warm itself. I also know that if he truly thought I was going to kill him, he would find the strength to fight me. I wonder if Cassandra knows he's a Player. I doubt it. If she did, she would kill him herself, despite my request, so that she could claim him as a trophy. But who does she think he is? And how did she know we were here in the first place? I've been wondering that since I turned to find her standing behind me, looking at me as if she'd come into the kitchen and caught me secretly eating one of the melomakarona our mother and aunts make at Christmastime. But there's been no time for explanations.

Right now I have to concentrate on putting on a show for her. Whatever I do, she has to believe that Boone is really dead. If she doesn't, she'll finish him off herself. But how am I going to do that? Unless his body somehow disappears, she'll be able to check whether or not he's still breathing.

I look at the entrance to the air shaft, which is just behind Boone, and I get an idea. I don't know if he can survive another trip into the water. He's barely able to stand now. But it's his only chance. *Our* only chance. Because now there's no denying it—we're a team. Who we're fighting for, I still don't know. And if he doesn't survive the next few minutes, it won't matter. I pray to the gods that he does make it.

I hold the knife up so he can see it. With my eyes, I try to tell him to trust me. I say, "I'll do you the favor of reuniting you with your brother." He looks at me, and his brow furrows for a moment. Then he gives the slightest of nods, and I know that he understands what has to happen.

I stab him in the stomach. He bends as if the knife has really gone in, but really I've only grazed him. Just enough to make the blood flow. I get some on my fingers and wipe it on the blade. Then I pretend to pull the knife out and I shove Boone toward the shaft. He spins, holding his hands to his stomach, so that his back is to me and Cassandra, and staggers the short distance to the opening. He plunges headfirst into it. There's a soft splash as he hits the water, then nothing.

It all happens very quickly, and I'm not sure it's convincing enough.

I turn back to my sister, wipe the blade on my pants, and return the knife to my boot. The whole time, I expect Cassandra to express her doubts that Boone is really dead. However, all she does is lower her gun and say, "Who was he?"

"An American," I answer. "A soldier. Not a very good one."

"He couldn't have been completely incompetent," Cassandra says. "He wounded a Player."

"A lucky strike," I say as I retrieve the box. "And now he's dead, or soon will be."

"What did you mean about his brother?"

So she did hear. "His brother was also a soldier," I lie, although this is not entirely untrue. Jackson Boone was a Player, like his brother. "He was killed in the war."

"It sounds like an interesting story," Cassandra says. "You can tell it to me on the trip."

She's walking up the stairs. I follow her. I hate leaving Boone behind, but I really have no choice. I have to keep pretending that he means nothing to me. Not knowing whether he's alive or dead is horrible, but for now I have to bury all my emotions as deeply as possible. Not only is Cassandra trained as a Player, but she's my twin. We have a bond that is beyond the normal sibling relationship. Each of us knows what the other is feeling and thinking without having to ask. Sometimes, this is a gift. Other times, like when we had to fight each other in training, it could go either way. Now it puts me at a disadvantage.

If I lie to her and she detects any trace of nervousness, she'll know.

Ironically, after everything I've been through in the past 48 hours, the most difficult thing is going to be pretending things are normal between me and my own sister.

Cassandra makes her way through the New Museum as if she's been here a hundred times. I'm not surprised. She has a photographic memory, and I'm sure she's memorized every map she could find of the building. I still don't know, however, how she knew to come here in the first place, or why. What I do know is that she's dying for me to ask her, so I don't. We've only been in each other's company for 20 minutes, and already we've slipped into our familiar patterns.

"It's too bad about Europa," Cassandra says as we exit the museum. "Also about Theron, Cilla, and Misha." She looks at me, and I know she's trying to read my expression. "Four Minoans dead. I hope what's in this box is worth it."

That she is placing the blame for the deaths of our linesmen on me is obvious, and it makes me furious. She has no idea what I've been dealing with since arriving in Berlin, how difficult the past six months have been working inside the MGB. She's brave, yes, and capable. But while I've been here, risking my life every day for our line, she's been at home in Crete.

"Every war has its casualties," I say, keeping my voice even.

"And Sauer?" Cassandra asks.

"Dead," I tell her. "Suicide."

"Anyone else?"

Again I think about Boone's brother, whose body is still in the trunk of a car parked nearby. I think too of Lottie and Bernard, Jackson's wife and son, who are waiting in a borrowed apartment for us to return. If Boone can't get out of the museum alive, what will become of them? They aren't my problem now that I have the box containing the weapon, but I find myself worrying about them anyway. I know Boone has given them instructions on what to do in the event we don't come back, and I hope they'll be safe.

"No," I say. "Not from our side, anyway."
"How many sides are there?" Cassandra asks.
"I'm not certain," I say, and this is the truth. "Things became complicated."
"Which is why I'm here," my sister says. "To uncomplicate them."
There they are, the words she's been wanting to say to me all along. I knew she wouldn't be able to resist forever. This is what she's been waiting for, the chance to tell me how I've failed.
"When we couldn't reach Theron, Cilla, or Europa, we knew that something had gone wrong," Cassandra continues. "And then we had word that Misha had been killed."
So there was someone else inside the MGB spying for them. For us. I'm not surprised. In fact, I assumed there was. I do wonder who it is, though. I don't ask. I'm not ready to give Cassandra even the smallest bit of satisfaction.
"The council decided it would be best for me to come see if you were in trouble," she says.
"Of course," I say. "And since you look like me, it would make it easy for you to assume my role as Player without arousing the suspicions of anyone else who might be involved."
"The look on the American's face when he thought he was seeing double was worth the trip," Cassandra says. "It was almost as if I'd broken his heart."
Her words are not lost on me. Again, though, I ignore them. We've reached the street. Cassandra stops at a car, takes some keys from her pocket, and unlocks the door. She gets inside, and I walk around to the other side. When she pushes the door open, I get in. "Are we driving back to Heraklion?" I ask as she starts the engine.
"Train," she says as she pulls away from the curb. "It will take a little more than two days, so we'll have lots of time to catch up. I have a bag for you, so we can go directly to Berlin Friedrichstraße. Unless there's something else you need to do."

She looks over at me. I look back at her. "No," I say. I pat the box I'm holding in my lap. "Sauer is dead. We have the weapon. That's what I came for."

Cassandra grins. "Good," she says. "This will be fun. Just the two of us, with nothing to do but talk. It will be like when we were children."

That's what I'm afraid of, I think as I grin back at her and say, "I'm glad you came."

CHAPTER 2

Boone

As I sink through the water inside the air shaft, all I can think about is how cold I am, how my muscles won't do what I tell them to, how hopeless I feel. Without any light, I'm in total blackness. I can't turn around in the cramped space, so I have to keep going down, back into the flooded chamber where Sauer's body is. Then I have two choices: I can either come back up the shaft, or I can go back into the elevator and climb up the cable again. Neither one seems possible. I barely made it up the elevator cable the last time. Now my body is even more worn out and damaged.

To make things worse, the only thing waiting for me if I do manage to get out is a whole bunch of problems. My brother is dead. The weapon I worked so hard to find is gone. The thought of going home and telling my council that I failed my assignment, and that the Minoans now have the weapon, is horrible. Even worse is the idea of telling my mother that Jackson didn't actually die in the war, but that now he's dead, and it's because I couldn't save him.

Then there's Ariadne. I don't want to believe that she betrayed me, that she played me like a fool in order to get her hands on the weapon. And part of me doesn't believe that she did. She could easily have killed me, or let her sister kill me, but she didn't. Why? I'm no longer any use to her. She doesn't need me. Any good Player would have used the opportunity to take me out. And Ariadne is an excellent Player. So why am I still alive? Why did she give me a chance?

Maybe, I think, she doesn't believe I can make it out. Maybe she's hoping the freezing water and the darkness will do what she couldn't bring herself to do.

And she might be right. I can feel myself growing more and more exhausted. It would be easy to just close my eyes and wait for the air in my lungs to run out. I can practically hear the cold whispering in my ear, telling me to give up. It would be so easy.

I feel myself pass through the bottom of the shaft and into the chamber where, somewhere, Sauer's body still floats. I can't see anything, can't even really orient myself to know which way to go. The explosion caused by the grenade Ariadne dropped down the shaft has filled the room with pieces of debris, which further confuses me, as things keep bumping against my body. And I'm running out of time.

I feel my thoughts slowing down. Instead of thinking clearly and quickly, making decisions, I'm lost in a fog, following one idea for a short time and then stopping. The darkness is closing in. All I want is to go to sleep and wake up somewhere else.

Then the voice of Fawn Flowers, my harshest trainer, cuts through the darkness. "The human body has limits," she says, and I instantly picture her standing over me as I lie in the mud. It's sleeting, I'm soaked through, and I'm completely worn out after running for what seems like a thousand miles through a snowstorm. My feet are covered in blisters that tear and burn with every step, my hair is frozen into icicles that sting my eyes, and now she tells me I have to turn around and run all the way back the way I came.

Fawn doesn't help me. She just stands there, scowling as she lectures me. "No matter how strong a body is, it can become too damaged to work. But sometimes the mind can push us past those limits. If you ever get into a situation where you think you can't physically go on, think about the person you love most in the world. Think about how you need to get from where you are to where that person is. Don't think about how tired you are, or how much you hurt, or how impossible it seems. Just think about that person and start moving."

That day, I thought about my mother. I pictured her waiting for me back at our house. I thought about never seeing her again. Then I imagined the look on her face when I came through the door. I kept that image in my head as I forced myself to get to my knees, then to my feet. I kept my mother's face in front of me as I stumbled a few feet, then as I began to walk. I kept telling myself that she was so close. When my blistered feet screamed for me to stop, I ignored them. When I slipped in the snow and fell, I shut my eyes and saw my mother smiling at me, telling me how much she loved me, and I got up again.

I ran the whole way home like that, one step at a time. And when I finally did reach our front door, I went inside and collapsed in my mother's arms. Even though my body was wrecked, I'd never felt so happy.

I think about her now. I see her face, looking at me with that expression she has that means she's worried but doesn't want to let me know. I can tell she wants me to come home. I try to move my arms and legs, to move toward her, but I feel so heavy. I'm being dragged down into the black water, and my mother's face starts to fade away.

Then something unexpected happens—I'm looking at Ariadne. She's standing in front of me just like she was a few minutes ago. Her eyes are locked on mine, and without saying a word, I know she's asking me to trust her. And I do. I know I shouldn't. Every Player instinct I have is screaming at me to fight her and her sister, even though I have almost no chance of winning. Instead I look into her eyes and know that I'm here now because she cares about me, that she sent me back into the cold and the dark because it was the only chance she had of saving me.

Suddenly I want more than anything to be with her again. She and Cassandra are probably on their way out of the museum already. I don't know where they're going, or how I'll find them. I only know that I have to try.

At the other end of the room is the elevator and the shaft leading up to an office. But I don't think I can climb back up the elevator cable again. In the room above me are my clothes, and getting back into them is my best chance of surviving. If I can get back up the air shaft. First I have to find the opening. I swim up until my outstretched hand touches the ceiling tile. Fortunately, I haven't moved too far away from where I entered the room, and a few moments later I find the edge of the shaft opening. I swim into it and kick as hard as I can, which isn't very hard at all. Still, I move up, and every inch brings me closer to air. I keep Ariadne's face in my mind and keep going.

When my head breaks the surface of the water, I gasp in air. My burning lungs expand, and the pounding in my head and chest calms. But I'm not safe yet. Far from it. I still have to get up the rest of the shaft and into the cellar. The longer I stay in the water, the harder it will be, so although it seems impossible, I set my back against the cold metal wall of the shaft, force my knees up until my feet are pressed against the other side, and slide upward one agonizing inch at a time.

The entire time I'm working my way up the shaft, Ariadne is there in my head, urging me on. I never take my eyes from hers, and this is the only thing that keeps me going. Even then, there are a couple of times when I don't think I can go any farther. That's when her voice fills my head, telling me not to give up. For her, I don't. For her, I keep going even though I can no longer feel anything in my fingers or toes.

Then I'm at the end. It takes everything I have left to reach up and pull myself over the edge of the shaft and onto the floor. I crawl to the pile of my clothes and pull them on with fingers I can see now are torn and bloody from clawing at the walls of the air shaft. When I manage to get my coat on, I start to feel just the tiniest bit more alive. I have on clothes. I've survived. And I have a purpose.

I stagger up the steps and through the halls of the museum. Outside, dawn is still some time away, and the world is gray and still. I find my way back to the car and try not to think about my brother's body in the trunk as I get in and start the engine. I turn the heater up as high as it will go and wait for the air to warm up. When my hands are working well enough to operate the shifter, I put the car in gear and drive back to the apartment we've borrowed from Lottie's acquaintance Anaïs—where, I hope, Lottie is still waiting.

She is. When I come in, stumbling, she runs over and helps me into the bathroom.

She starts the water flowing into the bathtub, then helps me take off my clothes, as my fingers still aren't working quite right. When I'm down to just my boxer shorts, she helps me into the tub. I sink down until only my head is above the water, letting my frozen body thaw.

Lottie perches on the toilet, watching me.

"I'm not going to drown," I promise her, trying to lighten the mood.

"What happened?" she asks. "Where's the girl?"

"We found the weapon," I say. "Well, parts of it. And some plans."

Her face brightens for a moment, and she opens her mouth to speak.

"But there were complications. One complication, anyway. A big one."

I tell her everything: about Cassandra, and about my trip back down the air shaft into the flooded chamber. Her eyes widen with each new detail. When I'm done, she says, "So the weapon is lost. The Minoans have it."

"For now," I say.

"You're going to go after them?"

I nod. "That's my plan."

"How will you even find them?" she asks. "And if you do, how will you get the weapon back? Once they have it, surely they'll keep it protected."

"Of course they will," I say. "As for finding them, I have some ideas."

Lottie shakes her head. "I hope you have a secret weapon."

I picture Ariadne. "I think I might," I say.

She sighs. "Are you sure you're all right?"

"Never better."

She stands up. "I'll go make something to eat, then."

She leaves, and I close my eyes. The truth is, I'm still cold. I feel like I'll never truly be warm again. But I'm alive. The water feels great, but I know I can't stay here long. There is a lot to be done, and with every second that passes, Ariadne and Cassandra are getting farther and farther away. I need to go after them, and soon.

There's a knock on the door. Lottie opens it and steps inside. She's holding a small stack of folded clothes, which she sets on a chair. "Apparently, Anaïs has a gentleman friend," she says. "I found these in one of the dressers." She bends to retrieve my pile of wet things. "I'll hang these up to dry."

I stay in the bathtub until the water begins to cool, then get out and dry myself with one of the towels. I dress in the clothes Lottie has found. They're a little big for me, but they're warm. When I'm dressed, I go out into the other room. Lottie is in the kitchen, stirring something in a pan on the stove.

"There were tins of soup in the cupboard," she says as she dips a spoon into the pot.

"I'm starting to feel like Goldilocks," I say as I take a seat at the table. "I wonder what Anaïs will think when she comes home and finds people have been sleeping in her bed, wearing the clothes in her dresser, and eating her food."

I take a bite of the soup. It's made with beef, hearty and thick, and I eat half the bowl before I say another word. Lottie sits down across from me and waits. I can tell she's anxious to hear why I've returned alone, but she doesn't rush me. When I'm done, I push the bowl away. "We need to talk about what happens next," I say. "Do you and Bernard have somewhere safe to go?"

"Safe?" Lottie says. "Safe from whom?"

"Too many people know about the weapon," I remind her. I think about Jackson's body lying in the trunk of the car. She can't have forgotten what happened. "If someone thinks you know anything about where it is, they might try to harm you."

Lottie's face hardens, and I know she's now thinking about Jackson as well. "There are places where we will be safe," she says stonily.

"And where we can bury Jackson."
"Where?"
She looks like she doesn't want to tell me. "In France," she says.
"I'll need to know where you are," I say. "In case I need your help."
"What can I do?"
"I don't know, exactly," I admit. "Maybe nothing. But when this is over, I know my family would like to meet you and Bernard."
Lottie shakes her head. "I don't think they would like that at all," she says. "They will blame me."
I can't tell if she really believes this or if she's the one who doesn't want anything to do with us. I don't argue with her. There will be time for that later. Right now, we both need to get going. There's one more thing I need to discuss with her first.
"What can you tell me about Karl Ott?" I ask her.
Lottie shrugs. "I've known him since we were children. Our fathers worked together."
I sense that this is something else she's reluctant to talk about. But I need information, and so I press on. "What's his real name?"
She hesitates a moment before saying, "Tobias Falkenrath."
"Jackson said his father was imprisoned by the Allies."
"Yes," Lottie says. "The Soviets."
"Could Ott be working with someone?"
Lottie looks at me and wrinkles her brow. "What do you mean?"
"Somebody tipped off the people who came and took you from the safe house," I say.
"It could have been any number of people," Lottie replies tersely.
"Yes, it could," I say. But I have my doubts. I can't help thinking about how Ott disappeared so quickly during the fight at the factory, and how determined he was to get the weapon.
"Karl wouldn't betray us," Lottie says, as if the matter is settled. She stands up. "I need to get Bernard ready to leave."
I don't argue with her. Now that I know Ott's real name, I can find

out more about him on my own. Still, I'm not happy having his whereabouts unknown. He's a wild card, and I'd feel better if I knew what he was up to.

While Lottie goes and wakes Bernard, I wash the dishes and put them away. When Lottie and Bernard are ready, I make one last trip through the apartment, making things look the way they did when we arrived. My clothes are still damp, and I don't want to put them on and risk being cold again, so I'll be borrowing Anaïs's friend's clothes permanently. Hopefully, she'll just convince herself he took them, and won't even know someone has been here. Not that it matters. Still, I've been trained not to leave any evidence behind, and it's important to stay sharp.

We leave the apartment and go down to the car. Before Lottie and Bernard get in, I give them each a hug. I also give Lottie some of the cash I took from the safe house. "This should be enough to get you to France," I tell her.

She tucks the money into the pocket of her coat, then hands me a piece of paper. "The address where we'll be," she says. Then she kisses me on each cheek. "Good luck, Sam."

She gets into the car, starts it, and drives away. I watch until she reaches the end of the street and disappears. Once she's out of sight, I turn and start walking. I'll be leaving Berlin myself shortly. First, though, I need to make a call.

CHAPTER 3

Ariadne

The waters of the Aegean are choppy, as they often are in winter, and the caïque rocks a little as we make the crossing from Piraeus to Heraklion. But after more than 48 hours cooped up in a train compartment, it's a pleasure to be out in the open air. I only wish my homecoming were under different circumstances.

Manos Theodorakis is at the helm of the *Amphitrite*, and as we motor, he talks to me and Cassandra about the civil war that has been waging in Greece for the past four years.

"I think we are nearing the end," he says. "Now that Stalin has withdrawn support from Tito, the Communists will not be able to maintain their positions. Already they are calling for Vafiadis to be replaced. It's only a matter of time."

Ianthe Pavlou, who is sitting at the small table in the cabin with me and Cassandra, takes one of the pieces of the weapon from the box that sits open in front of her, and inspects it. "If the rest of the country had fought the way Cretans did against the Germans, the war would have ended much sooner."

Ianthe is talking about the Battle of Crete, which occurred in the summer of 1941, when the Nazis sent paratroopers to invade the island in an attempt to secure it as a seaport. They were met with fierce resistance from the local population—most of whom are of the Minoan line—who defended their ancestral home and defeated the invaders. Cassandra and I were only 10, but we had already been training for several years, and we assisted the older fighters by acting as scouts and relaying information back and forth. Ianthe, who is older than we are by 15 years, killed a dozen soldiers herself, and has a thick scar running down the left side of her face as a reminder.

She sets the piece in her hand back in the box and stands up. "I need a break," she says. "Ari, want to come outside for a smoke?"

I can tell that she wants to talk to me alone. I nod and follow her out of the cabin and onto the deck. Ianthe leans against the rail that runs along the side of the boat. She takes a pack of cigarettes from her pocket and taps one out. She offers it to me, but I shake my head. She puts the pack away, places the cigarette in her mouth, and cups her hand around it as she strikes a match and touches it to the tip. When it takes, she tosses the match into the sea and blows out a cloud of smoke.

Even though it's winter, the temperature is warm and the skies are blue. The change from Berlin is remarkable. I realize how much I've missed Greece after more than half a year away. I look out over the seemingly endless expanse of the sea. We've been motoring for only a few hours, so Crete is not yet visible, but I search the horizon for its familiar hills anyway. At the bow, dolphins break the surface, swimming alongside us, and it feels as if they've come to escort me home.

I should be elated. The weapon is in our hands, and it could change everything about how Endgame is played. But the worry that began when I first saw my sister in the museum has slowly grown into a feeling of dread. During the train trip, Cassandra acted as if everything was fine, catching me up on the news from home. Never once did she ask about Boone, or for details about what occurred in Berlin. Rather than being comforting, this lack of questioning has only made me more wary. It's as if she is trying too hard to make me feel at ease, which has had the opposite result. Equally distressing is that when I asked her why and how the council had decided to send her to assist me, she said only that she didn't know their reasons, and that I would have to ask them myself.

"How was the journey from Berlin?" Ianthe asks.

"Uneventful," I tell her.
She laughs. "You mean boring," she says. "I imagine it was, after everything."
She's watching me. She knows something. I wonder how much. I decide I might as well find out. "What have you heard?"
She takes a drag on her cigarette before replying. "Four dead," she says.
I nod. What is there to say to this? Again I wonder how everyone knows what happened, when I've made no report myself. But I don't want to appear anxious, and so I say, "I hope what's in that box is worth it. Can you tell anything?"
Ianthe is a scientist, like Sauer. Her specialty is ancient civilizations. She shakes her head. "No," she admits. "But there are items in our collection that might be of some assistance. Things we've found over the years. We'll see."
She's being evasive. I can tell by the way she turns away from me and pretends to be looking at something in the water. I don't know if she really doesn't know anything, or if for some reason she doesn't trust me enough to tell me what she thinks. I stand beside her and look at the water too. It flashes in the sunlight, and the smell of salt and fish tangs the air around us.
"There's going to be an inquiry," Ianthe says, her voice almost a whisper. She doesn't look at me. "I thought you should know."
So that's it. Now I know why Cassandra was sent to Berlin. Someone thinks I've done something wrong, made mistakes. That I've failed as the Player. I'm not surprised. It's what I've been most afraid of. Having it confirmed doesn't make me feel better, but at least now I know what's waiting for me when we reach the island.
There's no point in asking Ianthe any questions. She's most likely told me everything she knows. She's not part of the council, and therefore not privy to their discussions. Probably she's heard the rumor from someone else. She's only told me now because of our friendship.
Now she turns to me and smiles. "I wouldn't worry," she says. "It's

routine when there are deaths."

I nod. She's right. However, the knot in my chest isn't loosening. There's something more going on. What it is, I won't know until I'm standing before the council. I expect that will happen shortly after our arrival in Heraklion. They will want to talk to me while the details of the past week are fresh in my mind. Not that I'm likely to forget them.

"If you two stare at that water much longer, Poseidon himself will rise up and claim you as his brides."

I turn to see Cassandra watching us. I wonder how long she's been there, and if she's somehow heard any of our conversation. I don't think so. Now she comes and joins us at the railing. She's right beside me, our shoulders touching.

"Remember the time the trainers took us out on a boat to practice deep diving, and when we came up, the boat was gone?"

"We had to swim twenty kilometers back to land," I say. "In the dark. When I said I couldn't swim any farther, you told me that if I didn't keep going, a sea monster would reach up and drag me down to eat me."

"And it might have," Cassandra says. "Who knows?" She laughs. "Speaking of sea monsters, I bet Theia Astraea is making kalamarakia krasata for your welcome-home dinner."

Again, my sister's cheerfulness is unnerving. If she knew that the council was unhappy with me, she would normally not miss the opportunity to make me feel bad about their displeasure. Acting as if this is an ordinary return from a successful mission is not normal. I catch Ianthe's eye for a moment. The look on her face is one of pity, which worries me as much as Cassandra's behavior.

"I'm going to sit in the bow for a while," I say. "I'm a little tired."

I feel Ianthe and Cassandra watching my back as I walk away. Will they talk about me? It annoys me that I'm now suspicious, that I'm letting the fact that the council is holding an inquiry bother me. It's not unexpected, but Ianthe's warning has made me uneasy.

When I reach the bow, I settle into a nest of fishing nets, curling up with my head resting on a buoy. I stare up at the sky, watching the clouds move slowly across the blue expanse like sheep on a hillside. The sun warms my face and makes me drowsy, and soon, despite my worries, I fall asleep.

I dream about Boone.

I'm in the flooded underground chamber. I've gone there to try to rescue him. It's dark and cold, and the water is filled with debris: papers and pieces of things that were hidden behind the cabinet doors before the grenade explosion ripped them open. I swim through the room, feeling my way with my hands. I touch a body, but it's not Boone. It's Sauer. His dead eyes stare at me, his mouth open and his tongue swollen from the poison he took. I push away from him and turn. Boone is behind me. When I see him, I'm filled with joy.

Then I realize that he's dead too. His body hangs in the water, his limbs limp as a marionette's. His eyes are closed. I reach out for him, and his eyes blink open. They're white, as if they've frozen. His hands grasp my wrists, the bloated fingers like manacles of ice. I fight him, but he doesn't let go. I scream, and the air in my lungs bubbles out. I try to breathe, but there's only water. It fills my mouth, and I choke. Boone opens his mouth, and even underwater I can hear him laugh as he watches me drown.

I'm awakened by the bumping of the caïque against a dock. For a moment I'm confused about where I am. Then I remember, and I realize that we've arrived. We're on Crete. Home. I climb out of my makeshift bed, stretch to rid myself of the lingering bad feelings from my dream, and try not to think about whether what I saw was prophetic or just a nightmare. I very much hope Boone is still alive, but I can't think about him at the moment.

I go and help Ianthe and Cassandra moor the boat, tying the bow and stern lines to the cleats anchored on the dock. Once the caïque is secured, Ianthe gathers up the box with the pieces of the weapon in it and we begin the walk to my parents' house. When we're halfway there, Ianthe and Manos break off to go their own ways. I hate to see the box leave my sight, but I know that it's safe with Ianthe, and it's one less thing I have to worry about. For the moment, anyway.

Cassandra and I don't talk, but she hums a tune as we walk. It takes me a moment to place the song. It's one we made up when we were children, about a girl who goes into the forest to find and kill a monster.

"You're singing the hunting song," I say.

"Am I?" she says. "That's odd. I haven't thought about that in years."

She sounds happy, as if she's the one coming home with a trophy. Which I suppose she is. But is it the box, or is it me?

When we reach our home, she lets me go in first. I take only a few steps inside before my mother appears and takes me in her arms, smothering my face with kisses. My father is next, and the two of them hug me so tightly I feel like an olive being pressed for its oil.

When they finally let me go, my mother stands and looks me up and down.

"You've lost too much weight," she declares.

"It's because I didn't have your moussaka and keftedes to make me fat," I tell her.

"You're in luck," my father says. "She and your *theia* have made enough of both to feed the entire Greek army."

I follow my mother into the kitchen, where my aunt is standing by the stove. Like me and Cassandra, my mother and her sister are twins. Astraea opens her arms and I endure the hugging and kissing all over again. As soon as she's done greeting me, though, my aunt hands me a wooden spoon and says, "Don't let the meatballs burn."

It feels good to be tossed right back into normal life. Nobody asks me about Berlin. Nobody talks about Endgame. We cook while my mother and aunt bicker over the best way to season the lamb. We drink glasses of sweet white wine. It all feels familiar and welcome, and it takes me a while to realize that there really is enough food for a large group.

"Who is all this for?" I ask.

As if in answer, there's a knock on the front door. My father disappears, and when he comes back, he's accompanied by five people: Effie Kakos, Nemo Stathakis, Ursula Tassi, Xenia Papadaki, and Venedict Economides. Individually, they are my third-year mathematics teacher, a bookseller, one of my trainers, the great-grandmother of my best friend, and the priest at the Agios Minas Cathedral. Collectively, they are the Minoan council.

"Welcome home, Player," Xenia Papadaki says as she embraces me and kisses me on both cheeks.

The others are more formal, shaking my hand. I notice that they greet Cassandra in a similar manner. Perhaps it is my imagination, but it seems they might be even more enthusiastic in their congratulations to her, as if she is responsible for bringing them the weapon. Or maybe, I think, they're congratulating her on returning her wayward sister to them.

I try not to think about it too much as my father shepherds us to the table, where we sit. Cassandra and I are seated across from each other, and throughout dinner I occasionally look at her to see if she shows any indication of this being her victory celebration and not mine. Each time, she returns my look and lifts her glass of wine in salute. I have several glasses as well, and this does much to ease my tension.

The food is delicious. The conversation alternates between politics, local gossip, and the coming new year. Again, nobody asks me about my mission. We eat for several hours. Then the table is cleared and plates of bougatsa and loukoumades are brought out along with small cups of dark, rich coffee. Only then does Effie Kakos, who as the senior member of the council is sitting at the head of the table, say, "Now, Ariadne, let us talk about this Samuel Boone."

CHAPTER 4

Boone

Like Berlin, Budapest is recovering from the war very slowly. Over a period of 50 days at the end of 1944 and the beginning of 1945, the city was virtually destroyed by fighting between the German and Soviet armies. Its buildings still lie in ruins, and its people walk through the city like ghosts haunting what I can tell was once a beautiful place. And, despite the devastation, it's still beautiful. They're rebuilding, and one day I want to come back and see it the way it should look, when the scars are healed.

Even now there are signs that the city and its people are coming back to life. The new year is two days away, and that always makes people hopeful. In my family, we each make a list of things we want to happen or to do in the new year. We put the list away, then take it out again on New Year's Eve and see how much of it has been achieved. My list from last year is tucked away in a drawer of my dresser back home. My list for the current year is sitting in front of me on the table in the café where I'm sitting, waiting for the person I've come here to meet.

I look at what I've written so far.

Find Ariadne
Get the box
Learn Spanish
Finish reading *Moby-Dick*

The last item has been on my list every year for the past five years, ever since my father told me I should read it because it's the greatest American novel ever written. I hate not finishing things, so I keep putting it there hoping it will give me the incentive I need to get through Melville's doorstop of a book. But in all this time, I've only made it through the first 100 pages, so I suspect it will be there again in 1949. I don't know how the guy found so much to say about whales.

As for the first two things on my list, I don't know yet how I'm going to get them done, but I'm determined to do it. Only now, looking at my handwriting on the scrap of paper, do I realize that I've put finding Ariadne first. Maybe it's coincidence. Maybe not. The longer I'm apart from her, the more worried I get that I'll never see her again. I've never felt this way about anyone, and it's making me more than a little anxious that perhaps I'm letting my emotions get in the way of what should be my primary concern—retrieving the weapon and taking it home. In order to get the box, I need to find her, so it's all tied together. But what if it wasn't? What if I had to choose one thing over the other? Would I look for her first, or the box?

"It's a little late for writing your Christmas list for Santa, isn't it?"

A man pulls out the chair across from me and sits down. I quickly pick up the piece of paper, fold it, and stick it in the pocket of my coat.

"Yeah, well, I never get that BB gun I ask for anyway," I say.

The man is older than I am, probably in his forties. He's tall and thin, with an angular face, dark eyes, and close-cropped black hair. His name—at least the one I've been given—is Charles Kenney.

"Your journey here was uneventful, I assume," Kenney says.

I know what he's asking. He wants to know if I think I was followed.

"Pretty boring," I tell him.

"I'm sorry I couldn't get here earlier," he replies. "I had business to attend to elsewhere."

It's been three days since I contacted my line back in America via shortwave radio. Using Morse code, I let them know that I'd located the item I was searching for, but that it had been lost again. I didn't tell them how. I said I could get it back, though. They responded by telling me to go to Budapest and meet the man who is now looking at me intently from across the table. I assume he's Cahokian, but I've never heard of him, and don't know who he is or what he does, so I wait for him to tell me.

"We've met before," he says. "Although you wouldn't remember it. You were only four years old, and it was only for a few minutes. I was one of the people who evaluated your brother to determine his potential as a Player. I left America soon after, and have been living in various places in Europe ever since. I'm sorry about what happened to Jackson."

I wonder if he's referring to the story we were all told—that Jackson died in the war—or if he knows about the incident in Berlin. I don't know what, if anything, I should say about that. Or about so many other things. Kenney is connected to my line, so I should tell him everything. Instead I find myself keeping secrets.

"Sauer is dead," I say, deciding to avoid the topic of my brother altogether for now. "He committed suicide in the room where the box was hidden, after triggering a booby trap designed to kill anyone in the room. He didn't want us to have it."

"Us?" Kenney says.

"The Cahokians," I say, quickly catching my mistake. I can't mention Ariadne or the Minoans to him.

"Ah," he says, nodding, as if maybe I meant something else. "I see. And did he say why?"

"He said it was too dangerous for anyone to have."

"And yet he never destroyed it himself," Kenney says. "Don't you find that interesting?"

I suddenly feel as if I'm being tested. I don't like it. "It was the most important thing he ever worked on," I answer. "He probably couldn't bring himself to do it."

"Possibly," Kenney agrees, although he sounds doubtful. "Or perhaps he was keeping it safe for someone else, and feared that if we took possession of it, the other party would never get it back."

"Could be," I say.

"It doesn't matter now, though, does it?" says Kenney. "So, you recovered the box, but then it was taken from you. Is that correct?"

This is the part I've been dreading the most. "Yes," I say. "I almost died getting the box and escaping from the flooded chamber for the second time. When I came out, there were people there. I was exhausted and injured. I couldn't fight them. There were too many. I figured staying alive was the priority, and I could always retrieve the weapon later."

Kenney is looking at me, his eyes locked on my face. I meet his gaze, knowing that he's searching for any indication that I might be lying. I hope that he takes any sign of nervousness as me being embarrassed at having failed as a Player. That would be a natural reaction for anyone in my position.

"Understandable," he says after a long moment. "And you say you know who these people are?"

I nod. This next part will be tricky. I have to play my role perfectly, or everything will fall apart. "The leader is a man named Karl Ott," I say. Even though I know this is not Ott's real name, I don't share this information, as I may be able to use that "new" information later to buy me more time if I need it. "He's the son of a scientist who worked with the Nazis. Sauer told me that Ott had been pressuring him for a long time to give him the weapon. He's part of a group of people who want revenge for what was done to the Nazis by the Allies."

"Sauer told you this?"

"Yes."

"I wonder why he would share that information if he didn't trust you to have the weapon yourself."

"Maybe to convince me that he really didn't think anyone should have it," I say. "To gain my trust and lure me into the room so he could kill me."

"There are easier ways to kill someone," Kenney says. "Why reveal the location of the hidden room and kill himself in the process?"

These are all legitimate questions, and I try not to let it bother me that Kenney is asking them. They're things any trainer or Player would wonder about. I keep my voice neutral as I say, "I think he was tired of keeping the secret." *Like the one the council kept about my brother,* I think, wondering again how much Kenney knows about that.

"Where do you think Ott has taken the weapon?" he asks.

I've given a lot of thought to how to answer this question, which I of course knew was coming. As far as my council is concerned, getting the weapon is the primary—the only—mission now. They don't know that the Minoans are involved, and they especially don't know that finding Ariadne is just as important to me.

"The Soviet Union," I tell him.

One of Kenney's eyebrows lifts. "Really?"

"Ott's father is in prison there," I explain. "I think he's going to try to get him out."

"Did his father work on the weapon with Sauer?"

"Possibly," I say, although I don't think this is true. As far as I know, only Lottie's father, Oswald Brecht, knows as much about the weapon as Sauer did.

"And so you want permission to go to the Soviet Union in search of Karl Ott, who you *think* has the weapon with him."

"I know it sounds like a wild-goose chase," I say. "The Soviet Union is a big place, and Ott might have taken the weapon somewhere else. But it's the best chance we've got to retrieve the weapon. Give me a week to see what I can find out. If I haven't gotten the weapon back by then, we'll go to plan B."

"Which is?"

I grin, hoping it comes across as confidence. "There is no plan B, so plan A has to work."

Kenney leans back and sighs. "This is not a good plan," he says flatly.

I worry that he's going to say no, and order me to return home. If he does, I don't know what I'll do. I hold my breath as he thinks. I can see the wheels of his mind turning, examining the various risks and potential rewards.

"You speak Russian?" he asks.

"Well enough."

"The Soviets are not fond of Americans," he says. "If you're caught and they think you're spying for the United States, we can't help you. Once you enter the Soviet Union, you're on your own."

"I understand," I tell him.

He nods. "All right. I'll get you money and an identity. It will take you a few days to travel there. Train is easiest. I don't like that this Ott fellow has a head start on you, so you'll need to leave as soon as possible."

If Ott really had the weapon, Kenney would be right. But Ott doesn't have it. Also, I'm not going to the Soviet Union, at least not right away. It's important that he think that's where I'm heading, though, so I say, "I've already looked at the schedules. There's a train leaving tonight that will get me as far as Minsk."

Kenney stands up. "Meet me back here in two hours," he says.

He leaves. I stay at the table for a little longer, finishing my coffee and thinking about my real plan. I have indeed looked into train schedules, but not to Moscow. I'm going to Athens. With a little bit of luck, I can be there in about 24 hours. What happens after that, I'm not sure. I assume that the Minoans will be concentrated in Crete, as that's where the line comes from. But I could be wrong. Even if I'm not, finding Ariadne won't be as simple as just asking around to see if anyone knows her.

There's also the possibility that she doesn't want me to find her. I try not to think about this too much. And I really don't think it's true. Still, lurking in the dark places of my mind is the fear that maybe she really was just using me to get the weapon. I still need to go to Greece to look for the weapon, so I try to convince myself that whether she wants me there or not doesn't matter. It does, though.

I finish my coffee and leave the café. For the next two hours, I walk around the city, thinking about how lucky I am that although the United States was drawn into the war and suffered casualties, our country was largely untouched in the way so much of Europe has been. Apart from the Japanese attack on Pearl Harbor and isolated incidents of submarines launching minor mortar attacks on the West

Coast, no enemy bombs touched US soil. Our cities weren't reduced to rubble. Our bridges and roads weren't destroyed. While we were all afraid of what might happen, our reality was nothing compared to what the people in places like Budapest must have endured.

I can't help but wonder what the aftermath of Endgame, when it comes, will be like. All I've been told is that only the people in the winner's line will be spared. Everyone else will die. But how? And what will happen to the world itself? Will those who are left be living in ruins? Will all the great cities be completely destroyed along with the people who live in them? I think about the destruction I've seen while traveling through Europe, the effects of the war on the people and places here. Endgame will be much worse than that war. Much, much worse. The thought of so many beautiful places being reduced to nothing makes me sad. The thought of all those people being reduced to nothing makes me angry.

I already know that even if I find Ariadne, if Endgame happens during our lifetimes, at best only one of us can survive it. More likely, we'll both die. That's not acceptable to me. Which means that I—we—need to find a way to change the outcome. I don't know how, but we have to try.

When it's time to meet up with Kenney again, I return to the café. He's already there, standing outside. When I approach him, he hands me an envelope. It's thick with what I assume is cash and identification papers.

"Here you go, Mr. Volkov," he says. "I believe your papers are all in order."

"Thank you," I say.

"Contact me in one week," Kenney says. "Use shortwave communication again. The same frequency. I imagine you'll be able to find equipment easily enough."

"I think so," I tell him.

He reaches out his hand. I take it. "Good luck."

He turns and walks away, and just like that, I'm a new person. I open the envelope and take out the identification papers. Alexander Volkov. I have a feeling this is sort of like being named John Smith back home—generic and forgettable—which is perfect. I return the papers to the envelope, stick the whole thing in my inside coat pocket, and start walking. I have a train to catch.

CHAPTER 5

Ariadne

The Cave of the Golden Horns is lit by torches. They flicker in the light breeze that comes in from the sea and travels down the narrow corridor that leads to the large central chamber in which I now stand. The cave is so named because, according to Minoan legend, this is where the first pair of golden horns was found, the symbol of King Midas and the bull-headed Minotaur who lived in the maze at Knossos. The horns that are placed upon every Minoan Player's head when she's chosen and crowned.

I'm wearing the horns now. They're always donned when a Player is called before the council in an official capacity, which is what's happening tonight. Only this isn't an ordinary meeting. I'm on trial.

I was informed of the trial following dinner last night, after it was revealed that the council knows about Boone. How they know, I haven't been informed. But they do. And they want to know exactly how and why I came to be working with him. I started to explain last night, but I was told to wait until now. The fact that nobody accused me of anything, and that the remainder of the evening was cordial, if not exactly pleasant for me, makes me hopeful that this is just a formality.

My mother, father, and aunt have all told me that there's nothing to worry about. The thing making me nervous is Cassandra. After the council left last night, she left as well. I haven't seen her since. I didn't hear her come in last night before I gave in to exhaustion and slept, nor have I seen her today.

I drive thoughts of her from my mind, and prepare to meet the council. I'm standing in the middle of the room, my bare feet on the sandy floor. I'm wearing a plain white robe and the golden horns. In front of me, opposite the entrance and arranged in a slight arc that mirrors the curve of the cave wall, are five chairs carved out of massive rocks. They look like thrones. They're empty now, but soon the council members will be seated in them.

As if I've summoned them with my thought, the council emerges from a smaller room located behind the stone chairs. They too are wearing white robes, only their feet are encased in sandals and their heads are bare. They enter single file, arranged in age from oldest to youngest. The oldest, Effie Kakos, takes the center chair. Flanking her are Venedict Economides and Xenia Papadaki, and on either side of them are the two youngest members, Ursula Tassi and Nemo Stathakis.

I kneel in the sand, my head bowed, and wait for Effie to speak the words that will begin the trial.

"We gather here tonight in the presence of the gods," she says, her voice strong and sure. "Player, rise and stand before us."

I get up and face the council. I've known all of them for my whole life. One, Ursula, trained me. I've eaten at Xenia's house hundreds of times. Effie taught me algebra, and I've bought books from Nemo and received the Lamb from Venedict's hand. But none of that matters now. Now they are a jury, and their task is to determine my guilt or innocence.

"Player," Effie says. "You are here tonight to answer questions concerning your recent mission for the Minoan line. Do you understand?"

"Yes," I say, keeping my voice clear and strong.

"And do you give your word that the answers you provide will be the truth and the truth alone?"

"Yes."

"Very well," Effie says. "Tell me, did you know that Samuel Boone was a Player for the Cahokian line?"

"Yes," I answer. "Not at first, but I came to learn it."

"And did you reveal to him that you are a Player of the Minoan line?"

"Yes."

"Why did you do this?"

The question comes not from Effie, but from Ursula. She sounds annoyed, as if she can't believe I would do something so reckless. I know that as a former Player herself, and as my trainer, she understands better than most how this might be a grave error.

"I believed it would create trust between us," I say.

"For what purpose?" Ursula asks.

"The Cahokian had developed a rapport with Sauer," I explain. "The scientist was reluctant to cooperate with me. He saw me as a threat. I thought perhaps I could use the Cahokian's relationship with him to my advantage. Also, he saved my life when Europa and I were attacked by MGB agents."

"Tell us about the death of Europa," says Nemo Stathakis. The bookseller is perhaps the quietest and gentlest of the council members. His life has been spent in a world of words, among imaginary friends. His grandest adventures have been in his mind. I don't believe he has ever left Crete, or ever intends to. Europa was his mother's mother. His mother was killed fighting the Nazis in the Battle of Crete, and I know his grandmother's death must be very hard on him. Still, when I look at him, he smiles back at me kindly.

I think about Europa, who went by Lydia in Berlin, and about how she had long been a hero of mine. "She was brave," I say, trying to forget how the MGB agent killed the old woman as if putting down a dog. "She fought hard. But we were outnumbered."

"And the Cahokian, he saved you?" Xenia says.

"Yes."

"Why did he not kill you?" Ursula asks.

I think about how I wondered this same thing when I woke up to find Boone sitting on the bed, watching me. At the time, I thought he was foolish. Now I know it's because his heart is not as hardened as mine is. Or as it was. Meeting him has thawed it.

I cannot tell the council this, and so I say, "I think he meant to use me in the same way that I used him."

"You believe he would have killed you once he had the weapon?" It is Venedict who asks this.

"I believe that was his plan, yes," I tell him. "We needed each other in order to get it."

I wait for more questions. They have not yet brought up the deaths of Theron, Cilla, and Misha. More of my failures. I know these must count against me as well. Yet when Effie speaks next, it is to say, "Will the witness please enter the chamber?"

Cassandra appears. She has apparently been waiting in the adjacent anteroom. Like me, she is wearing a white robe and is shoeless. She comes to stand beside me, but does not look at me.

"You witnessed the Minoan Player with the Cahokian Player—is that correct?" Effie asks my sister.

"Yes," Cassandra says.

"Can you tell us what you saw?"

"I saw her kiss him."

The words hit me like a fist. Did Cassandra really see me kiss Boone before he went into the air shaft to retrieve the box? It's true that she appeared not long after that, so it's possible. But why has she said nothing about it until now?

"Player, is this true?" Effie asks me.

There's no point in lying. "Yes," I tell the councillor. "It was part of my plan. As my sister can confirm, I also ultimately killed him."

"Did you witness the Cahokian Player's death?" Effie asks Cassandra.

She hesitates before answering. "I saw our Player administer a wounding blow," she says. "And I saw the Cahokian Player fall into the opening of a shaft. I did not see him die."

"So it's possible that he lived?" says Xenia.

"It's possible, yes."

"Possible, but very unlikely," I interject. "The Cahokian was suffering from hypothermia. His strength was spent. He made no effort at all to fight me."

"Witness?" Effie says, looking for confirmation of my claim.

"He did not fight back," Cassandra says. "It was as if he knew there was no reason to."

Her words are carefully chosen, as if she has been waiting to use them. Breaking protocol, I turn to her. "You know he couldn't have survived the water again," I say.

"The Player will refrain from addressing the witness," Venedict barks.

I return my gaze to the council. There is much I want to say, but I don't. In my anger at my sister, I've managed to convince myself that she's lying. Only she isn't. I didn't kill Boone. And Cassandra knows it.

"Witness, is it your opinion that the Player acted improperly?" Effie asks.

Cassandra's voice is steady as she replies. "I believe our Player is dedicated to the Minoan line."

For a moment I think I've misjudged her. Then she continues.

"However, I believe her judgment was compromised by her feelings for the Cahokian."

Again I want to deny everything. But I have already lost my temper once. To do so again would be disastrous for me. All I can do is stand there, attempting to control my emotions, and wait to be questioned further.

The council has no more questions, though. Instead Effie says, "The Player and the witness will go to the anteroom while the council discusses this matter. We will call you back when we have reached a decision.

Cassandra turns and walks out of the chamber. I follow her. When we are alone, I grab her by the arm. She pulls away.

"What are you trying to do?" I ask, keeping my voice low to avoid it being overheard by the council.

"I was asked to give a report of what I saw," Cassandra says. "That's all. I would have said the same thing even if the Player in question was not my sister."

"You know nothing about what happened in Berlin," I say.

She smiles. "I'm your twin. I know things no one else could. You didn't even try to kill the Cahokian."

I look away. There's no point in denying it to her. She's right—as my twin, she senses things. Also, she's been trained as a Player.

"You're right that he probably died anyway," she says from behind me. "Even if he didn't, it doesn't matter. We have the weapon. And if the Cahokians choose to have someone so weak continue to represent their line, it only makes our job easier."

I want to tell her that she knows nothing about Boone, that he's stronger than she could ever imagine. Before I can even begin speaking, though, a voice calls us back into the council chamber.

I walk in ahead of Cassandra. She once again stands beside me. But now there is a gulf between us as wide as the Bosporus.

"It is the council's opinion that the Player has acted imprudently," Effie announces. "It has also been decided that a vote of confidence will be taken."

My heart stills in my chest. A vote of confidence is only held when the council questions whether a Player is fit to continue Playing. It has occurred only a handful of times in the history of the Minoan line. And now I'm the one they're voting on. Everything I've worked for, everything I've ever been, might be taken away from me. It's all happening so quickly that I don't even have time to think too much about it.

"We will indicate our votes in the prescribed manner," Effie says.

Ursula stands. She holds out her fist and opens it. On her palm sits a white stone, which indicates she has found me worthy of retaining my role as Player. I look at her and silently send her my thanks. That one of my own trainers still believes in me makes my heart glad.

Next to stand, on the opposite end of the row of chairs, is Nemo. He holds out his fist and reveals his stone. Like Ursula's, it is white. Two votes for me.

Venedict rises, wasting no time in showing me his stone. It's black. He has found me unfit to be our Player. Somehow I'm not surprised. I am surprised, however, when Xenia also holds out a black stone. I think of her almost as my own grandmother, and to have her find fault with me is a pain worse than any punishment I can think of.

With two votes for me and two against, Effie is left to cast the deciding one. She is one of the wisest people I know, and I pray that she will save me.

When her fingers uncurl, a black stone is sitting on her palm. I stare at it as Effie says, "The council has voted. The Player is found to be unworthy of representing our line."

I think this is as bad as it can get. But it gets worse. Effie has more to say. "The council has also decided that the Player will be succeeded by her sister."

I can feel elation emanating from Cassandra. Effie steps down from her chair and comes over to us. She reaches out and takes the golden horns from my head. Turning to Cassandra, she places them on her. "In the presence of our gods, I crown you the Player of the Minoan line," she says.

I don't know what to say or do. I never imagined being in this position. Now that I am, all I want to do is disappear.

Effie turns back to me. "As the weapon has been recovered and brought to us, there will be no punishment meted out for your failings," she says, and her voice is not unkind. "Your service is noted and we thank you for it. Now you may go."

That's all. After everything I've endured to become our Player, after everything that's happened, I'm dismissed like a child being shooed away from a party where only adults are welcome. A party at which my own sister is the one being celebrated.

I don't look at Cassandra as I turn and walk out of the Cave of the Golden Horns. I don't look at the councillors. I look only ahead of me. Only when I'm out, when I'm standing under the stars and Orion is gazing down on me, do the tears come.

CHAPTER 6

Boone

I was concerned about being able to walk through the streets of Heraklion without being noticed, but my worries mostly disappear when I see the crowds filling the squares. Midnight is approaching, bringing the first day of 1949 with it, and it feels as if the entire city is out getting ready to welcome the new year. Stalls are set up, piled with pomegranates and what look like huge onions. There are also food vendors and musicians. Everyone seems to be having a good time, which lifts my spirits, even if I can't join in.

I've paid a man to bring me to Crete in his boat, but I still have no idea how I'm going to find Ariadne, or the weapon, and now that I'm here, I wonder if maybe I've made a mistake. For one thing, Cassandra knows what I look like. I've disguised myself as much as I can by dyeing my hair with boiled tea-leaf water, which is a trick my mother taught me. It's made the color only a few shades darker, and it will only last a few days, but it should help. Also, I was able to buy an old sweater, coat, and cap from the fisherman who brought me here. He thought I was crazy for wanting them, and they smell like fish and seaweed, but at least now I look like a lot of the other men in Heraklion.

Still, I'm a little nervous. I have a feeling strangers are quickly spotted here. Right now I'm protected by the crowds, the darkness, and the distraction of the New Year's Eve festivities, but that won't last forever. I need to do what I've come for and get out as quickly as I can. But I don't know where to start looking, I have no contacts here, and although I'm familiar with many of the languages spoken by the different lines, Greek is not one I've mastered.

For the first time since getting on the train in Budapest, I feel like I might not be able to pull this off. Maybe I should have been straight with Kenney and told him that the weapon has fallen into the hands of the Minoans. But then what would have happened? Would there be an all-out war between our lines? Would he have sent someone else to try to get the weapon? If so, who? Anyone else wouldn't hesitate to kill Ariadne.

If I'm honest with myself, I have to admit that I'm here just as much to find Ariadne as I am to find the weapon. Maybe even more because of her. That puts me in a dangerous position. Already I've kept things from my council and lied about my plan. Both things are probably grounds for punishment, if not out-and-out removal from my position as Player. Until now I've told myself that as long as I get the weapon, everything else will be unimportant. But that's not true. If I do find Ariadne, and she wants to be with me too, what then? Players from different lines can't be together. It's impossible given the rules of Endgame. Even once we age out and new Players take our places, it would be forbidden.

"You are American?" someone says in rough English.

A boy is standing in front of me. He's maybe eight or nine, skinny, wearing patched pants and a coat with sleeves too short for his arms. He's looking at me hopefully. When I don't answer right away, he tries again in French. *"Êtes-vous français?"*

I know I'm supposed to be Russian, but I don't think the kid is likely to speak that language. He's probably picked up some phrases from the soldiers who have come to the island during the war, and wants to practice using them. I probably shouldn't talk to him at all, in case he starts telling his buddies about the stranger in town, but I also don't want to be rude.

"English," I say, hoping the accent I attempt is convincing.

He grins. "God save the King!" he says, and laughs. "You soldier?"

I shake my head. "A traveler."

He grins again. "You need a guide? I show you around. Temples. Caves. Everything."

I start to say no, but then I get an idea. It's a risky one, but it's the only possible lead I have, so I decide to try. "I came here because I met someone from Crete, and he told me it was very beautiful."

"Yes," the boy says. "Very beautiful."

"His name is Calligaris," I say. "Maybe you know him."

"Many people with that name on Crete," the boy says.

"He has daughters," I say. "Twins."

"Ah," the boy says. "That Calligaris. Ariadne and Cassandra."

My heart skips a beat when I hear Ariadne's name. "Do you know where they live?"

The boy reaches out and takes my hand. "Come. I show you."

Before I can object, I'm following him through the crowd. No one pays any attention to us, but still I'm anxious. I don't know who my guide is, or where he's taking me. I can't just walk up to the door of Ariadne's house and knock. When the boy eventually leads me away from the main street to a smaller side one, I stop him.

"I want this to be a surprise," I tell him. "For the new year. Just show me where the house is, okay?"

"Okay," he says, and starts off again. I'm thankful he's young, and hasn't learned to be suspicious of people he doesn't know. I also envy him a little for this.

A few minutes later we turn in to a narrow lane, and he stops. "There," he says, pointing to a house. "Calligaris." He looks at me expectantly, and I realize that he's waiting for me to give him something. I reach into my pocket and fish out some coins. I'm not even sure what currency they are, as I have several jumbled up in there from my travels, but he doesn't seem to care. He sticks the money in his own pocket and trots off, back toward the noise and the crowds.

I turn my attention to the house. Assuming the boy has brought me to the right place, is Ariadne inside? For all I know, she's out celebrating like so many other people. Or maybe she's in there with her family. With Cassandra. Thinking about Ariadne's twin, I reach into my coat and check for my pistol. If I have to face her again, I'll be ready, and this time she won't be walking away with a smile on her face.

I approach the house and start scanning it, looking for the best way inside. Like most of the houses I've seen in Heraklion, it's constructed of stone and plaster, with several tall, open windows that can be covered with wooden shutters. Right now the windows are open, and light spills out from all of them. I wonder which one, if any, is Ariadne's bedroom.

As I'm standing there, the front door opens. I quickly dart into the shadows and watch as several people come out. When I see Ariadne among them, laughing and smiling as she puts her arm around the shoulder of a handsome young man, I get jealous. Then I remind myself that it might not be her. It might be Cassandra. My Player instinct kicks in, telling me that if it is, I should take her out.

Instead I let the group pass by me. The closer they get, the better look I get at the girl, and for some reason, I'm almost positive that it's Cassandra. There's a cockiness to her that seems out of place for Ariadne. Of course, the Ariadne I know might have been an act. Maybe this is the real her. But I don't think so. When I look at this girl, I see Ariadne's face, but I don't feel Ariadne there. I don't know how else to explain it. It's like looking at someone wearing an Ariadne mask.

When they've moved on down the street, I walk across to the house and risk peering into one of the lower windows. There's an older woman moving around, picking up dishes and carrying them into the back of the house. Ariadne's mother? I hear her say something in Greek. Someone else answers, and it sounds like Ariadne, but I can't see her. The two of them talk a bit more. It sounds to me as if they're arguing, but as I don't understand the words, it's difficult to say. Then the voices stop. The woman reappears. She seems sad.

If Ariadne is here, she's now in one of the upstairs rooms. I examine the exterior of the house, and see that it would be easy enough to scale the walls. The stones provide handholds and footholds. It's risky, as anyone passing by could see me, but I decide to chance it, and begin climbing. Pretty quickly, I'm level with the upper windows. I look in the first one and find an empty bedroom. The second window likewise reveals a room with no one in it.

I'm hanging there, trying to decide what to do next, when I hear a sharp intake of breath above me. I look up, and Ariadne is looking down at me. Like many of the roofs, this one is flat, and there's a rooftop garden up there. She's standing at the edge, regarding me with an expression of disbelief.

"Boone?" she says, as if she isn't sure. Then I remember my disguise.

I climb the rest of the way up and pull myself over the edge. I stand in front of her, and the two of us just stare at each other for a long moment. Then Ariadne pulls me into a hug, her arms closing around me. I hug her back and bury my face in her hair. It smells sweet and clean, and I close my eyes, letting the scent fill my nose as I hold Ariadne tightly.

"I knew you'd get out," she says softly. "But how did you find me?"

"Oh, you know," I say. "I just walked into the center of town and shouted, 'Does anyone know where I can find the Minoan Player?'"

She lets go of me and steps back. "I'm not the Player anymore," she says. "Cassandra is."

"What?"

"The council voted to remove me," she says.

She sounds angry, but also a little bit relieved. I wonder if she's been thinking about what this means for us. Now that she's not a Player, maybe she thinks we can be together.

"It doesn't change anything," she says, as if she's reading my mind. "If anything it makes it worse. They think I was colluding with you. And I guess I was. To them, that makes me a traitor. I'm lucky to have escaped punishment. If they think there's anything between us, or that I'm helping you, they would not be lenient again. It would mean death for me."

Death. Would they really kill her? As soon as I ask myself the question, I know that the answer is yes. This is Endgame. Everything about it is a matter of life and death. If her council thinks she's a danger to them, they wouldn't hesitate to kill her. And what about *my* council? Would they do the same thing? I can't recall a Cahokian Player ever being removed from action. What if I'm the first?

All of a sudden, I realize the position I've put both of us in by coming here. I've been reckless, stupid. "Do you want me to go?" I ask Ariadne.

She doesn't hesitate as she shakes her head and says, "No. But you can't stay. You have to get away from Crete. It won't take them long to know that you're here, and if they catch you, you'll be dead as well."

"Then come with me," I tell her. "Away from Crete."

"They'll follow," she says. "Wherever I go, they'll come after me. And I won't be any more welcome among the Cahokians than you would be here."

"You don't know that," I say. "My family are good people."

She smiled sadly. "So are mine, Boone. That's how I know."

I think about what she's saying. Her family loves her, just like mine loves me. And her family, her line, would never be able to accept us together because of the rules of Endgame. It's as simple as that. And she's right: mine would feel the same way. We've known this since the very beginning, but ever since I decided to come looking for her, I've thought there might be a way out. Now the reality of what our lives are stares me right in the face.

Nobody ever tells you that when your heart breaks, you can feel it. I feel it in my chest now, a sharp pain like the slice of a knife. At first I think it's just sadness about not being able to be with Ariadne. Then, the more I sort through the emotions swirling around in my head, the more I realize that it's also about my position as a Player. My whole life, I've been trained to think only of winning Endgame. Now, because of what I feel for Ariadne, that's also at risk. Especially if my council knows about Ariadne, which is a very real possibility given that hers knows about me. Even if I get the weapon and take it home with me, will my council be able to trust me? As I stand here with Ariadne, I see the two things that mean the most to me being taken away.

"There has to be another way," I say. "There has to. What if we buy our way out?"

"What do you mean?"

I think quickly, putting pieces together in my mind. "What do both of our lines want more than anything?"

"To win Endgame," Ariadne says.

"Right. And both of them think the weapon will help them do that."

Ariadne's eyes widen. "Are you saying we trade the weapon for—"

"For our freedom," I say. "We tell them they can't have the weapon unless they agree to leave us alone."

Ariadne shakes her head. "Do you have any idea what you're saying?"

"I know exactly what I'm saying," I tell her, although I'm not certain I do. I only know that right now I'll do anything to get her to be with me.

"It's insane," she says. "It will never work."

"Maybe not," I say. "But we can try. Do you know where the weapon is?"

"I think so," she says.

"Can we get to it?"

"Maybe."

"Then let's go. If we're caught, you can tell them I forced you to show me."

"And if we're not caught?" she asks.

I take a breath. "Then we leave Crete together," I say. "We take the weapon with us."

I expect her to immediately say no. When she doesn't, I know I have a chance. I take her hand. "Trust me," I say as I squeeze her fingers.

When she says, "Come with me," I think my heart might burst from happiness. She leads me across the rooftop garden and into the house, then into her bedroom, where she puts on shoes, takes a bag from her closet, and puts a few things into it. Then we go down the stairs, pausing to make sure no one sees us before leaving the house. Ariadne does not look back as we make our way down the street.

"The weapon is at Ianthe's house," she says. "They're trying to decipher the plans."

It takes us only 15 minutes to reach the other house. We keep to the side streets, avoiding the busy squares where people are congregating. Even so, I can sense that Ariadne is on high alert. So am I. It was dangerous enough when I was on my own. If we're discovered together, it could be even worse. There are a lot of things I want to ask Ariadne and talk to her about, but they all have to wait.

Unlike the Calligaris home, this other one is dark. There are no lights in the windows, no sounds of celebration coming from inside.

"Looks like no one is home," I say.

"Looks can be deceiving," Ariadne reminds me. "Let me go to the door. It won't seem unusual for me to come here."

"Even though you're not the Player anymore?"

"Ianthe is a friend," Ariadne says. "Wait here."

I watch her walk across the street. Again I think about how she must be feeling. Everything is happening so quickly, and I wonder if I'm doing the right thing, asking her to help me. Even though she's been demoted by her line, she's still Minoan. Her family is here, and her friends. If she's caught helping me, she could lose all of that too. Selfishly, I want her with me. But maybe I'm asking too much.

She knocks on the door and waits. Nobody comes to open it. She knocks again. When still there's no answer, she takes something from her pocket and inserts it into the door lock. The door opens, and she slips inside. I wait for her to signal to me that it's all right to join her, but she doesn't. I wait, wondering what's happening inside. No lights come on, and there are no voices. Then Ariadne emerges from the house and darts across the street.

"I've got it," she says, showing me a familiar-looking box.

"That was easy," I say.

"Too easy," she replies. "It was locked up, but still I was able to get it without much effort."

"What are you saying?" I ask her.

"I'm not certain," she says. "But we need to get away from here. Now. How are you getting back to the mainland?"

"I hadn't really gotten that far with my plan," I admit.

She shakes her head. "How did you get here?"

"I hired a boat."

"And you didn't tell him to wait for you?"

"I didn't know how long it would take."

"Sometimes I can't believe you're a Player," she says. "Come on."

"Where are we going?"

"To the docks."

Again she takes me through backstreets, avoiding the crowds.

When we arrive at a dock, she goes to a boat and begins untying the mooring lines. "You can pilot a boat, right?"

"Sure," I say. "I think."

"You think?"

"How hard can it be?"

Before she can answer, a voice behind us says, "So, it's true."

I turn and see a woman standing on the dock, watching us.

"Ianthe," Ariadne says.

"I told the others you would never betray us," Ianthe says. "I see now I was wrong."

"I'm not betraying anyone," Ariadne tells her.

Ianthe looks at me. "No?" she says.

Ariadne takes a step toward her. "This isn't about Minoans and Cahokians anymore," she says. "It's about all of us working together."

"Together?" Ianthe says. "You want to share the weapon?" She laughs, as if this is the stupidest thing she's ever heard. "Is that what this *boy* has promised you?"

I bristle at her obvious insult and want to say something. Ariadne glances at me as if to tell me to calm down, and I force myself to keep quiet.

"He hasn't promised me anything," Ariadne says. "We believe there's another way, a way we can all benefit from using the weapon."

Ianthe pulls a gun from her coat pocket. "You're not thinking clearly," she says. "But it's not too late."

As I wait for Ariadne to say something, a burst of gunfire erupts. Instinctively, I check myself for wounds, thinking the Minoan woman has fired at me. Then I realize that it was the sound of fireworks. It must be midnight, and people are celebrating the arrival of 1949.

Ianthe too must think it's gunfire, as she looks around. While she's distracted, Ariadne rushes at her and tackles her. The two of them struggle, rolling around on the dock. Then Ariadne gets Ianthe in a choke hold. The other woman tries to break free, but Ariadne retains her grip, and soon Ianthe passes out.

"Help me get her on the boat," Ariadne says.

"On the boat?" I say.

"We can't leave her here," Ariadne says, putting her arms under Ianthe's and lifting her. "She'll alert the others."

Not if we kill her, I think. But I know Ariadne won't do this. So I go and help her carry the unconscious woman onto the boat. Ariadne finds some rope and ties her up securely. Then she says, "I knew it was too easy. We need to go. Now."

She takes control of the boat, starting it as I finish untying the mooring lines. As we leave the harbor, I go and stand by her, looking out at the dark water.

"It will take us seven hours to reach the mainland," Ariadne says.

"And then?" I ask.

She looks at me. "And then we'll see."

CHAPTER 7

Ariadne

The last thing I expected to be doing on the first day of the new year is driving to France in a stolen car with the Cahokian Player after stealing from my own line, but that's exactly what I'm doing. Boone is slumped against the door of the Citroën, snoring as I navigate the roadway. We've been taking turns driving, and I'm supposed to wake him when we reach Belgrade, so that he can relieve me and I can sleep. However, I am not tired. Even if I were, my thoughts would make it impossible to rest.

I have committed treason. By now this will have been discovered. Ianthe will have returned to Crete and told everyone what happened. Hopefully, she will also deliver the message I gave her when we left her tied up in the boat at the dock on the mainland. "Tell them that there's another way," I said as she glared at me, her eyes filled with both anger and sadness. I know she thinks I've turned my back on my line. She's wrong. I still hope there's a way for us all to use the weapon for our mutual benefit. But will anyone believe that? And even if they do believe that it's what I want, will they ever agree to cooperate with other lines?

I don't know. And they will come after me. I know that. I do have an advantage in that they don't know where I am going. Depending on how much they know about Sauer—and I assume they know as much as I do—they might surmise that Lottie is the person with the most knowledge of the weapon. They might also think that the weapon is heading for the United States with the Cahokian Player. Either way, they will be looking both for the weapon and for me.

I wonder if I will ever see Crete again, or my family. I fear that I have made this impossible. As far as they are concerned, I might as well be dead. Perhaps they even wish me so. Cassandra, as our new Player, is the one most likely to be tasked with hunting down the stolen weapon. If so, she will also be told to get it at any cost, including, if necessary, my life. We are still sisters, still share the same blood in our veins, but we might as well be strangers.

Maybe we have always been enemies. At any rate, we have not been friends for a very long time. Now Cassandra has what she's always wanted. She's the Player. If the cost of this is our sisterhood, I believe it's a price she would more than willingly pay. Truthfully, I've often wondered why the council chose me over her. I imagine they are now asking themselves the same question. Particularly Ursula Tassi and Nemo Stathakis. Having declared their belief in my innocence, they will undoubtedly be even more disappointed. They might even find themselves suspected of disloyalty.

My mother and father I cannot bring myself to think about. The pain I have caused them is far more than they should ever be expected to bear. For them, this will be like a death. My name will cease to be spoken in the house. Their friends will pity them, or worse. What was once a source of pride and joy for them will now be a bitter taste in their mouths. Even though Cassandra will do everything she can to remove the tarnish from the Calligaris name, there will always be those who delight in reminding them that they birthed a traitor.

And what of me? The entire course of my life changed the moment I agreed to help Boone steal the weapon. Before that, even. If I replay the events of the past week (has it really been only a week?), I suppose it all began the moment I first had the opportunity to kill him, and didn't. That decision altered my destiny, although my grandmother would say that the Fates did that the moment they spun, measured, and cut the thread of my life. I don't believe that I am simply acting out a predetermined story, or that any of us are. I think we make our own fates.

What, then, have I determined for myself? Now that I am no longer a Player, everything is gone. I have nothing but the few things I brought with me: a small amount of money, some clothes, a pistol, several items of sentimental value. I no longer have access to the resources of my line. No safe houses. No weapons. No money or documents. No information. Only what's in the small bag in the backseat. And what Boone will share with me.

I don't want to be dependent on him. We are obviously now something more than two Players working together. I have cast my lot with him. I still don't know what this means, however. When this is all over, where will I be? Who will I be? All of my life, I've been a Minoan. For much of it, I've been a Player or training to be a Player. Now I am just a girl. A girl with unusual skills, yes, but what use are they to me now? What kind of life can I make with them?

Everything is a question. And I have no answers.

Boone stirs in his sleep. He stretches, then opens his eyes. When I look over at him, he grins. "Hi," he says. "How long was I out?"

"A couple of hours," I tell him.

"You were supposed to wake me."

"I'm not tired," I say.

"You mean you were thinking too much. Come on, pull over. I have to pee anyway."

I steer the car to the side of the road. Boone gets out and walks off into the field a little way. When he returns, he comes to my side and opens the door. "My turn," he says.

I get out and we switch places. When I'm sitting in the passenger seat, Boone reaches over and takes my hand. We sit there for a while, both of us looking out at the falling snow. I don't express my fears to him. I don't know why, except that I already feel too unsure, too vulnerable. I trust him, but I'm afraid of letting him see how much I've given up for him. Maybe he already knows. He probably does. But we don't talk about it, and I find myself wondering if he's just as unsure as I am.

After a few minutes, Boone starts the car and pulls back onto the road. I close my eyes and sleep fitfully.

We stop for the night in Krško, finding a small inn where the proprietor doesn't even give us a second look as he takes the money Boone offers and leads us upstairs to a small room with a single bed. It's freezing cold, and after washing up in the tiny bathroom, Boone and I climb into the bed still wearing our clothes, and pull the heavy woolen blankets over us. We're both exhausted, and within minutes I'm asleep again despite the nearness of him. We wake before dawn and get back in the car.

After another long day of driving, in the small hours of the morning we reach the tiny French village where Lottie is staying. When we knock on the door of the house, it takes a long time before anyone answers. When the door finally opens, we're greeted by a woman who looks less than pleased to see us. Boone addresses her in French, she closes the door, and we wait some more. The next time the door opens, Lottie is there.

"Come in," she says. She doesn't look any happier to see us than the first woman did.

She leads us into a kitchen, where we sit at a table as she brings us something to eat and drink. It feels good to be sitting in a real home after so long in the car, even if the home is not mine. I listen as Boone fills her in on what's taken place.

"You have the weapon?" Lottie says.

"It's somewhere safe," Boone says. We've agreed not to let Lottie know that we have it with us.

"What are you going to do with it?"

"We don't know yet," Boone tells her. "I'm supposed to be in Moscow, looking for Karl Ott. I told the Cahokian contact that he has the weapon."

"But you have it," Lottie says. "Why not just give it to them?"

Boone hesitates before answering. "We don't know if they should have it."

The way he keeps saying *we* is obvious, and not just to me. Lottie looks at me, then back to Boone. I can tell she wants to know what's going on between us, but she doesn't ask. Instead she says, "What do you need me to do?"

"After Sauer, your father knows the most about the weapon," Boone says.

"Yes," says Lottie. "But he's in prison."

"We're going to get him out."

Lottie laughs, not because this is funny, but because Boone has taken her by surprise. "Taganka Prison is not a place you simply walk out of."

"Karl Ott's father is there as well, isn't he?" Boone asks.

Lottie nods. "Yes. That's how I know how impossible what you suggest is. Karl's tried for the past several years to find a way to free his father."

This is exactly what Boone and I have been counting on. Now Boone says, "Perhaps if he had people with special training assisting him, it could be done."

Lottie's expression changes. "The two of you?"

"Not to brag, but few people are as well equipped for something like this as Players," Boone says. "And you have the two best Players in the world sitting right here."

This flash of cockiness reminds me of when we first met. Then, it annoyed me. Now, it endears him to me. His self-confidence is reassuring. I find myself suppressing a smile as Boone keeps working on Lottie.

"Ariadne has spent a long time living and working with the Soviets," he says. "And both of us are trained in every type of combat and rescue technique you can think of. If Ott can help us get into Taganka, we can get your father out."

"Why should he?" Lottie asks.

"Because we'll also be springing his father," Boone reminds her. "And because he still really wants to get his hands on the weapon, and we'll let him think he has a chance if he helps us."

"But you have no intention of letting him have it."

Boone shrugs. "Like I said, I don't know what we'll do with it."

Lottie thinks over what he's said. "I don't know that my father will help you," she says, and I can tell from her tone that she means this. "His relationship to that work is . . . complicated."

"Let's worry about that once we get him out," Boone says. "Whether he will or won't, I'm sure he'd rather not be sitting in that place. From what I hear, it's brutal. Especially for political prisoners."

A shadow of worry passes over Lottie's face. I know she's thinking about her father being in the Soviet prison, about what might be happening to him. Boone is right: Taganka is a terrible place. The MGB I worked with used to refer to it as the Devil's Playground because of all the unimaginable things that await the prisoners there. Almost nobody who passes through its gates comes out again, and if they do, they're forever changed. If there's a chance that Lottie can get her father out, she should take it.

She does. "I'll contact Ott," she says, standing up. "I'll let you know what he says. In the meantime, there is a room upstairs where you can rest. You'll have to share."

She looks at me, and I don't look away. Her unspoken question hangs in the air, and I answer it by saying, "I think we can manage." Lottie smiles briefly, and I think that despite our past, despite everything that happened in Berlin, she is happy for us. Having lost Jackson must surely be a huge blow to her, and maybe she sees the possibility of Boone and me being together as a sliver of hope in the darkness.

She shows us to the room, then leaves us alone. When she's gone, Boone says, "Did that just work?"

"I think maybe it did," I say as I open my bag and take out some fresh clothes. I'm hoping the bathroom we walked by has a bathtub in it, but I'll settle for washing my face.

Boone sits on the bed and bounces on it like a little boy. When I look at him, he stops. "Sorry," he says. "I'm just kind of excited. I know everything is weird, but it feels good to have something to do."

"Once a Player, always a Player," I remark.
He stands up and comes to me. "Sorry," he says again. "I didn't mean to make you upset."
"I'm not upset," I tell him. "Not about this." And I'm not. Because Boone is right: it is nice to have something to focus on other than my personal worries. Something like going to Moscow to break into one of the most notorious prisons in the world is a problem I know how to work with. It will involve planning and skill, but it can be done. Unlike fixing the rest of my life.
He still looks sad, so I lean up and press my mouth to his. It's the first time we've really kissed, and when our lips meet, my entire body comes alive. I have to force myself to pull away. "It's okay," I reassure him. "I'm going to go see about a bath. I'll be back."
I leave him in the bedroom and go next door. There is a bathtub, and it does work, although the water is only lukewarm. That's good enough. I fill the tub, add some bath salts from a jar, and then sink into water that smells like roses. I take a bar of soap and rub it on my skin, enjoying the way the lather washes away the feeling of being in a car for two days. When I'm done, I feel, if not like a new person, then at least like someone who has more options than she did a few hours ago.
I rinse off, wrap a towel around me, and return to the bedroom. I half expect to find Boone already asleep, but he's not. He's sitting on the bed, the box with the weapon pieces in it open before him. He's holding up a piece and looking at it.
"Is it wise to have that out in the open like that?" I ask as I shut the door and lock it.
"No," he says. He hasn't looked up yet, as he's too busy examining the piece in his hand. "But I've risked a lot for this stuff, and I wanted to see what all the fuss is about. It's weird to think that this was made by people from outer space, isn't it?"
I walk over to the bed and stand in front of him. I let go of the towel, and it falls to the floor. The air is cool on my naked skin, and I shiver

a little. Boone looks up. The piece of the weapon in his hand tumbles from his fingers, and he scrambles to catch it.

"Oh," he says. "Wow. Um . . ."

He seems so unnerved that for a moment I almost pick up the towel again. Have I made a mistake? Is he not interested in me this way? Then another thought enters my mind: *Maybe he's never been this close to a naked woman.*

I sit down next to him and take the weapon piece from his hand. I put it back in the box, then close the lid, pick up the box, and set it on the floor. Boone is reclining against the pillows, just watching me.

I lean over and kiss him, softly at first, then more deeply. Again he hesitates, but only for a moment. Then he kisses me back. His hands grip my arms, and he pulls me down beside him. I feel like I'm falling, tumbling through space after letting go of a lifeline that has tethered me to something safe and familiar. Now I'm floating in unfamiliar territory, where the rules no longer apply and I don't know what will happen. It's frightening, but at the same time, I've never felt so free.

CHAPTER 8

Boone

The village has a very old church, built centuries ago and dedicated to Saint Roch, who Lottie tells me is the patron saint of, among other things, dogs. This explains the half dozen mutts curled up on blankets below a statue of the saint that is surrounded by lit candles. One of them opens an eye as we walk by, then goes back to sleep.

"The villagers bring them food," Lottie says. "They consider them good luck."

We continue through the sanctuary, then down a set of stone stairs into a room beneath the church. It's bitterly cold here, and our breath fogs the air. In the room are several wooden tables, on which rest simple coffins. There are three of them.

"They store the dead here during the winter," Lottie tells us. "The ground is too hard to dig, of course, so they rest here until the spring."

We've come to see Jackson. Well, not to see him, as I'm not about to open the coffin. But I do want to pay my respects to my brother. Not wanting to upset Bernard, we've left him playing with a neighbor's boy. The woman whose house they're staying in, who I've learned is Lottie's friend Bérénice, is watching them.

"Jackson's is the middle one," Lottie says. "I'll be upstairs." She turns to go.

"I'll go with her," says Ariadne.

"No," I say. I reach out and take her hand. "Stay with me."

I can't help but think about what happened between us last night. I haven't told her that it was my first time, but I'm pretty sure she knows. Even though I might not have been as good as I could have been, it was still absolutely amazing.

I feel weird thinking about this in a church and in front of my brother's body. Then again, I think Jackson would be happy for me. There's so much going on right now. So much uncertainty. Ariadne is one thing I can count on. One real thing that I can touch and hold. One person I can believe in.

I no longer worry that she's playing me. She's taken a huge risk by helping me, and by taking the weapon from her own line. She's trusting me not to hurt her, which for someone who was trained as a Player is the biggest thing she can do for someone else.

Ariadne keeps hold of my hand as I walk to Jackson's coffin and put my other hand on it. I stand between them, my brother and my—what, girlfriend? That seems like such an inadequate word to describe how I feel about her, like we're just two normal people who go to the movies together. We're more than that. Much more. I don't know what the word for it is, though. I do know that she's my future, and Jackson is my past. The living and the dead, with me in between them.

I want to say something to my brother. But what? I'm sorry? I love you? I wish we hadn't lost so much time, and that we had more now? All these things are true, but saying them out loud feels weird, like reciting lines written for a play. I feel them, but my mouth can't bring itself to say them.

"Where do Minoans believe we go when we die?" I ask Ariadne.

"It's said that heroes go to Elysium," she tells me. "A kind of paradise where they're rewarded for their bravery in this life."

"And everyone else?"

"It depends who you ask. Some think there's an underworld. Some think we just die. What do Cahokians believe?"

"Different things," I say. I think about my mother, who spends every Sunday morning at the Methodist church, while my father only goes to Christmas Eve services or if someone's getting married. Jackson sometimes went with my mother on Sundays, but I don't know what he actually believed. We never talked about it.

"Wherever you are, Jackson, I hope you're happy," I say, and touch my fingers to my brother's coffin. "Maybe I'll see you again someday."

I'm done talking, but I'm not ready to leave, so I stand there for a while longer, my arm around Ariadne. We have a long, difficult road ahead of us, and for the moment I want to just stand in this quiet room, far from the world of Endgame and everything associated with it. As soon as we leave, it's all going to become more and more complicated.

We stand like this for a while, not talking. Then I take Ariadne's hand and walk back up the stairs. With each step, I feel the weight on my shoulders grow heavier. At one point I pause on the stairs, and Ariadne moves ahead of me, gently pulling me along with her. It's as if she's leading me back into the world. I could hold back, fight against it, but I go with her, and together we enter the church. Lottie is sitting in one of the pews, waiting. She has a strange look on her face, and is staring at something. I follow her gaze and see that she's looking at the crucifix on the wall. Christ hangs on it, his sad eyes looking heavenward.

"I tried to pray," Lottie says. "I couldn't. I don't think God is there. Or if he is, he isn't listening."

I want to say something to make her feel better, but I can't think of anything.

"If it's true what they say," Lottie continues, "about Endgame. . . . If it's true, then where is God? Where is the hope?"

Ariadne squeezes my hand. I think about the conversation we've just had in the crypt below the church. These are big questions. Questions I haven't given a lot of thought to, honestly. Mostly because they're hard, and I don't know that there are answers, or at least not answers that will bring anyone any satisfaction.

"These creatures that made the weapon," says Lottie. "Are they gods?"

"It's said they can be killed," Ariadne replies.

Lottie snorts. "Many cultures have gods that can be killed," she says. "Does that make them any less gods?"

Again I have no answer for her, and this talk is only making me more uneasy.

"We should be getting back," I remind them.

As we leave, a dog enters the church doorway, covered in snow. It shakes, then trots by us to join the other dogs at the feet of Saint Roch. It was snowing when we left the house, and now it's begun to fall more thickly. We walk through the streets, returning to the house. The visit to the church has made us all quiet, and I wonder what Ariadne is thinking about. I don't know much about Minoan religion, about their gods and beliefs, except for what she's told me about the afterlife. I want to ask her more about it, but Lottie seems upset now, and it's important to keep her calm given what we have left to do today.

When we get to the house, Bernard is outside with the neighbor boy and Bérénice. They're making a snowman. Already the bottom and middle balls of the body are in place. Now they're setting the head on top of these. They're too short to reach, so they're being helped by a man. It's Karl Ott.

"Ah," he says when he sees us. "There you are."

Lottie goes to him and hugs him. Ariadne and I are less enthusiastic. I extend my hand, which Ott accepts. Ariadne does the same. I'm surprised when he takes it, as they have been at odds since their first meeting.

"I did not expect to see you again," Ott says. "At least not so soon."

"Yeah," I say. "You disappeared pretty quickly during the fight at the factory."

His smile doesn't waver. "It was important to get my family to safety," he says. "You understand."

I think about my brother, lying dead in the church, and say nothing.

"Let's go inside," Lottie suggests, perhaps sensing the tension. "Bernard, you and Paul can finish the snowman with Bérénice. I'll bring you a carrot and some coal for his face."

We go inside, where we take off our coats and go into the kitchen.

Lottie busies herself getting the carrot for the snowman's nose, and I fill a kettle with water and put it on the stove to get hot. Then I join Ariadne and Ott, who are seated.

"We spend a lot of time around kitchen tables, making plans," Ott says.

"You got here quickly," Ariadne says. "You are living nearby?"

"Not far," Ott says, but offers no details. "Lottie says that you want to go to Moscow."

He's not wasting any time. This is fine with me. My deadline for contacting Kenney is coming up in two days. I want to be in Moscow by then. Preferably with something to show for it, although I don't think that's possible.

"Yes," I tell Ott. "We're going to get Oswald Brecht out of Taganka."

Ott laughs. "You can't be serious."

"We're very serious," I say. "We'd like your help to do it, but we'll do it on our own if necessary."

"What makes you think I can help you?"

"Your father is there," I say. "I think it's safe to say you've spent a lot of time thinking about how to get him out."

Ott shrugs. "Of course. But my methods would be less—how should I put this—direct than yours."

I nod. "I understand. I bet you've been cultivating relationships with people who might be able to help."

He doesn't respond, so I know that I'm right. "We don't have that kind of time," I continue.

"What is the rush?" he asks.

"Brecht has become of interest to other parties," I tell him. "Parties that might prefer he never leave Taganka alive."

I know Ott understands my meaning. I also know that he very much wants me to tell him who these other interested parties are. I don't. I'm bluffing, at least in part. I don't really know that anyone else knows about Brecht, but it's plausible, and having Ott think that the scientist's life is in jeopardy might be incentive for him to help us.

"This is of course connected to the weapon," he says. "I assume that you have it in your possession once more."

"We know where it is," I say. "And it's safe. For the moment."

He smiles. He knows how the game is played. "And I'm supposed to help you because, in return, you will help me get my father out of Taganka as well."

"That's about it," I confirm.

Ott drums his fingers lightly on the tabletop. Behind us, the kettle whistles. I get up and attend to it, giving him time to think. When I return to the table and set a mug of tea in front of him, he takes it and drinks. He still hasn't spoken. I give a mug to Ariadne, and our eyes meet. She raises her eyebrows, and I shrug slightly. I don't know what's going through Ott's head, or which way he will go.

"Do you know who my father is?" he says.

I wasn't expecting this, and I shake my head. I don't know. I haven't had time to find out.

"His name is Helmut Falkenrath," he says.

Ariadne, who has been quiet throughout the conversation, says, "The scientist who headed up Uranprojekt?"

"That's what he was accused of," Ott says. "And yes, he worked on the project. But he was not the leader. In reality, he was just the only one left to blame."

"Uranprojekt was a Nazi attempt to develop nuclear weapons," Ariadne tells me. "Many of the scientists who worked on it defected to other countries when the Nazis rose to power. Mostly to the United States."

"That's correct," Ott says. "My father helped many of them do so, but he himself remained behind for too long, and then it became impossible to leave. Those men went on to help the Americans complete the Manhattan Project. But after the war, the Americans allowed my father to be blamed. They did nothing to stop the Soviets from putting him in prison. He was deemed expendable."

He's looking at me as if this is somehow my fault because I'm

American. Before I can say anything, he adds, "And you don't even know his name."

"Look," I say. "If you don't want to be part of this, that's fine. We can do it on our own. But let's get something straight—I'm not responsible for things my government did."

"No," Ott says. "You're not. And I will help you."

He says *help* as if we've begged him to come along. As if we can't possibly do this without him. It makes me angry, but the truth is, we do need him. And right now I'm just relieved that he's said yes, even if it all seems to have happened too easily.

"You are correct that I have some contacts within the Soviet Union. Some even within Taganka itself. Still, this is no simple matter. Do you have resources available to you?"

I understand that he's asking about more than whether we have access to weapons, or cash. He wants to know whether the Minoans and Cahokians are working together. I don't want him to know that Ariadne has fallen out with her line, and so I say, "We have enough."

I don't know if this is actually true. I have money, but not weapons, at least not enough to break into a prison. I'm hoping Kenney will be able to help with that once I contact him.

"And the weapon?" Ott asks again. "Where is it?"

"Safe," I say, in a tone that makes it clear he won't get any additional information.

He smiles but says nothing, and I wonder what he's thinking.

"This is not much of a plan so far," he says. "Go to Moscow. Break into a heavily guarded prison. Extract two high-profile political prisoners and get out of the country."

"Sounds pretty straightforward to me," I say.

Ott sighs. "And then what?"

"Then what what?"

"What do you expect Brecht to do for you? Build the weapon?"

"At least tell us what it is and what it does," I say.

"Of course," he says. "Your interest is purely scientific."

"Perhaps your father can help too," I say.

"Perhaps he can," says Ott. "Provided he has sufficient incentive to do so."

I'm not sure if he's talking about money or about control of the weapon. At this point it doesn't matter. I'm not promising him anything. The possibility of getting his father out of the Soviet Union has to be enough right now.

"There are two ways to get to Moscow," he says, not pressing the issue. This actually worries me more than if he had made demands, as it suggests he's planning something of his own, or holding a winning hand that he'll reveal when I'm not in a position to counter. "Car or train. Plane as well, although that is much more difficult. I suggest we drive. It gives us more control."

"Great," says Ariadne. "More time in the car."

"It will take two days," Ott says. "If we don't stop."

Two days. That means if we leave soon, we'll be there sometime on January 5, the day I'm supposed to contact Kenney.

"All right," I say. "Let's get going."

CHAPTER 9

Ariadne

Listening to the conversation going on around the table, I'm reminded how much Russians enjoy arguing, particularly about politics. And how much they enjoy drinking, which makes the arguing even more impassioned.

The journey to Moscow was long, and I am tired. All three of us are exhausted—myself, Boone, and Ott. I still call him Ott, even though I know his real name; he prefers it, and it's how he is known by the people we are now with. We are in an apartment in one of the city's overstuffed tenements, where spaces built for two people are inhabited by four, six, eight, sometimes more. Smells of cooking food—cabbage and onions and boiled meat—fill the stairwells and seem to seep right through the walls along with mumbled conversations and the occasional shouting.

Moscow has been gripped by a killing cold, with temperatures dropping at night to the point that just breathing hurts and exposure of more than a short time invites death. The building's heating system is inefficient, and it wheezes like an old man with not long to live. Most of the residents wear coats, scarves, and gloves even inside. The apartment we are in is heated by a small gas cooktop, the burning blue rings performing double duty as they heat the kettle and pot of simmering soup seated atop them.

"Stalin cannot last much longer," says a man named Yuri. He is a bear of a man, massive and hairy, his black beard a thicket on his cheeks and chin. He pounds his fist on the table, making the glasses and plates clatter. "His popularity is falling after what he did in Poland and Hungary."

A woman seated across from him and to my left, whose name is Oksana and whose eyes are the bluest I've ever seen, points a finger at Yuri and says, "Yes, but look at what is happening in China. The Communists will win there, mark my words. The people are desperate to believe the promises made by these so-called leaders. Just as happened here."

I tune them out and try to relax. These people are Ott's friends, and I am wary of them because I am wary of him. I understand the necessity of working with him for now, but I am not happy about it. Even though he was nothing but pleasant during the trip here, I do not trust him. I especially don't like having to depend on him for anything. I wish, as I have more than once over the past few days, that I had my Minoan connections to call on. That, of course, is impossible, however. It's unsettling to me how nearly every aspect of my life was tied to my line, and how without them, I have to rely on others. It is a position of weakness, and not one I enjoy being in.

I sense someone looking at me, and look up to see Ott watching me from across the table. When our eyes meet, he gives me a little smile, lifts the glass of vodka in his hand, and takes a sip. The voices of the two Russians flow between us like a river, and we stand on opposite sides. I pick up my own glass and drink. The vodka burns my throat, but it also warms me a little. I set the glass down, and almost immediately Yuri fills it from the bottle that sits in front of him.

The apartment door opens, and Boone comes into the room accompanied by another man, who they call Tolya. He is not much more than 16 or 17, skinny and twitchy. He is also, apparently, a radio operator. He and Boone have been in the building's basement, where there's a hidden shortwave radio and where Boone was to try and communicate with his Cahokian liaison.

"Did you reach him?" I ask as Boone takes the empty chair beside me.

Yuri and Oksana stop their conversation and look at him too.
"Yes," Boone says.
I can tell he doesn't want to say too much, but he has little choice. Tolya has heard everything, and although Ott assured us that the boy understands almost no English, I suspect this is a lie. He has most likely understood everything that Boone transmitted to his contact, and everything that was sent back. Because of this, I'm also sure that Boone communicated in coded language.
"I told him that I need a few more days to complete my mission," Boone continues. "Hopefully, we will be done by then."
Yuri grunts. "Done or dead," he says, then laughs loudly. "That is the plan, anyway." He gets up and joins Tolya at the stove, where he is stirring whatever is cooking in the pot. Yuri dips a ladle into the pot, slurps loudly from it, and then picks up a bowl. He ladles some more of the pot's contents into it and brings it over, along with a pile of spoons, which he drops in the center of the table.
"Borscht," he says as he hands me the bowl. "Very good."
I pick up a spoon and taste the soup. It is good, and warming. Yuri brings more bowls, and soon everyone is eating. Yuri talks as we eat, and it occurs to me that perhaps he gave us the soup so that we would be too busy to interrupt him.
"I work as guard at Taganka," he says. "In part of prison where Falkenrath and Brecht are kept. "Oksana works in kitchen. Ironic, since at home I do all cooking and she is better shot with pistol." He laughs again, and Oksana makes a gun shape with her thumb and finger and pretends to shoot him.
"Often I transfer prisoners from one place to another," Yuri continues. "Plan is that I bring in new prisoner—Sasha." He indicates Boone. "Also, there is new girl working in prison infirmary." He looks at me. "What name is on your papers?"
"Irina Guryeva," I say.
"Irina is new girl in infirmary," Yuri says.
"Infirmary?" I say. "Why not in the kitchen with Oksana?"

"No girl needed in kitchen," Yuri says. "But needed in infirmary. Oksana tell them her friend nurse and will come help. Your Russian is good. You will be fine. Mostly it is cleaning and sewing up knife wounds. You can do that?"

"She can do that," Boone says, and gives me a wink. I think about how I stitched him up after he saved me from the MGB attackers. At the time, touching his bare skin made me feel oddly off balance. Now I know why.

"Excellent," Yuri says. "Now you both inside Taganka."

"Okay," Boone says. "But how do we get Falkenrath and Brecht *out*?"

Yuri shrugs. "I do not know," he says. "I only get you in."

"What?" Boone says. He looks at Ott. "This is the big plan? Get us inside and then make it up as we go along?"

Yuri shrugs again and holds up his hands. A moment later, just as I'm about to speak, he and Oksana burst out laughing.

"Yuri is joking," Oksana says. "There is a plan."

"Yes," Yuri says. "There is plan. Plan is, new prisoner Sasha will get into fight with Falkenrath, so that he has to go to infirmary. There, nurse Irina will give him injection that will make it like he is dead. We then take body out."

I look at Boone, who, like me, seems skeptical. "You've used this drug before?" I ask.

"Three times," says Yuri.

"And it worked?"

"One time," he says. "Right, Tolya?"

Tolya, who is leaning against the wall as he eats a bowl of borscht, nods brusquely.

"Tolya was good as new once we give him antidote. No problem."

"And what about Brecht?" I ask. "How are we getting him out? Are you going to drug him as well?"

"His health is not good," says Yuri. "And two deaths would be suspicious, so we cannot use drug. To get Brecht out, we need explosion."

"Explosion?" Boon says.

Yuri waves a hand. "It not as dangerous as it sounds. Always things exploding in Taganka. Prisoners make illegal stoves. Also, things for making vodka."

"Stills," Oksana says.

"Stills, yes," says Yuri. "They make stills out of coffee cans, teakettles. All kinds of things. We make it look like one of them explode. Makes big mess. Lots of noise. Prisoners will start to riot as they always do. While other guards getting them under control, we sneak Brecht out."

I shake my head. "This is the worst plan I've ever heard," I say.

Yuri shrugs. "You have better one?"

"Can't we bribe someone?" I suggest. "Everyone I ever met in the MGB could be bribed."

"Possibly," Yuri says. "If you have enough money. But takes time, and you do not have time."

"Or money," Boone reminds me. "Not that much, anyway."

Yuri nods at him, then looks at me. "You have other plan?"

I think for a minute. "I guess not," I admit.

Yuri holds up his hands. "I think not. So, we use my plan."

"What will Ott be doing?" I ask.

"Waiting in ambulance," Yuri says. "To drive body away. We will also put Brecht in van. Hide him underneath place where body is. It will, how you say, use one stone to hit two birds."

We spend the next few hours going over the plan again and again, using the rough map of Taganka Prison that Yuri draws on a piece of paper. Yuri will use his position as a guard to bring in a new prisoner, Boone. He will put him in the same cellblock as Falkenrath. Boone will pick a fight with the scientist and injure him enough to require a trip to the infirmary, where I will be waiting pretending to be a nurse. I will administer an injection to him that will make him appear to die, at which point they'll call for his body to be removed to the ambulance waiting outside. Ott will be driving the ambulance, and will accept the body. In the meantime, Yuri and Boone will be setting up an explosion in the cellblock to create chaos and allow them to sneak Brecht out as well.

The more we talk about it, the more unsure I am. There are so many places where the entire plan could go wrong, so many things requiring luck. Yuri assures us that he has some friends inside Taganka who will help, or at least not interfere, but I'm still not comfortable. I don't like having so many variables, so many moving parts that need to come together for this to work.

Boone can sense that I'm wary. His hand finds mine under the table, and he holds it while we go over the various steps in as much detail as we can. Every time Yuri glosses over something, or tells me not to worry when I raise a concern, Boone tightens his grip, reminding me to calm down.

It's after three in the morning when Yuri finally says, "I think that is enough. We go at six, so we should sleep."

"Six?" I say. "Why so early?"

"Shift changes at seven o'clock," Yuri explains. "This way, everyone tired from being up all night. Less likely to pay attention or notice anything out of place. Explosion will take them by surprise—BOOM! Also, will still be dark outside, so easier to get away."

He gets up, as if the meeting has been adjourned, and goes over to the couch, where he lies down. "Good night," he says, and almost immediately he begins snoring.

"He can sleep anywhere," Oksana says as she covers him with a crocheted afghan. "He learned it fighting in the war. I, however, cannot sleep with his snoring, so I will be in the other room. You are welcome to sleep there too. We have no beds, but blankets and pillows."

Ott and Tolya stay in the kitchen as we follow Oksana into the apartment's tiny bedroom, which is divided in half by a sheet hung on a line. Oksana gives us the promised blankets and pillows, then leaves the room. We hear the door to the tiny bathroom shut, and then the sound of pipes banging as water is turned on. Boone and I create makeshift beds with the blankets and use the opportunity to talk while we're alone.

"What did you tell Kenney?" I ask him.

"Not much," he says. "That kid was hovering, although he was pretending to do something else, and I didn't want to say too much in front of him. I think he understands more English than he lets on. And anyway, I didn't want Kenney to know too much either. I'm sure the Cahokians have people in the Soviet Union, but I don't want them involved. The less everyone knows, the better it is for us."

"This plan is shaky," I say.

"Like an earthquake," he says. "But it's the best we've got. Too many people know about the weapon now, and Brecht is the logical person to go to. We've got to get to him before someone else does."

"I wish we had more time," I say. "And money. And equipment. And pretty much everything else."

"Hey," Boone says. "We have the most important things. Each other."

"You just want to see me in a nurse uniform," I tease. His remark is sentimental, but I can tell he believes it. I do too. Being with him is the only thing I have right now besides the years of training that are making it possible for me to—hopefully—pull off what we have planned.

"We'll make this work," he says, kissing me.

I don't know if he means the plan or us. Before I can ask, Oksana comes back.

"The bathroom is free," she says as she disappears behind the sheet.

"Ladies first," I say to Boone, and head for the door with my bag.

The bathroom is tiny, the water a cold trickle, but it feels good to splash some on my face and brush my teeth. As I do, I look at myself in the cloudy mirror. I look like any number of girls getting ready for bed. But in a few hours, I'll be in the middle of a mission that could end in the deaths of more than a few people. Perhaps even mine. I think of all the other girls in all the other apartments in this building. What are they thinking about right now, the ones who aren't asleep and dreaming? Are they wishing they had a new dress, or that the boy they like liked them back? Are they worried about their futures, or filled with hope for a better new year?

I rinse my toothbrush and put it away. Will I be doing this again tomorrow night? Or will everything be different? I don't know. I turn off the light and return to the room where Boone is waiting. Until it's time to get up and prepare for the mission, I'll lie with him, his arms around me, and, hopefully, dream the dreams of a normal girl.

CHAPTER 10

Boone

From the outside, Taganka Prison is actually beautiful, at least what I can see of it in the predawn darkness through falling snow. It's an imposing brick structure, with high walls, towers, and barred windows. I know terrible things happen inside, but as Yuri and I approach one of the side doors, I feel as if we're entering a castle.

"Talk little," Yuri reminds me as he inserts a key into the lock of the door. "Your accent is not so good. Perhaps you act simple, yes?"

I nod. At the moment, all I want is to get inside. I'm supposed to be a prisoner, and Yuri has dressed me as one. I'm wearing pants and a thin shirt underneath a tattered old coat. No socks, and a pair of old shoes with holes in the soles. When the wind blows, I feel as if I'm back inside the flooded chamber underneath the New Museum.

"I will have to be rough with you," Yuri says. "I apologize. It is necessary."

With the door open, he pushes me through, yelling at me in Russian to hurry up. I know this is for the benefit of anyone who might be inside, so I play my part, stumbling in and trying to look frightened. But the only one there is an old woman who is washing the floor with a mop, and she doesn't even look at us as Yuri takes me by the arm and leads me down a hallway.

As he predicted, the prison is mostly quiet. But there is some activity. As we move deeper into the building, a handful of guards appears. They glance at me and say a few words to Yuri. Nobody asks who I am or why I am there. I imagine they've seen so many people come in that they no longer care. Prisoners are just more bodies to manage, not people with names or stories of their own.

I see some of these prisoners as I'm marched up a flight of stairs and down more hallways. They are crowded into cells. Most are asleep, but some are up. They gaze out with little more interest than the guards showed, maybe sizing me up, maybe looking to see if I'm someone they know. None speak to me or to Yuri, and I avoid their eyes, trying to be as unmemorable as possible. The smell is the worst, a combination of harsh soap and unwashed bodies. I suspect the soap is used more for the floors than for the prisoners, as I see more women like the one downstairs, all of them tiny and hunched over, pushing puddles of dirty water around as if it will help.

Eventually, we stop in front of a cell and Yuri takes out his ring of keys. A door is unlocked and slid open. Yuri whispers in my ear, "Do it soon, before the shift change." Then I'm inside, and the door is slammed shut.

The cell is small, no more than eight feet across. Bunk beds are pushed against one wall, and there is a small window high on the far wall. The glass has a hole in it, and the winter cold blows in. A form is wrapped in a thin blanket and curled in the bottom bunk. Helmut Falkenrath. Ott's father.

I've debated about how much to tell him about what is about to happen to him. Part of me thinks that if he knows, it will not be as frightening. Another part thinks that it will all be much more believable if he knows nothing. However, I'm also afraid that if he fears he might be killed, he might have a heart attack or something.

I hear noise in the hallway. Guards are talking. I recognize Yuri's voice. The shift change is beginning. It's time to act.

I go to the bed and kneel down. I reach out and touch Falkenrath's shoulder. To my surprise, he is not asleep. "I have cigarettes," he says in Russian. His voice is timid, and I can feel him trembling. Probably, he has been afraid since hearing someone new enter his cell. He's offering me a bribe not to hurt him. He keeps his back to me, curled tightly.

"I am your son's friend," I say in German. "I am here to get you out."
He hesitates, then rolls over. It is hard to see him in the dim light, but I can see the gleam of his glasses. "Tobias?" he says, as if he can't quite remember.
"Yes," I say. "I am a friend."
I feel bad saying this given what else I have to do, but I need to give him some hope to help him get through the next few minutes.
"Is he here?" he asks.
"Yes," I say. "He is waiting for you outside."
The voices of the guards grow louder. They are walking down the corridor. It's time.
"You must trust me," I whisper to Falkenrath. "You will be all right."
Before he can answer, I drag him from the bed. "I said that one is mine!" I yell in Russian.
Falkenrath cowers before me, obviously not understanding. He looks at me with confusion on his face. I have to remind myself that I'm here to save him as I punch him in the stomach. I don't hit him as hard as I could, but even still, he cries out and falls backward. I reach down and pick him up by his shirt, which rips as he feebly claws at me with his hands.
Hearing the commotion, prisoners in the surrounding cells stir. I hear the sound of running feet. The guards are coming. I have only moments to do what needs to be done.
"I am king here now!" I shout. I pull the knife that has been hidden in my jacket out and hold it up. Falkenrath, seeing it, squeals in fear.
"Help!" he cries. "Someone help me!" Despite what I have told him about being here to get him out, he obviously doesn't believe that's what's happening. I don't blame him.
I cut him with the knife, aiming for the soft part of his stomach, the spot someone who was really trying to kill him would go for. But I don't go deep, just enough to make the blood flow. Falkenrath screams as if I've stuck him like a pig at slaughter, however, clutching

himself and throwing himself on the floor. I don't think he's acting, but it's exactly what I need him to do.

I crouch over him, yelling threats and holding the knife up as the guards reach the cell door and open it. As planned, one of them is Yuri. He comes in first, knocking the knife from my hand with one giant paw and throwing me onto my back. He kneels over me and yells to the other guard, "Is that one dead?"

The other guard checks Falkenrath. "Only bleeding," he says.

"Take him to the infirmary," Yuri orders. "I'll take care of this troublemaker."

The other guard helps a moaning Falkenrath get to his feet, then removes him from the cell. Yuri says to me, "Play along," then jerks me to my feet.

"Not five minutes in here, and already you think you run the place?" he bellows. "I think I need to teach you how things work in Taganka."

He punches me, but not too hard. I fall against the bunk beds, making as much noise as possible. From outside the cell, the sound of other inmates shouting drowns out our voices. Some are calling for me to kill the guard. Others are calling for him to kill me. A few rattle things against the bars of their own cells, clacking and clanging, creating a soundtrack to the fight.

Yuri and I make it sound convincing. Several times he throws me into the bars of the door, all the while yelling at me that I need to learn my place. I pretend to fight back at first. At one point, Yuri shoves me a little too enthusiastically, my face connects with the floor, and my nose really does start to bleed. It hurts, but it makes things seem more real, so I don't try to stop it. Yuri hauls me to my feet and drags me from the cell.

"Perhaps some time alone will change your attitude," he says as he parades me down the hallway.

By the time we reach the stairs, the whole floor is buzzing. Also, more guards have appeared. As Yuri marches me by them, they eye me like a prize that they wish they'd been lucky enough to catch.

"Do you need help administering his lesson?" one asks.

Yuri laughs. "Get your own student, Kirill," he barks.

I can tell that the men relish the idea of being allowed to hurt me. Their hunger is evident in the way they leer and joke. I can't even imagine what it must be like for the prisoners who have to live here. Especially ones like Falkenrath, who have so little fight left in them to begin with. The years here must have been hell for him. I hope that our plan to get him out works.

Yuri manhandles me down more stairs and into a small storage room, where he shuts the door. "Good," he says, switching to English. "Falkenrath should be on his way to infirmary. Sorry about nose. Now we get Brecht."

"Where is he?" I ask, wiping my nose on my sleeve. The bleeding has mostly stopped.

"Other wing," says Yuri. He takes a bag out from behind a stack of boxes. "Put these on. You just promoted from prisoner to guard."

The bag contains a uniform like the one Yuri is wearing. I quickly put it on. Then Yuri hands me a pistol. I put it into my pocket. It feels good to have a weapon other than the knife, which anyway was left behind in the cell upstairs. I stuff my prisoner clothes into the bag, which Yuri tosses into a trash can.

Yuri takes out another bag, and we bring this one with us as we head for the part of the prison where Brecht is housed. I keep my head down, in case anyone recognizes the prisoner who came through earlier, but nobody pays any attention to me. If they do, we've prepared a story about my being a new guard Yuri has been charged with showing around Taganka.

The area where Brecht is looks exactly like the one where Falkenrath was. Cell after cell is filled with prisoners. Now, though, they are waking up. Somehow, word of the events in the other wing has reached here, and there is an undercurrent of unrest. The guards who are ending their shift are anxious to leave, and the ones coming on are not pleased to be here. It's exactly what we hoped for.

"They will open the cells soon for morning showers," Yuri says. "We must be ready to go."

We've decided that the best time to act is while the prisoners are going back and forth to the communal bathroom at the end of the hall. The bag Yuri carries contains a small, simple explosive device that he and Tolya have made. It's designed more to make noise and smoke than to destroy anything. Once we light the fuse, we have a short time to get away from it.

A guard blows a whistle indicating that the first group of prisoners should file into the corridor and walk to the bathroom. We know that Brecht ought to be among them. We pretend to patrol the hallway, looking for him. When he appears, coming out of a cell halfway down the hallway, Yuri nods at me. We walk toward his cell but do not address him in any way.

The line of men shuffles toward the washroom. When they have passed us, we slip into Brecht's cell. Yuri takes the bomb from the bag and tucks it underneath the bed. He lights the fuse, and we walk quickly out of the room, heading back in the direction of the bathroom. We are almost to the door when there is a loud noise and black smoke billows out of Brecht's cell.

Immediately, people begin running and yelling. Guards come rushing down the hallway, both to see what has happened and to keep control of the prisoners. They're yelling for them to get back in their cells. Many comply, but others are refusing to go. The guards grab them and push them. Soon the hallway is a confusion of bodies.

Yuri and I duck into the bathroom. A few men are already in the showers and haven't heard the racket. Others are lined up, waiting their turn. They look at us as we walk among them.

"Back to your cells!" Yuri shouts. "Now!"

The men are used to obeying, and most obey. Brecht is one of them. As he walks by us, I take him by the arm. "Not you," I say in German. He startles, surprised to hear me use his native language. I lean in and say, "Come with me. Your daughter sent me."

These are apparently the magic words, as Brecht doesn't hesitate to walk with me and Yuri as we leave the bathroom and press into the crowded hallway. Fighting against the tide of bodies, we manage to get to the end and into the stairway. There Yuri removes his coat and puts it around Brecht, who is swallowed up in it. He is not at all convincing as a guard, particularly as he is not wearing shoes, but it will have to do.

We hustle him down the stairs. Either because most of the guards are upstairs, or through sheer luck, we make it without encountering anyone. Yuri pushes a door open, and we're in a courtyard where there is a GAZ-55 ambulance waiting. Ott is sitting in the driver's seat. We usher Brecht to the ambulance and push him inside.

"You stay here," Yuri tells me. "Wait for Falkenrath."

He turns and goes back into the prison. I climb into the back of the ambulance and pull the door shut. One side of the interior is filled with a stretcher and the sole passenger seat. Brecht is sitting on the seat. Ott, in the front, is turned to him. Their hands are clasped.

"Is it really you, Tobias?" Brecht asks.

"Yes," says Ott. "It is good to see you again, Oswald."

"Are we escaping?" Brecht says. "What are we waiting for?" he asks.

"My father," Ott tells him.

"Helmut?" he says. "You're getting him out as well?"

"We're trying," I say.

I wonder what's happening inside Taganka's infirmary. By now, Falkenrath should be there, and Ariadne should be playing her part in the operation. It's a risky part, for everyone involved, and a lot could go wrong. There's nothing I can do about it, though. Nothing but wait.

As Ott and Brecht talk, I sit with my eyes glued to the door to the prison. If all goes well, it should be opening at any moment. If it doesn't, we will leave with Brecht, and Ariadne will be on her own. I stare at the door, willing it to open. *Come on,* I think. *Come on. Get out of there.*

The door opens, and someone comes out. But it's not someone bringing Falkenrath to the ambulance. It's someone I've never seen before. And he's holding a gun.

CHAPTER 11

Ariadne

Helmut Falkenrath is not a good patient. A quick glance at his wound tells me that Boone has not injured him badly. But there is a lot of blood, and the scientist is frightened, which probably contributes to his hysteria.

"I'm dying!" he wails in German as I clean the cut with antiseptic wash.

"You're not dying," I tell him, also in German.

This calms him somewhat, although he continues to moan and gasp with every touch of the cotton on his skin. I wish I could inform him that, if all goes well, he'll soon be out of Taganka Prison and reunited with his son, but the risk of exciting him further is too great. And if he knew what he's going to have to endure before that reunion, he would likely get up from the bed on which he's lying and run screaming from the infirmary.

The syringe containing the drug that will "kill" Falkenrath is in my pocket. Before I administer it, I want to tend to his wound. This also gives Boone and Yuri time to liberate Brecht and get him to the ambulance as well. When Falkenrath was brought into the infirmary by two guards, it was a great relief to know that the first part of our plan had worked so well.

The nurse in charge of the prison hospital is a sour, pinch-faced woman who is more concerned with drinking her morning tea and eating the vatrushka sitting on a plate on her desk than she is with attending to the patients, so I have been left alone to do all the work. There are eight men in the beds that line both sides of the room. Most have wounds from fights of various kinds, although two have deep, rattling coughs that suggest something more serious. From what I've been told, it is our job to patch them up and get them back into their cells as quickly as possible.

I take a needle and pass the catgut through its eye. Clamping the needle between the jaws of a driver, I prepare to begin sewing Falkenrath up. This should take only a few minutes, after which it will be time to give him the injection. I still don't know exactly what is in the syringe, but Yuri has assured me that it will be effective at mimicking the symptoms of cardiac arrest, after which Falkenrath will go into a coma state and appear dead, at least to anyone who does not examine him carefully, which I don't believe the nurse in charge will do. She has made it clear by her indifference that the lives of prisoners are not valued commodities at Taganka, even the lives of men like Helmut Falkenrath. I think of all the scientists, writers, dissidents, and other intellectuals who are living inside these walls, imprisoned here because of supposed crimes against the powers in charge, and how most of them will simply disappear, never to be heard from again. It's such a waste of life, and it saddens me.

I am about to push the needle through Falkenrath's skin to make the first stitch when a male voice behind me says, "Be careful with that one, Strekalova. We would like for him to live."

I start to respond that I will do my best, when I realize what he has called me. Strekalova. My name when I was undercover with the MGB. My blood runs cold. I turn slowly and look at who has spoken. I recognize the face. He is someone who worked in the MGB office in Berlin, although we never had occasion to work together. It takes me another moment to recall his name, but I am able to retrieve it.

"Morozov," I say.

He smiles. He is not holding a weapon that I can see, but his hands are in his pockets, and so it is possible he is armed. More important, he is blocking my way out of the room, standing between me and the only door. The head nurse is seated behind us, and she does not appear to have heard what he's said to me.

"I am surprised to see you here," Morozov says. "I did not know you were a nurse."

I smile even as every nerve in my body tenses for action. "You learn many things when you serve in the army," I say.

"Indeed," he says. He takes a few steps closer, until he is standing beside the bed across from me, with Falkenrath between us. The scientist is listening to our conversation, but he says nothing. "I was greatly surprised when I heard that you had left Berlin," Morozov continues. "It was very sudden."

So, he knows. But what is he going to do about it? Perhaps he thinks that he has me trapped in the room with nowhere to go, and so he is not concerned. This would be a mistake on his part. Still, it is not only myself I am worried about. I am supposed to be getting Falkenrath out of this place. Now I don't see how I can do that without a fight. A fight I don't have time for.

"It is too bad what happened to Utkin," Morozov says. He lifts his hand and draws an extended finger across his throat. Then he laughs. Falkenrath is looking from me to Morozov. He senses that something is going on, although he has no idea what it is. He is also still in pain from his wound, which I have not sewn shut. The needle remains in my hand, poised above his abdomen. Now I hold it up to show Morozov.

"If you will excuse me, I have a patient to attend to."

Morozov's face hardens. He reaches into his pocket. "I think perhaps someone else should take over for you," he says. "Nurse! Come here."

The head nurse looks up. "What do you need?"

Morozov turns his head to answer her. As he does, I leap out of the chair I am sitting in. At the same time, I draw the loaded syringe from my pocket. Before Morozov knows what's happening, I jab the needle into his arm and depress the plunger. He roars and pulls his arm away, the needle still stuck in it. But it's too late. Whatever is in the syringe is now coursing through his body.

"Get up!" I say to Falkenrath.

"I'm wounded!" he objects.

"You'll be worse than that if you stay here," I tell him, pulling him out of the bed.

He comes with me, clutching his stomach. Morozov attempts to grab us, but already his body is racked with spasms. His face reddens and contorts, and his mouth opens in a silent roar as he clutches at his chest. Falkenrath and I slip past him and head for the door as the nurse screams behind us.

Unfortunately, her screams draw the attention of the guards in the hallway. They turn and look as I leave the infirmary with Falkenrath ahead of me. When they see a prisoner they think is attempting to make an escape, they draw their guns.

"Get down!" I tell Falkenrath.

He doesn't listen. What's happened in the infirmary has frightened him, and he panics. He runs toward the guards yelling for them to help him. They ignore him, firing their weapons. Falkenrath falls to the floor, blood pooling out from half a dozen wounds. I can tell that he will not get up again.

It hits me with full force that I've lost Ott's father. But I have no time to waste mourning for a man I've never met before today. I have to think of my own survival. For the moment, the guards think that I am a nurse chasing an escaping patient. They lower their guns as I approach Falkenrath's body and kneel beside it, pretending to check for a pulse.

"Are you all right?" one of them asks as another runs to the infirmary to see why the other nurse is still shrieking. I have only a few seconds. I do not have a gun, but there is a knife tucked into the pocket of my nurse's uniform, and I've always preferred fighting with a knife. I draw it and throw it at the nearest guard. It enters his eye, and he falls. I pull the knife out, get up, and run down the hallway. I know that Ott is waiting in an ambulance in the courtyard. That's where I need to get to. I have memorized the map Yuri drew of the prison, and I have only to run down this corridor, turn left, and go to the end. There the door will open into the outside.

As I turn the corner, I see someone else running. It's a man. He's ahead of me, and he hits the door to the courtyard and goes out. I hear him yell. I don't know who he is, but I know he's bad news for me and for whoever is waiting for me in the courtyard.

I run hard for the door, waiting to hear shots. I do not. Behind me there are shouts. The second guard has discovered his friend dead, and now his booted feet pound on the floor as he comes after me. There is nowhere to hide. I have no cover if he starts shooting. I have to get out.

The first shots are fired from behind me just as I reach the door. They hit the wall over my head as I push the door open and burst into the courtyard. There I find the man who was ahead of me, standing with his gun pointed at Boone, who is climbing out of the ambulance with his hands raised.

The man with the gun turns. I kick out with one foot, pivoting at the hip, and connect with his arm. The gun fires, but I've thrown him off balance, and the bullet strikes the building behind me. Before the man can collect himself, I'm on top of him, using my knife to make him no longer a problem.

"We have to go!" I call to Boone. "There are more coming."

"Where's Falkenrath?" he asks.

"Dead," I tell him.

Boone looks shocked. So does Ott, who has gotten out of the ambulance. He looks around, as if perhaps his father is somewhere and he just hasn't seen him. "Dead?" he says.

"The guards killed him."

Before I can say anything else, Ott gets back into the ambulance. It starts up just as the door behind me flies open and the guard who has been chasing me comes out. I turn to meet him, and hear the ambulance roar away. Boone yells something, but I'm too busy with the guard to hear what it is. I make quick work of him, then turn my attention back to Boone.

"That wasn't part of the plan," I say, every doubt I've had about Ott's loyalty now ringing like warning bells in my head.

"He was probably afraid and wanted to get Brecht to safety," Boone says, but he sounds unconvinced.

The door to the prison opens once more, but this time it is Yuri who emerges. He looks at the two dead guards and says, "You must go. Now. Return to apartment. I will be there when I can."

Boone and I don't wait for him to tell us twice. We run out of the courtyard. Thankfully, it is still dark, and we are able to hide from the flashlight beams that shortly begin sweeping the area. We hear the voices of the guards calling to one another, but they don't know where we've gone, and we're able to slip away from Taganka and into the streets without being seen.

It takes us some time to return to the building where Yuri and Oksana live. When we get there, Tolya lets us in. When we ask him if Ott has been there, he shakes his head no.

"Where do you think he's gone?" I ask Boone.

"I wish I knew," he says.

"Do you think he's crossed us?" I ask. It's what I've been wondering since hearing the ambulance drive away.

"I wish I knew that too," Boone says. "For right now, let's just assume he was afraid that Brecht would also be killed if he waited."

I can't help noticing that Tolya seems edgier than usual. He's walking around the small apartment, fidgeting and looking nervous. I suppose he could simply be worried about his friends, but this seems to be more than that.

"What do you know?" I ask him in Russian.

He glances at the door, as if he is thinking of running.

"You won't make it out," I say. "I promise you that."

Surprisingly, he laughs. "None of us will make it out," he says bitterly. He looks at me, and now the shy boy is gone, replaced by something with a harder edge. "Do you know what they did?" he asks. "Stalin's army? During the war? They sent children to fight. They sent *dogs* to fight. Dogs with bombs strapped to their backs. They starved them, then tossed meat underneath German tanks so that the dogs would go to get it and the bombs would explode."

He looks haunted, as if he is remembering something unspeakable. "I was only eleven when I was taken to fight," he says. "Given a rifle and told to shoot anything that didn't look like a Red Army soldier. Then they assigned me to the dogs, because I was good with them. They liked me. When I saw what they were doing with them, I cried, so I was beaten for being weak, for caring about dogs more than about my countrymen. And so I learned not to cry. Instead I was kind to the dogs, because I knew they were going to die, and I wanted them to know that someone loved them."

He looks away. "Stalin does not care about us any more than he cared about those dogs. We are just tools for him—things with no purpose but the one he assigns to us. And when he is done with us, or when we refuse to do as he asks, we disappear."

I think I'm beginning to understand. "What did Ott promise you?"

"A weapon," he says. "A weapon to help us regain our country for ourselves."

I look over at Boone. I don't know how much of our conversation he's understood, as it's all been in Russian, but from the look on his face, I think he has the general idea.

"What was his plan?" he asks Tolya.

"To get his father and the other scientist out of Taganka, then convince you to reveal the plans for the weapon."

"And then?"

"Either share it—or kill you."

"And in exchange for helping, he would let you use it on whatever targets you have in mind," Boone says.

Tolya nods.

"And you trusted him to actually do this?" I say.

"We do not have many options," Tolya says. "And Ott despises the Soviets as much as we do."

This is true. And maybe Ott would allow them to use the weapon, as long as it suited his purposes. However, I think there is more going on than any of us know. More to Ott than we even suspected.

I am about to say as much when there is a knock on the door. Boone stands, removes his pistol, and moves so that he is out of sight. I nod at Tolya to go to the door, keeping my hand on my knife, as my pistol is still in my bag in the bedroom.

Tolya goes to the door. "Who is it?"

A child's voice responds. This does not mean there is no reason to worry, however. I think back to the incident in Europa's apartment in Berlin. It could be a ruse. So as Tolya undoes the locks and opens the door, I do not relax at all.

The child is alone. It is a boy of maybe six or seven. He hands Tolya an envelope. "I was told to bring this to you."

"By whom?" Tolya asks.

The child shrugs. "A man," he says. "He gave me fifty kopecks to bring it."

The boy leaves, and Tolya shuts the door. He opens the envelope and takes out a piece of paper. He looks at it, then hands it to me. "It's for you," he says. "From Ott."

I take the paper and read it.

"He wants us to meet him," I say. "To talk."

"Talk about what?" Boone asks.

"He doesn't say," I tell him. "But I'm guessing it will involve the weapon and not killing Brecht. He probably wants to make a deal. There's only one way we're going to find out."

"When and where?"

"Tonight. In Gorky Park."

"What do we do until then?"

I crumple the note up and toss it on the table. "We wait," I say. "And we make a plan."

CHAPTER 12

Boone

The Moscow River is a frozen ribbon dotted with fishing huts, the lanterns inside spilling golden light onto the black ice. The snow that was falling most of the afternoon has stopped, and stars diamond the clear sky as Ariadne and I make our way along the walking path and deep into Gorky Park. The temperature has tumbled to well below freezing, and not many people are out. Those that are bustle by quickly, heading for shelter and warmth. No one looks at us. It's as if the park is filled only with shadows sliding silently in and out of the trees.

We've had all day to discuss what Ott might want. We still aren't sure. Tolya had little else to tell us, and when Yuri and Oksana returned to the apartment, they were equally unhelpful. The incident at Taganka is being blamed on Nazi sympathizers, and the death of Helmut Falkenrath credited to the bravery of the guards who thwarted the "terrorist activity." The escape of Oswald Brecht has been covered up for now, although Yuri says that, privately, the prison authorities are in a panic and terrified that they will face stiff consequences for his disappearance. The government does not like it when prisoners slip through their fingers, especially political prisoners. Someone will have to pay.

At first we weren't sure if we should even stay in the apartment, after finding out that Ott had promised the group use of the weapon in exchange for their help. But we had nowhere else to go, and Ariadne argued that we were better off knowing what they were up to than leaving and wondering. And she was right. Both Yuri and Oksana seemed genuinely surprised by Ott's behavior, and I think they honestly believed that we would willingly help them with their cause in exchange for their assistance.

We are still having a conversation about them as we walk to Gorky Park.

"They are part of a group that is looking for any way out of their current situation," Ariadne says. "They are small, and without resources. Their battle seems impossible to win, and probably it is. It's no surprise they would agree to help Ott."

She's right. It's something I can't really imagine living with, being so afraid of what your government might do to you that you would risk everything to try to stop them. I think Yuri, Oksana, and Tolya are good people. Ott, I'm not so sure about. Although he says his interest is in fighting oppression, I think he really wants the weapon to take revenge on the people who put his father in Taganka Prison. And now maybe Ariadne and I are also on that list. His father died while we were supposed to be getting him out. I'm sure he blames us.

"He's going to try to trade Brecht for the weapon," Ariadne says.

It's the obvious thing. But I'm not so sure. "He needs Brecht to make sense of the plans," I remind her. "Without him, he's starting from zero."

"Maybe Brecht has agreed to help him," Ariadne says. "Maybe once Ott has the weapon, Brecht will help him anyway, and this is all a trick to get us to hand it over."

"He should know we wouldn't bring the weapon with us to Moscow," I say.

"Except that we did," Ariadne reminds me.

We did. It is not an ideal situation, but I was uncomfortable leaving it behind in France, so far away. While Lottie might have been entrusted with it, I don't entirely know where her loyalties lie, and at any rate, having it or knowing where it is would put her in more danger than she is already in. It was best to leave her ignorant regarding its whereabouts. And so we brought it with us, making sure that at all times one or both of us has been awake to keep it safe from Ott in the event that he went looking for it. This morning was the most perilous time, as we didn't dare leave it in the apartment while we were in Taganka, and had nowhere else to put it. Also, in the event that neither of us returned from the mission, we didn't want anyone who knew anything about the weapon to stumble upon it. In the end, we separated the tube containing the plans from the box holding the weapon pieces. The box we hid in the basement of the apartment building, tucked inside a broken boiler. Not the best place, but the best we could do given the circumstances.

The tube containing the plans we kept closer. It's sewn into the coat I'm wearing. Again, maybe not the smartest place to keep it, but I feel better having it nearby. If something goes wrong, it won't be too difficult for Ariadne to retrieve it. And if something goes *really* wrong, well, we won't be around to care, I guess.

Not that I think Ott will try to kill us. If he does, he loses any chance he has of getting his hands on the weapon, and I think that's more important to him than anything else. I also don't really believe he would hurt Brecht, who was his father's friend. So although I'm apprehensive, I'm not overly concerned about this meeting.

"Ott's only bargaining chip is that he thinks we really want the weapon to be built," I remind Ariadne. "He thinks we want Brecht because we need him to help us build the weapon."

The thing is, I'm not sure we really care about building the weapon anymore. If we ever did. Now that Ariadne is considered a traitor to her line, it's not like she'll hand the weapon over to them. Even if it would get her reinstated as Player. And I'm not anxious for the Cahokians to have it either, at least not without agreeing to share it or use it to change the course of Endgame for everyone. Mostly, I'm thinking that *we*—Ariadne and I—can use it as a bargaining chip, to negotiate some kind of way for us to be together. And we could probably do that even without Brecht. Really, the only reason I'm concerned about him is because he's Lottie's father and Bernard's grandfather. I figure I owe it to them, and to my brother, to keep him unharmed.

It's funny how my perspective on all of this has changed in such a short time. And it's all because of how I feel about Ariadne. Now I reach out and take her hand.

"What?" she says.

"You're always so suspicious," I say. "Can't I just want to hold your hand?"

"Sorry," she says. "It's that whole Player thing. Don't trust anyone and all that."

"Pretend we're on a date," I say. "I'm walking you home."

She laughs. It's the sweetest sound in the world. "You mean, pretend we're normal people?"

"I don't think we can ever be normal, exactly," I say. "Not after all of this. But maybe something close to it."

Ariadne doesn't say anything, and suddenly the atmosphere around us feels different. "Hey," I say. "Is something wrong?"

"No," she says, but she doesn't sound convincing.

I stop. "Talk to me," I say.

"There's nothing to talk about," she says.

"Come on, Ari. I can tell when you're holding out on me."

"Did you just call me Ari?"

"Yeah," I say. "I guess I did. Do you like it?"

"I do," she says, and this time, I know she means it. "Cassandra and I never even used nicknames for each other. It was always Ariadne and Cassandra."

"Well, *Ari*," I say. "What are you worried about?"

"Meeting a dangerous man in a dark park?" she suggests.

"Besides that. There's something else, isn't there?"

She hesitates before answering. "When do we stop running?" she says.

I don't have an answer for her, at least not one that will help. "I don't know," I say. "Let's just get through tonight, and then we'll worry about it."

It's not the answer she wants to hear, or the one I want to give her, but it's the only one I've got. Right now we seem so far away from everything that could be considered a normal life. And maybe it's too late for us to have anything normal. Probably it was too late the day we were chosen to train as Players.

"Let's throw the plans in the river and get out of Moscow," I say. "Go somewhere warm. I'm sick of snow and cold. I want to lie on the beach and not think about the end of the world."

She puts her arms around me and hugs me. "That sounds great," she says. "But we can't."

"Why not?"

"For one thing, the river is frozen."

"We could drop the tube through one of those fishing holes," I argue.

"For another, they'd still come after us."

I sigh. She's right. They would. The only way we'll get out of this is if we give our lines something they want.

"All right," I say, and kiss her. "Let's get this over with, then."

We walk the rest of the way to the rendezvous point in silence. When we get to the place Ott has chosen, a statue of a woman poised to dive off her pedestal and into the water, we stop. There is no one else in sight, although we have a few minutes until the agreed-upon time. We stand in front of the statue, back to back, surveying the area and waiting. I rub my hands together to try to warm them. It feels as if the cold has soaked into my bones and will never leave, and I think about how nice it would be to sit in front of a warm fire with Ari, with nothing to worry about. I wonder if that will ever happen.

Somewhere, a clock begins to chime midnight. Before it's counted out twelve hours, Ott appears, walking out of the darkness. He is alone. He stops a dozen feet away from us.

"A beautiful night," he says.

"Yes," I say. "It is."

"I'm sorry that our last meeting did not go as planned," Ott says.

"And I'm sorry that the guards killed your father," I tell him. I want him to know that it was not Ariadne's fault. "There were complications."

Ott nods. "Regrettable," he says. "I understand the Minoan was recognized."

I feel Ariadne stiffen beside me. I know that, like myself, she's wondering how Ott knows this. Brecht couldn't have told him, so that means he has some inside knowledge of what went on inside the Taganka infirmary.

There's no point in denying what happened, so I say, "She tried to get your father out."

"And failed," says Ott.

So, this is how he's going to play this. He blames us for his father's death, and now he wants some kind of reparation.

"How is Brecht?" I ask, trying to change the subject.

"As well as can be expected," Ott tells me. "After so much time in Taganka, I'm afraid his health is not at all good. He requires medical attention as soon as possible."

It sounds like a threat, a threat meant to make me inclined to do whatever it is he asks. "It will do no one any good if he dies," I remind him. "His daughter and grandson would like to see him again."

"I imagine they would," Ott says. "Much as I would like to have seen my father again."

I can tell he's not going to move past this issue, and so I decide to get to the point. "What is it you want?"

He laughs. "How American of you," he says. "Always in a hurry."

"Yeah, well, it's cold," I say. "And it's been a long day."

Ott's voice, when he replies, is icy. "What makes you think I want anything at all from you?"

This takes me aback. If he doesn't want anything, why did he ask us to meet him here? Obviously, he has something we want and we have something he wants. The only thing that makes sense is that he wants to trade, or come to some kind of partnership.

"We need to get out of here," Ariadne whispers to me. "Now." She reaches for my hand, but Ott speaks again, and I wait to hear what he has to say.

"Maybe what I want *is* you," he says.

"Boone," Ariadne says. "Now."

This time, I let her pull me away. Something is wrong. But we get only a few steps before a figure confronts us. It's Kenney. He has a pistol aimed at us.

"Leaving so soon?" he says. "I was hoping we could have a little chat. It seems there's quite a lot to talk about."

I turn and look at Ott, who has moved closer and is also now holding a gun. If Ariadne and I try to make a break for it, one or both of us will end up dead. Our only hope is to try to buy ourselves some time.

"All right," I say to Kenney. "Let's talk."

CHAPTER 13

Ariadne

In the Greek story of the hero Odysseus, he at one point in his journey is sailing his ship through the Strait of Messina, which is guarded on one side by the six-headed monster Scylla and on the other by Charybdis, who creates a deadly whirlpool by swallowing huge quantities of seawater in an attempt to sate her unquenchable thirst. Knowing that he cannot avoid both dangers, Odysseus is forced to choose one over the other. He elects to pass by Scylla, who devours six of his sailors, rather than risk losing his entire ship to Charybdis. It's a classic example of being faced with a decision that has no good outcome, and one that Minoan trainers famously use when teaching Players about making difficult choices.

As Boone and I stand between Ott and Kenney, I attempt to figure out which is Scylla and which is Charybdis. If I am forced to confront only one of them, which is the most dangerous? I know nothing about Kenney except that he is a Cahokian operative. As such, he will very much want the weapon for his line. If he knows I am a Minoan, he will be particularly interested in ensuring that I don't get it. But Ott also wants it for his own purposes, and he has the added incentive of thinking that he needs to avenge his father's death, for which he blames me. Both men would likely be happy to see me dead.

Because of how we are standing, I am facing Ott, and so he currently draws my focus. Boone, meanwhile, continues the conversation with his linesman.

"I understand you took a detour before heading to Moscow," Kenney says.

"I had to get the weapon back," Boone explains.

"Of course," Kenney says. "You might have mentioned that the Minoans had it, however. Although perhaps it wasn't the weapon you were most concerned with retrieving."

He's of course talking about me. I want to respond to him, remind him that I'm not a trophy to be collected, but it's important to keep things calm for as long as possible.

"I knew she could be useful," Boone says.

Kenney laughs. "I'm sure she is," he says. "Unfortunately, she presents a dilemma. A Minoan working with a Cahokian can end only one way."

Again, his meaning is clear. One of us has to die. And because he is Cahokian, his choice is much less complicated than that of Odysseus.

"Not necessarily," Boone tells him, obviously grasping his meaning as well as I have. "There are other options. We could share the weapon."

"An interesting suggestion," Kenney says. "However, one I think neither council would agree to."

"We won't know unless we ask them."

"I don't think that will be necessary," Kenney replies. "I've been tasked with bringing it home."

I feel things reaching a point of no return, and so I say to Ott, "What about you? Do you think he'll share with you? Is that what he promised?"

I still don't know how Ott and Kenney have come to be working together, but I know that it has to be because Ott was given a guarantee of some kind.

"Mr. Ott will be well rewarded," Kenney says from behind me.

Ott's gaze flickers from me to where Kenney is standing. Is there uncertainty in his look? Is he now doubting that Kenney will fulfill whatever promise has been made? If I can create a wedge between them, this might give us an advantage.

"He won't let you have it," I say to Ott. "Never. If he told you he would, he was lying."

"She's very convincing," Kenney says. "I can see why you fell for her lies, Samuel."

"She hasn't lied to me," Boone snaps. "Ever."

Kenney laughs again. It is a terrible sound, filled with scorn and malice. "Of course not," he says.

"Look," Boone says. "I have the plans and the pieces of the weapon. We can take them back to the council. Back to America. Just let her go back to the Minoans. They don't have anything now anyway."

"An excellent idea," Kenney says. "I'm pleased to see you're being sensible now. Although I imagine the council will require further explanation from you, having the weapon safely in Cahokian hands is really what we all want. And I'm sure your mother will be relieved to have you home again safe and sound."

It all sounds very reasonable, easily settled and wrapped up. All Boone has to do is hand over the weapon and the plans. Part of me, the part still hardwired into my Player brain, wonders if he really intends to do it. After all, it makes sense, and if Kenney really lets me go, we all walk away alive, if not happy. My heart, however, tells me he won't. Once the weapon is given up, he has no reason not to try to kill us. Besides, there's still a piece of the puzzle missing.

"What about Brecht?" I say. "Without him, the plans are useless."

"Not useless," says Kenney. "More difficult to work with, of course, and it would be easier if he cooperated. Then again, he might be persuaded if he thinks the lives of his daughter and grandson depend on it."

"You have Lottie and Bernard?" Boone says.

"You thought we didn't know about them?" Kenney answers. "Or about your brother?"

"Are they all right?"

"For the moment. Whether or not they stay that way will depend entirely on you and Brecht."

"That sounds reasonable," Boone says. "There's just one problem."

"Oh?" Kenney says. "What is that?"

"The Cahokians don't make threats against people's children."

Kenney snorts. "What kind of game do you think you're playing, Samuel? This isn't a playground, and this isn't hide-and-seek. We do what we need to win. And now *I* am through playing with *you*. Either cooperate with me, or first I kill the girl and then I give the order for your brother's wife and child to be dealt with."

Before Boone can reply, another voice says, "He is not who he tells you he is."

I recognize the voice. It belongs to Tolya. Turning my head away from Ott, I see him shamble out of the darkness. He is holding a gun of some kind.

"He came to the apartment," Tolya continues. "He tried to get Yuri and Oksana to tell him where the weapon is. When they told him they did not know, he killed them. I was hiding. I heard everything."

"Is this true?" It's Ott who has spoken. He sounds shocked and angry.

"Yes," Kenney says.

"Who are you?" Boone asks. "Who are you really?"

"Who I am does not matter," Kenney tells him. "What matters is that I am telling the truth about Brecht's daughter and her child. If you want them to come to no harm, you'll give me what it is I want."

"Ott, are you working with him?" I ask the man in front of me.

Ott shakes his head. "I knew nothing about Lottie and Bernard," he says.

"How did you come to be involved with him?" I say.

"Tolya remembered the frequency on which Boone transmitted the message to his council," he says. "I did not trust Boone to give me the weapon, and so I contacted them myself and told them I had it. This man replied and agreed to meet me."

Boone looks at Kenney. "How did you intercept my messages from Berlin?"

"So many questions," Kenney says. "Again, it is not important who I am or who I am working for. The only question is, are you going to give me the weapon? As you can see, I have no qualms about killing those who stand in my way."

"You have two guns trained on you," Boone says. "And two Players who would love a chance to get their hands on you."

"You're right," Kenney says. "So let's remove one of those problems."

He turns and fires at Tolya, who sees him move and tries to get out of the way. But he's hit, and he falls to the ground with a cry. Boone and I use the distraction to leap into action. As Boone reaches for the pistol in his coat pocket, I go for mine. At the same time, we dive and roll, making it more difficult for anyone to hit us if they fire at us. We come to our feet holding our guns.

Ott has ducked behind the statue of the diving woman, and attempts to shoot at me from behind the base. But he is a poor shot, and hindered by the darkness. Kenney is more adept, but Boone is firing at him as well, and he has retreated from the footpath and into the trees. It is difficult for any of us to see the others, even with the clear sky and the quarter moon.

I hear running feet, and realize that Ott has given up trying to battle me and is running away. He is going in the direction of the trees where Kenney has hidden himself and where Boone has also disappeared. I hear several shots, then nothing.

"Boone!" I call out.

"I'm all right," he shouts back, but his voice is moving away from me. I assume that he's in pursuit of Kenney.

Tolya is lying on the ground. I have to decide whether I'm going to go after Ott and Kenney or check on him. I know Boone can handle himself, so I decide to check the boy first. I run over to him and kneel. He's still alive, but barely. Kenney's bullet hit him in the chest. There is blood on the ground beneath him, black like water in the moonlight, and blood dribbling from his mouth. He is dying.

I take his hand and hold it. His fingers grip mine tightly. He says something, but I can't hear it. I lean down.

"Sobaki," he says in Russian. *"Sobaki layut."*

The dogs. The dogs are barking.

He smiles, and his eyes empty of life. There is nothing I can do for him, so I leave him there and enter the trees. I have heard nothing since those first shots, and can see nothing at all. I am blind as I move through the woods, searching for the spots where moonlight filters in through the branches. I know I am heading toward the riverbank, but I have no idea where Boone or the others are.

Then there is another series of shots. I call Boone's name again, and he calls back. I follow the sound, and find him on the riverbank. Ott is lying on the ground, and Boone is kneeling beside him.

"Where's Kenney?" I ask.

"He ran onto the river," Boone says. "I wounded him."

He points, and I see a spattering of darkness against the snow. Blood.

"I'll go after him," Boone says. "You stay here with Ott."

I nod. Boone gets up and goes off, following the trail of blood. I turn my attention to Ott. He's holding his hand to his shoulder, and also appears to have been shot.

"It was Kenney," he says, although I have not asked.

"He thought you were Boone," I say as I pull his hand away from his shoulder. A quick check shows me that the wound is not serious. The bullet has just grazed him, slicing through his heavy wool coat but not entering his flesh.

"No," he says. "He knew who I was. He was trying to kill me."

"You sound surprised," I say. "What did you think he would do?"

Ott starts to stand.

"Where are you going?"

"We need to get to Brecht before Kenney does," he says.

"Kenney knows where Brecht is?"

"Yes," he says. "And Brecht does not know not to trust him."

"Where is he?"

"At the home of an ally," he says.

I can tell he's hesitant to tell me any more than that. I don't blame him, although he's going to need to trust me if we're going to get to Brecht.

"Did Yuri or Oksana know where you took him?"

"No. They knew nothing."

"All right," I say. "But we can't go without Boone. Besides, he might catch Kenney anyway."

"We cannot wait to find out," Ott insists. "There is no time."

He's right. But if we leave, Boone will have no idea where we're going.

"We must go," Ott says. "If Brecht is lost to us, the weapon is useless."

This is not entirely true, as Kenney himself made clear earlier. Still, losing Brecht to Kenney would not be good. I don't know who he is working for, but he's already shown that he's willing to kill anyone who gets in his way. It's possible he's even working for another line. Regardless, Brecht is a key player in what's going on. We need to protect him.

Again I think of Scylla and Charybdis. Do I help Brecht and risk losing Boone if something goes wrong? Or do I go after Boone and hope that we catch Kenney before he can reach Brecht? My heart wants to go to Boone.

He's a Player, I remind myself.

He is. And although I no longer want the weapon for myself, for my own line, I don't want to lose Brecht to someone else who might be able to use what he knows. I have to believe that the Fates will bring Boone and me back together. How, I don't know.

"Let's go to the scientist," I tell Ott.

CHAPTER 14

Boone

Kenney has a head start on me, and the darkness makes it difficult to search for him. But he's also wounded, and occasionally I spy spots of blood on the snow and ice that blanket the frozen river. As I expected, he's running toward the fishing huts, probably hoping to cross the river and escape on the other side. If he's as smart as he seems to be, he will soon stanch the wound, making it almost impossible to track him. I need to find him, and soon.

I reach the first cluster of huts. As I run by each one, I peer inside, in case Kenney is trying to hide there. But all I see are the startled faces of fishermen who look up from staring down at the lines that descend through the holes they've drilled in the ice and into the waters of the river below. Several have caught fish, which lie on the ice beside them, gasping or already dead.

Then I hear a shout, a man yelling. I run toward the commotion and find an old man standing outside his hut, shaking his fist at a retreating fighter.

"He stole my skates!" he bellows.

Many of the fishermen have pairs of skates hanging on the walls of their huts, simple blades that strap to their shoes and make traveling on the river easier. I'm certain that it's Kenney who has taken the man's pair. If so, he will now be much faster than I am.

I leave the man yelling for the thief to go to the devil, and I look for my own pair of unguarded skates. I find them easily enough, and putting them on does not take long. I have skated for years, on frozen lakes and ponds and rivers, so I know how to balance, how to push with my thighs and let my weight propel me forward. As I shoot across the ice and into the night in pursuit of Kenney, I hope that he is less familiar with skating, and that I can catch him.

Once the fisherman behind me stops shouting, the night is silent, the only sound the scraping of the skates' blades on the ice and the in and out of my breathing. I concentrate on listening for the sound of Kenney skating somewhere ahead of me, hear it coming from my right, and correct my course to head for him.

I wonder who this man is. I don't believe he is Cahokian. There's something about him that's too calculating, too cruel, for someone from my line. Not that we are less determined than other lines, or want any less to win. But I have yet to meet a Cahokian who enjoys violence as much as Kenney seems to. Then again, maybe I'm being naïve.

If he isn't Cahokian, he has somehow intercepted my transmissions to the council. Shortwave radio channels are open, of course, so anyone could hear. But my messages were coded in such a way that they would be meaningless to anyone who didn't understand what I was really saying. He did. Which means that he is an insider of some kind. He knows too much about Endgame, about me, about my family and the weapon, for this to be some kind of bizarre coincidence.

I see him ahead of me, a black shape against the night, an almost imperceptible shifting of shadow back and forth. He has to know that I'm behind him, has to hear my skates against the ice. I try harder to listen to the pattern of his movement, to match mine to his so that he won't hear me. He can't risk turning his head to look for me, so sound is all he has to go on.

We keep skating like this, him not slowing down and me not getting close enough to fire at him. I'd hoped his wound would cause some difficulty for him, but either he is stronger and more determined than I gave him credit for, or he has not been badly hurt. All I can do is keep going, trying to keep him in sight. Soon, though, if we keep going in this direction, we will come to the edge of the river. Then what?

Will I be able to take him there?

Then it occurs to me—maybe instead of trying to stop him, I should let him go and follow him. Killing him would obviously eliminate a major problem. However, there might be something more important to be gained by not killing him. Information. I don't know who he really is or who he's working for. If I kill him, I will never find out. If I leave him free to go where he wants to, though, he might lead me to answers.

It's a difficult decision. If I follow him, I'm leaving Ariadne behind with Ott. I know she can handle him. I'm not worried about that. But where will she go? How will I find her again? And what if Kenney just leads me on a wild-goose chase? He knows I'm following him, so he'll try to lose me.

Unless he's trying to get somewhere before one of us does. Like to wherever Brecht is being kept. Kenney doesn't have the weapon, so the only thing of value he has is Brecht. Maybe Lottie and Bernard, but I have a feeling that was just a bluff to get me to go along with him. He might very well know where they are, but something tells me he hasn't yet taken them. He was most likely waiting to see what I would do first.

I decide to let him go. My gut tells me that Ariadne will persuade Ott one way or another to tell her where Brecht is. If that's also where Kenney is going, then we're now in a race to see who gets there first, in which case it's best for me to stay on his tail. Even if he knows, or suspects, that I'm following him, he still has little choice but to go wherever Brecht is. He can't risk Ott or Ariadne getting there first.

Now there are lights shining on the shore. We're nearing the far edge of the river. I keep pace with Kenney as it gets closer, but I change my course slightly so that I approach the shore to his right, rather than behind him. I see him scan the area as he stops to remove his skates, then hurries up a flight of steps. He doesn't see me doing the same farther down the bank. But I can tell he knows I'm here, as several times he stops and looks around him.

He walks quickly down the path that follows the river. I stay in the shadows behind him, not letting him out of my sight but not overtaking him. I suspect at some point he is going to need a vehicle, and I'm right. He stops beside a KIM 10-50 and does something to the door before pulling it open and slipping inside.

I waste no time doing the same, using the butt of my pistol to shatter the window on an Opel and opening the door. After that, getting it started is easy, and when Kenney pulls away, I'm not far behind. I drive with my lights off, which presents few problems as the road is not busy at this time of night. But that also means that I have to be more careful about not letting Kenney see me.

Fortunately, he seems far more interested in getting where he's going in a hurry, and tailing him is not difficult. When he stops in front of an apartment building, I stop too. And when he dashes inside, I'm only steps behind him.

Kenney races up the stairs, not bothering to look behind him, until he reaches the third floor. There he stops in front of an apartment. The door is already open. He steps inside, and a moment later I hear him curse loudly. He comes running back out, only to find me standing in the hallway, my pistol pointed at him.

"Didn't find what you were looking for?" I ask.

"Killing me won't help you," Kenney says.

"Did I say I was going to kill you?" I ask. "Besides, I don't see how you're in any position to try to bargain. I have the weapon."

"And I—we—still have Brecht's daughter and grandchild," Kenney says. "If he ever wants to see them alive, I need to live as well. If I fail to report in, my associates will be more than happy to make sure Brecht never gets the reunion he longs for."

"Maybe I don't care about that," I say.

"Oh, but you do," Kenney says. "After all, they are your brother's family as well."

When I don't answer, Kenney smiles. "Your love for your family is your greatest weakness, Samuel. And that includes your love for the

Minoan. You think it's what will save you, but in the end, it will be what causes your downfall."

"Who are you?" I ask. "You're not Cahokian."

"No," he says. "You're correct about that. Nor am I Minoan, or Nabataean, or La Tène, or any of your other so-called lines. But I have been associated with many of them. I suppose you could say I am a free agent. I go where I'm needed."

"Or where you're paid to go," I suggest.

"Money can be an excellent motivation, yes."

"If you have no line, what's your interest in Endgame?"

"Curiosity," he says. "And, as you pointed out, the financial reward can be most agreeable."

"How did you find out about Endgame?"

"You hear stories," he says. "All kinds of stories. Most turn out to be nothing more than that. Occasionally you stumble upon something that turns out to be real. Well, you believe it to be real, which is all that matters to me."

"You don't believe it?"

"I've heard and seen a great number of strange things, many of which people would consider unbelievable. Do I think that you and the others are truly involved in a game to decide who survives the end of the world? No. But it doesn't matter what I believe. It matters what you believe, and how I can profit from that belief."

"At least you're honest," I tell him.

He smiles. "That's not a word many have used to describe me." There is a long pause; then he says, "So, Mr. Boone, what do we do now? I assume the Minoan or Ott has removed Brecht from here. Or perhaps he fled on his own, although I doubt that."

"Meaning I have everything I need," I say.

"Except, as I've mentioned before, Brecht's daughter and grandson. And please don't try to tell me that you don't care what happens to them. As I've already pointed out, your devotion to family is a regrettable flaw in your character, at least as far as your position in this game is concerned."

"Maybe I'll surprise you," I say.

"I would enjoy that," Kenney says. "But before you decide, I should also tell you that you might not have as much as you think you do."

I don't understand, and this must show on my face, because Kenney grins. But before I can ask him what he means, the door to the apartment across the hall from the one Kenney has exited opens and a man comes out carrying a bag of trash. The door and the man block Kenney from my view. The man, looking up and seeing me holding a gun, swears loudly in Russian and throws the bag at me as he turns and ducks back inside. I knock the bag aside, but now Kenney is running down the hallway away from me. He reaches a door and goes through it as I start to chase him.

The doorway opens onto a stairwell. Steps go both up and down. I listen, and hear clanging above me. Kenney is headed up. I follow.

I burst out the door at the top of the next flight of stairs, and find myself on the roof. Kenney is also there, standing on the edge and looking around, as if he's hoping he can somehow escape from me. Hearing the door open, he turns and looks at me.

"It must have occurred to you that you retrieved the weapon and the plans rather easily in Crete," he says. "Have you asked yourself why?"

It has occurred to me. Even though Ianthe followed us, it did seem unlike the Minoans to leave such an important thing unguarded.

"The plans you have are fake," Kenney says. "A reproduction. You were allowed to take them, and the pieces, because we wanted you to have them, so that you would feel confident locating Brecht and liberating him. Also, it was a test of their former Player, to see where her loyalties truly lie."

I think about the tube with the plans, which even now is sewn into the coat I'm wearing. Are they really fakes? I want to believe that he's lying to me, but I don't think he is. It all makes too much sense.

"I'll admit that Ott contacting me was an unexpected development," Kenney says. "It would have saved a great deal of time had he done it earlier, or if I had been able to find him to suggest a partnership myself. Although admittedly it was easier to let you and his associates do the work of infiltrating Taganka. That was indeed impressive."

"If you knew the plans were fake, and you knew Brecht was here, then why come to the meeting in Gorky Park at all? Why not just take Brecht and deliver him to the Minoans?"

Kenney sighs. "I'm afraid I let my pride get the best of me," he says. "I wanted to get the girl as well. Oh, not for the same reasons that you want her. As I said, the Minoans allowed her to escape with you as a test. A test she failed. Now there's a bounty on her head. I meant to collect it along with the reward for delivering Brecht to them."

I despise the way he's speaking about people as if they're just things to be bought and sold. I think about how he's killed people who got in his way, or who couldn't give him what he wanted. He might not be playing Endgame, but he's playing a game nonetheless. However, his goal isn't the salvation of a line; it's money.

"I will return to my original question," he continues. "What do we do now? Assuming the girl has Brecht, which I think is entirely likely, that means you have one half of the puzzle while the Minoans have the other half. You also have something else they want very badly."

"Ariadne," I say.

"Indeed. I can see that what you would like most is to kill me. However, perhaps our interests would be better served if you allow me to broker a deal."

"Deal? What kind of deal?"

"The girl's life in exchange for the scientist."

"I give you Brecht, and the Minoans let Ariadne and me go?" I say.

Kenney nods. "I'm sure I can convince them to agree to that."

"Maybe the weapon is more important to me than she is," I say.

He laughs. "Maybe," he says. "But I don't think so."

He's right, but the way he seems so sure of himself makes me angry.

"I'm a Player," I say. "I'll do whatever it takes to win."

He laughs again. "Yes, you're a Player," he says. "Just not a very good one."

I shoot him. When the bullet hits him, a look of surprise flashes across his face, but only for a second. He stumbles backward. At the edge of the roof, he teeters for a moment. Then he falls, disappearing into the night.

CHAPTER 15

Ariadne

The body falls out of the sky, descending like an angel whose wings have been broken and are now useless. It hits the ground with a dull, flat sound. By the time I reach it, blood is already staining the snow around it.

It's Kenney.

Although the fall itself would almost certainly have killed him, I see that he's also been shot. I look up at the roof, and see someone looking down at me. Although I can't see the face, I'm sure that it's Boone. I wave, and he waves back.

I kneel and search Kenney's body. In the inside pocket of his coat I find a small leather-bound notebook. I slip it into my own pocket and continue looking, but find nothing else of interest, just some money and, curiously, a handkerchief with the initials *JEK* embroidered on it.

Behind me, Ott and Oswald Brecht stand gazing over my shoulder at the body. I stand up and say, "Let's go back to the apartment."

"What about the body?" Brecht asks.

"Leave it," I say. "This is Moscow. Nobody will notice one more body on the street."

We go inside and climb the stairs. When we reach the apartment, Boone is inside, waiting for us.

"You got here before me," Boone says, glancing at Brecht.

Despite the situation, I smile. "You know I don't like to lose a race," I say.

He grins. "I'm afraid our friend Kenney had a little accident."

"So I noticed." I take the notebook from my pocket and toss it to him. "I found this on him."

Boone catches the notebook. He opens it, flipping through the pages.

"Anything interesting?" I ask.

He nods. "Very interesting. He has names and contact information for at least seven lines in here." He looks at a few more pages, then shuts the notebook and tosses it back to me. "He told me he wasn't Cahokian. That doesn't surprise me, but I wonder how many other lines he's been playing against each other."

"And how many know about the weapon," I say as I look at the pages. As Boone said, there's a lot of information. Many people would kill for the intelligence Kenney has scribbled in his book.

At the mention of the weapon, a shadow passes over Boone's face. "That's another thing," he says. "He claimed the plans we have are forgeries."

I look up. "Really?"

"He says it was all a Minoan trap to test your loyalty. You said it felt too easy. Maybe you were right."

I think of Ianthe confronting me on the dock. I told her that my taking the plans wasn't about disloyalty to my line, but it was clear she didn't believe me. Still, she surely would have relayed my message back to the others. Would any of them believe what I said about wanting to use the weapon for a greater good? Would Cassandra?

"You have the plans with you?" Brecht's question interrupts the storm of thoughts raging in my head.

"Yes," Boone tells him.

"May I see them?"

"Will you be able to tell if they're fake?" I ask.

He nods. "Most likely."

I look at Boone, who says, "Can I borrow your knife?"

I reach into my boot and remove the knife, which I hand to him. He uses it to cut the stitches on the lining of his coat, then gives it back.

He slides the tube holding the plans out of its hiding place and gives it to Brecht.

Brecht sits on a sofa, opens the tube, and tips the plans into his hand. He unrolls them and places them on a coffee table in front of him. He looks at them for a moment, running his fingers over them.

"The paper is not the same," he says almost immediately. "And the writing, while very similar to that on the originals, is different."

"You remember them that well?" I question him.

He nods. "I've studied these plans in great detail," he says. "Sometimes I even dream about them." He looks up and smiles sadly. "It's not every day you discover something this important. Evrard and I devoted much of our lives to deciphering the plans. I suspect either of us could have re-created our half from memory, although now I don't know."

"Your half?" I say, not understanding.

"He didn't tell you?" says Brecht.

"Tell us what?" Boone asks.

"The plans were in two parts," Brecht says. "They were kept separate to prevent anyone from getting the full set. Evrard had only one half."

"Where's the other?" I say.

Brecht rolls up the set of plans on the table and places them back in the tube. "Cappadocia," he says. "Hidden. We never found it."

"Cappadocia?" Boone says.

"We believe so."

"Why didn't you find them?" I ask him.

"If the device is really as powerful as we think it could be, Evrard and I didn't want the people we were forced to work for to build it," he says. "We kept the existence of the second set of plans a secret between us." He looks at me. "Do you have the pieces as well?"

"Yes," I say. "Although those may be forgeries too."

He waves a hand at me. "That wouldn't matter. We re-created those pieces from the plans."

"They're not original?"

Brecht shakes his head. "The pieces we found were damaged. Evrard and I built the ones that were in the box. May I see them?"

He cannot. The box with the pieces is still hidden in the basement of the apartment building where Tolya and the others lived. At least, I hope it is. If Tolya was correct, Kenney didn't find it.

"The box is safe," Boone says. "We just need to retrieve it."

"Then we should go," says Brecht.

"Not so quickly," Ott says. He's been silent throughout the conversation. Now we all look at him. "Kenney threatened my family. And yours," he adds, looking at Brecht. "He might have been lying, but if there's any truth to what he said, we need to find out."

"There are addresses in the notebook," I tell them. "He at least knew where they lived."

"But there are a lot of addresses," Boone says. "Including my family's and Ariadne's family's. Kenney was obviously a collector of information. But who knows what he actually did with any of it."

"I need to contact my wife," Ott says. "And Lottie."

"Can you do that?" I ask him.

"With the radio back at the apartment, yes," he tells me. "Or I can at least try."

"And then what?" I say. I look at Boone. "We need a plan."

"We can talk on the way to the apartment," Boone answers.

We leave, getting into the car Boone has stolen. As we drive back to the apartment building, we continue our discussion. I'm not entirely comfortable talking in front of Ott and Brecht, but we have few options.

"If my line has the authentic plans, and they don't know about the second set, we still have an advantage," I say.

"Also, they don't have Brecht," Boone reminds me.

"But if they have our families, they have a bargaining chip," Ott remarks.

Only if you're willing to make the bargain, I think to myself. Although I do not want to see Ott's family or Jackson's family hurt, they ultimately have nothing really to do with me. I know this is my Player mind reacting to the situation, but it's how I've been trained to assess the situation. I wonder if Boone is thinking the same thing, or if he's thinking about Lottie and Bernard.

"Excuse me," Brecht says from behind me. "But what is your plan for the weapon if it can be built?"

This, of course, is the big question. How much Brecht knows about Endgame, or the Makers, is unclear to me. Will he understand, or believe me, if I say we want to use the weapon against its creators, to try to stop humanity from being almost entirely wiped out? It sounds ridiculous even to me.

However, the way I answer him may determine whether or not he continues to help us. After all, what incentive does he have for helping to build the weapon? Maybe, like Sauer, he would rather see it lost forever. Although I don't think so. If he did, he wouldn't have mentioned the second set of plans. Perhaps he has other motivations, though, ones that work counter to ours. This is a tricky situation, and I'm unsure how to proceed.

"We want to use it to stop bad guys," Boone says in his typically brash manner.

"Ah," says Brecht. "In that case, I suppose the question I should be asking is, who do you think the bad guys are?"

"We can talk about that later," Boone says. We have arrived at the apartment building. Boone looks at me and says, "Maybe just Ott and I should go in. I can get the box, and he can try to radio Lottie or his wife."

I know what he's doing. He's leaving me to talk to Brecht. I still don't know what I'm going to say, how I'm going to explain the situation we're facing, but I say, "All right. Be quick."

The two of them leave, and Brecht and I are alone. Before I can decide how to begin, the scientist says, "You cannot trust Tobias."

It takes me a moment to realize that he means Ott. "No," I agree. "I don't think we can."

"He's not a bad man," Brecht continues. "But he is an angry one, and that makes his thinking unclear."

I turn around and look at him. "What about you?" I ask. "Aren't you angry about what's been done to you?"

Surprisingly, he smiles. "I'm a scientist," he says. "I'm trained to look at situations impartially."

"That's easier to do in a laboratory than in a Soviet prison cell," I remind him. "Are you telling me you never think about revenge?"

He shrugs. "What's done is done."

His voice is calm, but I don't know that I believe him. "And what about your daughter?" I say. "Would you not do anything to save her and your grandchild?"

This time, he is slower to answer. When he does, it's a simple "yes." Then he looks into my eyes. "So let us hope no one has taken them."

I appreciate his honesty, although it does nothing to make me feel better about what might happen later on. I say nothing, but sit silently and wait for Boone and Ott to return. This game has become crowded with players, each of us with our own motivations. Yet we are all going to have to work together, at least temporarily.

A few minutes later, the doors open and Boone and Ott get back into the car. Boone is carrying the box. "Right where we left it," he says, handing it to me.

"What about Lottie?" I ask. "Did you reach her or Greta?"

My question is met with silence. Then Ott says curtly, "No."

"That doesn't mean something has happened to them," Boone says. "Just that we weren't able to get through."

He and I exchange glances. This is going to be a problem. If Ott thinks his wife and child are threatened, he's going to be even more on edge. And dangerous.

"We need to return to France," he says.

"May I see the box?" Brecht says before anyone can reply to Ott.

I turn and hand him the box. He holds it on his lap and opens it. He looks at the pieces inside.

"Are they forgeries?" I ask.

"If they are, they're very good ones," he says. "But it doesn't matter. Only one of them is truly important." He selects one piece and picks it up. "This one."

"Why that one?" Boone asks him.

"Because," Brecht says, "this is not part of the weapon."

"What is it?" I say.

"A key," he answers.

"A key to what?"

"If I am correct, to the place where the second set of plans is hidden."

"In Cappadocia," I say.

"Yes."

Our problem has now become more difficult. France and Cappadocia are in different directions from Moscow. Getting to either one will take several days. I know everyone in the car is thinking this.

"If we get the plans, we'll have something they want," Boone says.

"It might be too late by then," Ott counters. "They already think they have everything."

Again we've found ourselves between Scylla and Charybdis. I'd like to think that Boone and I are in control of what happens next, but the truth is, it's Brecht who is commanding the ship. If he refuses to cooperate, going to Cappadocia will be useless. And if he chooses to go there instead of France, we will have to deal with Ott's reaction.

Boone looks at the scientist, who is still holding up the key and looking at it. "Well?" Boone says. "What do you think?"

Brecht closes his hand around the key. "I think I want to see my daughter again."

ENDGAME

THE FUGITIVE ARCHIVES

VOLUME 3

THE BURIED CITIES

CHAPTER 1

Boone

The town we are walking into isn't on any map.

All around us, volcanic rock formations tower to the skies, many of them ending in rounded points, like giant stone mushrooms growing out of the earth. The surrounding landscape is harsh but beautiful, rocky and treeless, covered in a thin blanket of snow that crunches beneath our boots as we ascend a hill. It feels like we're walking on the moon.

"What's the name of this place?" I ask Oswald Brecht. The scientist is walking ahead of me, humming to himself. After years spent in a Soviet prison, he is now a free man, thanks to me and Ariadne, and he seems excited to be out of there.

"It has no name," he says. "Not officially. The people who showed it to us call it *yildiz erkekler şehir,* the city of the star men."

Hearing him say *yildiz,* the woman who is leading us turns and flashes a smile. Her name is also Yildiz. She's very old. Ancient. I wouldn't be surprised if somebody told me that she'd helped Noah load the animals onto his ark. Her face is a nest of wrinkles, her eyes cloudy, her mouth toothless. Her hair is white and her body is bent. Yet she walks as quickly as any of us.

"Yildiz," she says. She points to the sky, which like her eyes is also gray and cloudy. "Star."

Ahead of her is a girl of 12 or 13. Her name is Kelebek, and she's skinny as a laundry line and serious as Warren Spahn standing on the pitcher's mound facing a batter. Her dark eyes watch everything, and I haven't seen her smile once since we met her six hours ago. She's related to Yildiz in some way that I haven't quite figured out yet. She calls her "grandmother," but this doesn't seem likely given the great difference in their ages.

"I was surprised to find her still living," Brecht says to me in a low voice, nodding at Yildiz. "She was one of the guides when we first came here, in the summer of 1944. I did not expect to find her again. We are lucky."

We found Yildiz in a Turkish city called Malatya, where Brecht had directed us so that we could look for a guide who knew this part of Cappadocia. Too much time had passed since his last visit here for him to remember how to find this place again on his own, and anyway he had been brought here and returned by an SS military escort, and so had only a vague recollection of where it was. When he admitted this, I worried we might not find the city at all. But then he discovered Yildiz sitting in the same shop where he had last seen her, selling cups of tea. Kelebek was with her. The girl spoke English well enough that, between that and the Turkish that we know, negotiations were undertaken and an agreement reached for them to escort us here.

"Have you ever seen anything like this?" I ask Ari, who is walking beside me. I really want to take her hand and hold it, but we've decided it's best to keep our feelings for each other to ourselves. Well, Ari has decided, and I'm going along with her, although really I would kiss her right in front of everyone and not care what any of them think about it.

She shakes her head. "It's beautiful. It reminds me of the wildest parts of Greece, but even stranger."

"It's kind of like the badlands of North Dakota," I tell her. "We did a session there when I was training. I felt like I was on another planet."

"The landscape was formed by volcanos," Brecht tells us. "Over the centuries, wind and rain wore away the deposits, leaving these towers behind."

"It is not the only place like it," Ott says, as if he's seen a million of these cities. I shoot him a look, but he's too busy drinking from the flask of water he's carrying to notice.

"That is so," says Brecht. "There are a number of these underground cities scattered throughout Cappadocia."

"Underground?" I say, looking at the rock towers that go *up*.

"These so-called fairy towers are spectacular," says Brecht. "But the truly remarkable parts are underground. The rock is fairly easy to dig away, and the cities extend to great depths beneath the surface, in some instances hundreds of meters."

"Who built them?" I ask.

Brecht smiles. "That depends who you ask. Most archaeologists will tell you they were built by early Christians, to be used as places of refuge from persecution. And many of the underground cities do feature churches, some with beautiful frescoes painted inside them. But this place is different."

"Different how?" Ari asks.

Brecht raises his eyebrows and grins like an excited kid. "It's best to show you."

We keep walking. We have been traveling for several days, ever since we left Moscow after springing Brecht from Taganka Prison. The journey has been a difficult one, made more difficult, at least for me, by the presence of Karl Ott. Since he betrayed us in Moscow, attempting to turn us over to Charles Kenney in exchange for a reward, I have been even more suspicious of him than I was to begin with. Kenney himself is another worry. Claiming to be working for my own council, he turned out to be a rogue operative who had somehow found out about Endgame and decided he could make a profit by doing business with the lines. But which lines he made contact with, and what kind of deals he made with them, we don't know. And since I pushed him off the roof of a building, he can't tell us.

I don't really want Ott with us at all. We needed him in Moscow, where his connections helped us get into Taganka Prison, and he helped us because we were also supposed to be freeing his father.

Unfortunately, his father was killed in the attempt, and Ott turned on us. At first, he wanted to return to France on his own to check on his family. He was worried that someone else looking for the weapon might harm them or kidnap them to use as a bargaining chip. If I didn't think he might be running back to try to make another deal with someone else, I might have let him go. Then, after Brecht said he wanted to see his daughter again and make sure she and his grandson were safe, I thought we might all be going back to France. And since his daughter was married to my brother and his grandson is my nephew, I get being worried about them. But Endgame doesn't stop so you can check in on your family, so after some back and forth Ari and I convinced them that finding the second set of weapon plans would be the best way to make sure they got to see their loved ones again. The plan now is that once we find what we've come for, we'll go back to France and figure out our next moves.

So all of us are still together, although uneasily. Even though Kenney is dead, we don't know what information he might already have relayed back to the Minoans. Nor do we know if it is true that the Minoans, or someone else with whom Kenney was working, have taken Lottie and Bernard. Since we have no way of contacting them, we can't know for certain. We may be racing against a clock we cannot see. All we can do is hope that we've made the right choice.

One thing that I am not at all surprised about is that the Minoans have put a price on Ari's head. I'm sure Kenney wasn't lying about that. What worries me more is that Cassandra didn't make an appearance in Moscow. I'd have thought that once she knew where Ari and I were going, she would have made it a point to come after us. Since we haven't seen her, that means that she either didn't arrive in time to confront us, or that she has another plan. One way or another, I sense that we will meet again, and soon.

"If people know about this place, why hasn't it been studied like the other underground cities?" Ari asks.

"It's thought to be unlucky," Brecht answers. "Although people still reside in many of the underground cities, this one was abandoned centuries ago. The locals avoid it, and as you saw, there are no populated towns for many kilometers in every direction. That is not by accident. They fear this place. They say it's cursed."

"Cursed?" Ari says. "How so?"

"It's said that if anyone disturbs the secrets hidden here, he will suffer greatly."

"Just like in *The Mummy*," I say.

Yildiz turns again. "Boris Karloff!" she says, and gives me a thumbs-up. I return the gesture, and she cackles happily. Kelebek, watching us, scowls.

"Rather like that, yes," says Brecht. "Well, more like the real-life Lord Carnarvon, who financed the expedition to find Tut's tomb and died shortly after it was opened."

"Carnarvon died from a mosquito bite, not a curse," Ott says, snorting. "I suppose Hollywood didn't find that interesting enough."

I ignore him. "But you've already opened this particular place, haven't you?" I ask Brecht.

"Yes and no. We did a bit of excavation. But we were . . . interrupted."

I stop walking, which forces Ari and Ott to stop as well. Brecht turns and looks at us. Ahead of him, Yildiz and Kelebek keep going. "What?" Brecht says, wiping his brow with a handkerchief. Despite the cold, he is sweating.

"What have you not told us?" I say.

"Nothing," he says. "I told you that the second half of the weapon plans are here."

"Yes," I say. "And do you know where, exactly, they are?"

"No," he admits. "Not exactly."

Ari and I look at each other. Ott curses. Hearing him, Yildiz and Kelebek stop and wait to see what is happening.

"You might have mentioned this earlier," I tell Brecht.

"I told you the truth in Moscow," he says. "Just not, perhaps, the whole of it."

"What makes you so sure the plans are here, then?" Ott asks, voicing what we are all wondering.

"Information gathered at the site where the first set of plans was found," he says. "There was a map. It showed the location of this city, as well as details of the underground rooms."

This is better news. "And you recall the details of this map."

"Regrettably, it was destroyed," he says. "Shortly after we arrived here to begin our search."

"Destroyed?" Ari says.

"By one of the other guides," Brecht explains. "He claimed he was doing it to prevent us from causing a disaster. He was shot for his troubles, but the damage was done. The map was gone."

"And there was no copy?" I say.

"None. And no further work was done."

"Why not?" I ask.

"The tide of the war was turning against our employers," Brecht explains. "All available minds and bodies were recalled to Germany in an attempt to defend what remained of the Reich."

"Then how are we going to find the plans now?" Ari says.

"By doing what archaeologists and adventurers have done since the first robber broke into the first tomb," Brecht says. "Following the clues."

My heart sinks. "You've had four days to tell us this."

"If I had, you wouldn't have come," he says. "And I couldn't risk losing my daughter and grandson."

This I understand—although he's wrong. Even if he'd told us that we were coming on an expedition with no guaranteed outcome, I would have come. Ari and I have agreed that we need to do whatever we can to make sure the weapon doesn't fall into the wrong hands.

Next to me, Ari makes a noise suggesting she is less than happy with this new revelation. I put my arm around her. She tenses for a moment, then relaxes against me. "Come on," I say. "It will be like a Tintin adventure."

"You know the Tintin books?" She sounds surprised.

"How do you think I learned French?" I say. Then I address Brecht. "Where do we start?"

"Up there," he says, pointing to one of the rock towers.

We begin walking again, following Yildiz as she climbs a flight of steep steps carved out of the rock and passes through a small doorway. She enters easily, but most of us have to duck to avoid striking our heads on the lintel. Inside, another set of stairs curls up the side of the tower. Yildiz is mounting them, with Kelebek behind her. Brecht follows her, then Ari, then Ott. I bring up the rear. We slowly rise up the tower, our speed dictated by Yildiz's pace, corkscrewing around and around until we empty out into a small chamber at the very top. Narrow windows spaced around one half of the room let in light and air. The other wall space is taken up by a series of crude paintings. I examine them along with the others. There is a central figure painted in white and blue. It is humanoid in shape, but without discernible features. Around it are many smaller figures, painted in brown and yellow.

"They look as if they're worshipping it," I say. "Is it a god?"

Yildiz says something in her language. Kelebek says, "It is one of the star men."

I look at Ari, and an unspoken question passes between us: *Does she mean the Makers?*

Yildiz says something more, and again Kelebek translates. "The stories say the star men first came many centuries ago. They brought with them secrets that they shared with the people here. They taught them to build cities."

"Has she ever seen one?" I ask.

Kelebek says something to Yildiz. Yildiz shakes her head and replies. "No," Kelebek says. "She says she is not that old. They stopped coming long before that. But she has seen lights. When she was a girl. Lights from their ships in the heavens."

I don't contradict the old woman. Perhaps she has seen lights. Many people have. I doubt very much they belonged to spaceships of any kind.

"Why are we looking at this?" Ott asks, sounding impatient.

"We're looking at *this*," Brecht says, walking to another part of the painting. He points to another group of brown-and-yellow figures. Some of them are holding what appear to be weapons, which are aimed at one of the tall blue-and-white figures. Yellow light appears to be bursting from the weapons and surrounding the taller figure.

Yildiz speaks.

"The people turned against the star men," Kelebek says. "They called them demons and killed them with the star men's own weapons. But then they turned against one another as well, arguing about what should be done with the weapons and the other technology the star men left behind. Many died. And so some of them who were wiser than the others destroyed the weapons to stop the fighting."

Again Yildiz says something. Her voice never wavers, as if she has told the story many times before.

"But two of the people—sisters—hid what was left of the weapons, each putting some of the parts in a secret place known only to her," Kelebek translates. "Along with the instructions for building it. In case it should be needed again. One of the sisters was our ancestor, and her story has been passed down from mother to daughter until now."

"I believe one set of pieces was hidden in the other city, where we found the first set of plans," Brecht tells us when Kelebek is finished. "I believe the second set is here, hidden somewhere below."

"But how do we find it without a map?" Ott says.

"A map would be helpful, yes," Brecht says. "But perhaps we don't need one. Before the map was destroyed, I was able to identify one point of interest, what I believe is a door. But I couldn't figure out how to open it."

"And now you have?" I ask.

"I had a lot of time to think while I was in Taganka," Brecht says. "And it occurred to me that the answer might be right in front of us. Do you have the box with the pieces?"

I nod. We've brought it with us, and I'm carrying it in a pack on my back. Now I set the pack down, open it, and remove the box.

"Open it, please," Brecht says.

I unlatch the lid and raise it. Inside, the pieces of the weapon rest inside their compartments. Brecht comes over and looks at them, then takes one out.

"All this time, we thought these were pieces of the weapon," he says. "But I think this one may be more than that."

"What do you think it is?" I ask.

Brecht turns the piece in his fingers. "I believe it is a key."

CHAPTER 2

Ariadne

"You *believe* it is a key?"

I look at Brecht, who is gazing at the piece in his hand with a peculiar expression. I wonder what he's thinking. Myself, I am thinking that we might have come a long way for nothing. I hope I am wrong.

Brecht holds the key up as if it's a holy relic. "I do," he says. "Of course, we won't know until we put it in the door."

"Which is where?" Boone asks him. He sounds impatient, and I can tell he is annoyed. As am I. Brecht has just made our mission even more difficult.

Brecht points a finger toward the floor. "Down there," he informs us. "In the underground city."

Boone sighs wearily. "Don't tell me," he says. "You're not sure exactly where it is."

Brecht shrugs. "I have an idea," he says. "The map was not entirely specific, so we might have to try a number of possibilities."

Suddenly I feel very weary. These are questions Boone and I should have asked before we even began the journey here. That we didn't is worrying to me. It suggests that we are losing our edge as Players. Or perhaps we are afraid to admit that we are running out of options, and are hoping that if we only keep moving forward, everything will be all right. More and more, I am finding it difficult to separate my personal feelings from what I should do as a Player of Endgame. Then I remind myself that as far as my line is concerned, I am not a Player anymore. Now I am Playing for myself alone, or perhaps for myself and Boone. Maybe even for humanity itself. But to what end? I still don't know. But something keeps me Playing. I want to win, even if I don't know what winning means anymore.

"I know where it is."

We all look at the girl, Kelebek. She is standing beside the old woman.

"The door," she says, in case we have not understood her meaning. "I know where it is."

Yildiz says something in rapid-fire Turkish. I don't understand all of it, but I get that she's telling the girl to be quiet. She sounds almost fearful. Kelebek silences her with a curt nod of her head, then says, "My friends and I have spent many hours here. I can take you to the door."

"You play here?" Brecht says. "Despite the legends?"

"I am not afraid of legends," Kelebek says.

Brecht laughs. "Brave girl," he says. "Very well, then. Let's be on our way."

Kelebek shakes her head. "It is getting dark," she says. "We must wait until morning."

"What difference does it make?" Ott asks. "Underground it's always dark. We'll have to use flashlights whether it's day or night."

"We won't," the girl says. "You'll see. Tomorrow. Tonight, we camp."

She doesn't wait for a reply from any of us, but turns and walks out of the room and down the stairs. Brecht laughs again. "I suppose we have no choice," he says, and starts off after Kelebek.

Ott looks at me and Boone. "Are we taking orders from a child now?"

"Unless you know where the door is, I think we are," he says.

Ott grunts. I look over at Yildiz, who still seems upset by what's happened. "Are you all right?" I ask her in Turkish.

She nods, but the worried expression is still on her face. She leaves the room, followed by a still-fuming Ott. Boone and I are alone. "Do you think she really knows where this door is?" I ask him. "Or that there's really anything down there anyway?"

"I don't know," Boone says. "I guess we'll find out."

This doesn't make me feel any better. I'm used to Boone being the optimistic one, the one who believes everything will work out. In only a short time, I've come to welcome his particularly American attitude. Or maybe all the months I spent with the dour Russians rubbed off more than I realized. Whatever it is, I suddenly need him to tell me it will be all right. I take his hands and hold them tightly in mine, staring into his eyes.

"Don't worry," he says, giving me one of his lopsided smiles, which, despite my worries, makes my heart skip a beat. "We're on an adventure, remember? Like Tintin."

I nod. "In search of buried treasure," I say.

He kisses me. I do feel better, at least a little. Mostly, I realize, I'm tired. So much has changed in the past weeks, both in my life and in how I think about things. Huge changes that have broken my world apart. I'm here now to, what, try to find a way to piece it back together? Truthfully, I don't know. My goal has been to find the second set of plans for the weapon. What happens after that, I'm not sure.

"Come on," Boone says, taking my hand and leading me out of the room. "If we stay up here any longer, everyone will wonder what we're up to."

Part of me resists leaving. I know we can't stay in the fairy tower forever, but just for a moment I want to pretend that we can, that we can live in the sky with only the sun and the moon and the stars. I want to forget about weapons, and fighting, and especially about Endgame. I want life to be normal. But I don't even know what that looks like, and so I go with Boone, leaving the mural and the narrow windows behind and returning to the real world.

Outside, the others are waiting. The sun is low in the sky, the early winter dark coming on quickly. The temperature is dropping now that the sun is fading, and soon it will be night. We need to figure out our shelter.

Kelebek, it seems, has already thought about this. "Come with me," she says, and starts walking toward a cone of rock that rises out of the ground ahead of us. There is a single opening in the volcanic rock wall, a black mouth into which the girl disappears. We follow her inside and find ourselves in a spacious room. Just how large it is becomes apparent when Kelebek strikes a flint and lights some tinder placed inside a fireplace that is carved into the rock. The smoke disappears up a hidden flue.

Brecht looks into the fireplace. "It must vent outside somewhere above."

He and I dart outside for a moment and look up. Sure enough, approximately 25 meters above, we see tiny plumes of smoke exiting from a seemingly solid spire of rock.

"Ingenious," he says. "And all done without modern technology. The builders must have scraped that chimney out one spoonful at a time."

We go back inside. Kelebek and Yildiz are kneeling by the hearth, opening packs and taking out food. Already, dishes of dates and olives are laid out. Small paper-wrapped parcels follow, and are unwrapped to reveal dolmas—grape leaves stuffed with a mixture of ground lamb, spices, mint, and raisins. Smelling them, my mouth begins to water, and I realize how famished I am after our trek.

We sit cross-legged on the floor, eating with our hands and drinking water from our flasks.

"Don't worry about water," Kelebek says when she notices me taking small sips. "There are wells here. The water is good."

"You've explored here often?" I ask her. She reminds me a bit of myself—wary of letting too much of herself show—and I hope to earn her trust by getting her to talk.

She nods, but says nothing further.

I lean over. "I used to go into the caves by my home when I was your age," I whisper, as if I am telling her a great secret. "My grandmother told me they were filled with monsters. She thought that would keep me away, but it only made me want to see them for myself."

This story earns me a smile. Kelebek glances at Yildiz. "She does not like it that I come here."

Yildiz looks up and frowns. Kelebek and I laugh together.

"What do you think is hidden here?" Kelebek asks me.

I don't know what to tell her, and so I say, "I am not sure. What do you think it is?"

"Something important," she says. "Something worth a lot. I remember the last time people came. During the war." She looks at Brecht, and her face hardens. I wonder what she's remembering. I think for a moment she will tell me, but she doesn't. Suddenly she's as wary as she was before.

"We are not like those people," I assure her, but she only shrugs and resumes eating.

When we are done, Brecht goes outside again. This time it's to smoke a cigarette. I find him sitting atop a tall rock, the flat surface of which is reached by a set of steps carved into the back. I climb up and join him. Above us, the cloudy afternoon sky has cleared, and the stars are visible against the cold blackness of space.

"One of the things I missed most while in Taganka was being able to see the night sky," Brecht says. "The daytime sky is more or less always the same, except for clouds. And they are random. But the night sky, it changes in an orderly fashion as the stars move across it. When I was a boy, my grandfather taught me the names of the constellations. Often he would wake me in the middle of the night and take me out into the yard to look up at the sky, so that I would learn what it looked like at different hours and in different seasons. My mother always knew when he did it because the next day I would be late getting up for school."

He takes a puff on his cigarette and blows the smoke out. "I hope to do the same with Bernard." Then he turns his head to look at me. "And what do you hope for?"

I think about it. "I don't know," I tell him. "For now, finding the second set of plans."

"Yes," he says. "But what then?"

This is, of course, the question hanging over all of us. We have each come here for our own reasons, reasons that may ultimately be at odds with one another. Brecht, I think, is mostly driven by scientific curiosity, a wish to finish what was started when he and Evrard Sauer realized what they had found. Also, I think, he hopes that the weapon might be used to buy the safety of his daughter and grandson, if that becomes necessary. Ott, too, I think, believes that the weapon can be used as a bargaining chip. He hides this behind talk of using it to prevent another war, but I believe he would be just as happy to use it to start another one.

When I don't answer Brecht's question, he tries another tack. "The world is filled with legends about items with unbelievable power. Items that have been hidden to prevent greedy men from finding them and using them for their own ends. Always someone finds them, and always the outcome is ruin."

"You think we should leave whatever is hidden here alone?"

"Everyone who goes in search of power believes that they will be the exception," he says. "That they will be the one with the wisdom to use the power for the right purpose." He stands up. "But what do I know? I am a scientist, not a philosopher."

He leaves me alone on the rock, looking up at the stars. But I am not alone for long. A few minutes later, Boone joins me. He sits down beside me and takes my hand. Alone in the dark, we can do this without worry, and I lean against him.

"What were you and Brecht talking about?"

"Opening Pandora's box," I say. "Finding the lost Ark of the Covenant. Wearing the Ring of Gyges."

Boone whistles. "That sounds like some conversation."

"He asked me what we plan on doing with the weapon."

"Ah," Boone says. "And what did you tell him?"

"Nothing," I say. "What would you have told him?"

"No fair," he says. "You're trying to get me to answer the question for you."

He's right. And I do want him to answer it. He doesn't.

"Are we still Playing Endgame?" I ask.

"I'm still the Cahokian Player," he replies.
"And I am still not Cahokian," I remind him.
He pulls me closer. "One thing at a time," he says. "Let's see if this key of Brecht's really is a key, and if the door is even a door. And what the hell is the Ring of Gyges, anyway?"
"It's from Plato," I tell him. "Don't they teach you anything in your American schools?"
"Just readin', ritin', and 'rithmetic," he says. "So, what does it do?"
"Makes the wearer invisible, so that he can do anything he likes without being caught. The story asks us whether or not people will behave morally if they don't fear being caught or found out."
"And what's the answer?"
"Plato says it depends on the nature of the man."
"The weapon could change everything," Boone says after a moment. "For us. For the lines. For everyone."
Before I can reply to this, Brecht appears behind us. Instinctively, we pull apart.
"You need to come down," Brecht says. "There is a problem."
"What's happened?" I ask as Boone and I get to our feet.
"It's Ott," he says. "He's disappeared. And so has the girl."

CHAPTER 3

Boone

When we get back inside, Yildiz runs up to us, speaking wildly in Turkish. She's talking so fast that I can't understand a word she's saying, but Ari does.

"She says Kelebek went to get water. A few minutes later, she realized that Ott was gone as well."

"Maybe he just went out to smoke," I suggest. "Or walk around."

"The key is gone too," Brecht tells me. He holds up the box containing the weapon pieces. It was tucked into my pack, but someone has obviously removed it.

I look at Ari. We should never have left the box unattended. It was a stupid thing to do.

"We have to find him," I say. I turn to Yildiz. "Do you know where the well is?"

She nods enthusiastically, and beckons with her hand. "Come," she says.

The three of us follow the old woman as she leaves the room and goes outside. She hobbles quickly in the opposite direction of the stargazing rock, heading for the doorway of another fairy tower. Once inside, she begins to descend a set of stairs that spiral down into the earth. It's dark, so Ari, Brecht, and I turn on our flashlights. The beams cross one another as we hurry behind Yildiz, casting looming shadows on the stone walls.

The stairs corkscrew down, as if a giant has plunged them into the dirt. I estimate we descend about 50 feet before they stop and we find ourselves in a tunnel just tall enough for me to walk in without having to bend over. It's maybe four feet wide, and we have to walk single file.

"They designed these tunnels so that enemies would have to enter one at a time," Brecht says from behind me. "It made them easier to pick off."

"That's very reassuring," I tell him. "Anything else we should watch out for?"

"Oh, all manner of traps," he says. He sounds excited. "Pitfalls. Falling rocks. In the other city Sauer and I explored, there was a room that filled with sand, burying anyone who became locked inside it. The architects of these places were very clever."

Ahead of me, Yildiz begins calling out Kelebek's name. I try to quiet her, in case Ott is hiding somewhere, but she ignores me, her frantic cries echoing through the stone tunnel. There is no answer, and she calls out some more.

My fear is that Ott took the key and followed the girl, then forced her to show him the door and open it. But since we don't know where the door is, we could be going in the totally wrong direction. All I can do is continue to follow Yildiz as she races through the tunnel. When we come to a fork, she does not hesitate as she takes the path to the left. Then there are more stairs, another tunnel. The whole time we are moving, she continues to call out Kelebek's name.

Finally she gets an answer. The girl's voice comes back, echoing through the tunnel. She doesn't sound scared, which makes me feel a little less worried. When we emerge from the tunnel into a small room, we find her standing calmly in front of what looks like a trough carved into the rock. It's filled with water. Then I hear the muffled sound of someone loudly cursing. It seems to be coming from beneath the floor.

"Is that Ott?" I ask.

Kelebek nods. "He threatened to harm me," she says coolly.

"How did he get down there?"

Kelebek steps on one of the stones, and it tips beneath her foot, pivoting on an unseen hinge. Ott's voice becomes louder for a moment, then is dampened again as the stone slides back into place.

I kneel beside the stone and test it with my hand. Once again it tips. This time I stop it from closing by holding it open. I shine my flashlight into the darkness below. Ott's face is illuminated as he looks up at me from the bottom of a narrow pit about 15 feet deep. He shields his eyes with his hand.

"Get me out of here," he says. "I think my damn leg is broken."

"Maybe you shouldn't have tried to force the girl to open the door for you," I suggest.

"I didn't," he says. "I went after her when I realized she'd taken the key."

I look at Kelebek.

"He's lying," she says instantly.

"Search her," I tell Ari.

Ari moves toward the girl, who backs away and pulls a small knife out of somewhere in her clothes. "Don't touch me!"

"Looks like he's telling the truth," I say as the girl pokes her knife at Ari.

"Of course I'm telling the truth," Ott snaps. "Now get me out of here."

"We'll need to get some rope," I tell him. "And something to make a harness out of."

I hear a grunt, then some more cursing. This time, it comes from Kelebek. Ari has disarmed her easily, and now has her arms around the girl, who is thrashing wildly and clawing uselessly at Ari. Yildiz is talking to her in Turkish, trying to calm her down, but the girl is too busy being angry to listen.

"Stop it!" Ari says. "Nobody is going to hurt you."

Kelebek, probably more worn out than she is ready to listen, stops struggling. When she's no longer trying to break away from Ari's grasp, Ari slips a hand into the girl's pockets. She pulls out the key from the weapon case.

"Why did you take it?" she asks.

"I didn't," the girl says. "I took it from him."

"Before you tricked him into stepping on the stone?" Ari says.

Kelebek nods. "I told him I would open the door for him. He gave me the key."

"She's lying!" Ott bellows. "I was going to take the key from her, but I stepped on that damn trapdoor and fell in here."

I look at Ari. I honestly don't know which of them to believe. Based on what I know of him, it's far more likely that Ott took the key and tried to get the girl to open the door for him. But something about the way the girl is acting makes me think she might not be telling the truth. Normally I would say that she's just frightened and intimidated, but I'm not sure those are feelings she's capable of.

Ari lets go of the girl, who immediately steps away and glares at all of us like an angry cat. When Yildiz attempts to put an arm around her, Kelebek shrugs her away and stands with her arms crossed over her chest.

"I'll go back and get some rope from our packs," I tell Ari. I look down at Ott and say, "Sorry, but you'll have to sit in the dark for a little longer." I let go of the rock, and as it slides back into place, once again sealing him in the pit, I hear him muttering in German.

"I'll be back as soon as I can," I say.

It's easy enough to find my way back through the tunnels. I memorized the route on the way in, and now I just reverse it. Ott is in no immediate danger, and I know Ari can handle whatever might happen, so this time I go a little more slowly and appreciate the enormous amount of work that went into creating this place. I try to imagine how it was built, how long it took to carve the stairs and tunnels out of rock, to go so deep into the ground. It's an amazing feat of engineering. I think about how much Jackson would love this place. Then I remember that my brother is dead, his body lying in a crypt beneath a church in France. I push that thought from my mind and climb the last set of stairs, back to the surface.

As I walk outside and toward the room where our gear is, I'm startled by someone coming out of the door. For a moment, my flashlight shines on the face of a boy. I have just enough time to see that there is a thick scar running across it, and that his right eye is missing. Then he turns and takes off at a run.

"Hey!" I call out. He ignores me, disappearing into the darkness.

I run after him, shining my flashlight in a sweeping motion to try and catch a glimpse of him. But he's vanished, as if he's a ghost and not a flesh-and-blood boy. There are dozens of doorways into which he could have slipped, and I know it's useless to keep looking for him, so I return to the room to see how much damage he's caused.

First I check to make sure he hasn't taken any of the weapon pieces. Fortunately, it appears that he's only taken food. A couple of the sacks have been emptied onto the floor, but the boy has really just made a mess. Still, I'm now worried. We're too far from any inhabited villages for this to be an accident. The boy must have either followed us or been sent by someone. Either way, he now knows we're here, and that could be a problem. We need to get what we came for and get out.

I put the scattered items back into the packs, then carry them two at a time to the second fairy tower, where I stow them just inside the door. It's not a whole lot better than leaving them unattended in the old location, especially if the boy is out there watching me, but it's better than nothing. I don't have time to go get Ari and the others, and I can't carry six packs with me, so it's going to have to do for the moment.

I shoulder my own pack, which contains rope and other things I might need, and I make the trek back to the room where Ari and the others are waiting for me.

"What took so long?" Ari asks when I appear.

I laugh as I slip my pack off. Of course, being a Player, she would know exactly how long it should have taken me, enough to worry that I wasn't back in time.

"We had a visitor," I tell her. I describe the boy. When I mention the scar and the missing eye, Yildiz starts to chatter, grabbing Kelebek's arm.

"You know who it is?" I ask the girl.

"I know," she says. "His name is Bilal. He plays here sometimes."

"With you and the others?"

She shakes her head. "The others make fun of him, because of his eye and his scar. I do not. I tell them to leave him alone."

"Did he take anything?" Ari asks me.

"Just some food," I tell her. "I don't think he's anything to worry about. Even if he goes back to town and tells someone about us, it will take him hours to get there. Hopefully, we'll be done by then and on our way."

I turn my attention to getting Ott out of the pit. First I take a length of rope from my pack. Then I fashion a kind of harness out of some blankets, just something for him to put under his arms so the rope doesn't hurt him too much. When it's done, I push open the stone covering the trapdoor to the pit and call out, "Incoming!" as I drop the harness down to Ott.

He puts the rolled-up blankets under his arms and threads the rope beneath them, crossing it in the back and looping it around his chest a couple of times. When it's secured, I tell him to sit with his back to the wall. Then Ari and Brecht help me pull him up, a little at a time. He yelps a couple of times as his injured leg is jostled, but eventually his head appears in the opening. Ari and Brecht hold the rope, and I pull Ott the rest of the way out. He lies on the floor, groaning, as I inspect his leg.

"Is it broken?" he asks as I run my hands along it.

"Nothing feels broken," I say. "I don't think we'll have to amputate it."

He doesn't find my joke funny. I get him to stand, but when he tries to put pressure on his foot, he stumbles and cries out. I can tell there's no way he's going to be able to walk. I help him sit again, and he leans against the wall. I motion for Ari to come with me into the hallway.

"He won't be able to come with us," I tell her. "And we can't leave him by himself. I don't trust him."

"You think he did go after Kelebek."

"I don't know," I say. "To be honest, I don't trust her, either. But it doesn't really matter. We need her, at least until we get through this door we're looking for. And now that we've had company, I think we need to do that as soon as we can. That boy might just be here by accident, but I don't want to risk waiting until morning now. Which means that—"

"One of us will have to babysit Ott," Ari says.

"Yeah," I say. "Want to flip for it?"

"Flip for it?"

I fish in my pocket and pull out a coin. A 25-kuruş piece. I hold it up. "Heads or tails?" I ask Ari as I toss the coin into the air. It flips over several times; Ari says, "Tails," just before I catch it again. I slap the coin onto the back of my other hand and hold it up for her to see.

"Have fun with the baby," Ari says, grinning.

I look at the coin and groan. I'm stuck with Ott.

"Don't let him stay up too late," Ari teases. "And no sweets before bedtime."

We return to the room where the others are waiting to see what we've been discussing. Ott looks miserable, Kelebek looks defiant, and Brecht looks hopeful.

"Ott and I will stay here," I announce. "It's probably best if Yildiz stays as well. Ari will go with Kelebek and Brecht to try and open the door."

"And once it's open?" Ott asks.

"One thing at a time," I tell him. "Now let's get going. Well, you three get going. The sooner you find the door and see if that key works, the sooner we can all get out of here."

Yildiz speaks in a low voice to Kelebek, who seems reluctant to go without her. But then Ari says to her, "You'll have to lead the way. Can you do that?"

Kelebek nods, but I can tell that she's pleased to be the most important person in the room, at least for now. She walks out, and

Brecht follows. As Ari passes by me, I stop her. "The packs are at the top of the stairs. Good luck." I want to kiss her, but I settle for giving her a wink.

"See you soon," she says, and winks back.

When they're gone, I sit next to Ott on the floor. "Did the girl really steal the key?" I ask him.

"Does it matter?" he says. "I don't think you'll believe me either way."

I laugh. "Probably not," I agree.

He's quiet for a moment, then says, "Do you know what the problem with Americans is?"

"No," I say. "But I have a feeling you're going to tell me."

"The problem with Americans," he says, "is that you don't know what it is to lose. And when you've never lost, you never know what it's like to be pushed to the point where you will do anything to win."

I think about what he's said. Maybe he's right. Maybe never losing a battle makes you forget what it's like to have nothing left to lose. But I'm not just American. I'm also Cahokian. And a Player. For me, losing isn't an option.

I wish I was with Ari, instead of here with this man I don't trust and don't like. I look over at Yildiz. She has tucked herself into a corner of the room, where she now appears to be sleeping. I wish I could do the same thing.

For some reason, the scarred face of the boy flashes across my thoughts. I wonder if I should be more worried about him showing up here. Where did he go? Why was he here in the first place? I want to think he's just curious, or was here for another reason. Whatever it is, there's nothing I can do about him at the moment. I have to stay here and remain alert for any signs of trouble.

I just wish I could shake the feeling that it might show up sooner than I would like.

CHAPTER 4

Ariadne

The trapdoor in the well room is only the first of many obstacles hidden in the underground city. After getting our packs, Kelebek leads me and Brecht down twisting corridors and through room after room, she points out many more. The people who built the city wanted very much to protect it, and themselves. But what were they protecting themselves from? Brecht mentioned that the cities were designed to guard the occupants from Christian invaders, and that is probably true in some instances. This one, however, seems designed to do more than that. It's built to make penetrating the inner rooms a deadly undertaking.

"How did you discover all these traps without setting them off?" I ask the girl as she points out yet another pitfall.

"We did set some of them off," she answers. "Bilal lost his eye to one when he peered through a hole and a sharpened stick came out. Another had her leg crushed by a stone. My friend Nesim went through a doorway in one of the towers and never came out again."

Brecht also provides information. "Those holes in the ceiling," he says as we pass beneath a stretch of corridor. "Heated oil would be poured from somewhere up above, drenching the unlucky invaders trying to come this way. I imagine there are also arrow slits in the stairwells. And that stick that took your friend's eye," he adds, speaking to Kelebek, "it might have been tipped with poison. Probably ineffective after all these years. He's fortunate; it might have killed him."

The scientist is enjoying this, as he should. Exploring places like this is his life's work. He examines every new discovery with the excitement of a child opening a gift. I, meanwhile, am wondering if our flashlight batteries will hold out long enough to complete our task. I have noticed simple straw-and-pitch torches spaced here and there along the corridors, and what look like clay oil lamps in some of the rooms, but I would prefer not to use them, if they are even still in working order after all these years.

"We are almost there," Kelebek informs us as we descend more stairs. I have been counting, and we are now nine levels underground. I feel like one of the figures from the myths, on a katabasis into the underworld in search of something precious. It's unbelievable how large the city is. What is seen on the surface is beautiful and awe-inspiring, but it only begins to hint at what lies beneath. Corridor after corridor, room after room, has been carved from the earth. This is a fortress buried underground, massive and well defended, as if a giant opened its mouth and swallowed it whole.

Ahead of me, Kelebek suddenly seems to disappear, passing through a solid wall. For a moment I think she's tricked us somehow. Then I reach the spot where I last saw her, and discover that it's an illusion. The corridor does indeed seem to end, but there is a narrow opening on either side, just wide enough to slip through. Hearing voices, I pass through the one on the right, and step into a chamber. Kelebek is there. Brecht steps in after me.

"Had you gone to the left, you would have had your head smashed in by a log on a pendulum," Kelebek says, smiling. "We tried that way first. Luckily, Nildag was not tall enough to be hit by the log."

"It's a good thing I went to the right, then," I say. She smiles again, and I wonder if she's making a joke, or if she was hoping I would choose incorrectly.

I focus on the wall she is standing in front of. The other walls are the same ordinary brown rock that the entire city is carved from. This one is different. Inlaid all across it are small rocks of some kind, arranged in seemingly random patterns. Scattered among them are empty holes. I walk over and touch one.

"Thieves must have prized some of them out," I remark.
"No," Kelebek corrects me. "Those are, I think, the keyholes."
I look at her, surprised.
"Look here," she says, and shines her light on the wall. Now I can see that the stones are set within a large circle, the edges of which at first seem to be carved into the rock. Upon closer inspection, I see that the circle is actually a separate piece of rock entirely, set into the larger wall. It's about three meters across.
"I think it must be a door of some kind," Kelebek says.
Brecht, who is examining the wall himself, laughs. "Clever child," he says. "I believe you're correct. And I suppose all we have to do is insert the key into the correct keyhole to open it."
"It can't be that simple," I say.
"Of course it isn't," Brecht agrees. "My guess is that if we choose the wrong hole, something decidedly unpleasant will come of it."
"Then how do we choose the right one? And what are these stones?"
"Opals, I think," Brecht says, tapping one with his finger. "They're not uncommon in this part of the world, although these are unusually large ones."
"And what is their purpose? They must have some meaning."
Kelebek is standing by the wall opposite the door. She reaches her hand up and does something. A moment later, there is a grinding, and a slab of rock begins to turn beside the opening we passed through, shutting it. I rush to it, but there is no way to stop the massive stone from sealing us in.
"It is all right," Kelebek says when I turn on her angrily. "Look." She nods at the wall of stones.
When I turn back, the wall is glowing. Actually, it is the stones that are glowing. Something is lighting them up from within, filling them with a pale luminescence.
"I didn't know if it would work at night," Kelebek says. She sounds pleased.
"What do you mean?"

"I've only seen it work when the sun is out," she explains. "That is why I said we should wait to come here during the day. We thought the light came from sunlight reflected in mirrors from above somehow. It seems we were wrong."

I look at Brecht. "I have heard of something like that before," he says. "A temple in the Amazon jungle had a map that could only be read when the sun shone through an opening in the wall and was reflected off a series of mirrors. I suppose the same could be done to bring light down here."

"But moonlight?"

"That is less likely," he admits.

"Besides, the moon is barely past the first quarter," I say. "And the night is cloudy. This is something else."

"Perhaps the ones who made the weapon left more than that behind," Brecht says.

I look at the wall in wonder. Could it really be that this is Maker technology? Despite all my Endgame training, I've never seen anything like it before. The glowing lights seem so out of place in this ancient, primitive place, and I can't imagine what is powering them. Whatever it is, it's both beautiful and mystifying. I step back and look at the placement of the opals in the wall. Something about it seems familiar, like a pattern, almost, but I can't place what it is. I stare at it a bit longer. Then it comes to me. "It's a map of the night sky. Part of it, at any rate."

I walk to the wall and touch a series of glowing opals. "That's the constellation Cygnus," I say. "And here is Delphinus."

"Ah!" says Brecht. "I see now. And there are Hercules and Vulpecula." He laughs excitedly. "How wonderful this is!"

"And each constellation has one missing star," I continue. "See? There is a hole in Cygnus where Deneb should be."

"So there is," Brecht says. "Instead of a stone, it's a keyhole."

I notice that Kelebek has come to stand beside me. She is gazing at the map of the constellations, a look of awe on her face. "Which one opens the door, then?"

"That's the question," I say. "What do you think?"

She studies the map, her brow wrinkled in concentration. "Perhaps the one in Hercules? He was the strongest man. He could move a stone this large."

It's a good guess. I take the key from my pocket. It's a simple shape, a cylinder about 10 centimeters long, with several notches along the sides and indentations on one end. I hold it up to the hole where the star cluster called Rasalgethi in Hercules should be. It's the same diameter as the hole.

"Let's see if he can move this one," I say, and push the key into the hole.

At first, nothing happens. Then a grinding sound fills the air. For a moment I think that the door Kelebek shut is opening. Then I turn around, and realize that the back wall is advancing toward us, pushed forward by an unseen mechanism. The room is closing in.

"That doesn't seem to be the correct keyhole," Brecht remarks.

I pull the key from the hole. The wall does not stop advancing.

Brecht looks at the wall, then at the size of the room. "I estimate we have approximately thirty seconds before we become a good deal thinner," he says.

I look at the remaining constellations. "Any ideas?" I ask.

"Perhaps it's Aquila, the eagle," Brecht suggests. "He carried the thunderbolts of Zeus. Maybe the lock needs a bolt from a god to open it."

It makes as much sense as anything. However, I fear that if I choose incorrectly again, something even worse than the advancing wall will be the result. Although if I choose nothing, it won't matter anyway.

As the grinding sound reminds me that time is rapidly running out, I keep studying the map and thinking.

Then I have a thought. "If the thing hidden behind the door is a weapon, then perhaps you need a weapon to open the door."

"Sagitta?" Brecht says. "The arrow? It's one of the least visible of the constellations. Only four stars."

"All the better," I say. "Easily overlooked in favor of the more familiar constellations."

I consider it some more. It's as good a line of reasoning as any. The fact is, this is all a guessing game. How would the people who built this door and its locking mechanism think? What kind of riddle would they use to protect their secret? There's really no way of knowing.

"What happens if you're wrong again?" Brecht says.

"Let's hope I'm not," I say.

Again I insert the key. It slides in with only a slight bit of hesitation. I feel the end connect with something and stop. I let go and wait. Then all the lights wink out. For a brief, horrible moment, I think I have chosen incorrectly again. But, very slowly, the circular door sinks into the floor, until finally the top edge of the stone disappears and we are looking into the opening of yet another corridor. This one is circular, and the entire surface is studded with glowing opals.

"It seems the journey isn't quite over," Brecht says.

I shine my flashlight into the corridor. I cannot see the end of it, so I have no idea how long it goes on for, or where it ends. Nor do I know what kinds of traps might be waiting for us. But we have no choice. The three of us step into the tunnel. Once inside, we all turn and watch as the back wall of the chamber inches closer, until finally it meets its opposite and, with a soft thumping sound, the doorway is once more sealed. We won't be going back that way, so I pray that there's another way out.

This corridor is as narrow as the previous tunnels, so we have to go single file again. I take the lead, with Kelebek coming next and Brecht last in line. As we walk through the dark passageway, the opals light the way. It feels as if we are walking in space, traveling among the stars. It's breathtaking. But I wonder if we are walking to our deaths.

"I suspect if the architects wanted us dead, we would be," Brecht says from behind me. "Perhaps this is just a bit of pageantry before we reach the treasure room."

"Or perhaps they want us to believe we are safe," I say.

"Believe me," Kelebek says. "In this place, you are never safe."

Of the three of us, she has the most experience in the hidden city. She has seen its dangers firsthand, and survived them. I find myself thinking that she would make an excellent Player. Had she been born elsewhere she very well might have been. Instead she is just a very brave girl in a very dangerous place.

The corridor continues on for approximately 100 meters. As we walk through it, I notice that in addition to the stones, there are occasionally holes in the walls and ceiling, just as there were in the door. I suspect these could be used to shoot oil, poisons, or other deadly things into the corridor. With every step, I fear tripping a trap or alarm, for something sharp to come flying at my head. But we keep going without incident.

And then the corridor ends. Not at a door or a set of stairs—it just ends. There is a hole in the floor, and when I shine my flashlight into it, I see that the walls keep going down, like the shaft of a well. But the beam disappears into the darkness. I cannot see what, if anything, is at the bottom.

"Now what?" Kelebek says. "We can't go back."

"We go down," I tell her. I slip the pack from my back and set it down. Opening it, I take out a coil of rope. "I'll go down. You two will have to hold the rope on this end." It's a risk, but one I have to take.

"I'm lighter," Kelebek says. "I can go."

I shake my head. "We don't know what's down there." I smile. "But it's very brave of you to offer."

She nods curtly, but I can tell she is pleased. When I have the rope tied around my waist, I give the other end to Brecht. "Hold this," I tell him. He nods and braces himself as I walk to the edge. Kelebek helps him hold the rope as I sit on the edge. "I'll lower myself down," I tell Brecht. "Then I can look around and see what's going on."

I slide over the edge, and Brecht and Kelebek anchor me. I place my feet on the wall and walk down it, hand over hand. All goes well for about 10 meters. Then I take a step and the wall seems to disappear beneath my feet. There is just nothing there. My other foot slips, and all of a sudden I am hanging in open space.

"Are you all right?" Brecht's worried voice comes from above me.

"The wall ends," I shout back. "I'll have to keep going on just the rope."

I pause for a moment, holding on with one hand while I use the other to shine the flashlight around. My flashlight searches for a bottom to the shaft, but there's nothing. I'm suspended in darkness. I don't know what to do. The rope is about 25 meters long, and I'll soon run out. I don't know how much farther down the shaft goes. It could be hundreds of meters. I could climb back up, but then what? We can't go back the way we came—the entrance is sealed off. Perhaps this really is a trap—and we are stuck down here to die.

And then as if in answer, there is a soft whooshing sound, and something swings across the shaft above me. The rope is severed, and I fall.

CHAPTER 5

Boone

After half an hour of listening to Ott complain about his leg, I'm ready to kill him. Fortunately, he wears himself out and somehow falls into an uneasy sleep. Both he and Yildiz are out, which gives me some much-needed quiet time. I'm enjoying the silence when I hear a sound come from the corridor. It sounds like a cough, and it happens only once, but in the quiet it's enough to make me startle. I get up and take a look. I leave the two sleepers in the room and venture into the tunnel, choosing not to turn my flashlight on. By now my eyes have adjusted to the darkness down here, and I can move down the hallway without stumbling.

Then I hear voices, low and unintelligible. I can't even make out what language is being spoken, but I can sense urgency in the exchange. Ahead of me is the point where this corridor joins the one leading outside. Whoever is speaking is standing at the Y where the tunnels split into two. I draw my pistol.

A beam of light slices the darkness ahead of me, shining down my corridor. I press myself against the wall and crouch, the light swinging above me. I hear footsteps advancing into the hallway. My options are to meet the intruders head-on or retreat to the chamber where Ott and Yildiz are sleeping. I choose to prepare for a confrontation.

Then, unexpectedly, the light is extinguished. I decide to keep going. Moving quietly, I creep down the corridor until figures begin to take shape ahead of me. I can make out two people standing in the main passageway. One is Bilal, the boy I saw earlier. The other is a man. His back is to me, and I can't see his face. Bilal is pointing farther down the corridor, in the opposite direction of our hideout. Both figures start walking.

Again I follow them, shadowing from a safe distance. Neither of them speaks, and I wonder where Bilal is leading the man.

The corridor empties into a room of some kind. A moment later, Bilal cries out. I hear the sounds of a struggle; then the boy screams again. Instinctively, I step into the room. When I do, a flashlight blinds me. Then, surprisingly, I hear someone laugh.

"Looks like I found you after all, buddy," someone says.

Something about the voice is familiar enough that I don't shoot. The man lowers the light out of my eyes, and speaks again. "This little guy promised to help me find you, but I think he was trying to lead me down a dead end. Emphasis on *dead*. I should have known better than to trust a street rat."

I turn my own flashlight on now, so that the room is lit up enough to see what's going on. I look at the man standing there, one arm around Bilal's throat, the other holding his own light.

"Hicks?" I say. "What are you doing here?"

I can't believe my eyes. I'm looking at my best friend from back home. Tom Hicks looks back, grinning. "Surprised?" he asks.

Surprised is an understatement. Hicks shouldn't be anywhere near this desolate place. For a second, I think I must be imagining him. Then he lets go of the boy's neck and gives me a hug, slapping me on the back.

"The council hadn't heard from you in days. They thought you might have gotten yourself into some trouble, sent me in to help." Hicks's tone is light and joking, as if we're back home, hanging out in my bedroom and chatting about the new Captain America comic book.

I have a million questions. I start with, "How did you know we—I was here?"

"The council was contacted by a guy named Kenney. Said he had some information about you. Said you might need extracting."

I don't contradict him, but something isn't right. Kenney didn't know we were coming here. Not unless Brecht said something to him before I pushed him off the roof in Moscow. Even then, I don't see how he would have had time to contact my council. And if he *did* contact them, what else did he tell them? My thoughts flash to Ari. Maybe Hicks isn't here to help a friend. Maybe he's the new Cassandra.

"I found this little guy in Malatya," Hicks says. His arm is back around Bilal's neck. The boy looks terrified. "Said an American had come out here and he would help me find him."

Again, something isn't adding up. I first saw Bilal more than an hour ago. Was Hicks already with him, then? And why didn't he just call out my name?

Like me, Hicks is trained as a Player. The council always has a backup, of course, usually several, ready to take the place of the main one. Just like I was the backup for my brother, Jackson, Hicks is mine. I've known him since we were kids, and he's like a brother to me. I should be thrilled to see him.

But it just doesn't feel right. Partly this is because I'm worried about Ari; partly it's because Bilal is looking at me like an animal caught in a trap. "You can let him go," I say to Hicks. "He's not going to do anything—are you, Bilal?"

"You know his name?" Hicks says, giving a little laugh.

"He's friends with the girl who guided me here," I say.

Hicks relaxes his grip. Bilal slides out from under his arm and moves away, rubbing his neck.

"Speaking of guides," Hicks says. "Have you found what you came here for?"

"Not yet," I say.

"Well, now I can help you look," Hicks says. "I bet together we'll find it in no time. But how about you put that thing away? You're making me a little nervous."

I look down at the pistol in my hand and realize I'm still holding it as if I might need to use it. I put it away. Hicks steps forward and opens his arms. I hesitate a moment before giving him another hug. He pats my back. "It's good to see you alive. You had me—us—worried. Your mom has been a wreck since you went quiet."

"Yeah," I say. "It's been a wild couple of weeks. Tell me more about what Kenney told the council."

"I don't know everything," Hicks said. "Just that you had come here chasing after something you thought was important, and that you might have gotten in over your head. Boy, I never thought I'd be making my first plane ride to a place like this."

He's trying to change the subject, which makes me more wary. But I have to keep pretending I'm happy to see him until I figure out exactly what's going on.

"So, what should we do now?" Hicks says.

I decide that I can't put off telling him about Ott for much longer. "Come with me," I tell Hicks. "I'll explain more."

He follows me back down the corridor. Bilal tails us, and Hicks ignores him. When we reach the place where the passageway branches, Bilal trots down the hallway leading to the outside. I call after him, but Hicks says, "Let him go. We don't need him anymore."

The boy gives a quick glance over his shoulder, and I think I see him shake his head, as if he's telling me not to believe what Hicks is saying. Then he's gone.

"How much do you know about why I went to Berlin?" I ask Hicks.

"Just that you were trying to find some guy who used to work for the Nazis," he says. "Another scientist. The council didn't give me too many details."

Just like they didn't give me too many, I think. *Only what we need to know to get the job done.*

I'm not sure what I should tell him about Ott. If he doesn't know about him, I could make up anything about who he is and why he's here. I think about it as we walk back to the chamber where I left Ott and Yildiz, but as we reach it, I still haven't made up my mind.

It turns out that it doesn't matter. We have a bigger problem. Yildiz is gone, and Ott is slumped on the floor. His throat has been cut, and a puddle of blood has formed around him. I kneel beside him and feel for a pulse. There isn't one.

"Is that the guy?" Hicks asks.

I ignore him. I'm trying to figure out what the hell happened here. Ott was wounded, sure, but he still would have fought for his life. And I didn't hear anything at all, which means he must have been overpowered really quickly.

"We have to find Yildiz," I say.

"Who?"

"The old woman who guided me here," I tell him.

"I thought a girl guided you here—the kid's friend?" Hicks says. "Who's this old woman, and what did *he* do to make her so angry?"

My brain is churning, trying to figure out what's going on. I don't think Yildiz did this. But then who did? And where is the old woman? Someone waited until I was out of the room. Or, I think, someone *lured* me out. And I fell for it.

I stand up and face Hicks, a knot of fear and anger forming in my stomach. "You're not alone, are you?"

"You saw the kid," Hicks says. "But I don't think he could do this, do you?"

I shake my head. "And I don't think he did do it. So, who did?"

Hicks cocks his head. "Now how would I know?"

His demeanor has changed. Everything has changed. "Why are you really here, Tom?" I ask him.

He sighs and looks away for a moment. When he looks back, it's not my friend looking at me. It's another Player. "I'm wondering the same thing about you, Sam. Why are you here? And who are you here with? See, I've been hearing some pretty unbelievable stories about you. Things I'm having a hard time believing are true about my best friend. So maybe you can clear up a couple of things."

"Like?"

"Like, is it true you're here with a Minoan girl?"

I notice he hasn't said "with the Minoan Player." I consider lying to him, telling him that Ari is dead. Instead I say nothing. Hicks waits a little while, then shakes his head. "I was really hoping it wasn't true," he says. "I was really hoping our Player hadn't turned."

"I haven't turned," I tell him. "You don't understand what's going on."

"No," he says. "I guess I really don't."

"I can explain everything," I say. "To you and to the council. When we get home."

Hicks looks at me with a sad expression. "I wish it could wait," he says. "I really do, Sam. But the council has heard everything they need to hear."

"What are you talking about?"

"They know about the girl. And how you went to Crete to get her, instead of coming home or even reporting in."

"I went to get the weapon that we—that I—recovered in Berlin," I argue.

"And then you went with her to Moscow," Hicks continues. "You have to admit it doesn't look good."

"We needed to get Brecht out of prison," I say. "He was the only one who knew where the second set of weapon plans was."

"And where is he now?" says Hicks. "With the girl? Getting the weapon, or plans, or whatever is hidden here? While you sit at home waiting? That's not what a Player does, Sam. It's not what the Sam I knew would do. This girl has done something to you."

"She hasn't done anything," I say. "She—"

"I can't say I blame you," Hicks interrupts. "If she's identical to her sister, she must have been hard to resist."

"Cassandra," I say. I look at Ott, dead on the floor. "You're here with Cassandra. She's the one who killed him."

"She's a little spitfire, isn't she?" Hicks says. "I hear you had a run-in with her yourself. Almost makes me hope Endgame doesn't start while I'm the Player. I'd hate to have to take her out."

What he's said registers in my brain. "Player? You?"

"I'm really sorry about it, Sam," he says. "The council thought it would be best if you took a break from the game."

"A break?"

Hicks pulls at his earlobe, which is what he always does when he's nervous. It's how I always knew when he was getting ready to make his move during training, and how I always beat him. He used to wonder how I knew, and I never told him. "More like retirement," he says. "See, the Minoans contacted the council and told them what was going on with you and their Player."

"So it wasn't Kenney," I say.

Hicks shakes his head. "He did contact them, but he was trying to get them to pay for information. The Minoans gave it to them for free. Guess I should have just told you right out."

"Where's Cassandra?"

"My guess is, going after her sister," Hicks says. "She was pretty anxious for a reunion." He laughs. "It's weird, huh? A Cahokian-Minoan joint mission. Kind of like if the Sub-Mariner and the Human Torch had to work together. The council sure was surprised when the Minoans suggested it."

He's been sent here to kill me, just as Cassandra has been sent to kill Ari. But I might still have a chance. I know Hicks doesn't *want* to kill me. Also, he's after a bigger prize—the weapon.

"Ariadne—the Minoan—is going right now to get the weapon," I tell him. "If we wait, we can take out her and her sister, get the weapon, and take it back home."

"Fawn said you would try that," Hicks says. Of course she did—of all my trainers, Fawn was the toughest. "She also said I should kill you before you had a chance to talk, but I couldn't do that. I thought I at least owed it to you to say good-bye. This isn't personal or anything. You're still my friend."

We stare at each other for a long time, neither of us saying anything. I can't believe it's come to this, my best friend sent by our council to kill me. When all of this started on Christmas Eve, I was supposed to come out a hero. Now I'm a traitor.

"We've fought a lot of times," I say to Hicks. "And I won every time. What makes you think you can win this time?"

He grins. "Things change," he says, and rushes at me.

I prepare to meet him. Then, unexpectedly, he stumbles. A puzzled look appears on his face. He gasps, then collapses to the ground. Someone is standing behind him, in the shadows.

"You," I say, and go for my pistol.

Something stings my neck. A strange burning sensation spreads out, and my throat constricts. I fight to breathe, and my vision blurs. I stagger back, fumbling for my gun, but my hand doesn't seem to work. I fall, and the last thing I see before I slip into blackness is my attacker stepping over Hicks's body and coming toward me.

CHAPTER 6

Ariadne

I fully expect to die.

As I fall through the darkness, I do not scream or cry out for help.

I look up at the faint, bluish glow coming from the opening above me. It is like looking into a blue eye, an eye that watches me without blinking. I marvel at the ingenuity of the people who built this place. Whatever is hidden here, they did not want me to reach it. I am only sorry that I have failed in my quest. Also, that I will never see Boone again.

Then I land on something not entirely soft, but also not the hard rock or pointed spikes I expected. The force of my fall pushes me down; I choke as something fills my mouth, and at first I assume I am in water. But this is thicker somehow. I fan my arms to slow my fall, then head back up. My body is floating on some kind of liquid, and I smell a strange odor. The breath has been knocked out of me, so it takes a moment for me to realize what it is: oil. It's unpleasantly slick on my skin, and it clings to my clothes. When I can breathe properly again, I splash around in it, seeing if I can touch the bottom. I can't. Curiously, I have managed to hang on to my flashlight, and I shine it around.

I am just in time to see a massive mechanical arm swinging down toward me out of the blackness, its hand clenching an unlit torch. The torch breaks the surface of the oil with a splash; then the arm is still. I run my light up it until I see where it is connected to one of the walls in such a way that it can move up and down.

At first I don't understand its purpose. Then it occurs to me that had the torch been lit, the oil in which I am swimming would now be on fire, and I would be burning with it. It's yet another deadly construction, and I have survived it only because the torch for some reason failed to light. A lucky break.

Just in case, I need to get out of the oily pool as soon as possible. I shine the light around until I see a ledge of rock. I swim over to it and pull myself out. I kneel on the rock and look around. In front of me I make out a narrow doorway in one of the smooth walls.

From above me, Brecht's voice breaks the silence. "Are you alive?"

It's a perfectly reasonable question, but it sounds so ridiculous that I laugh. "Yes," I call back. "I'm fine."

"I don't suppose there's an easier way down?" he shouts. "A set of stairs, perhaps?"

"I don't see one," I tell him. "You're going to have to jump. Use what's left of the rope to go as far as you can, then let go. And don't linger at the end, or you might lose your head."

"How reassuring," he says.

As I wait, I inspect the doorway. Given that every new leg of the journey has presented an opportunity to be maimed or killed, I have no idea what to expect next. There is nothing extraordinary about the doorway at all, no carvings or decorations. It's suspiciously uninteresting. Which is exactly what makes me fear it.

A moment later, a small splash causes me to turn around. Kelebek is sputtering and choking in the pool. Then she is swimming over to me. Not long after, there is a larger splash as Brecht too makes the plunge from above. They swim to the ledge where I'm standing, haul themselves up, and try to scrape as much oil from their bodies as they can. I point out the stone arm dipping into the pool.

"Whatever they used to set the torch ablaze must have dried out over the centuries," I say.

"Fortunately for us," Brecht says. "That would be a most unpleasant way to die."

"Was the other box guarded this heavily?" I ask Brecht.

"No," he says. "Although I suspect it had already been taken from its original hiding place, as we found it with some other artifacts. I must say, I prefer that kind of archaeology." He looks up. "We can't go back, so I suppose we have to go forward. I wonder what else they have in store for us."

I indicate the doorway. "There's only one way to find out."

We approach the opening, and I peer inside with my light. Beyond it is a small, round chamber approximately three meters across. As in every other room we've seen, the walls here are smooth rock. However, in this one there are rough metal rods about 30 centimeters long sticking out of the walls at random places beginning about two meters up. I shine the flashlight beam around and see that the walls extend upward with no visible ceiling. It's as if we're standing at the bottom of a well.

In the center of the room is a solid block of stone. On top of it sits a metal box.

"Do you think that's it?" Brecht asks. "It's roughly the same shape and size as the other one."

I wonder if our search has finally come to an end. But I sense that there is danger here, too. An unseen threat that lurks in the darkness. What might the builders of this hidden city have in store for this last challenge?

Suddenly, Kelebek darts past me and into the room. I call out to her, but she ignores me. She runs to the box and puts her hands on it. I freeze, waiting for something terrible to happen. But nothing does. I grab her arm and pull her back.

"I was only looking," she says.

Brecht comes in and also examines the box. As he runs his fingers over it, there is a soft clicking sound. Circular openings appear on each end. Brecht bends down and shines his flashlight inside.

"There appear to be handles inside," he says. "You must reach in and turn them simultaneously to release the lid."

Before I can tell him not to, he puts his hands into the box.

I hold my breath. Just because we can't see the danger doesn't mean it

isn't there. I have a bad feeling about this.
"Just as I thought," Brecht says. "The handles inside turn. Like so."
He makes twisting motions with both hands. There's another click.
But no lid rises. Instead, Brecht grunts.
"What?" I ask.
"Something has closed around my wrists," he says. "A band of metal."
He tries to pull his hands free, but they're stuck.
There's another click, and this time Brecht cries out in pain.
"They're tightening," he says. Again he tries to pull them loose, to no avail. He tries to lift the box from the block. "It's fastened somehow," he says.
A moment later, blood begins to drip from the openings in the box.
Brecht howls like an animal with its leg in a trap. More blood appears, flowing quickly.
"My hands!" Brecht gasps. "It's cutting off my hands!"
I hear a sickening crunch—the sound of bones being broken. Brecht wails. Kelebek grabs my hand, and I feel her trembling. But there's nothing I can do. Brecht is screaming wildly now as the machinery of the box eats away at his flesh and bone and muscle. Then he pulls his right arm away. A stump emerges from the box, the end raw and bloody. A knob of bone protrudes from the ravaged meat, and blood sprays thickly from the severed artery. He pulls his left arm out and it too is maimed. He cradles his ruined arms to his chest.
Then the top of the box opens to reveal a familiar-looking, smaller box, the twin to the one we already have in our possession. Before I can think twice, I reach inside and snatch it out. I don't even try to open it, but tuck it into my pack, still dripping in Brecht's blood.
Brecht is breathing heavily, but has stopped screaming. He sinks to his knees as blood pours from him. He's going to die soon. There's nothing I can do.
"It seems they needed one final sacrifice before giving up their treasure," he says.
I kneel beside him and try to tend to his wounds. But before I can

begin, there is another sound, a hissing. I look up. Kelebek is standing below one of the metal spikes that protrude from the walls.

"Gas," she says, sniffing.

Brecht looks at me. "Go," he says.

"Where?" I say.

He looks toward the ceiling. "Up. Climb the spikes."

Now the final trap makes sense. By removing the thief's hands, the builders removed the one chance he might have of surviving. Opening the box to reveal the contents was meant only to show him what he had given his life for. But I still have my hands.

"Go," Brecht says again. "Now."

I stand up and run to Kelebek. Lifting her under the arms, I hold her up until she can grab the lowest of the iron spikes, which I now see have holes in the ends for the gas to pour out of. "Climb!" I yell at Kelebek. "Climb as fast as you can!"

She begins to scale the wall, reaching for the next spike above her and grabbing it. She is just tall enough to get from one to another. As she begins her climb, I turn back to Brecht. As I do, there is a scratching sound, and the lowest spike bursts into flame. I jump away so that it doesn't ignite the oil that still covers my body.

"You can build it," Brecht calls to me. "Now go!"

I have to leave him. I leap up, avoiding the burning spike, and grab the next. My fingers are slick with oil, and I almost slide off. But I manage to hold on and pull myself up. I reach the next spike just as another blossom of fire opens between my fingers. Somehow, the spikes are timed to erupt in sequence. For anyone climbing too slowly, it would mean a painful ending.

I look up and see Kelebek moving steadily but slowly. I call out to her to hurry, then follow my own advice. We will have to climb a very long way to get back to the surface. If the chamber even goes that high.

It could be another trick, a final horrible ordeal meant to torment anyone lucky or clever enough to get this far.

It occurs to me as I climb that whoever hid the weapon and its plans here wanted to provide a chance, however small, of success. Had they wanted to ensure the death of anyone entering the gauntlet of traps, they easily could have. But after each trap there has been a way of escaping. Perhaps they hoped a worthy champion would someday come along. Am I that person? I have the treasure. However, I have it only because Brecht gave up his hands and his life for it. Had he not done so, would I be the one bleeding out on the floor below?

More of the spikes are now breathing fire, and the heat is rising all around me. Now there is smoke, too, which burns my lungs. I cough, then push myself to climb more quickly. Soon I am right below Kelebek, whose shorter arms and smaller size make it more difficult for her.

"You can do it!" I say to her. "Climb like a monkey in a date tree!"

The heat and the smoke become more intense, and our bodies grow more and more weary, but we keep climbing, as if we are escaping the mouth of hell. The skin on my hands burns. My eyes sting. Every muscle in my body screams out for me to stop. But still I climb.

Eventually, I notice that the chamber is growing narrower, closing in on itself until it is barely two meters across. This forces the smoke rising from below to grow thicker, and it becomes more and more difficult to see or breathe. I am grasping for spikes, grabbing whatever I can find. I pray that Kelebek can do the same, and with every pull upward I fear I will either find her collapsed and hanging from a spike or hear her fall past me.

Then, like a miracle, I feel a breeze. We are approaching open air! This gives me renewed determination, and I force myself to climb some more. My blistered hands scream for mercy, but I give them nothing.

Then I am out. Hands are pulling me up, away from the smoke. I roll over onto my back and look up at the stars. Then I see the face of Yildiz looking down at me. She pours fresh, cool water into my mouth from a flask. I choke, then drink deeply. Nothing has ever tasted so sweet.

I sit up. Kelebek is sitting not far away. Her face is grimy with oil and smoke, but her smile is triumphant. "I told you she was worthy," she says. At first I think she is speaking to me. Then I realize that her words are directed at Yildiz.

"We call it the devil's chimney," Yildiz says, nodding at the hole from which we've just emerged. "Only the one who can beat the devil escapes it."

I don't understand what she's saying. Did they know about this? But before I can ask any questions, she says. "Come. We need to go. There are others here."

"Others?" I say.

The old woman nodded. "Two," she says. "One like the boy. One like you."

"Like me? You mean she looks like me."

"Like a mirror," she says.

Cassandra. Cassandra is here. How, I don't know. But I am not surprised.

"Where's Boone?" I ask Yildiz.

She smiles down at me. Suddenly I feel overwhelmed by fatigue. Unnaturally tired. I look at the flask still in Yildiz's hand. "What have you done to me?"

"Sleep," she says. "You will see him soon."

CHAPTER 7

Boone

I wake up curled on the floor with my hands tied behind my back. I pull against the ropes, but they're knotted too tightly, and all I manage to do is make them cut into my wrists. My thoughts are still foggy, and I shake my head, trying to clear it.

"Do not struggle," a man's voice says.

We're bobbing up and down, and at first I think that I'm on a boat. Then I notice the flame. I look up and see something large looming overhead like a black moon. It's a hot-air balloon.

"Who are you?" I ask, my voice thick and raspy. "Where are we going?"

"Soon," he says. "And do not try to get out of the ropes. I will kill you if I must."

I shut my eyes and try to remember. The last thing I saw was Hicks lying on the floor. But there was something before that. Something important. Then I remember. Bilal. The one-eyed boy. He was standing behind Hicks, holding a tube to his mouth. A blowgun of some kind. That's what the stinging in my neck was, a dart, tipped with a sedative, apparently. I assume Hicks was knocked out with the same thing. But where is he? And where is Ari? And Cassandra?

The man piloting the balloon is whistling. The sky around us is still dark, and I wonder how long I've been out, how long we have been sailing through the night. And, of course, I wonder where we are going. Does this have something to do with the Minoans? Or is someone else also involved? I have many questions, and no answers.

I try to rest, to conserve my strength for whatever is coming. The man's whistling goes on and on, and I wish he would stop.

Not long later, I feel the balloon begin to descend. Then there's a slight bump as we land on something. The man jumps over the side of the basket, then returns and pulls me to my feet. I climb out, which is difficult with my hands tied, and find myself standing on what seems to be a platform carved into the side of a mountain. There's a doorway in the rock, flanked by burning torches.

And we are not alone. A man stands in front of the doorway. He is very old, with a beard that reaches to his waist. He looks like someone I would see selling dates in a Turkish marketplace, or sitting on a stoop, smoking. When I step closer to him, though, I see that his eyes are clouded over. He's blind.

"Welcome," he says in English.

"Who are you?" I ask. "Where am I?"

"My name is Doruk," he says. "And you are at the eastern gate of the Mountain of the Star People." He looks at the man who piloted the balloon, who is standing beside me. "You may untie him."

The man moves behind me and works the ropes loose. As soon as my hands are free, I rub my wrists to get the blood flowing back into them. "Why am I here?" I ask Doruk. "And where is Ariadne?"

"The others are being delivered to their gates," Doruk says.

"Others?"

"The four of you," he says. "The ones who attempted to find the treasure hidden in the underground city, and the ones who came to stop them."

"I don't understand," I say. "Ari went looking for the weapon. Did she find it?"

Doruk shakes his head. "There was no weapon," he tells me. "Not in the buried city. Nor is what you already found a weapon. It is not even part of one."

Now I'm really confused. "Then what is it?"

"A test," Doruk says. "Designed to find someone worthy of taking the real weapon. Clues to a larger mystery."

What he's saying starts to sink in. "You're telling me that the pieces

and plans we have are worthless?"
"Not worthless, no. But not what you believed them to be."
"People died for those things," I say. "My brother died. The scientist who guarded them died. Other people too. Good people."
"I am sorry to hear that," Doruk says.
I still don't understand what any of this has to do with why I'm standing on the side of a mountain. At the moment, I'm trying not to think about everything that's happened because of the plans that Doruk is now telling me aren't actually plans.
"There is a weapon," he says. "A weapon of enormous power. I am part of a group whose lives have been devoted to keeping that weapon hidden, safe from those who would misuse it. For centuries, our people have kept its secret, waiting for someone to come claim it."
"Great," I say. "Well, here we are. Didn't Ariadne find whatever was hidden in the other place?"
Doruk nods. "She survived the ordeal, yes."
Hearing him say this, I find myself smiling. I knew Ari would do it.
"Then didn't she pass the test? Shouldn't she be given the weapon?"
Doruk says, "There is a final test. The girl bested our traps, and did so admirably. She won the chance to compete for the bigger prize. Now she must best her enemies. Or, perhaps, they will best her. And you are being given the chance to help her, or to win the prize for yourself, if you choose to turn against her. Each of you will enter the mountain through a separate gate. You will find your way to the center, where the thing you seek is hidden."
"A race," I say.
"Not just a race," Doruk answers. "No one can reach the center on his own. You may have to assist your enemy in order to advance, or ask for assistance yourself. Whether you survive what awaits you inside depends on your ability to choose wisely."
"Do we get any weapons?" I ask him.
"There are weapons of various kinds to be found inside," he says. "But your greatest weapon is yourself."

"You sound like one of my trainers," I tell him.
"And you get this." He steps forward and hands me something. It's made of some kind of bronze-colored metal and looks like an orange slice. The surface is etched with designs, and there are raised dots all over it.
"What is this?"
"A key," Doruk says. "Or part of one. You each have been given a part. But only together will the key work."
"So someone needs to get all four parts," I say.
"Or work together and combine them," he suggests.
I laugh. "I don't think that's going to happen." Doruk says nothing to this, so I say, "When does this race start?"
Doruk looks at the man who brought me to the mountain. "Give the sign," he says.
The man draws a flare gun from inside his *cübbe*, and aims it skyward. He pulls the trigger, and a flare shoots into the night with a shriek. A moment later, it bursts in a shower of sparks. Shortly after that, there are answering whistles from around the mountain.
"And so it begins," Doruk says. "You may enter."
He steps aside, and I approach the doorway in the side of the mountain. For a moment it looks like a mouth waiting to close around me. I stand there, peering inside. I'm exhausted and annoyed, tired of searching for a weapon that always seems to be just out of reach. If it even exists at all. I don't know who set all this up, but I wonder what would happen if I refused to play this latest game. Would I be allowed to leave? Somehow I don't think so. And I won't find out, because I'm going to Play. Not just because I want to see if there really is a weapon, but because it might be the only way I'll get to see Ari again. And if Hicks is one of the other people Playing, I'm sure as hell not going to let him win. Him or Cassandra.
I walk straight into the mouth of the mountain, daring it to eat me. Almost immediately, a stone door descends, sealing me inside. But it's not dark. There are torches mounted on the walls, and they provide

light to see by. Almost everything that I had in my pockets has been taken from me, so I look around for anything that might be useful as I face whatever is ahead of me. There is nothing.

With only one way to go, I walk forward. The corridor goes on for 10 yards or so, straight into the mountain. Then it ends abruptly, and I am standing at the mouth of a cavernous space. It's as if the mountain has been hollowed out. Torches flicker all over the place, but there is not enough light to see exactly how large the space is. I can't see all the way up or all the way down, but it looks as if there could be hundreds of feet of empty space in both directions.

In front of me is what looks like a narrow bridge made of wood slats. Rope handrails stretch out into the darkness, attached to poles on either side. I go back and take up one of the torches, then start to step onto the bridge, when a voice calls out, "Don't." The echo in the hall distorts it, but I would know it anywhere.

"Ari?" I call back.

"It's not anchored to anything," she calls back. "If you step on the end, it will tip down and you'll fall."

I put my foot on the first slat and press down. Just as Ari said, it tips.

"Where are you?" I ask Ari.

A light flares directly across from me, and I see Ari's face illuminated by the flame of a torch. She is about 50 feet away. Seeing her, my heart jumps in my chest, and I want to run across the bridge to her.

"How do we get across?" I call.

"I'm guessing there are four bridges," she says.

"That would be correct," says a voice to my right. I turn and see Cassandra standing on a ledge.

Hicks appears on my left, also holding a torch. "I bet something is holding them up in the center," he says. "Like that time the trainers made us balance on the ends of a board on top of a rock. Only here there are two of them. They're like the blades of a fan, or a weird crossed teeter-totter. The only way to get to the middle is for the four bridges to be equally weighted. That will balance the whole thing."

"And what happens when we get to the center?" I say.

"Only one way to find out," Hicks shouts back.

I shine my torch around, trying to better assess the situation. I'm assuming that the doors the other three came through are shut like mine is. And there's no way to climb up or down. We have to go out onto the bridges.

"Hicks and I weigh more than you do," I call to Cassandra and Ari. "We need to be closer to the center. Are we all agreed on that?"

"Agreed," Ari says.

"Cassandra?" I ask when there's no answer from her.

"We go on three," she says, ignoring me. "One. Two. Three."

I've barely had time to think about it, but she's not waiting for anyone else. I see her torch move as she darts onto her bridge. We all have to scramble to do the same. I step onto the walkway and feel it start to dip under my weight. I quickly take some steps toward the middle, and it corrects itself. But the others are moving as well, making it difficult to know how far I need to go. I feel the whole apparatus start to move like a Tilt-A-Whirl at the county fair. I drop the torch I'm holding in order to grab the handrails, and it tumbles away into the darkness. I can see it falling end over end. Then there's a splash, and it goes out.

At least now I know what's beneath us, and water is better than rocks. But that's not my immediate worry. The platform is still tipping. Ari's end is rising, while mine is falling. I have to get closer to the center. Holding the ropes, I propel myself forward enough that it evens out. But Hicks has had the same idea, and now the platform swings the other way.

"Everybody stop!" I shout. "We need to work together!"

To my surprise, the others listen. The bridges are now more or less even, but the smallest movement will cause them to tilt. To make things more difficult, three of us have dropped our torches. Only Hicks has managed to hang on to his.

"We all need to move toward the center," I say. "One at a time. Hicks, you go first. See if you can tell what we're working toward here."

Off to my left, Hicks's torch advances a little. The platform tilts, but not much.

"There's something in the middle," Hicks says. "A kind of wooden post with things sticking out of it. I can't tell what they are. I need to get closer."

"Everybody take three steps in," I say.

Again the platform bobbles a little, but remains steady.

"Can you tell what it is now?" I ask Hicks.

"It's knives," he says. "Knives stuck in a piece of wood."

Suddenly my end of the platform starts to tip down. I realize too late that Cassandra is running across her bridge. At the same time, Hicks realizes what's happening and tries to beat her to the weapons. The entire platform sways as the distribution of weight changes dramatically.

"Stop!" I shout. But it's too late. The platform lurches. I grab on to the rope handrails, but my feet slip, and I'm hanging out over empty space. I hear Hicks yell as he falls. There's a splash, and then a second one.

"Ari?" I call out.

There's no answer. The platform tilts even more, so it's now almost vertical. I try to wrap my leg around the rope handrail, but I can't swing myself up enough to reach it. Then I hear a chopping sound coming from above me, and the rope gives way. Someone has cut it.

I tumble into the darkness. I try to remain vertical, so that I enter the water feet first and minimize the impact. When I do, I immediately curl into a ball, slowing my downward motion. The water is surprisingly warm, but it also stings my eyes more than water should. As I swim for the surface, it occurs to me that minerals from the rock have probably dissolved in it, making it more alkaline.

My head breaks the surface. Torches on the surrounding walls throw flickers of light over the water, but it's still difficult to see. I hear splashing nearby, and turn toward the sound, ready to fight if need be. But it's Ari.

"Water again," I say, thinking about how often I've been wet while searching for the weapon. "At least this time it's warm."

"The water isn't the problem," she says. "We're not the only things in here."

CHAPTER 8

Ariadne

I don't know what is in the water with us, but I know that it's large.
"Some kind of fish, I think," I tell Boone.
"Fish?" he says. "Inside a mountain?"
"I've seen all kinds of things in the caves in Crete."
"Well, I don't want to wait around to find out what it is," he says. "Let's get out of here."
"And go where?" I say. "We have no idea how large this lake is."
"Is there any sign of the others?" he asks.
In answer, there is splashing to our right. Someone is swimming. I'm guessing it's the other man, the one Boone called Hicks, as Cassandra would never make so much noise. I still don't know who he is, and would like to ask Boone about him, but there are more pressing matters.
"The tower the bridges are attached to is over there," I say. "Maybe we could at least get out of the water."
It's as much of a plan as I have at the moment. I wish I knew where Cassandra was, as my bet is that she's more dangerous than anything lurking in the water. "Do you know what happened to my sister?" I ask Boone.
"Last time I saw her, she was trying to kill me," he says. "She got her hands on at least one of the knives."
"That's one knife too many," I say as we begin to swim.
We don't get very far before I feel something pass by my leg.
"I think we need to swim faster," Boone says, and I know he's felt it as well.

We increase our pace. The stone tower that is our goal is not far ahead. Then I again feel something beneath me. This time I receive a hard bump, as if whatever it is has hit me with its head. I'm lifted from the water a little bit. I think of dolphins, and how they investigate objects with their snouts. But I'm sure this is no dolphin.

"What the hell?" Boone says.

I look over in time to see him thrown into the air. He rises at least two meters, then splashes down again. As he does, I see something white slithering just above the water. Before I can make out exactly what it is, it sinks below the surface again.

"I really wish we had one of those knives," Boone says, treading water beside me.

I am about to tell him to keep swimming when a scream issues from the darkness, accompanied by frenzied thrashing. Something is attacking Hicks, and it's happening just out of our sight. All my instincts tell me to swim away from it, but I can't.

"We can't let it get him," I tell Boone. "We need his part of the key."

I start swimming. Boone is right beside me, matching me stroke for stroke. We follow the screams. I try not to think about what might be attacking him.

I find out soon enough. Suddenly the screams are cut off. As Boone and I pause, looking around, the water right in front of us erupts like a geyser. A beast emerges, pale white and slick with slime that glistens in the firelight. Its huge head is fishlike in appearance, and its eyes have the telltale milky appearance that indicates blindness. It opens its mouth, revealing translucent teeth that hang like icicles in the cavernous maw.

Just as quickly as it appears, it dives again. The water underneath me surges as it passes directly below where Boone and I are floating, helpless, with nothing to protect ourselves but our bare hands. Then the water breaks again, and Hicks appears. He gasps for air and claws at the water. He flails, trying to get to me and Boone, more afraid of the thing that pulled him under than he is of us.

He's almost to us when the beast rises again behind him. He turns, sees it, and screams in fear and rage. "Get away from me, you goddamn bastard!" he yells.

The thing seems to obey him, ducking down. But it's only toying with him. It strikes, pulling him under by the legs. His arms fly up as he's sucked down, his hands waving frantically for a moment before the water closes over them.

"Jesus Christ," Boone says. "We can't fight that thing."

"The key," I remind him. "We can't lose it."

There is another splash, this time as something falls from above. Cassandra. I see her body, not more than a shadow, as it slips beneath the water and disappears.

"Things just got worse, didn't they?" Boone says.

"Maybe not," I tell him. "If she has a knife, that creature will feel it pierce its heart."

"And she'll also get Hicks's piece of the key," Boone reminds me.

There's nothing I can do about that at the moment, so I wait to see what happens next. I don't have to wait long. Moments later, the water parts as the monster comes back up. This time, Cassandra is clinging to its side, like Perseus battling the sea serpent. Her knife is buried in its flesh, and she's hanging on to it. Something—blood, or whatever pumps through this creature—flows from several wounds in its side.

Even though we are enemies now, I have to become her ally, at least for this battle. I dive down, kicking hard in the direction of where they are. I can see the thing's body coiled below the surface, thick and ghostly. It's even larger than I thought, at least 10 meters long. Its strength must be enormous. I have no idea what I can do against it.

There is something else there as well. Hicks. He floats in the water, facedown and unmoving. His limbs are splayed out and lifeless. I change course and head for him. If I can find the piece of the key he was given, I don't need to help Cassandra fight the beast. Although if it takes her, then her piece of the key will be lost. No, we need to work together. We have already failed at that on the bridges above. We can't fail again.

I decide to go for the key first. Something knocks against me, and I startle, thinking it's another creature. But it's Boone. He points in the direction of the monster. I understand. He will go try to help kill it, while I go to Hicks. He disappears, moving with strong strokes away from me, and I turn back to the body in the water.

I reach Hicks and hold him by the belt, searching his pockets as quickly as I can. There is nothing in the pocket of his shirt, or in the ones in his pants. Also, I am running out of breath. I need to surface soon. I make one last try, running my hands over as much of his body as I can cover. This time, my hand finds something inside one of his boots, a bump that feels out of place. I fumble for the laces, trying to untie them as the last of the air in my lungs runs out. I manage it, and slip my fingers inside the upper part of his boot. There is something there.

Before I can pull out what I'm sure is the piece of the key, there is a violent tug and Hicks is ripped away from me. Off in the distance, I see the creature that Cassandra and, presumably, Boone are still wrestling with. This means there is another one. At least one.

I push for the surface, breaking through and taking a breath.

"There are more!" I call, not knowing if Cassandra and Boone can even hear me.

While the presence of more eel-like things is worrisome, I am more concerned about not getting the piece of the key that was secreted inside Hicks's boot. Although I fear it will be futile, I dive down again, scanning the water for any sign of him. I see nothing at first. Then there is a flash of white beneath me, deeper down. I turn and head for it. Something is swimming away from me. Then it circles back, heading directly for me.

I hover in the water, waiting for it. As it nears, I see that it has Hicks's body in its mouth. His head is thrown back, his legs flapping in the water. His boots are still on, which gives me hope. If I can grab on to him, maybe I can still get the piece of the key. And as long as he remains in the creature's mouth, it won't be able to bite me.

Not that its teeth are its only weapon. Its size alone could be deadly, as could the tail that writhes and coils behind it. *It's just a beast,* I tell myself as it hurtles toward me. *And beasts can be killed.*

As it nears, it rises above the water, intending to swim over me, perhaps to crush me with its tail. I reach out and manage to grab Hicks's limp hand, as if he has extended it in help. My fingers interlock with his, and I am pulled along beneath the monstrous fish. Water surges up my nose, and I start to choke. I cannot see. I cling to Hicks like I would a lover, and am lifted up and up.

The creature breaches. As it does, it emits a horrible shriek, as if it's communicating with its companion. I've never heard such a peculiar, awful cry. The other monster answers, and its reply is even worse, filled with pain and rage. Although my thoughts are focused on not losing my grip on Hicks's body, I recognize the sound as one of a wounded animal. Whatever Cassandra and Boone are doing, it seems to be working.

I suck in air right before we dive again and the water closes over my head. The beast heads down, most likely in an attempt to drown me. We pass through a cloud of something dark, and I realize that it's the blood of the other animal. The one holding Hicks in its mouth suddenly opens its jaws, and Hicks falls out. I fall with him, both of us sinking. The creature passes over us, and as it leaves, it flicks its tail, which hits me with great force, pushing me even farther down.

I wrap my arms around Hicks and we spin away. I can see nothing, and now I don't even know which way is up and which is down. My lungs ache, and there is a pounding in my head that makes it difficult to think. The rough skin of the fish has scraped my arm raw, and it stings badly.

I ignore all of this and work my way down Hicks's body to his feet, where I find the boot still in place. I reach inside and pull out the piece of the key. Gripping it tightly in my hand, I swim away from Hicks, glad to leave his corpse to its watery grave and return to the surface.

On the surface, everything is still. In the distance I hear the same keening cry I heard the animals make before, moving farther away. There is the gentle splashing of someone swimming. Then Boone is there.

"Where's Cassandra?" I ask.

"She swam off," he says. "I don't know where."

"And the monster?"

"Dead," he says. "At least I assume it is. Your sister carved it up pretty good, and I destroyed at least one of its eyes."

"I'm glad Cassandra didn't carve you up as well," I tell him.

"She tried," he says. "And she got a couple of good slices in. Not all the blood in here belongs to the giant fish monster. But I'll survive. Did you find Hicks?"

"I got the piece of the key," I tell him. "Hicks is dead."

"They sent him after me," Boone says. "My council."

He says nothing else, but he doesn't need to. I understand very well what he's saying. We are now both fugitives from our lines. I reach out and take his hand. "We can't let Cassandra get the weapon," I remind him. "We have to keep going."

"I know," he tells me. "Besides, I'm not going to wait around here to become fish food."

As if it heard him, the remaining creature howls again. We need to go.

"I say we find one of the walls and swim along it," Boone says. "It's as good a plan as any. If we get to land, we get to land. If we get too tired and drown, we drown. And if that thing comes back and eats us, at least Cassandra will never get all the parts of the key and will never get to the weapon."

So we start swimming, hoping to reach a wall. We've swum fewer than 100 meters, though, when the water starts churning again.

My first thought is that the sea monster has come back. Then the water begins to form a whirlpool, spiraling inward. Something is pulling us down from underneath, like a great mouth opening up and swallowing the water.

"Now what?" Boone says moments before a tremendous force sucks us beneath the surface.

We are pulled away from each other. I try to swim, but realize immediately that it's futile. The power of the water is too great. I am flung around like a ragdoll as the maelstrom spins, faster and faster, drawing me toward the bottom of the lake.

CHAPTER 9

Boone

By the time I'm pulled through a long tunnel in the rock and spit out onto the floor of another cavern, I'm more than half dead. I lie on the stones, trying to clear the bitter water from my lungs. Somewhere inside the mountain, the tunnel I've just passed through closes again and the water falling onto my face slows to a trickle. The sound of coughing nearby jolts me awake. Ari! I roll over.

It's Cassandra.

I stagger to my feet, hoping to gain an advantage on her before she fully comes to. But before I can get to her, someone blocks my way. Actually, several someones, as suddenly there are at least half a dozen children standing between me and Ari's sister. At least, I think they're children. They're definitely the *size* of kids. But they're also wearing metal masks sculpted into grotesque faces with large, gaping mouths and angry expressions. Where there should be eyes, there are openings for the children to see through.

All of them are holding weapons—and they're pointed right at me. Some have long spears with wicked-looking metal tips. Others are carrying knives with razor-sharp blades. And some wield sticks studded with metal spikes. They form a weird little army. I think I could take out a bunch of them before they hurt me too badly, but for the moment I stand with my hands raised, letting them know that I'm not planning anything.

Cassandra is stirring. I notice that she's lost her knife in the trip through the water pipes. This doesn't stop her from leaping to her feet and assuming a fighting posture. "Who are you?" she snarls.

"Who they are is not important," a voice says. The group of children parts, and an elderly woman passes through them. Her gray hair is worked into a thick braid that hangs down her back, and she moves slowly. "They are here to judge you."

"Judge us?" Cassandra says. She laughs. "Children?"

The woman says, "Players of the Minoan and Cahokian lines, come with me. Your trial is about to begin."

"How do you know who we are?" I ask. Water drips from my clothes, but the air here is dry and warm, and I am not shivering.

The woman looks at me. Her eyes gleam. "We receive news of what occurs in the world, even here," she says. "And we have seen other Players at other times and in other places."

"What line are you?" Cassandra snaps.

The woman shakes her head. "We are of no line. We are merely observers and guardians."

"What gives you the right to keep the weapon from me?" Cassandra presses.

If Cassandra's manners are irritating, the woman doesn't show it. She responds with the same neutral tone she's been using all along. "Our right is that we are in possession of it, and you are not. And if you wish to find it, you will need to pass what awaits you through there." She nods, indicating a set of stone doors I didn't notice before.

Cassandra has not looked at me once. "Get on with it, then."

"Not yet," I say. "Where is Ariadne?"

The woman says, "I do not know what became of the other two. All I know is that the two of you are here."

She walks away. One of the children takes my hand and pulls me along. Another tries to do the same with Cassandra, but she yanks her hand away and walks alone. The child's hand in mine feels oddly rough, as if it's made of the same stone the mountain is. I want to ask more questions about what happened to Ari, or go look for her, but that clearly isn't going to happen, at least not now.

"There are three trials," the woman explains as we walk. "Each one presents you with an opportunity to win an item that could greatly aid you in one of the final trials."

She pushes on the doors, and they swing outward. We walk into a large chamber maybe 50 feet in diameter and half that high, the entire thing lit up by dozens of torches mounted on the walls. The floor seems to have been scooped out and filled with loose sand. All around the sides are tiers carved into the rock. I recognize it immediately as some kind of stadium.

The children file into the seats. The old woman points to iron spikes set into the walls and to rings set into the ceiling. There are also a number of thick hemp ropes hanging at random intervals from the top of the room. And in the very center, also hanging from the ceiling, is something that gleams as it slowly turns. I can't tell if it's a sword or something else, and it doesn't really matter. Whatever it is, that's the prize, and I need it.

"The goal is simple," the woman says. "Collect the item and return with it to this starting point. You may attempt to injure each other, but if one Player is killed, the other will be terminated as well."

"Why?" Cassandra asks.

"Because this is not the final test," the woman tells her. "Begin."

Before I realize that she's told us to start, Cassandra shoves me, hard. I go flying into the sand and sprawl on my face. As I'm getting up, she is already scaling the wall, climbing from spike to spike with amazing speed. She is far ahead of me. Unless I take a shortcut.

There is a rope hanging above me, just out of reach. I run and leap onto the first tier of the stadium, landing on the ledge just in front of a group of watching children. From there I jump again, and I grab the rope. As it swings, I begin to haul myself up it hand over hand. I've done this in gym class a million times, as well as in training, and I'm good at it. Cassandra is just reaching for the first of the iron rings that will take her across the ceiling, and I'm already within five feet of getting there myself. Plus, I started my climb in the middle of the room, which means I'm closer to the first object. I still can't tell what it is, but I see it hanging there for the taking.

I climb the rest of the way and reach out for the object. It's a foot long, and made of metal, but I have no idea what it is. My hand wraps around it and I pull. It comes free. Triumphant, I look to see where Cassandra is. She is still making her way across the ceiling, swinging with strong, assured movements. But she is too late.

Or so I think. As I begin my descent, the prize tucked into the waistband of my pants so that I can use both hands, Cassandra grabs on to a ring. Using her forward momentum, she swings her legs hard and lets go. She flies through the air and reaches for another of the ropes. It swings in my direction. Then Cassandra's legs are around my waist and her hands are tearing the metal tube from me. I try to grab it back from her and slip. One hand holds on to the rope, and I slide down, tearing the skin from my palm. Cassandra hangs on, sliding with me. Then she pushes away and falls the rest of the way to the ground. She lands in a crouch, holding up the object she stole from me like the trophy it is.

I slide to the end of my rope and land on my feet. My hand is bleeding. I press it against my thigh. It stings, but I don't want Cassandra to see that I'm injured in any way. It's bad enough that she has the first prize.

"Very clever, Minoan Player," the old woman says. "You have won the staff."

"What does it do?" Cassandra asks, examining the item.

"Press the button in the center of the grip," the woman tells her.

Cassandra does, and the staff magically extends on both ends until it is a good six feet in length. Cassandra laughs. "This will be very useful." She looks at me and sneers. "Too bad you couldn't keep it in your possession, Cahokian."

Around us, the masked children are filing out of the stadium, leaving through a door that opens in the far wall. The old woman motions for us to follow them. We do, going down a set of stairs that turns several times before leading into another open space. The air here is incredibly hot, and I soon see why. We are standing on a long, narrow ledge. Before us is an expanse of bubbling, stinking . . . something. Tar? Sand? I can't tell. But the heat is almost unbearable, as is the stench. Rising from the mess are stone pillars of various heights. Looking at them, I have a feeling I know what's coming. A moment later, the old woman confirms it.

"On top of one of the pillars is the second object," she says. "Find it and return here with it, and it's yours. Fall into the boiling sands, and you will be burned so severely that you will wish you had died."

"Better watch your step, Cahokian," Cassandra says.

"Remember," the woman continues, "if one of you dies, the other does as well."

This time, when the woman gives the command to start, I'm ready. I jump from the ledge and onto the nearest pillar. As I land on it, I realize that it's not as wide as I thought it was. I stagger and almost fall, but catch myself.

"Try not to kill yourself, Cahokian," Cassandra shouts as she picks her route through the steaming landscape. "You'll deprive me of the pleasure of doing it for you later."

I have no idea where the item we're after is, so I don't know if I should follow Cassandra or find my own way through the muck. Then I remember what the old woman said about us both needing to survive this. I don't want to get too far away from Cassandra, in case something happens. Also, if she *does* find the object first, I want to be able to take it from her if I can. So, I go in the direction she's going, leaping from pillar to pillar. I have to really throw myself into the air to make it.

We search for maybe 10 minutes without either of us finding anything. Then, while jumping from one pillar to another, I see something flash like a beacon through the steam. Cassandra is not far off, and she sees it at the same time.

We race for the pillar where the light is coming from. Both of us take wild leaps as we move from pillar to pillar. We reach the blinking light at the same time. I can see that it's coming from a small metal ball that is nestled in a hollow on top of a pillar.

Cassandra and I both jump for the pillar. She lands first, bending and snatching up the ball. I land right beside her. There isn't enough room for both of us, and the force of my body colliding with hers knocks Cassandra off balance. She starts to fall backward. Instinctively, I throw out my hand and grab hers. She takes it, but the ball she is holding flies out of her grasp. I try to grab it with my free hand, but I miss. It sails past me, over my shoulder, and falls with a sickening plop into the steaming swamp.

I pull Cassandra up onto the pillar. She stares at the spot where the ball is sinking into the muck, as if she's thinking of diving for it.

"Good catch, Cahokian," she says bitterly. "I thought Americans were supposed to be good at baseball."

She turns and heads back to where the old woman and her army of children are waiting for us. "Which of you has the ball?" the woman asks.

"Neither of us," Cassandra tells her.

"It was lost," I say.

"What was it?" Cassandra asks.

"It doesn't matter now," the woman replies. "We must move on to the third trial." She looks at me. "You will not be participating."

"What?" I say. "Why not?"

"The third trial is only for those who have won an item," she says. She turns to Cassandra. "This trial is for you alone."

Cassandra smirks at me. "Looks as though you'll be going into the next trial empty-handed, Cahokian," she says.

"Perhaps not," the old woman says. "You have a choice to make, Minoan Player. You may keep the item you've won, or you may give it up. If you choose to do so, you may then ask me three questions regarding the nature of the remaining trials and final location of the weapon you seek. The other Player will not hear the questions or answers. Which do you choose?"

Cassandra takes the staff from her waistband, where she's been carrying it, and hands it to the woman. "I don't need this to win," she says. "I choose the questions."

"Very well," the woman says. She then moves away with Cassandra, back into the stairwell. I remain surrounded by the masked children. Not long after, I hear a muttered curse and Cassandra storm through the doorway. She's enraged. "Give me back the staff!"

Before she can reach me, several of the children block her way. She puts her hands on them and starts to shove them away. The next moment, she is flying backward at high speed. She smacks into the rock wall and slumps to the floor, stunned. The children are massed together, their false faces turned toward her. Cassandra scrambles to her feet and, with a roar, reaches out and rips one of the masks off. Then she recoils.

As if on cue, all the children reach up and remove their masks. Underneath they are not children at all. Although their bodies resemble humans, their faces are made up of metal gears that click and turn like the insides of clocks.

The old woman appears in the doorway. She looks at Cassandra, then at me. I shake my head.

"What are they?" Cassandra says.

"They are the architects of this place," the woman says. "The minds that built it."

"And who built *them*?" I ask.

"It is time for you to go," the woman tells us. "Pass through that doorway and continue on your quest." She points to a door at the far end of the rocky ledge.

Cassandra runs for the door. I don't want her to get ahead of me, but I can't help myself. I look at the old woman. "What happened in there?" I ask.

I don't think she'll answer, but she does. "I told her the truth."

CHAPTER 10

Ariadne

I wake up hearing the voices of angels. There are no words, just ethereal notes of pure beauty. I lie in the darkness, not knowing where I am. My body aches, and there's something wrong with my left arm, but I am in a nest of soft blankets, and for the moment I am grateful for the rest.

"I told you she would not die. You owe me fifty kuruş."

I open my eyes and look at the boy sitting cross-legged on the ground beside me. He is peering at me out of one eye with interest. The other is gone, his face on that side scarred over. Then I see another face. It belongs to the girl, Kelebek. She tilts her head and says, "She could still die. Look at her arm. The poison is spreading."

"You're betting on my life?" I croak. My throat is raw, as if I have swallowed an entire desert of sand.

"We saved it," Kelebek says. "So we have the right."

Now I remember. The lake. The creatures. The rush and suck of the maelstrom. I sit up. Pain tears through my arm when I attempt to put my weight on it, and I buckle. I try again, using just my right arm. This time I am successful, although my head is throbbing, and I feel I might be sick.

Then I am. I throw up a combination of water and bile. Kelebek and the boy move to get out of the way. I heave again. Now I feel as if a fire is burning in my stomach.

"It's the poison," Kelebek says. "It's killing you."

I look at my arm. There is a wound on my wrist, a deep puncture. The skin around it is dark purple, and there is a yellowish pus oozing from the opening. More alarming are the tendrils that snake up my forearm, almost to the elbow. They are the same blackish-purple color, but also tinged with green and yellow. The girl is right: there is a poison in me.

"The things in the lake are venomous," Kelebek says. "You must have been bitten."

"Is there an antidote?" I ask.

She shakes her head.

"But you could still live," the boy says hopefully.

"You are Bilal," I say, remembering Boone's description of the boy.

He nods.

"You want those fifty kuruş very badly, don't you?" I say.

He grins. Kelebek shakes her head. "He will only use them to buy sweets," she says.

"Bilal, I will make you a deal," I say. "If you help me find my friend, I will give you five times that many kuruş."

The boy's eyes widen. Kelebek, however, shakes her head again. "He is probably dead," she says. "Even if he is not, we are forbidden to help you."

"But aren't you helping me now?" I ask, not understanding.

Kelebek bites her lip and does not answer.

"I am the one who pulled you from the water," Bilal says. "She would have left you to drown."

Kelebek swats him, and he yelps. "You know the rules," she snaps. "If the elders find out, we will be in trouble."

"I don't think she'll tell them," Bilal replies. He looks at me. "Will you?"

I shake my head. "All I know is that I woke up here," I say. "Not that I know where here is."

"We call it the cave of angels and demons," Kelebek tells me.

"Because of the voices," Bilal adds. "They're made by the wind blowing through holes in the mountain. Depending on how it is blowing outside, the sound inside changes."

I listen again to the peculiar sound filling the air. The tone has changed, and beneath the beautiful notes there is something more sinister and threatening. The wind outside has changed direction. I wonder if it's a portent of what's to come for me inside the mountain.

"You don't know for certain what happened to Boone?" I ask. "Or to my sister?"

"They were sucked into the channels beneath the lake," Kelebek says.

"Probably," Bilal adds.

"And where do those channels lead?"

"We've already interfered too much," Kelebek says.

I force myself to stand up. Although moving my arm is painful, I can still move it, at least for now. "I need to go," I say. "Will you at least help me find my way to the next trial?"

Kelebek and Bilal look at each other. An unspoken argument occurs between them. Bilal must lose it, because it's the girl who speaks. "The poison is going to keep spreading. You will weaken and die."

"I would rather die trying to win than lying down listening to the angels and demons singing me into the underworld," I tell her.

Bilal leaps up. "I will show you," he says. Kelebek frowns, but a moment later she stands as well. She says nothing as she turns and walks away. Bilal grins at me. "Come on," he says, cocking his head.

We pass out of the cave and move into a corridor that winds its way in a slow downward spiral. We are going deeper into the mountain. I have no sense of what time it is, whether it's night or day, or how long I've been inside this place. I feel as if I am in a dream, one that began a lifetime ago and may never end. It occurs to me that perhaps I am dead, and that these children are my guides into the realm of the ancestors. And then I think of the poison in my arm, and how it is killing me. Can it really not be stopped? How much time do I have left before it runs its course?

Somewhere inside this mountain, Boone and Cassandra are also either dead or moving closer to the place where the final treasure lies waiting for the winner to claim it. How far ahead of me are they? Are they together? What trials have they endured that I have not?

All these questions play at my mind as we journey through the rocky passageways.

"We will take you to the hall of the guardians," Bilal says. He has been beside me the whole way. I know he is watching to see if the poison causes me to stumble, and I appreciate his kindness.

"Who are these guardians?" I ask him. Then I think of the lake creatures whose poison is even now killing me. "Or *what* are they?"

"You will find out for yourself," Kelebek says before Bilal can answer. This is obviously a warning to him to keep whatever he knows to himself.

"It's not much farther," Bilal says quietly.

We come to a set of stairs that leads down. Kelebek stops. "This is as far as we take you," she says.

I reach out my hand to Bilal, who takes it. "Thank you," I tell him. "If I survive this, I will give you the kuruş."

"It's all right," he says. "Good luck."

I lean down and kiss him on both cheeks. Then I turn to Kelebek. "Thank you for helping me."

She nods. We have been through a great ordeal together, the two of us. I remember her climbing up the devil's chimney, and how she never once faltered while facing a challenge. Even though she was willing to let me die earlier, I respect her for adhering to the rules of the game her people have devised—and for breaking them. "I think you are the bravest girl I've ever met," I tell her.

A flicker of a smile passes over her face. Then it is gone, and she says, "Good-bye, Player."

I walk down the stairs, leaving them behind and heading toward whatever is awaiting me below. I am unarmed, and the poison is weakening me more and more, but I am determined to face whatever is in the so-called hall of the guardians. I wonder if that will include my sister. I pat the pocket in which I stowed the two pieces of the key. I still have them. But will they ever be joined with the other two, or have those been lost? I will have to wait to find out.

The stairs end at an open doorway. I step through it and into a huge rectangular hall. Unlike the other rooms, which have all been lit by torches, this one is filled with a bluish light that shines from inside enormous gemlike stones set into the rock. They are very much like the ones in the tunnel in the first city, but on a much larger scale. Their light illuminates the faces of statues that have been carved out of the rock. They stand at least 20 meters tall, lining both sides of the hall. They are identical to one another: humanoid in shape, with stern but handsome faces that are neither male nor female. Each has its hands cupped in front of its body, holding another of the glowing rocks. Curiously, several of the statues have been broken. One has had its head knocked off completely. It lies in the middle of the hall, the eyes looking up at the ceiling. Others are missing hands, and random pieces have been chipped from the bodies by some unknown force. On each wall, there are several doorways similar to the one I have just come through. At the far end of the hall, a set of wide steps leads to a set of doors that lock as if they protect something valuable. I sense that behind them lies what I have come deep into the mountain for.
I step into the hall, alert for any signs of trouble, and begin investigating. I see something in the sand, and go to look at it. It's a small metal ball with a piece of glass set into one end, and a button of some kind on the other. I have no idea what it is, but I put it into one of my pockets and resume searching. I soon find several other unusual items: a bow without a string lying beside two unused arrows, a knife that has been broken in two, a handful of bullet casings. This place has obviously been the scene of one—or probably several—battles. But against what? Between whom?
As I'm holding the bow and looking at it, someone runs into the hall through one of the doorways. I look up to see my sister standing not 10 meters away from me. She looks angry, and her mood does not improve when she sees me watching her. But we have no time to exchange pleasantries before Boone runs into the room as well. For a moment, he and Cassandra stand side by side, both of them with

their eyes trained on me. Then Cassandra notices the bow in my hand. Immediately, her eyes begin scanning the area in search of other weapons.

Boone runs over to me. When he touches me in an attempt to embrace me, I wince. Then he notices my arm. "What happened?"

"The things in the lake are venomous," I tell him.

"How did—"

I cut him off. "Later," I say. I nod at Cassandra, who is picking something up from the sand. It looks like a spear. "We have to prepare for whatever is coming."

Normally, Cassandra would have attacked one or both of us before searching for weapons. I know why she hasn't—she wants us alive long enough to help her defeat whatever is coming. Then, she thinks, she will kill us and take the pieces of the key we have. Of course, I am thinking the same thing. Cassandra is deadly, but I am weakened by the poison in my body, and I don't know if Boone and I alone can fight whatever the final guardian of the treasure is.

I reach into my pocket and take out the metal ball. "I found this," I tell Boone. "I'm not sure what it is."

"I think I know," he tells me. "Or I have an idea, anyway. When the time comes, press the button. The glass eye will blink. When it does, throw it at whatever you're trying to kill and then duck."

A grenade of some kind. It will come in handy. I put it back in my pocket, then turn my attention to hunting for weapons. Boone does the same, making sure not to let Cassandra out of his sight. The three of us are like wolves, circling and waiting.

Boone is searching in some rubble. He bends down and picks something up. As he does, there's a grinding, cracking sound. It's coming from above us. We look up and see a hole opening in the ceiling as two stone slabs slide away. A shadow appears in the opening, huge and black. Then something falls out of the hole toward us. We scatter, taking shelter behind whatever we can find.

The thing lands in the center of the hall. At first it looks like an enormous ball of iron. Then it unfolds itself and stands up. It's a man, but not one of flesh and blood. This one is made of metal. He stands as tall as the surrounding statues. Like Talos, the great bronze giant made by the god Hephaestus to protect the island of Crete, he is somehow alive. He turns his head, and I see his eyes blazing blue with the same light that fills the hall.

I look at Boone, who is staring at the metal man in amazement. "Holy Isaac Asimov," he says. "It's a robot."

CHAPTER II

Boone

The thing I'm looking at shouldn't exist outside of a story in *Astounding Science Fiction*. The robot—and I'm absolutely sure it's a robot—looks very much like I've always pictured they would. Only this thing is real, and it's looking at me. Well, if the two glowing blue things in its face are eyes, it is. Probably they're sensors of some kind. I'm so fascinated by it that I almost forget that I'm supposed to be fighting it.

Then it raises one giant hand and points a finger at me. Its fingers have openings in them, and I'm not about to wait around to see what comes out of them. I run to my left and dive behind the giant stone head sitting there. I'm just in time, too. Seconds later, a blast of something hits my hiding place. I don't know what it is—electricity, maybe, or some kind of sonic wave—but it's powerful. The head cracks, splitting down the center, and the two halves roll aside, leaving me exposed.

The giant robot has turned its attention to Cassandra. Instead of running from it, though, she does the opposite, and races toward it, still holding the length of wood she found in the sand earlier. It's exactly the right thing to do. The robot is powerful, but it's also big and clumsy. Cassandra zigzags, so it can't draw a bead on her. She runs directly under its legs. At first, I don't understand what she's going to do with the wood. Then I see her jam it into one of the robot's leg joints. It goes deep.

But this is not a flesh and blood thing. Her attack would have easily disabled an animal or human. The robot just takes a step, splintering the wood as though it's nothing. It swivels, following Cassandra as she runs toward me, and this time I see the blast come from its fingers. Blue light erupts and sizzles through the air. It clips Cassandra, who is still running a jagged pattern, and she spins around from the force of it. She falls to the ground, twitching. The robot takes a step toward her and keeps coming. It means to crush her beneath its huge feet.

I'd love nothing more than to see her turned to jelly under the giant's foot. But we need her piece of the key, and she might still be of use in this fight. So I run to her and grab her under the arms, dragging her away from the approaching robot. I find a spot behind some rubble and stop there. Cassandra is stirring, and she says, "The eyes."

"What?" I ask.

"The eyes," she repeats. "We need to take out the eyes. It's one of the things the old woman told me."

I leave her there and go back to confront the robot. Ari has beaten me to it. She's standing in front of it, holding the metal ball in her hand. As I watch, she presses the button, and the red eye begins to blink red.

"Aim for its eyes!" I call to her.

She pulls back her arm and throws. The ball sails through the air. It arcs up and heads right for its target. It connects with the robot's head. There's a loud boom as it explodes. When the smoke and sparks die down, I see that the metal of the giant's head is scorched in places, and one of its blue eyes has gone dark.

This gives me hope. If we can take out one eye so easily, surely we can take out the other and bring this thing down. Ari feels it too, and turns to me with a triumphant expression. She raises her fist as if defying the robot.

She doesn't even see the burst from the thing's hand, the gobs of what look like molten lava. I do, though, and I run to her and shove her out of the way. She falls, and a blob of liquid fire spatters against my chest. Immediately the cloth of my shirt dissolves. My skin is next. Although the shirt has taken the worst of it, there's enough left to cover half of my chest in a tarry goo. It feels like I've been set on fire. Instinctively,

I try to wipe it away, and only succeed in getting some on my hands, which also now start to burn.

I fall to the ground, burying my hands in the sand on the floor. This helps a little, but not enough. I grit my teeth and scream, trying to drive myself through the pain. I rub my burning hands together, hoping the sand will rub away whatever is on my skin. It does, but it takes a lot of my skin with it, leaving my hands raw and bleeding.

The robot is moving again, walking with slow, thunderous steps in my direction. Ari is on her feet. "Run!" she yells, and I do, dodging to the right and heading along one side of the hall while Ari does the same on the other. The robot can't aim at both of us at once, and it chooses to try for Ari. More of the fiery gunk shoots from its hands, splattering against the wall just above her head. She keeps going.

The hopefulness I was feeling a moment ago is gone. I have no idea how we're going to fight this thing. It's massive, and practically impossible to hurt without the right weapons. The only one we had, we've now used, and while it worked, the robot isn't slowing down. I don't know how we're going to take out its other eye, or what will happen if we do. For all I know, the thing will just keep shooting until it kills us all.

Cassandra appears, looking a little groggy but standing. I run to her. "What else did the old woman tell you about how to stop it?"

She looks at my chest, at the raw, singed flesh and the black gum dripping down my torso. I think I see a corner of her mouth lift in a smile. She doesn't answer my question, just runs toward the robot. She picks up speed as she goes, and when she vaults off a piece of rock, using her hands to push off, she flies through the air, tumbling and landing on the robot's outstretched arm. She scales it and leaps onto its shoulder, then begins hammering at its remaining eye with a stone in her hand.

The metal giant reaches up and flicks her away as easily as a horse brushing off a biting fly. Cassandra once more is flying through the air, but without any grace. Her arms and legs flail, and when she hits one of the statues flanking the hall, she crumples. All the strength in the world can't stop the mechanical monster.

Now that it's shown us that there's little we can do against it, the robot seems determined to finish us off. It picks up a chunk of stone, and hurls it at Ari. She ducks away just in time, and the stone makes a crater in the wall behind her. The robot keeps picking up rocks and throwing them, forcing her to run back toward me. Chunks of wall and statue fly through the air with each hit.

The thing switches from throwing rocks to blasting us with more of the burning tar. Ari and I take cover as it sprays everywhere, turning the hall into an inferno. Cassandra is still unconscious on the ground, and somehow she isn't hit by any of it. But it's only a matter of time until she is.

Now I understand exactly how people felt during the war when they were trapped in their houses during bombing raids. They didn't know exactly *when* they would be hit, but they knew it was coming. It's a horrible feeling, being helpless, but I can't think of a single thing to do against the robot. It's a mechanical nightmare, relentless, its only purpose to kill us, even if it destroys the entire hall to do it.

Ari and I prepare to make one last attempt at stopping the thing. She holds a broken knife in her one working hand, while I pick up an arrow and grip it tightly. I know it's ridiculous, but if we're going to die, we're going to die fighting.

"Hey!" a voice calls out. "Over here, you blockhead!"

I look toward the voice. Standing in one of the doorways is Hicks. His face is bloated and purple, the same color as Ari's arm. He's swaying on his feet, and he looks as if he'll fall over at any second. Yet somehow he manages to stagger into the hall, right in the path of the robot. He stands there, rocking back and forth. There's something in his hand.

I run over to my friend. Despite everything, I'm happy to see him alive. When he sees me, he grins. "Sorry I'm late," he said. "I kinda got lost."

There's no time to ask him how he got here. The robot is preparing to attack, raising its arms. Hicks turns his attention back to it. He raises his own hand, and I see that the thing in it is a makeshift slingshot he's somehow cobbled together from a forked stick and a piece of rubber tubing.

"You walk far enough in this place, you find all kinds of things," he says as he stoops to pick up a rock. He places it against the rubber band.

"You have to hit it in—"

"The eye," he says. "I figured that out."

He aims at the robot, pulls his arm back, and lets go. The rock flies straight and true. It connects with the giant's remaining eye, which explodes. Hicks turns to me, triumphant. "Just like shooting cans off a stump back home."

He's looking at me, so he doesn't see the robot stumbling forward, falling. He doesn't see it as it comes down, its massive hand outstretched. I do see it, and I rush toward Hicks, forgetting everything except that he is my best friend. But I can tell there's not enough time to get there and push him out of the way, so I yell, "Move!"

He doesn't. Instead, he turns just in time to see the hand before it hits him. When it does, he falls beneath it, crushed. I kneel down beside him. Blood is dribbling from his mouth, and the light in his eyes is quickly fading.

"Guess old Goliath didn't like me taking him down," he says. He tries to laugh, and blood sprays from his lips.

I never imagined saying good-bye to my best friend like this. I reach out and touch Hicks's face. The skin is cold and slick with sweat.

"Promise me something," he whispers.

"What's that?" I ask him.

"Don't let that Minoan get whatever this thing is guarding. Okay?"

"Sure," I tell him. "I won't."

Hicks smiles. "Knew you weren't a traitor," he says. "See ya, Boone."

His eyes close. He breathes one last time, then he's gone.

Ari has come over. I stand up and put my arm around her. I see her looking at Hicks's mottled face, wondering if her turn is coming next. The poison is making its way through her veins, farther up her arm. I can sense her exhaustion. Whatever is going to happen next, we need to finish it, and soon. "Let's check on Cassandra," I say.

I turn to look for her, and she's right behind me, holding a rock in her hand. "Sorry, Cahokian," she says as she brings the rock up toward the side of my head. "I need to speak with my sister. Alone."

CHAPTER 12

Ariadne

"You don't look well, sister."

Cassandra drops the rock she's just used to knock Boone out. At first I think she might have killed him. But his ruined chest is still rising and falling. Of the three of us, only Cassandra appears more or less unscarred, although I know the blow from the mechanical man must have hurt her badly.

She reaches into the pocket of her pants and pulls something out. She holds out her palm. On it is her piece of the key. "You have yours."

It is not a question. She knows that I do, that I would not have gone through all of this if I did not.

"You're going to die, Ariadne," she says. "The poison has advanced too far." She glances at the body of the dead Cahokian, Hicks. "That will be you soon enough."

She's right. I can feel the poison, thick and deadly, creeping through my veins. It has become more difficult to breathe. My arm is almost useless. How much longer do I have left? Not long, I think.

"What do you want?" I ask my sister. She knows that she could kill me. Or she could simply wait for the poison to finish its job, then take the pieces of the key from me and from Boone.

Cassandra comes over to me. I don't flinch as she raises her hand and places it against my cheek. "You know you've lost," she says. "I will open the door, take the weapon, and return with it to Crete. I will be the hero of our line. Your name will be forgotten. Already our parents no longer speak it. It's as if you were never born, that there were never two of us. Only one."

She looks down at Boone. "I will kill him, too, of course. Then everything you've done will be for nothing." She looks back at me. "Tell me, was it worth it? Losing everything? For him?"

I stare into her deep brown eyes. Eyes exactly like mine, in a face I share. How is it, I wonder, that two bodies so similar can have hearts that are so different? Or are we really that dissimilar? Before meeting Boone, I might have felt as she does now. Loving him, even for such a short time, has changed me. "Yes," I tell her.

Her face hardens. This is not the answer she wanted. She wants me to say that I regret it all. At that moment, I realize that what Cassandra wants more than anything in the world—perhaps has always wanted—is to be capable of love. Maybe at one time she was. Before training turned her heart to stone. Before her jealousy of me poisoned her just as the beast's poison has doomed me. We are both dying, only Cassandra doesn't know it.

She kneels down and begins going through Boone's clothes. She quickly finds the piece of the key that he has been carrying, and stands up. She takes me by the wrist and drags me along behind her as she walks the length of the hall to the stone doors. Too weak to struggle, I don't resist. When we reach the steps, I stumble up them.

"Give me the other pieces," Cassandra says.

"You'll have to kill me," I say.

She laughs. "A final display of bravery? Admirable. But you want to see what's behind those doors as much as I do. I'm allowing you the chance."

As much as I want to defy her, she's right. I do want to see what's inside the next room. My entire life has been devoted to this. Everything I've done has led up to it. To die now, without knowing, without seeing, is unimaginable. She's already won. I won't defeat her with a final display of resistance.

I take the two pieces of the key out and give them to her. She plucks them from my hand, then presses two of the pieces together to form a half. There's a clicking sound as they join. Cassandra puts the other two pieces together, then adds them to the first pair. Now she has a completed ball in her hand. She walks over to the doors, where there is a round indentation in the wall beside them. The key fits into it perfectly.

The doors slowly swing inward. Cassandra steps through them, and I stagger forward. Inside is a small chamber less than three meters across. There is nothing grand or unusual about it. The walls are bare, without carving or adornment. There are no statues standing sentry, no torches, no anything except for a stone pedestal with a metal box resting on top.

Cassandra walks up to the box and places her hands on it. I manage to follow, and stand behind her as she lifts the lid. When she turns to me, the look on her face is one of victory. "Would you like to see what you've lost?" she asks.

I bring my hand up. In it is the arrowhead I've been holding in my palm. I plunge it into Cassandra's belly and draw it up in a sharp, tearing motion. Her skin parts, and warm blood pours out over my hand. Her mouth opens, and her hands scrabble at me as she tries to push me away. I look into my sister's eyes. "I will see you soon, sister," I say as I push the arrow into her heart.

Cassandra falls. I catch her in my arms and lower my sister to the floor. My heart aches under the weight of her. I have killed the other half of my soul. But there is no time to mourn. I close my eyes, willing myself not to pass out yet. When I open them again, I look into the box. There, laid out before me, is what appears to be a gun of some kind. I stare at it for a moment, then turn away. My life force is swiftly fading, and before it leaves me completely, I want to see Boone again.

The walk out of the chamber seems to take forever, even though it is only a handful of steps. When I get outside, I find that I am not alone. There are others in the hall. Some I recognize: Bilal, Kelebek, Yildiz. Most I do not. At first, I think they must be apparitions, hallucinations caused by the poison as it consumes my mind. Then Kelebek and Bilal run to me and take me by the hands. They support me as I stumble down the stairs, then lead me through the group of onlookers and over to where Boone lies on the ground.

I fall down beside him, reaching out to stroke his face. I think maybe he has succumbed to Cassandra's blow after all, but then his eyes flutter and open. His eyes are unfocused for a moment. Then he looks at me and smiles.

"Hey there," he says. One hand comes up to hold mine. Then he sees the blood, and a shadow of worry passes over his face.

"It's not mine," I tell him.

"Cassandra?"

"Dead."

"The weapon?"

"It's there," I say. "In the chamber."

"I want to see it."

He sits up, holding his head, then stands. I can't, and so he reaches down and pulls me to my feet. Then he picks me up, cradling me in his arms, and walks to the chamber. When we are inside, he sets me down. I am able to stand by leaning on him. I do not look at my sister's body lying on the floor. Together, Boone and I look at the weapon in the box.

"We won," he says, but his voice is flat.

"Yes," a voice behind us says. "You have won." Yildiz is standing in the doorway. "You may take it and go," she says. "We will return you to the other city."

"What about Ari?" Boone asks her. "Can you heal her?"

Yildiz shakes her head. "That is beyond our powers."

"I'm not leaving you here," Boone says to me.

My body is on fire. The poison is burning me up from the inside. I look at Yildiz's eyes. "Do you have something to make death come quickly?"

She hesitates only a moment before nodding.

"Bring it to me," I say. "Please."

Boone starts to protest, but I stop him by placing my fingers on his lips. "I'm not afraid," I tell him.

He looks at me for a long time. His eyes are wet. Then he nods. Yildiz turns away and says something to someone outside the chamber.

Boone helps me sit on the ground. We lean against the pedestal that holds our prize, our hands interlocked. Yildiz continues to stand in the doorway.

There are so many things I want to say to Boone, so many conversations we have not had, so many things we will never get to talk about. Now there is no time. All I can do is hold his hand, feel his pulse against my palm. His heartbeat soothes me.

I do have one question. "What will you do with the weapon?" I ask him.

Before he can answer, I see Kelebek come running up the steps. She hands something to Yildiz, then glances at me before turning and leaving. Yildiz walks over to me. She holds out a vial. "Drink this," she says, "and the end will come swiftly."

I don't have the strength left to reach for it, so Boone takes the vial. Then he says to Yildiz, "What will happen to the weapon if I don't take it away from here?"

"It will stay here forever," she says.

"Nobody else can claim it?" Boone says.

Yildiz shakes her head. "It is your prize. You may do with it as you wish, but no one else may take it. If you leave it here, the chamber will be sealed and the key destroyed. The ways into the hall will also be sealed."

"But someone could always find a way in," Boone argues.

"Only if they destroy the mountain itself," says Yildiz.

Boone has another question for her. He holds up the vial. "How much of this will it take?"

"Only a few drops," Yildiz says.

The old woman leaves us. Boone and I sit in silence for a minute. Then he gets up and goes outside. I hear a grinding sound, and the doors begin to close. Boone reappears, resuming his seat beside me.

“What did you do?” I ask.

He holds out his hand. He is holding the key. “Making sure no one can get in,” he says. “I know she said they would seal the entrances, but I want to be sure.”

He has locked us inside the chamber. Us and Cassandra’s body.

“Nobody needs this weapon,” he says.

I believe he is right. Before meeting him, I did not. I thought the most important thing in the world was securing any advantage I could for my line. But I was wrong. Cassandra and Hicks are dead. Boone and I may die too. Our lines will anoint new Players to take our place. And the game will continue. Now I see that there is no way to win. Not unless the lines can be persuaded to work together. And I do not think they are ready to do that. Each one wants to be the victor, and as long as that is the case, nobody will win except the beings that have forced us to Play.

Boone takes my hand in his, the vial of whatever Yildiz has given him pressed between our palms. “Ready?” he asks.

“Yes,” I say.

He raises our joined hands and tips the vial into his mouth. Then he holds it to my lips. I drink. The contents are bitter, but not terribly so. I swallow.

I lean against him, feeling his heartbeat against my back. We do not say, “I love you.” We both know how we feel. Instead we sit together and wait. The game will go on. We have not stopped it forever. But for now—for us—it is over.

And we have won.

Follow the Players from *Endgame: The Calling*—before they were chosen. Keep reading for a sneak peek at:

MINOAN MARCUS

When Marcus was a little kid, they called him the Monkey.

This was meant to be a compliment. Which is exactly how Marcus took it.

At seven years old, he monkeyed his way 30 meters up a climbing wall without fear, the only kid to ring the bell at the top. Ever since then he's made sure he always goes higher than the other kids, always gets to the top faster. Always waits at the summit with a cocky grin and a "What took you so long?"

He can climb anything. Trees, mountains, active volcanoes, a 90-degree granite incline or the sheer wall of a Tokyo skyscraper. The Asterousia Mountains of Crete were his childhood playground. He's scrambled up all Seven Summits—the highest mountain on each continent—including Antarctica's Mount Vinson, which meant a hike across the South Pole. He's illegally scaled Dubai's 800-meter-high Burj Khalifa without rope or harness, then BASE jumped from its silver tip. He's the youngest person ever to summit Everest (not that the world is allowed to know it).

If only someone would get around to building a tall enough ladder, he's pretty sure he could climb to the moon.

Climbing is an integral part of his training. Every Minoan child hoping to be named his or her generation's Player learns to scale a peak. They've all logged hours defying gravity; they've all broken through the clouds. But Marcus knows that for the others, climbing is just one more skill to master, one more challenge to stare down.

No different from sharpshooting or deep-sea diving or explosives disposal. For Marcus, it's more.

For Marcus, climbing is everything.

It's a fusion of mind and matter, the perfect way to channel all that frenetic energy that has him bouncing off the walls most of the time. It takes absolute focus, brute force, and a fearless confidence that comes naturally to Marcus, who feels most alive at 1,000 meters, looking down.

He loves it for all those reasons, sure—but mostly he loves it because he's the best.

And because being the best, by definition, means being better than Alexander.

It was clear from day one that Alexander Nicolaides was the kid to beat. It took only one day more to figure out he was also the kid to hate.

Marcus's parents called it camp, when they dropped him off that first day. But he was a smart kid, smart enough to wonder: What kind of parents dump their seven-year-old on Crete and head back to Istanbul without him? What kind of camp lets them do it?

What kind of camp teaches that seven-year-old how to shoot?

And how to arm live explosives?

And how to read Chinese?

It was the kind of camp where little kids were *encouraged* to play with matches.

It was most definitely Marcus's kind of place—and that was even before he found out the part about the alien invasion and how, if he played his cards right, he'd get to save the world.

Best. Camp. Ever.

Or it would have been, were it not for the impossible-to-ignore existence of Alexander Nicolaides. He was everything Marcus wasn't. Marcus could never sit still, always acted without thinking; Alexander was calm and deliberate and even broke the camp's meditation record, sitting silent and motionless and staring into a stupid candle for 28 hours straight. Marcus mastered languages and higher math with brute mental force, thudding his head against the logic problems until they broke; Alexander was fluent in Assyrian, Sumerian, ancient Greek, and, just for fun, medieval Icelandic, and he was capable of visualizing at least six dimensions. Marcus was better at climbing and shooting; Alexander had the edge in navigation and survival skills. They even *looked* like polar opposites: Alexander was a compact ball of tightly coiled energy, his wavy, white-blond hair nearly as pale as his skin, his eyes as blue as the Aegean Sea. Marcus was long-limbed and rangy, with close-cropped black hair. If they'd been ancient gods, Alexander would have had charge over the sky and the sea, all those peaceful stretches of cerulean and aquamarine. Marcus, with his dark green eyes and golden sheen, would have lorded it over the forests and the earth, all leaves and loam and living things. But the gods were long dead—or at least departed for the stars—and instead Marcus and Alexander jockeyed for rule over the same small domain. Marcus was the camp joker and prided himself on making even his sternest teachers laugh; Alexander was terse, serious, rarely speaking unless he had something important to say.

Which was for the best, because his voice was so nails-on-chalkboard annoying that it made Marcus want to punch him in the mouth.

It didn't help that Alexander was a good candidate for Player and an even better suck-up. The other kids definitely preferred Marcus, but Marcus knew that Alexander had a slight edge with the counselors, and it was their opinion that counted. Every seven years, the counselors invited a new crop of kids to the camp, the best and brightest of the Minoan line. The counselors trained them, judged them, pushed them to their limits, pitted them against one another and themselves, and eventually named a single one as the best. The Player. Everyone else got sent back home to their mind-numbingly normal lives.

Maybe that kind of boring life was okay for other kids.

Other kids dreamed of being astronauts, race-car drivers, rock stars—not Marcus. Since the day he found out about Endgame, Marcus had only one dream: to win it.

Nothing was going to get in his way.

Especially not Alexander Nicolaides.

Tucked away in a secluded valley on the western edge of Crete, the Minoan camp was well hidden from prying eyes. The Greek isles were crowded with architectural ruins, most of them littered with regulations, tourists, and discarded cigarette butts. Few knew of the ruins nestled at the heart of the Lefka Ori range, where 50 carefully chosen Minoan children lived among the remnants of a vanished civilization. Tilting pillars, crumbling walls, the fading remains of a holy fresco—everywhere Marcus looked, there was evidence of a nobler time gone by. This was no museum: it was a living bond between present and past. The kids were encouraged to press their palms to crumbling stone, to trace carvings of heroes and bulls, to dig for artifacts buried thousands of years before. This was the sacred ground of their ancestors, and as candidates to be the Minoans' champion, they were entitled to claim it for their own.

The camp imposed a rigorous training schedule on the children, but none of them complained. They'd been chosen because they were the kind of kids who thought training was fun. They were kids who wanted to win. None more than Marcus. And other than the thorn in his side named Alexander Nicolaides, Marcus had never been so happy in his life.

He endured Alexander for two years, biding his time, waiting for the other boy to reveal his weakness or, better yet, to flame out. He waited for the opportunity to triumph over Alexander so definitively, so absolutely, that everyone would know, once and for all, that Marcus was the best. Marcus liked to imagine how that day would go, how the other kids would carry him around on their shoulders, cheering his name, while Alexander slunk away in humiliated defeat.

He was nine years old when the moment finally arrived.

A tournament, elimination style, with the champion claiming a large gold trophy, a month's worth of extra dessert, and bonus bragging rights. The Theseus Cup was held every two years as a showcase for campers—and a chance for them to prove their worth. There were rumors that the first to win the Theseus Cup was a shoo-in to be chosen as the Player. No one knew whether or not this was the case—but Marcus didn't intend to risk it. He intended to win.

He swept his opening matches effortlessly, knocking one kid after another senseless, even the ones who were older and bigger. Bronze daggers, double axes, Turkish sabers—whatever the weapon, Marcus wielded it like a champion. Alexander, who'd started off in another bracket, cut a similar swath across the competition. This was as it should be, Marcus thought. It would be no fun to knock him out in an early round. The decisive blow needed to come when it counted, in the championship, with everyone watching.

The two nine-year-old finalists stepped into the ring for a final bout. Personal, hand-to-hand combat. No weapons, no intermediaries. Just the two of them. Finally.

They faced each other and bowed, as they'd been taught.

Bowing before you fought, offering up that token of respect, that was a rule.

After that, there were no rules.

Marcus opened with a karate kick. Alexander blocked it with ease, and they pitted their black belts against each other for a few seconds before Alexander took him in a judo hold and flipped him to the ground. Marcus allowed it—only so he could sweep his leg across Alexander's knees and drop him close enough for a choke hold. Alexander wriggled out and smashed a fist toward Marcus's face. Marcus rolled away just in time, and the punch came down hard against the mat.

The camp was on its feet, cheering, screaming Marcus's and Alexander's names—Marcus tried not to distract himself by trying to figure out whose cheering section was bigger. The fighters moved fluidly through techniques, meeting sanshou with savate, blocking a tae kwon do attack with an onslaught of aikido, their polished choreography disintegrating into the furious desperation of a street brawl. But even spitting and clawing like a pair of animals, they were perfectly matched.

The fight dragged on and on. Dodging punches, blocking kicks, throwing each other to the mat again and again, they fought for one hour, then two. It felt like years. Sweat poured down Marcus's back and blood down his face. He gasped and panted, sucking in air and trying not to double over from the pain. His legs were jelly, his arms lead weights. Alexander looked like he'd been flattened by a steamroller, with both eyes blackened and a wide gap where his front teeth used to be. The kids fell silent, waiting for the referee to step in before the two boys killed each other.

But this was not that kind of camp.

They fought on.

They fought like they lived: Marcus creative and unpredictable, always in motion; Alexander cool, rational, every move a calculated decision.

Which made it even more of a shock when Alexander broke.

Unleashing a scream of pure rage, he reached over the ropes to grab the referee's stool, and smashed it over Marcus's head.

Marcus didn't see it coming.

He only felt the impact.

A thunderbolt of pain reverberating through his bones.

His body dropping to the ground, no longer under his control, his consciousness drifting away.

The last thing he saw, before everything faded to black, was Alexander's face, stunned by his own loss of control. Marcus smiled, then started to laugh. Even in defeat, he'd won—he'd finally made the uptight control freak completely lose it.

The last thing he heard was Alexander laughing too.

* * *

"You always tell that story wrong," Marcus says now. "You leave out the part where I let you win."

Xander only laughs. At 14, he's nearly twice the size he was at that first Theseus Cup, his shoulders broader, his voice several octaves deeper, his blond hair thicker and forested across his chest. But his laugh is still exactly the same as it was on the day of the fight.

Marcus remembers, as he remembers every detail of that day.

You never forget the moment you make your best friend.

"Yeah, that was really generous of you, deciding to get a concussion and pass out," Xander says. "I owe you one."

"You owe me two," Marcus points out. "One for the concussion, one for the cheating."

They are hanging off a sheer rock face, 50 meters off the ground.

They will race each other to the top of the cliff, 70 meters above, then rappel back down to the bottom, dropping toward the ground at a stomach-twisting speed.

Marcus has heard that most kids his age fill up their empty hours playing video games. He thinks this is a little more fun.

"I most certainly did not cheat," Xander says, trying to muster some of his habitual dignity. Most people think that's the real him: solemn, uptight, deliberate, slow to smile. Marcus knows better. Over the last five years, he's come to know the real Xander, the one who laughs at his jokes and even, occasionally, makes a few of his own. (Though, of course, they're never any good.) "Not technically, at least," Xander qualifies. He jams his fingers into a small crevice in the rock face and pulls himself up another foot, trying very hard to look like it costs him no effort.

Marcus scrambles up past him, grinning, because for him it actually *is* no effort. "Only because no one ever thought to put 'don't go nutball crazy and smash furniture over people's heads' in the rules before," Marcus says.

"Lucky for both of us," Xander says.

Normally, Marcus would shoot back a joke or an insult, something about how it's not so lucky for him, because Xander's been clinging to him like a barnacle ever since. Or maybe something about how it was luckier for Xander, because now, with Marcus as a wingman, he might someday, if he's lucky, actually get himself a date.

But not today.

Not today, the last day before everything changes. Tomorrow, they will find out who has been selected as this generation's Player. It'll surely be either Marcus or Alexander; everyone knows that. They're the best in the camp at everything; no one else even comes close.

It's what brought them together in the first place. After all that time wasted hating each other, they'd realized that where it counted, they were the same. No one else was so determined to win—and no one else was good enough to do so. Only Marcus could melt Xander's cool; only Xander could challenge Marcus's cockiness. In the end, what else could they do but become best friends? They pushed each other to go faster, to get stronger, to be *better*. Competition is all they know. Their friendship is built on the fact that they're so well matched.

Tomorrow, all that changes. Tomorrow, one of them will leave this place as a winner, and embark on his hero's journey. The other will leave a loser, and find some way to endure the rest of his pathetic life.

Which means today is not a day for joking. *I couldn't have made it through this place without you,* Marcus would like to say. And *no one knows me like you do.* And maybe even *you make me want to be my best self.*

But he's not that kind of guy.

"Yeah, lucky," he agrees, and Xander knows him well enough to understand the rest.

They climb in silence for a while, battling gravity, scrabbling for purchase on the rock. Marcus's muscles scream as he stretches for a handhold a few inches out of reach, finally getting leverage with his fingertips and dragging the rest of himself up and up.

"It's probably going to be you," Xander says finally, and they both know what he's talking about. Marcus can tell Xander's trying not to breathe heavily, but the strain in his voice is plain.

"No way. Totally you," Marcus says, hoping the lie isn't too obvious.

"It's not like Endgame is even going to happen," Xander says. "Think about it—after all this time, what are the odds?"

"Nil," Marcus agrees, though this too feels like a lie. How could Endgame *not* happen for him? Ever since Marcus found out about the aliens, and the promise they'd made to return—ever since he found out about the Players, and the game—some part of him has known this was his fate. This is another difference between him and Xander, though it's one they never talk about out loud.

Marcus *believes.*

When they were 11 years old, Marcus and Xander spent an afternoon digging for artifacts at the edge of the camp's northern border. It was Xander's favorite hobby, and occasionally he suckered Marcus into joining him. What else were friends for? That day, after several long hours sweating in the sun (Marcus complaining the whole time), Marcus hit gold.

Specifically a golden *labrys*, a double-headed ax. The labrys was one of the holiest symbols of the Minoan civilization, used to slice the throats of sacrificial bulls. Marcus gaped at the dirt-encrusted object. It had to be at least 3,500 years old. Yet it fit in his palm as if it had been designed just for him.

"No one's ever found anything that good," Xander said. "It's got to be a sign. That it's going to be you who gets chosen."

"Whatever." Marcus shrugged it off. But inside, he was glowing. Because Xander was right. It did have to be a sign. The ax had chosen him—had *anointed* him. Ever since then, he's believed he will be chosen as the Player. It is his destiny.

But that's not the kind of thing you say out loud.

"It doesn't even matter which of us gets picked. Without Endgame, being the Player's just a big waste of time," Marcus says now. "Though I bet you'd be a chick magnet."

"But what good would it do you?" Xander points out. "It's not like you'd have time to actually date."

This is a game they play, the two of them. As the selection day draws closer, they've been playing it more often. Pretending they don't care who gets picked, pretending it might be better to lose.

"Imagine getting out of here once and for all," Xander continues. "Going to a real school."

"Joining a football team," Marcus says, trying to imagine himself scoring a winning goal before a stadium of screaming fans.

"Going to a concert," Xander says. He plays the guitar. (Or at least tries to.)

"Meeting a girl whose idea of foreplay isn't krav maga," Marcus says. He's still got an elbow-shaped bruise on his stomach, courtesy of Helena Loris.

"I don't know . . . I'll kind of miss that part," Xander says fondly. He's been fencing regularly with Cassandra Floros, who's promised that if he can draw blood, she'll reward him with a kiss. "But not much else."

"Yeah, me neither," Marcus says. "Bring on normal life."

He's a few meters above Xander, and it's a good thing, because it means Xander can't see his sickly, unconvincing grin. A normal life? To Marcus, that's a fate worse than death.

A fate he'd do anything to avoid.

The counselors try their best to give the kids some approximation of a normal upbringing. In their slivers of free time, campers are allowed to surf the Net, watch TV, and flirt with whomever they want. They even spend two months of every year back home with their families—for Marcus, these are the most excruciating days of all. Of course he loves his parents. He loves Turkey, its smells and tastes, the way the minarets spear the clouds on a stormy day. But it's not his world anymore; it's not his home. He spends his vacations counting the minutes until he can get back to camp, back to training, back to Xander.

Deep down, he knows this is another difference between them. Sure, Xander wants to be chosen. But Marcus wants it more.

Marcus *needs* it.

That has to count for something.

Marcus is happy to pretend that he and Xander are evenly matched, that the choice between them is a coin flip. It's easier that way; it's how friendship works. But surely, he thinks, their instructors can tell that it's an illusion. That Marcus is just a little better, a little more determined. That between the two of them, only Marcus would sacrifice everything for the game, for his people. That only Marcus truly believes he's meant to be the Player—and not just any Player, but the one who saves his people.

They're both pretending not to be nervous, but deep down, Marcus really isn't.

He knows it will be him.

It has to be.

He reaches the top with a whoop of triumph, Xander still several meters behind. Instead of savoring his victory or waiting for his best friend to catch up, he anchors his rappelling line, hooks himself on, and launches himself over the cliff. This moment, this leap of faith, it's the reward that makes all that hard work worth it. There's a pure joy in giving way to the inexorable, letting gravity speed him toward his fate.

Tomorrow, everything changes.

And it can't come fast enough.

THEY HAVE ONE GOAL.

TAKE FATE INTO THEIR OWN HANDS.

STOP ENDGAME.

The Zero Line Chronicles follow an underground group whose mission is to track down and kill each of the twelve Players—and save the world.

Also available as a paperback bindup *Endgame: The Complete Zero Line Chronicles*.

HARPER

An Imprint of HarperCollins*Publishers*

WWW.THISISENDGAME.COM

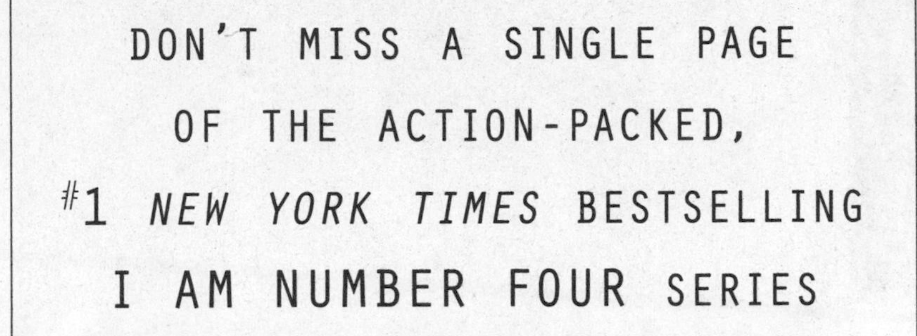
DON'T MISS A SINGLE PAGE
OF THE ACTION-PACKED,
#1 NEW YORK TIMES BESTSELLING
I AM NUMBER FOUR SERIES

THREE ARE DEAD.
I AM NUMBER FOUR
PITTACUS LORE
I AM NUMBER FOUR SERIES
THE POWER OF SIX
PITTACUS LORE
I AM NUMBER FOUR SERIES
THE RISE OF NINE
PITTACUS LORE
I AM NUMBER FOUR SERIES
THE FALL OF FIVE
PITTACUS LORE
I AM NUMBER FOUR SERIES
THE REVENGE OF SEVEN
PITTACUS LORE
I AM NUMBER FOUR SERIES
THE FATE OF TEN
PITTACUS LORE
I AM NUMBER FOUR SERIES
UNITED AS ONE
PITTACUS LORE